Don't close your eyes...

By Jamie Freveletti

DEAD ASLEEP
THE NINTH DAY
RUNNING DARK
RUNNING FROM THE DEVIL

THE COVERT ONE SERIES
ROBERT LUDLUM'S THE JANUS REPRISAL

JAMIE FREVELETTI

Dead Asleep

HARPER

An Imprint of HarperCollinsPublishers

This is a work of fiction. Names, characters, places, and incidents are products of the author's imagination or are used fictitiously and are not to be construed as real. Any resemblance to actual events, locales, organizations, or persons, living or dead, is entirely coincidental.

HARPER

An Imprint of HarperCollins*Publishers*
10 East 53rd Street
New York, New York 10022–5299

Copyright © 2012 by Jamie Freveletti
ISBN 978–0–06–202519–7

First Harper premium printing: November 2012

Printed in the United States of America

Visit Harper paperbacks on the World Wide Web at www.harpercollins.com

10 9 8 7 6 5 4 3 2 1

For Alex and Claudia,
with love and laughter

ACKNOWLEDGMENTS

I'd like to thank my agent, Barbara Poelle, and her husband, Travis, for the title suggestions, my publisher, Liate Stehlik, editor Lyssa Keusch for her editorial input and another great cover, the graphic artists and cover specialists who put it all together, and Shawn Nicholls for his online assistance. Thanks to everyone at HarperCollins for their support year round, and my publicists, Danielle Bartlett, Pamela Spengler-Jaffee, and Dana Kaye, who keep my schedule straight when I can't.

Thanks again to Darwyn Jones, who read the manuscript in a weekend despite the fact that he was swamped with his own work.

Thank you to the readers. Your encouragement is greatly appreciated.

And, of course, to my family.

Dead
Asleep

Emma Caldridge found the bloody offering on her credenza just before midnight. She had been working late preparing samples and organizing slides in the makeshift lab set up in the rented villa's spacious garage, and returned to the main house for another cup of coffee.

A small votive candle flickered next to the pile of feathers and hacked-off rooster foot, all arranged in a triangle on top of a pentagram drawn in a red substance that looked like blood. Emma's lab, Pure Chemistry, was located in Miami, and she had seen Santeria altars before, with their animal sacrifice and elaborate rituals, but this was nothing like that. This was voodoo.

She stayed still and listened for any sound that might indicate that someone was still in the house. The room was dark, the world asleep. She heard the rush of waves in the distance, the sound of a breeze moving through the trees outside, but nothing that indicated intruders. Her heart thudded in her chest, but she remained motionless, silent. If the intruders were in the house and expected to hear her scream or otherwise react, they would be disappointed.

Emma was used to facing danger. While she hadn't been tested in quite a while, her instincts had come back quickly when needed. Now, she remained quiet. The dark arts were a frightening thing, but she knew that the danger in the message wasn't from the mass of feathers, the dead animal, or the pentagram. In her experience, the danger came from the humans who created the mess and would be part of the corporeal world.

That she remained still came from a more practical consideration as well. She knew that if the intruders weren't in the house, it was entirely possible they were outside waiting for her to burst out of the front door and run to her car. Again, they would be disappointed. She rarely acted out of panic.

Emma pulled a pencil out of a cup next to the phone and used the eraser to lift the mass of feathers. Underneath, she found the doll. Its body was fashioned of hastily stitched burlap that sported brown yarn for hair and two black felt dots for eyes. A toothpick jutted from the center of the doll's forehead.

Emma snorted at the crude scare tactic. She was unafraid of ghosts or demons and things that went bump in the night. If it made noise, then a human, animal, or physical element created it. She heard the sound of breaking glass in the distance. The intruder was in the garage.

She dropped the pencil and ran through the darkened house, out the French doors at the back of the kitchen and onto the lawn. The garage held her work. Work that she needed to keep Pure Chemistry functioning as a going concern. Her heart thudded when she thought of someone destroying it. As she neared the garage she saw the shape of something that may have been a man, standing in front of her carefully prepared slides. He swept something across the table and she watched in disbelief as bottles, jars, and the containers holding a week's worth of work went crashing to the cement floor. She ran toward him, barely noticing the sharp gravel of the drive on the soles of her bare feet.

The garage's overhead light cast a yellow glow over the tables that Emma had set up to form the work space. The man upended the nearest table, sending another set of Petri dishes, test tubes, and even a microscope tumbling to the floor.

"Stop it!" Her voice was harsh. He froze. As she neared she could see the machete in his hand. It was what he'd used to sweep the bottles off the table. "That's my work. You have no right to be here." The man stayed still, saying nothing and keeping his face turned away. Emma heard the gravel crunch behind her.

"He responds only to me."

A woman stood at the corner of the drive. The weak moonlight lit her dark skin. She wore a scarf wrapped around her head and a pareo was knotted at her hip. She smiled, and her teeth, straight and white, glowed in the night, giving her a feral appearance. Emma leveled a stare at her. The woman's hard eyes were what bothered her most. They revealed a person without a soul, like the witch women in the Sudan who rode with marauding armies, wore black robes, and beat on drums while soldiers killed everyone in the village. The woman at the corner of the drive reeked of depravity. It was all Emma could do not to take a step back, away from the force of ill will that flowed from her in waves.

"He's my slave," the woman said. "A zombie."

"Don't be ridiculous," Emma replied, her voice sharp. She knew better than to show fear or acquiesce to the woman's bizarre claim, but found it difficult to maintain her ground. She hadn't expected to meet with evil in the middle of the night on a beautiful Caribbean island. Yet she managed to remain in place. "He's a trespasser. And so are you." Her anger fizzed at the deliberate destruction of her work. The woman moved closer, walking in an exaggerated, swaying motion.

"*You* are the outsider on this island. We belong here. Leave. And take your bottles and experiments with you."

Emma glanced at the man, but he remained still, not moving a muscle. His stillness was strange, and a frisson of a chill ran through her. She wished that she had thought to bring her cell phone. She was loath to leave these two even for the time it would take to retrieve it. If she did, she was afraid they would destroy even more.

"I saw the mess you made in the entrance hall,"

she said. "I'm going to call Island Security about your breaking and entering."

The woman chuckled, but the noise sounded wicked. "Island Security knows better than to interfere with a bokor priestess."

Emma was glad that the man stayed frozen during this exchange. She didn't want to grapple with both the woman and him. She took a step toward the woman.

"But *I* don't know better, and I'm telling you one more time to leave. Now. And take your companion and absurd talk of zombies with you."

The woman raised an eyebrow. "Ahh, the scientist in you doesn't believe? Be warned. You have no idea what you're dealing with here. With one word from me he'll cut you to ribbons. There's no negotiating with him."

"I don't recall offering any negotiation. I said leave. Both of you." Emma kept the man in her peripheral vision. With the machete in his hand, he didn't need to be a zombie to hurt her. Flesh and blood human would be enough.

The woman flicked her hand. "Kill her," she said.

The man burst into motion. He raised the machete and sprinted to her, closing the distance between them in seconds. His hair hung in thick Rasta braids down his back, and his face was contorted in a strange spasm. His eyes pointed straight to the sky even as he ran toward her, swinging the machete. It was as if he was not in control and that his body was responding to a force outside of his mind. His tongue whipped right and left, adding to the horrific sight. He started screaming in a high-pitched wail.

Emma spun and ran toward the villa. She heard the priestess's harsh laugh and the man's feet on the gravel driveway behind her. She had the fleeting thought that the man was insane and if he were to catch her would show no mercy.

She made it to the French doors and wrenched them open, tumbling through the entrance and slamming them behind her. She turned and flipped the dead bolt just as he crashed into the glass with his hands. The machete's blade made a clanging sound on the pane.

He stood there, breathing heavily, his weirdly canted eyes still staring upward. She crossed to the phone on the kitchen counter, dialed the emergency number and glanced back.

He was gone.

Cameron Sumner sat at the blackjack table and watched the croupier deal out the cards. The woman to his left watched as well. She had long blonde hair, a full figure, pretty face with brown eyes, and wore no wedding ring. He estimated her age at about twenty-eight, just a couple of years younger than him. It was unusual that such a young woman played the casinos alone. Perhaps she had a gambling problem, he thought, but rejected the idea as soon as he had it. She didn't appear desperate or stressed at all, and wasn't sweating with the thrill of the game, as most chronic gamblers did. Sumner had noticed that whatever table he joined, she inevitably appeared. She didn't speak to him, but played her hand with intelligence and calm, hitting when the odds were against the dealer and sticking when they weren't. She won three out of four hands.

He kept playing, lightly scratching the table with his cards to indicate to the croupier that he wanted a hit, making a small wave to stick, and watched the woman do the same. When the cocktail waitress appeared, Sumner ordered a Maker's Mark whiskey, the woman seltzer water with lemon. It was at that moment that he knew she was staking him out. She was on duty and not drinking.

He completed the hand, tipped the croupier, took his chips and pushed away from the table. The Maker's Mark came with him to the roulette wheel, where he played his favorite number: 32. A former girlfriend used to despair of his adventurous side until she'd become interested in numerology. After that she proclaimed his life path number to be 32, shrugged, said it was in his blood, and embraced it wholeheartedly. He didn't believe in numerology, but playing the number reminded him of her, and he smiled.

Twenty minutes later the blonde joined a nearby wheel. Close enough to see him, but not at the same table. She would move closer, he was sure of it. After twenty minutes more she strolled over and took the empty seat next to him. He smiled inwardly. After a few moments she made an attempt to reach across the roulette wheel to place her chips on a number located at the far side.

"Excuse me," she said as she leaned over him. He smelled her perfume and was treated to a full view of her chest in her low, but not too low, blouse.

"Of course," he said. He shifted his chair back to allow her access. The wheel turned and landed on 32. The croupier doled out Sumner's winnings and pushed them across the felt tabletop with his stick.

Sumner was on the small island of St. Martin on business. As a supervisor in the Air Tunnel Denial program, he flew intercept planes for the United States Southern Hemisphere Drug Defense program. Generally he and his crew operated out of Key West, but the recent upsurge in the areas of the Caribbean and West Indies islands had altered the ATD's focus. Sumner's job was to locate suspicious flights, usually flying under radar, warn them against crossing into United States territories and, once they did, arrest or intercept the planes before they landed. He was also charged with investigating the origin of the flights and putting an end to the drug operation.

He figured the woman could either be an undercover security officer hired by the casino, a member of the small island's police force, undercover, or a foil hired by the drug cartel to compromise or eliminate him before he had a chance to shut down the operation. He hoped she wasn't part of the cartel, but he thought that the most likely scenario.

Sumner won two rounds in a row, decided that was the best he would do against the house, and once again collected his chips. He swallowed the last of the whiskey before strolling to the window to cash out. After pocketing his winnings he headed to the exit. The blonde woman intercepted him.

"Leaving already?" Her voice was low and husky. She stood in front of him holding a stack of chips in one hand and her own drink in the other.

He nodded. "Quitting while I'm ahead."

"The house isn't going to like that." She smiled at him.

"It's such a small amount, I doubt they'll care."

"Maybe you should stay and have a drink in the bar. It's quite early by island standards." Her words were light but her gaze pointed. Sumner thought that perhaps she was a call girl working the casino, except for what he saw in her eyes. He thought he read a warning in them.

"Do you work for the casino?"

She looked surprised and shook her head. "Not at all. What gave you that impression?"

"You seem reluctant to let me leave."

She raised an eyebrow. "Just thinking that you'll enjoy yourself more here than at home."

"I have a good book." She looked a bit stung, and he said, "But I thank you for your concern. I'll enjoy the quiet."

She shrugged. "I hope you do. Good-bye." She turned and walked back into the maze of tables.

The balmy air smelled of saltwater and engine grease, a combination that wafted off a nearby pier. Sumner crawled into the small rental car and started back home. He drove carefully, keeping with the flow of traffic on the narrow road with one lane in either direction.

His rental was actually the beach house for a much larger estate. St. Martin's crime rate had been escalating in recent years, and as a result the estate was gated, with two large dogs that roamed the grounds. Sumner hit the button and watched behind him in the rearview mirror while waiting for the gate to open. In the distance he heard the dogs barking. He'd have a few minutes, if he was lucky, to drive through before they swarmed over the road. The gate swung closed behind him just as the dogs appeared. They were in full howl, and the largest, an Akita with an impressive ruff around his neck, began snapping at the car tires. Sumner proceeded ahead at a slow pace, using the car bumper to nudge the dogs out of the way. One, a large Rhodesian ridgeback incongruously named Susie, put her paws on the driver's side window and peered in at him, her big nose sniffing at the glass. Her bark turned to a sound of welcome once she recognized him.

The big house sat on the bluff above, with lights blazing. Even at the distance of four hundred yards, Sumner could hear the beat of heavy dance music as the inhabitants partied. He drove through the palm trees on either side and down the winding road to the beach. His place was considered a small guest house despite its three bedrooms, dedicated pool, and location on the water. He killed the engine and stepped out of the car.

He was alone. The dogs had followed him halfway down before heading back to the entrance. A sliver of moonlight shot across the gently moving waves, and he stood there a moment, enjoying the sound of water lapping against the shore. He heard a padding noise and then Susie loped into view, her long tail wagging as she approached. She pushed her head against his knee in greeting.

He reached down to scratch her ears before turning to the door. He was three steps away from the entrance when Susie began to growl.

He paused, straining his ears to pick up any hint of what the dog had noticed. He focused his senses around the heavy bass still pounding from the house above. Hearing nothing else, he took another step toward the door. Susie's growls grew louder and she began to pace in front of him. He kept moving forward and the dog subsided, walking alongside. When they reached the entrance, Susie sniffed at it in loud inhalations, her sides heaving. She snorted then and shook her head, stepping back.

Sumner paused again. The back of his neck tingled and he wondered if something, or someone, was waiting for him on the other side of the panel. He reversed himself and moved away. The beach house had a second, rarely used rear door off the laundry room that led onto a backyard with a clothesline stretched across it. He headed that way, keeping his head down and moving as silently as they could. Susie stayed with him. Reaching the door, he slid his key into the lock. It turned with a snick and he slipped inside. Susie pushed in after him, knocking the door wider with her big body. He grabbed her collar to hold her in place.

He decided against turning on a light as he worked his way down the hall. The dog's nails clicked against the floor and for a moment he wished he'd left her outside, except he had no weapon other than Susie. In full howl and enraged, she made a formidable sight. He peered into the darkened living area. A far bank of windows faced the ocean, taking full advantage of the view. To his left was the front door.

A glance at it told him everything he needed to know. A tangle of wires ran from what looked like a car battery to the door handle. An LED display glowed red. Sumner couldn't see what it was and didn't bother to stay. He spun around, dragging Susie with him, and ran back the way he'd come. His heart beat in a crazy rhythm and his hand on the dog's leather collar was suddenly slick with sweat. He made it into the laundry room and managed to slam the door closed when the bomb exploded.

3

Sumner felt the house shudder with the explosion's force. Two small pictures fell off the wall next to his head. They hit the tile floor and the glass in the frames shattered. He flung open the laundry room door and released Susie, who shot into the yard. He followed, running fast, keeping behind her and racing up the road to the big house. The Akita soon appeared on the path's fringe and joined them. When he was far enough away he looked back. Flames leapt out of the front of the beach house and he could hear the piercing sound of a fire alarm.

At the top of the drive, Sumner saw several people milling around the big house's massive back deck. He climbed the last of the hill and took the steps two at a time up to the platform, where he saw Ardan Kemmer, who owned the estate.

A burly man, Kemmer had purchased the house during the era when Dutch citizens could utilize the islands of the Netherlands Antilles to avoid paying the full tax burden of their homeland. In recent years the treaties protecting funds held off-shore were constantly being chipped away, and Kemmer faced multiple charges of tax evasion in his home country. Now, he was actively trying to sell the real estate and offload the mortgage. He wore a shiny black shirt open at the throat, gray cotton chino pants, and sandals.

"What the hell is going on?" he asked.

"Someone rigged a bomb to the front door," Sumner said.

Four young women surrounded Kemmer. To Sumner, they all looked alike, young, with streaked blonde hair, eyebrows plucked to a skinny line, and huge lips that must have benefited from collagen injections. Kemmer owned a series of bars and brothels in Amsterdam, and Sumner assumed the women were employees. One looked scared at his announcement about the bomb blast, but the others seemed unconcerned. Kemmer's eyes lit up.

"Was the house totaled?"

"I don't know. But it's burning. You'd better call the fire department." The girls ran to the edge of the deck to stare down at the beach house. Trees blocked the view but a trail of smoke could be seen rising from the general direction of the beach. "Never mind," Sumner said, hearing sirens in the distance. "The alarm must have signaled them." He watched as Kemmer seemed disappointed rather than relieved at the news that help was on the way. "I take it the house is insured?"

Kemmer nodded. "To the max. There's nothing of great value there." As an afterthought he added, "Glad you didn't get hurt."

Sumner wondered if that was indeed true. It was no secret that Kemmer was liquidating assets as fast as he could and moving the money into protected offshore accounts on other islands. It was also no secret that while Kemmer's business, both in women and in hashish, was legal in Amsterdam, he was not above transporting the occasional bit of illegal contraband throughout the Netherlands Antilles. Sumner had rented the beach house under an assumed name while investigating illegal drug flights, in the guise of a tourist on vacation, but the presence of the blonde at the casino and now the bomb told him that his cover was blown.

The blaring of a fire truck horn indicated that the department had reached the entrance. Kemmer went inside the house to press the button on the intercom that opened the gate, and Sumner watched the truck roll down to the house. When Kemmer reappeared, he was smoking a cigar, and strolling toward him with the air of someone completely unconcerned that at that very moment his beach house was burning to the ground not five hundred yards away. He returned to Sumner's side and handed him a cigar.

"You smoke?" he asked.

"Not usually."

"They're good. Honduran. Hand rolled." Sumner took the cigar and the lighter that Kemmer offered. "Any particular reason someone would want to blow you up?"

Sumner took his time to pull on the cigar. He'd only smoked cigars twice in his life and was no connoisseur, but this one was by far the smoothest he'd tried.

"None that I know of," Sumner said.

"How about you tell me your real name," Kemmer said. He pulled on his own smoke, his eyes never leaving Sumner's.

"You know my real name. It's on the lease." Sumner watched Kemmer's look change to skepticism. "Was the blonde at the casino one of yours?"

Kemmer snorted. "I don't have any girls working the Antilles. I don't have a license for the brothels. It's illegal here."

"I'm not in the business of busting call girls. You can tell me the truth."

Kemmer laughed. "Listen to you, talking about truth." He pointed in the direction of the beach house. "Someone wants you dead real bad. If I were you, I'd worry about that."

"Or you. It's your beach house, remember. I'm just passing through. Anyone want you eliminated?"

Kemmer shrugged and waved toward the road. "I didn't get this far in my business without collecting a few enemies, I'll admit. What was the blonde up to?"

"She tried to warn me off coming home. If she had been successful I wouldn't have been anywhere near the house. That leads me to believe the bomb was meant for you, not me." Kemmer scowled, then gave Sumner a sideways glance.

"Or she just liked a pretty face."

Now it was Sumner's turn to snort. "She was working. At what, I don't know."

The two men walked down the road together and turned a corner to find the fire department hosing down the front of the beach house. Smoke still rose into the sky, but the stream seemed to be weakening. A massive hole was all that was left of the front entrance. One of the firemen spotted them and headed their way. He flicked a glance at Sumner before addressing Kemmer.

"The fire's contained and should be out soon. This was arson, pure and simple. Do you have any idea who would want to do such a thing?" Kemmer gave the fireman the same story that he gave Sumner.

"How'd he get in here?" Kemmer asked. "I maintain security cameras on the front gate. Something tells me he didn't crawl in that way."

The fireman gestured at the ocean. "We think he drove a boat right up to the beach. Got any cameras there?"

Kemmer shook his head. "I don't need to see pictures of myself or my guests when they swim naked."

The fireman gave him a wan smile. "I advise you to set one up now. Whoever did this is bound to try again once they discover they failed." He eyed Sumner. "Are you the renter?"

"I am. Can I go in? I don't have much there, but my clothes are still hanging in the master bedroom."

"The bedroom was untouched, but I doubt that you'll want to keep your clothes once you smell them. Once the smoke gets in the fabric it's almost impossible to remove. You're welcome to see if you can salvage anything."

Sumner struck out around the snaking fire hoses and past the gaping hole of an entrance, reentering at the laundry room and taking the hallway to the bedroom. The smell of burnt fabric, scorched carpeting, and blackened drywall hung in the air. He went into the bedroom and winced when he saw the thick cloud of smoke that filled it. He opened the closet door, grabbed the sleeve of a jacket and brought it to his nose. The ashy scent was unmistakable. The fireman was right; he'd have to buy all new clothes. Sumner grabbed his tablet computer, removed the leather cover and tossed it into the garbage. He opened a drawer in the nearby chest and removed a small titanium case. He left everything else there, including his leather shaving kit. When he walked out, he saw Kemmer standing at the property's edge.

"You're welcome at the big house," Kemmer said.

Sumner was surprised. "Aren't you worried that I'm the target?"

Kemmer sighed. "Yes, but more worried that I am. You strike me as a useful type of guy to have around."

"Well thanks, but I'll be moving on." Sumner put the computer on the passenger seat of his car and slid behind the wheel. Kemmer leaned in, putting a hand on the open window ledge.

"If that blonde comes back this time, you listen to her."

Sumner smiled. "You bet I will." On his way out he paused at the gate to pat Susie's head when she ran up and put her massive paws on the door. "Thanks for the tip," he said to the dog. Susie merely snuffled before dropping down again. Sumner continued along the twisting drive, using his brights to illuminate the dirt road and trees around him. At the base he stopped.

The blonde woman's body hung from a tree at the side of the road.

4

Sumner threw the car into park and flung open the door. He ran up to the body. A dried trickle of blood came from a bullet hole in her temple. Her eyes were closed. He reached up to touch her bare calf. The body was cold. He hadn't been gone from the casino that long. She must have been killed shortly after he left.

An all encompassing anger started to bubble up from deep inside him. He stood there, staring at her. This was not the first time Sumner had encountered death, but the sight of the woman who had been so alive only a few minutes before now hanging from a tree, gone forever, outraged him. After a moment a beeping noise from the car invaded his consciousness. He returned and reached in to turn off the engine and pull the key out of the ignition.

"Such a waste."

Sumner looked up at a woman who stepped into the moonlight. She was dressed in black and

wore a balaclava over her face. He felt adrenaline kick into his system but relaxed when he saw
that she didn't have a weapon. Her voice seemed
familiar somehow, but he couldn't place it.

"Did you kill her?" he asked.

The woman shook her head. "No. I only wish
I'd been able to stop it. Forgive me for not revealing my name, but my cover hasn't yet been blown
and I can't. Yours has, though, so you need to get
away from St. Martin as fast as you can."

"I'm simply a tourist."

"No you're not, Mr. Sumner." That stopped him
in his tracks. His cover was well and truly blown.

"Why should I believe what you say?"

"Banner asked me to collect you and take you
to see him. Drive out and turn right. I have a
red car parked on the other side of the gates. I'll
follow you to the airport. Across the street from
the terminal is a dock where we have a boat waiting to take you to St. Barths. I'll cover you to be
sure you make it there alive."

The name Banner was all Sumner needed to
hear. Edward Banner and Carol Stromeyer ran a
contract security company with high level clearance called Darkview. Sumner had never met
Stromeyer, but Banner had saved his life in two
prior situations, and Sumner made it a habit to
do whatever Banner asked whenever possible. In
this case, though, he waited for the code word
to verify that the information truly came from
Banner. He stayed still. The woman seemed to
notice his inaction and said, "Oh, forgot to say.
The code word is 'alchemist.'" He knew then that

she was a Darkview operative, and the sound of her voice made the memory fall into place.

"Nice to meet you, Ms. Stromeyer," he said, "even if I can't see your face."

She didn't react in any way that he could see, but then, it was dark and she wore the balaclava, so he couldn't gauge any surprise at his use of her name. She said nothing in reply, merely turned and headed into the trees.

"We should call the police," Sumner said, not moving.

She stopped, turned back and shook her head. "The fire department will find her soon enough. There's nothing we can do for her now."

"Was she one of yours?" he asked. He assumed not, because if he was correct and the woman in black was Stromeyer, she wouldn't be as cool about the loss of a fellow agent.

"No, but I'm pretty sure she was working for one of the large estates on the island. If not Kemmer, then another one of the wealthy landowners."

"Wealthy and dirty?"

She nodded. "To the core. I've been tracking their activities for two months now, and I can tell you there's not much they don't have their fingers into. Prostitution, drugs, money laundering, and now murder." She indicated the body hanging from the tree.

"She tried to warn me about the explosion," Sumner said.

"Huh, she must have taken a liking to you," she said. Sumner shook his head.

"Nothing special about me."

The woman gave a low laugh that Sumner found incredibly appealing. His mental vision of Stromeyer as a buttoned-up executive turned into something far more scintillating. Now he understood Banner's admiration for her. He wished he could see her face.

"Why is your boat taking me to St. Barths? I don't have a plane that I can use." From the top of the hill behind him, he heard the sound of a large truck. "That must be the firemen," he said.

In an instant the woman melted into the trees, disappearing into the darkness. Sumner gave one last look at the body hanging from the tree before putting the car in gear and continuing on his way.

He was only two kilometers from the estate when he picked up the tail. True to her word, the woman he thought of as Stromeyer was following him in a red convertible, a flashy car that he wouldn't have chosen for a tail, though it had the advantage of being easy to spot in the dark.

Behind her, though, he saw another vehicle, a black Land Rover with shaded windows and a huge silver grill. The road to the airport was one lane in spots and curved often, so it was entirely possible that the Land Rover was simply another tourist or islander heading home after a late night at the casinos, but he doubted it.

Sumner turned off the road and into a neighborhood, squeezing his car down a narrow lane rimmed with parked cars on one side and dilapidated shacks on the other. The light of a tavern sign with a silhouette of a naked woman arching her back was the only illumination other than the moon. After a minute he saw the Land Rover again, behind the red car, which was still following him. The Rover was moving slower now, since its size made the street barely passable. Something about the hulking piece of metal working its way through the narrow lanes made him wary. He reached to the seat behind him and grabbed the titanium case. He typed in the code on a small electronic keypad and the lock opened. His nine millimeter gun lay inside. He had the right to carry a weapon in the United States, but each island had its own rules, and he hadn't registered it with the authorities in St. Martin when he'd flown in. He suspected they knew that as a member of the ATD, he had one, but they hadn't bothered to probe too deeply.

The airport came up on his left and the dock across the road directly in front. His high beams illuminated the area, revealing a sleek cigarette boat tied up at the dock. A man leaned against a wooden support smoking a cigarette as he watched the car pull closer. Sumner killed the engine, put the gun in his waistband and climbed out. Stromeyer's red car pulled to the curb and idled across the street fifty feet away. He watched the Land Rover slow before turning left onto the airport frontage road that ran along the water. It, too, stopped about fifty feet away. The taillights went black when the Rover's engine was shut down.

Sumner picked up the tablet computer and gun case and started walking toward the dock. The

smoking man pushed off the support and began
a slow stroll toward him. He was tall, taller than
Sumner's six feet plus, with dark skin and close-
cropped hair. He walked with a swagger Sumner
was used to seeing in the States but that seemed
out of place in St. Martin. Like an islander trying
to act ghetto and not quite pulling it off. It telegraphed the man's opinion of himself and told
Sumner that he was dealing with an amateur. In
fact, Sumner never worried much about shows
of aggression. In his experience, the most deadly
adversaries were those who telegraphed nothing
before the strike. The man stopped when he was
about ten feet away.

"You the one needing the ride to St. Barth?" He
spoke in the singsong patter of Jamaica.

Before Sumner could respond, he heard the
door of the Rover open. Swinging to the left,
he pulled his weapon out of his waistband. The
driver in the car had made one crucial error. In
opening the door, he hadn't killed the overhead
light. It lit the area and reflected off the gun in
the man's hand. Sumner aimed, pulled the trigger, and shot him through the arm as he swung
it up to fire. He heard the attacker grunt as the
bullet entered his bicep.

He spun around then as the Jamaican on the
dock pulled a knife. Sumner shot at him, too,
deliberately targeting a spot a few inches from
the man's face. The Jamaican yelled and dodged
left. Sumner moved toward him, keeping his gun
high. The man dropped the knife, letting it thud
onto the boards.

"Don't be shooting, man," he said. "Me only doing what I was paid to do." Sumner was upon the Jamaican now, staring into his dark, frightened eyes. The sodium lights above his head fizzed, but gave enough illumination for Sumner to see when his gaze flicked to the right.

Sumner's skin crawled and he heard the creak of the dock boards a second later. He let his legs collapse, dropping straight down, but knew his odds of beating a bullet in the back were slim. He turned his head to the right in time to see the new gunman take careful aim at his skull.

The man's body jerked and he stumbled, coming down on one knee. Sumner shot him then, full in the chest, but it was clear that his bullet wasn't required. The man fell to the ground, a wound in his neck pouring blood as the carotid artery pumped it out and onto the wooden deck. Seconds later he heard the unmistakable sound of a bullet being chambered.

The woman in black whom he'd assumed was Stromeyer passed over to the Jamaican.

"Give me the keys to the boat. Now."

"That ain't my boat."

She put the gun to his forehead.

"All right, all right." The Jamaican fished a set of keys out and handed them to the woman.

"Tell Raynaud that the next time he crosses me, he'll regret it."

The Jamaican shook his head. "Wasn't Raynaud."

"Then who?"

"Never got his name. European guy. Sharp suit

and skinny face. Said he owed that one a bullet."
The Jamaican waved at Sumner, who regained
his feet.

"Owed me a bullet?" Sumner said.

The Jamaican nodded. "You and some dude
named Caldridge."

5

E mma hung up the phone and started toward
the front door to wait for Island Security, passing through the house on the way to the sleeping areas. When she entered the bedroom section
it felt empty and quiet. Emma was certain that
the voodoo priestess and her strange companion
hadn't made it this far into the villa, because they
would have crossed paths. She walked to the tall
armoire that contained her clothes and opened
a drawer beneath the shelf, removing the gun
that she'd placed there. She was licensed to carry
firearms and had requested to bring hers to the
island. Island Security denied the request, but the
owner of the villa, a wealthy newspaper mogul,
had arranged for one of his bodyguards to leave
his weapon behind for her use. As she checked
the gun's clip she noticed that her hands were
shaking. The image of the man with the twisted
face kept running through her mind. While
Emma still didn't believe in voodoo or zombies,

the incident rattled her and his violent destruction of her work had enraged her.

The villa's doorbell sounded through the house. Island Security was quick, she thought. She carried the weapon with her and walked to the front, passing the voodoo offering on the credenza, reached for the door, then paused. She doubted the two visitors would take the time to ring the bell, but she released the safety on the gun anyway. She twisted the handle and opened the door, expecting to find Duncan Moore, the head of Island Security. Instead, it was a man she knew by reputation but had never met before: Richard Carrow, the lead singer of Rex Rain. He looked at the pistol in her hand.

"Rough night?"

He appeared unruffled at the sight of the gun. He was of medium height, maybe five-foot-eleven and rocker thin. Emma stood five-foot-seven and thought that her 125 pounds would be only about fifty pounds less than what Carrow weighed. His long, straw blond hair was a riot of curls down to his shoulders, and his face sported a five o'clock shadow. He wore faded jeans and an equally faded blue vintage-looking tee shirt with a gold rectangular banner on the front that read RADIO LUXEMBOURG in white letters. The appearance of a famous rocker at her door was almost as surreal as the earlier attack, but at least she knew who he was and that he owned a villa on the island. He held a bottle of liquor in his hand and took a swig from it.

"Sorry about the gun. A man with a machete just tried to attack me," Emma said.

Carrow looked incredulous. "This is Terra Cay. We don't have crime here. Illegal activity, yes. Crime, no."

"There's a difference?"

He gave her a cocky grin. "One hurts others, the other only hurts oneself."

"Interesting shade of gray you've got going there with your philosophy, but I think machete attacks fall under the crime heading."

"You look massively angry. Don't shoot me." Carrow took another swig of the liquor, looking completely unconcerned.

"He destroyed a week's worth of work. I was under a tight deadline and now it just got tighter."

Carrow tried to peer past her. "Was it some sort of crazed landscaper? They're the only ones I see use machetes. Is he still here?"

Emma stepped out onto the front porch and glanced around the lawn. A soft breeze ruffled her hair and the stone portico felt cool under her bare feet. She heard the leaves rustling in the trees and the frogs making their creaking up-and-down chirping sound. The ocean waves in the distance rushed against the sand, adding a rhythmic pulse. It felt peaceful. Idyllic. And foreign and elemental and ancient. It felt and sounded nothing like the modern world. She headed back to the garage at a fast clip. Carrow trotted along beside her.

"What are you going to do?" he said. Emma scanned the area, watching for signs of the two intruders.

"I'm going to protect my work."

"What if they're still out there?"

"Then I'll deal with them." For a brief moment Emma hoped that they *were* out there. She'd love to give them as deep a scare as they had given her.

"And the machete man?" Carrow said. Emma held up the gun.

"Gets shot."

Carrow grinned. "Remind me not to mess with your work."

To Emma's relief the garage area seemed deserted. Neither the woman nor the crazy man had returned. She stepped in, shoved the gun into the waistband of her jeans and reached down to right the table. Carrow put his bottle on another table and grabbed a corner to help her.

They got the table back on its legs and Emma began rooting around in the broken glassware. The native plants, water samples from the mangrove, and three vials of natural algae were destroyed. A small container that held prepared slides was on the ground. The slides were cracked, as if someone had crushed them with a boot heel. She sighed and swallowed as she picked up shards of glass.

"These samples alone took me four full days to acquire. Some are from the mangrove. My company was hired to undertake an extremely lucrative contract to acquire, analyze, and report on them. It's time sensitive, though. I don't produce on schedule and we don't get paid." She shut off the lights, waved him out of the garage, and pressed a keypad. Ten seconds later the garage door closed. She'd leave it closed for the night.

She swallowed both her anger and her fear. Carrow gave her a sympathetic look and stepped closer. The scent of cologne wafted toward her, mixed with sweat and a smoky smell that wasn't from cigarettes. He showed her the bottle that he gripped by the neck. Emma leaned in to see it in the dark. The label said LAPHROAIG.

"Whiskey?" she said.

"Scotch. Single malt. One of the best. Try it." Emma looked at the bottle and felt a moment of déjà vu. It seemed that every man she knew tried to push whiskey on her when the going got rough. She shook her head.

"I'm not much of a drinker."

He cocked his head to the side. "Didn't you just say that a man with a machete tried to kill you?" He used his tee shirt to wipe off the opening and held it up to her. His eyes were serious.

"You've got a point," she said. She took the bottle and downed a swig. Unlike the whiskey she'd had in the past, this was smooth and rich. Still, she coughed. But only once. "That's excellent." She gave it back to him.

His serious look softened. "Yes, it is. I'm Richard Carrow." He put out his hand. Emma nodded.

"I know. I saw you perform on the Grammy awards. I'm Emma Caldridge." She shook his hand.

"Did you call Island Security?"

She nodded. "I should go to the front of the house to wait for them." She started back, this time at a much slower pace, while scanning for any signs of movement. They reached the front door and both of them stepped into the foyer. Carrow's eyes fell on the mess on the credenza.

"What's that?"

"A voodoo offering."

Carrow took a swallow from the bottle. "Are you joking?" Emma shook her head. He moved in closer, peering at the feathers, and frowned. "Martin would know what this meant. Too bad." He looked at her. "I came here to talk to you about him."

Emma did her best to follow Carrow's stream of consciousness. She was fairly certain the Martin that he referred to was a member of Rex Rain, but she couldn't be sure. Still rattled from her two strange visitors, she was having a hard time focusing on what he was saying.

"I've been told that you're some sort of genius chemist, and I was wondering if you could assist me with a problem I'm having at my villa."

Emma looked at her watch. "It's two o'clock in the morning."

"It's a really bad problem." He waved the bottle in the air. "And frankly, I'm at my best at two in the morning." He spread his arms wide and grinned. "As you see." He swayed a bit to the side of the hand holding the bottle. It was as if his balance was so precarious that the extra weight was throwing him off. He took another swig. His expression turned serious. "You look really pale. They scared the shit out of you, didn't they?" Emma hated to admit it, but they had. The vision of the man's crazy, upturned eyes kept coming back to haunt her.

"That, Mr. Carrow, is an understatement," she said. He once again offered her the bottle. She took hold of it and downed another swallow without bothering to clean the neck. This one was even better. She felt a pleasant buzz begin, and even looking at the dead rooster didn't seem so awful.

"Is your problem a chemical one?"

"You could say that."

Emma was getting a bit frustrated. "Why don't you just spell it out for me?"

He took a deep breath. "My drummer fell asleep."

She shrugged. "And?"

"And hasn't woken up. For over twenty-four hours."

"Mr. Carrow . . ."

"And if you've heard anything about Rex Rain, you've heard the party stories, I'm sure."

Emma *had* heard the stories about Rex Rain and their legendary drug use. Some of the more fantastic tales involved satanic ritual and devil worship. She'd always dismissed the tabloid reports as gossip of the worst type.

"Well the stories are, for the most part, true," Carrow said.

"I don't believe that."

Carrow looked surprised. "You don't?"

"Satanic ritual and selling your soul to the devil for a number one hit? Nope. Don't believe it."

He smiled. "Okay, well maybe *that* story isn't true, but Martin has been known to visit mediums and conduct séances. In fact we have a famous medium staying at the villa right now. He also loves using the Ouija board." Carrow took a deep breath. "But honestly, I don't think I've ever seen him sleep this long. I've seen him pass out, mind you, but I don't think I've seen him actually sleep."

She heard the sound of an engine in the distance. The noise escalated and then lessened as the vehicle drove the curved road that led up the mountain to her rental villa. The house, called Blue Heron, sat on a rise overlooking the ocean in the distance. It had a narrow lap pool, two buildings connected by an open breezeway, and a small koi pond. Her staff consisted of a gardener, a maid, and a cook who lived in a row of one bedroom town houses located at the end of the property behind a stand of trees.

"That's probably Island Security," she said. "You'd be better off calling Terra Cay's doctor. I presume there's one on the island?"

"I'd rather you come. There's a pile of powder in the room that I can't identify." The noise of the engine grew louder.

"Worried that the doctor will identify it and then he'll be busted?"

Carrow nodded. "That's definitely part of it. We're here to party for the holiday, of course, but also to record. I can't afford to have him hauled to the mainland to face charges, but if I knew what it was, I'd just sweep it under the rug and call the doctor. What bothers me is that I don't." He gave her a pointed look. "And you can believe that I've seen it all before, so if I don't recognize it, then it must be real trouble." The noise of the car engine whining as it crawled up the steepest part of the hill had grown much louder. Carrow turned his head to listen.

"Please don't tell Island Security. Duncan Moore's an ass. He doesn't like me and he hates Martin."

Emma didn't respond. Instead she stashed the gun in the credenza's cabinet and opened the door. A dark green Jeep pulled into the drive with Moore at the wheel. His small vehicle sported three antennas of various lengths and a green logo of dual palm trees bending toward each other with the word SECURITY on the side. Moore killed the engine, got out and walked toward them. He wore a short-sleeved sand-colored shirt and dark green cargo shorts. He gave Carrow a curt nod before turning to Emma.

"You called Security?" he asked. Before she could answer she heard a noise and her name called. She looked over to see Latisha Johnson, the cook, hurrying toward them. Johnson was nearing forty, with thick dark hair that she kept in braids and then wrapped into a bun. She wore a robe and her arms were tightly wrapped around her middle as she approached, holding the robe closed. Latisha looked at each of them, her eyes widening when she recognized Carrow, and then she turned to Emma.

"Someone broke into the garage. I'm sorry to tell you that they tossed your test tubes on the ground."

Emma nodded. "I know. I called Security." She indicated Moore.

"You didn't talk about bottles in a garage," Moore said. "You said you'd been attacked."

The cook sucked in her breath. "What?"

Emma told her what had happened. When she was done, she noticed that Carrow looked fascinated, Johnson appalled, and that Moore didn't look as surprised as she would have expected. He exchanged a look with Johnson, whose face had become set.

"It could have been anyone," Moore said. "Access to the island is easily accomplished by boat from the mangrove side. The mountain blocks the view of their landing."

His response struck Emma as pat, safe. If she had to guess, she would have said he was hiding something. She looked at Carrow, whose return glance was filled with speculation. Then he took a swallow of the liquor and cast a suspicious look at Moore. Clearly, he didn't buy the man's explanation either.

"Tough to get through the mangrove," he offered in a mild voice.

Moore bristled at that. "I just said it was possible. There could be other explanations as well." Carrow gave a noncommittal shrug, which didn't seem to mollify the Security man.

"He appeared to be suffering from some sort of seizure," Emma said. "His eyes didn't focus on me, but upward, and his face was contorted in a tic. And I found this in my hallway." She stepped back and waved Moore and Johnson into the house.

Johnson gave a low moan. "Oh no, voodoo," she said, seeing the offering.

Moore snorted. "This voodoo stuff is getting out of hand. Until recently there was very little on the island."

Terra Cay sat in the middle of a row of islands in the Bahamas that reached down toward Puerto Rico. It was an exclusive enclave of the very rich. Access was only available to those who could afford to rent a house or charter a yacht big enough to handle the open water for days on end. The island had only one small hotel and a hundred villas, some of them for rent. Each renter was required to pay for a minimum staff of three people, including a cook. Everything on the island had to be imported, with the possible exception of the fish sold at the small marketplace. As a result, provisioning a rental villa was costly as well. Emma's stay was funded in part by a worldwide cosmetic company eager to find a new source of botany to add to their antiaging cream line. Currently, it touted the use of sea kelp as a miracle ingredient.

"But voodoo is practiced on the out islands," Johnson said. "And in Nassau."

"Nassau is not Terra Cay," Moore declared in a lofty manner that Emma found annoying.

Terra Cay was known for its snooty manners. The island's founding by the English, the extreme wealth of its citizens, and its ironclad rules made for a lovely place to vacation. The surrounding islands were the product of their Caribbean and West Indian ancestry. Carrow had been following the exchange between Moore and Johnson and he glanced at Emma and lifted an eyebrow.

"Don't many of the staff members on the island practice voodoo?" he said to Johnson, who nodded.

"They do. For many it's their heritage. Especially the Haitians. They believe that a voodoo priest or priestess can cure any illness, even cancer."

"Which is ridiculous," Moore interjected. Emma noticed that Johnson pressed her lips together. There was an awkward silence.

"Would you search through the house with me?" she said. "Once we've done that I'll lock it up." She looked at Carrow. "Then I'll be free to go to your house."

Moore looked at his watch. "It's almost two-thirty in the morning."

"Someone's always awake on the West Hill," Carrow said. Moore frowned even harder. Emma thought Carrow had made mention of the West Hill specifically to annoy him. "I'll wait in my Jeep. Whenever you're ready," he said to Emma. He sketched a wave at Moore and then gave the cook a deep bow. "Ms. Johnson, I recall your excellent cooking at the last party at the Blue Heron. It's a pleasure to see your lovely face again." Emma was astonished to see the solid, dependable Johnson almost flutter like a schoolgirl.

"And you, Mr. Carrow," she said. Carrow sauntered off.

"Let's look around," Moore said. "I'd also like you to come to the office tomorrow so that we can file an official report."

"I'll clean up the mess," Johnson said.

"Wait." Emma took out her cell phone and

snapped a photo. "Okay. Thank you." Johnson bustled off to the kitchen.

Twenty minutes later all vestiges of the voodoo offering were gone; they had canvassed the house and found nothing. Emma walked with Moore to his Jeep. Twenty feet away she saw Carrow sitting in his, thumbing away on a smartphone. He didn't look up. Moore climbed back into his vehicle.

"Watch yourself with him," he said. "Carrow and his group are wild characters. You don't strike me as that type." Emma smiled.

"Thanks. I'll keep my wits about me." She crossed her fingers and held them up for Moore to see. "Promise." He looked somewhat mollified as he threw the Jeep into gear and drove off.

She strolled up to Carrow.

"Moore done with his excuses?" he said.

Emma nodded. "I saw that you didn't believe the mangrove story. What do you think is going on here?" He slipped a key into the ignition and gave her a serious look.

"I think someone is sending you a message."

6

Carrow handed her the scotch, the top now screwed on, and threw the Jeep into first gear.

"Buckle up. We have to go straight down the hill and back up. I nearly lost my bass player on the lower curve just last week. Wouldn't have been a huge loss, you understand, but in this case I'd hate to deprive the world of that brain."

Emma smiled at him. He smiled back, threw the car into first and hit the gas. The wheels spun a bit on the dry ground but grabbed quickly enough, and then his Jeep shot down the road at a breathtakingly fast speed. They reached Dead-man's Curve. Carrow took it at forty miles per hour. Way too fast, she thought as the Jeep tilted sharply to one side. She clutched the handle above the door and willed herself not to say anything. Despite his speed, Carrow handled the car with confidence as he wound around the side of the mountain. At the halfway point he took a switchback, downshifted again into second, and the Jeep began to crawl upward, its engine whining with the effort to climb the hill, which blocked the low lying mangrove swamp from the rest of the island.

When they were at the top, Carrow's house came into view. It was a series of structures, all one or two stories interconnected with pathways and open air courtyards. Emma knew from the other island residents that Carrow employed a staff of fifteen and that the house was almost always filled with celebrities and the glitterati of the music world. It was two days after New Year's, and the entire island was full to the brim with rich, globe-trotting people anxious to play as hard as they could until driven back to their daily lives after New Year's. Carrow screeched into the horseshoe drive and slammed on the brakes. He reached over and indicated the bottle.

"May I?" he said.

She handed it to him. "Sure."

He unscrewed the top and Emma watched him gulp down some more of the liquid. He offered it to her but she waved it off.

Music echoed on the night air and a babble of voices came from behind the villa. The front of the house blazed with light thrown by two enormous lanterns placed on either side of a massive, carved wooden door. Carrow waited for her to climb out of the car and then got out himself and started toward the entrance, his right hand firmly clutching the bottle's neck.

A woman strolled out from next to the house, wearing only a white string bikini bottom with ties at each side and flip-flops. She was tall, emaciated, and had sharp-edged cheekbones and long honey-colored hair that reached the middle of her back. She carried an open whiskey bottle in one hand. Not the same brand that Carrow had, Emma noticed. She recognized the woman's face but couldn't place the name. She glanced at Carrow, but he seemed unconcerned at the woman's topless state.

"Hey, there you are," the woman said. "We were just looking for you." She peered at Emma. "Who's that?"

"Ms. Emma Caldridge, meet Britanni Warner."

The woman's face lit up. "Oh, yeah, the botanist!"

Carrow shook his head. "Chemist, isn't it?" He directed his question at Emma.

"Both, actually. I study plants for their use in cosmetic applications," Emma said.

"That's right," the woman said. "Cindy told me about her. Her lab makes the 'Pure Colors' makeup line that Cindy reps." Emma realized then where she had seen Warner before. She was a famous model, and the face that represented a second line of makeup sold in high-end department stores. "Are you here for vacation?" Warner asked her.

Emma shook her head. "Work. The company that you mentioned is the one paying for me to be here. I'm on the search for new botanicals."

"She's staying on the East Hill at Blue Heron."

"I know it. Nice location," Warner said.

"The view is spectacular," Emma said.

"I'm taking her to Martin's room."

Warner grimaced. "He's still sleeping. I hope you can help him. I'll be at the pool." She nodded to them, and Emma listened to the sound of her flip-flops snapping away.

Carrow waved her into the front door. The living room lights were set low. Wicker furniture and bamboo coffee tables sat on dark wooden floors. A bank of glass doors spanned the far wall, and through them Emma could see the outlines of a large infinity pool. At least thirty people lounged around it under the flames of citronella torches, while others in swimsuits floated on inner tubes. The whole scene appeared out of place, late as it was. She saw Warner walk to a lounge chair and pick up her swimsuit top. Music played, but not Rex Rain. Emma knew most of Carrow's hits, and the current selection wasn't one of them. The house was set high on the hill, and beyond the pool the ocean view would have been sweeping had it not been night. Now all she could see was the occasional wave as it undulated under the moonlight.

"Is the whole house awake?" she asked.

Carrow nodded. "After eighteen months on tour and playing gigs every night, we have become essentially nocturnal."

"Eighteen months is a long time."

He gave her a glance. "It will be two and a half years before we're done. In that time I'll have had all of four weeks off. These two and another two in March."

A woman in her mid-forties stepped in through the French doors that led to the pool area. She had black hair and wore a bathing suit with a sheer white tunic top over it and flip-flops decorated with rhinestones. Emma recognized her as Belinda Rory, a woman made famous by the cable show *The Other Side*. She claimed she could speak to the dead, among other things. Her arresting brown eyes passed over Emma in a focused assessment.

"Is he awake?" Rory said to Carrow. He shrugged.

"Dunno. Going there now."

"If you need me just let me know." She nodded once at Emma and started across the living room to a swinging door on the opposite wall. When she pushed through it, Emma saw the front panel of a stainless steel refrigerator. The door closed behind her.

"Wasn't that the famous television medium?" Emma asked.

Carrow nodded. "Martin invited her. He wanted to speak to Jimi Hendrix."

Emma raised her eyebrows. "And how did that go?"

Carrow gave her an amused look. "Apparently he was otherwise occupied." Emma suppressed her own smile. In her travels she'd seen many things that appeared unexplainable, and had learned not to dismiss too readily anything that was new or unusual. Still, she didn't believe in mediums, or that they could speak to the dead.

They entered a hallway and passed into a bedroom. This room, too, had glass doors where the wall should be and another breathtaking view of the ocean. Emma moved toward a large four-poster bed made of teak with a mosquito net pulled back on each side. A man lay there, sleeping. His eyes were closed and his face had a peaceful look. A sheet was pulled up to his chest.

"He's wearing clothes," she said.

"He was drinking right before." Carrow pointed to a carafe on a nightstand that was filled with red wine. Next to it was a glass, and next to that a pile of powder. Emma stepped closer.

"Is this it?" she said.

"Yes."

Emma reached to a lamp on the nightstand and moved it closer, taking care not to disturb the powder. It was a dirty, beige color. "What's his usual powder of choice?"

"Not powder, pills. Roxy's."

OxyContin. Emma wasn't surprised. The prescription pill had taken over the drug world. What was on the nightstand wasn't it, though, that was clear. OC was blue. The color was off.

"He sometimes uses China White, so I initially thought this was just some cheap stuff he'd picked up on a nearby island on his way here, but that's not heroin." Emma didn't want to ask Carrow how he could be so sure it wasn't heroin, but she needed to know if he'd taken it himself. If he had and hadn't fallen asleep, then perhaps the powder wasn't the culprit.

"Did you try it? Is that how you know it's not?"

Carrow shook his head. "I don't do heroin, or Oxy, but I've seen plenty of both, and this isn't it. Plus, Martin said he wasn't going to do heroin anymore."

"He could have been lying."

Carrow grimaced. "Martin lies a lot, but I believed him when he said it."

Emma moved closer to the bed, and her toe hit something. She bent down to retrieve whatever it was and her hand closed on a dry shape that felt like wood. It was the root of a plant, bent with two tendrils that twisted downward. She held it up to show Carrow. He leaned in to get a closer look.

"Is it ginger root?"

Emma turned it over, looking at it from all sides. She'd never actually seen the root. She didn't think it was indigenous to the island, but it was easy to grow and required only abundant moisture and warm temperatures, both of which were plentiful in Terra Cay.

"It's mandrake."

"What's mandrake?"

"A plant that acts as a narcotic when ingested." The root was the exact color of the pile of powder on the nightstand. "It looks as though he grated it into a powder and drank it. Probably with the wine." Emma watched Carrow closely. She could see his expression harden.

"What a fool that man is. If it's a drug, Martin will take it. Will he come awake? Or do I need to get him to a clinic?"

"It can be dangerous. When added to wine it will make the person ingesting it fall asleep and be insensible. The ancient civilizations used it as an anesthetic when stitching wounds, and it's said that it was administered in Rome to those being crucified so they wouldn't feel the pain. Gave some of the Roman soldiers a fright when the crucified were taken down because they'd come back to life. Where did he get his hands on this?"

Carrow sighed. "I haven't the slightest idea. It's no secret that Martin spends most of his time drunk or high, but honestly he's always taken drugs that are commercially available. I've never known him to make his own from a root. This is new."

Emma handed him the plant. "I don't think mandrake is native to the island so you'd better look around your villa to see if he's cultivating it somewhere." Carrow took the root from her with a look of distaste.

"We're supposed to start recording in two days and I need him to be awake. If I find it I'll be sure to yank it all out. His little drug garden will be gone."

"Be careful with that. The legends say that mandrake screams when you pull it from the ground and if you hear it you'll die."

Carrow gave her an appalled look. "Screams? Are you serious?"

"Some say that the ancients used to tie a rope to a dog's tail and have the dog pull it out. They would blow a trumpet at the precise moment to muffle the scream." Carrow leaned closer and his cologne wafted over her. She didn't recognize the scent but it smelled delicious. She could see a glint of humor in his eyes.

"I'll be sure to rip it out during one of our re-cording sessions. Half the critics complain that we don't make music at all. Just a tremendous amount of noise. Mandrake screams have nothing on Rex Rain."

7

Emma drove herself home in one of Carrow's spare Jeeps. Carrow had decided to give it a little more time before he notified the island doctor. He'd offered to drive her back but she waved him off. He'd continued drinking steadily the entire time that she was with him and she didn't want a repeat of the wild ride up the hill.

Her house and grounds were filled with sounds, but good, natural ones rather than crashing glass and incoherent screams. Tree frogs sang their up-and-down tones and moths fluttered around the solar-powered lights that lined the driveway. The ocean waves made a rhythmic rumble as they washed against the beach below. She used her key and stepped into the cool foyer. The lights were low, the house quiet. Despite the apparent peacefulness, or maybe because of it, Emma retrieved her gun from the cabinet and made another quick circuit of the house before entering her bedroom. She grabbed her nightgown from a hook behind the bathroom door, dropped her clothes in the hamper, placed her gun within reach on the nightstand, and fell asleep in minutes.

She woke the next morning when a bar of sunlight shot through the edge of the wooden shutters on the window and landed on her face. A quick glance at the clock told her it was almost nine, far later than her normal rising time of seven. The late night had taken its toll. She yawned, stretched, and headed to the armoire to get some clothes. She opened the panels.

A human skull sat on the shelf.

Emma swallowed the shriek of surprise at the sight of it. It stared back at her with its black hole eyes. It couldn't have been placed there before she and Moore took their turn around the house, because she'd opened the armoire to get the gun. Somebody had entered after she left for Carrow's. The idea that an unknown intruder had waited and watched made her skin crawl. She wondered if the priestess was the culprit.

Emma kept her eyes on it while she opened a drawer beneath. She pulled out a pair of shorts and a top and dressed. She removed a pair of running socks and put them on her hands, took a deep breath and lifted the skull from the shelf. Holding it out in front of her, she walked with it through the hall and into the kitchen, where she placed it in the stainless steel sink. It looked authentic, but she knew that it likely was not. The sharp intake of breath behind her told her that Latisha Johnson, the cook, was back.

Emma turned and saw her standing next to

a large man in army green overalls. The delivery-man had a large water balloon on his right shoulder. His skin was pale and his head shaved clean. A name tag embroidered on his shirt read CARL. He gave Emma a dull look and glanced at the skull with the same lack of curiosity.

"You should remove that immediately," Johnson said. "It brings death. It shouldn't be in the house."

"Where do you want me to set this up?" the deliveryman asked.

Johnson didn't respond. The stark fear on her face prompted Emma to once again pick up the skull. Its black socket eyes seemed to watch her. She carried it past both Johnson and the deliveryman. Johnson cringed away as Emma crossed next to her, but the man just flicked his eyes between the skull and Emma. He stared at it with an impressive calm.

"Lady, I got fifteen more deliveries to make. Where do you want this?" Emma heard the man ask again as she went out the back door, taking care to walk on the grass rather than the gravel of the driveway. The lawn felt warm under her feet. Hearing footsteps behind her, she looked back to see Johnson following at a safe distance. Emma kept going toward the garage, past the large green delivery truck parked in the driveway with the words SPRINGFED WATER emblazoned on the side. Once she reached the garage, she placed the skull gently on one of the tables. Johnson came to stand next to her.

"Miss Emma, you should leave. That's a message."

Emma had no doubt that it was, but she was intrigued that someone would go so far to try to frighten her, and in such a bizarre fashion. Wild men hacking at her with machetes scared her; Halloween props did not. She put her hands on her hips while she contemplated the skull. The deliveryman appeared behind Johnson holding a clipboard.

"Voodoo bokor killed my neighbor when I lived back in Haiti," the man said. He stepped closer to Johnson and thrust the clipboard at her. "Free trial is thirty days. You don't like it you call the company and I'll come back and take it away. Need to sign." He handed Johnson a pen. While she read the paper on the clipboard, the man looked at Emma. "You don't mess with a bokor. They bad. That skull means the evil one comes to get you."

"I don't believe in voodoo," Emma said. The man held her gaze with his dull eyes and emotionless face.

"Voodoo bokor gonna kill you," he said.

"That's enough!" Johnson snapped out the command. "I'll have no such talk around me." The man shifted his look to her.

"Sorry, ma'am," he said. He flashed Emma a sour look, turned and sauntered away. Emma watched the truck reverse down the driveway and disappear out the gate. Johnson frowned.

"What an unpleasant man," she said. She folded the yellow contract copy that he'd given her. "I'm not sure that I believe in voodoo either, but I do believe that humans have an almost unlimited drive to destroy each other when they want something that someone else has."

"Interesting choice of words. What do you think they want to take from me?"

"I think they want to stop you from collecting the plants."

Emma thought so, too. It was the only logical explanation for both the man's destruction in the garage and the skull in her bedroom.

"It's not going to work. The contract I have requires that I collect them, analyze them, and deliver my results in record time. I'm not giving up. My company needs this contract. After breakfast I'm going to pay a visit to Security. Find out who is currently on the island."

Half an hour later she returned to the garage. She started the car and shifted it into reverse.

"Don't you leave that awful thing in here! Take it with you," Johnson called to her from the driveway's edge. Emma nodded.

"Could you hand it to me?"

Johnson shook her head. "Oh no, I'm not touching it."

Emma sighed before putting the car back into park. She returned to the skull, put the socks back on her hands, and placed it down into the foot well. Then she reversed out of the driveway and headed to the airport.

Terra Cay was only twenty miles long and four miles wide. The mangrove swamp sat on the farthest end and the airport ran along the length. The short landing strip created a challenge for pilots, because it ended at the base of one of the hills. A mistake in landing could mean smashing into a wall of rock and dirt. Inclement weather only increased the risk. Several planes had crashed over the years, killing three pilots and four passengers. Extending the strip was not an option, because the other end managed to butt up against a bog. The area was chosen for the landing strip precisely because it was unsuitable for any other use.

Island Security was located in a small clapboard ranch house a quarter mile up the hill from the landing strip. It had the advantage of being close to the airport and in full view of arriving airplanes. This was also its disadvantage. Emma winced at the noise of an incoming plane. She parked in front of the building and lifted the skull out of the foot well. She closed the door with her foot and headed up the stairs to the front porch of the house. The door opened before she knocked.

"Latisha told me you were on your way," Moore said. He looked down at the skull in her hands. "Bring it in. We'd like a look at it."

Emma moved through a narrow hallway and into the main room on her right, which was large and airy. Potted ferns and soft yellow walls made the room inviting, as opposed to imposing. Most of the island kept this image of tropical living without a care in the world. Several desks placed in rows held computers and phones. In the back there was another, rectangular office that ran along the width of the room. It had a picture window through which Emma could see two large flat screen televisions. One was set to the Weather Channel and the other displayed a view of the small airport immigration office and its baggage claim area, which was open air and covered only by a roof.

A dark-skinned man in a short-sleeved white shirt with an Island Security logo on the front sat at one of the nearby desks. He looked about thirty-five years old, with neatly trimmed hair and a tiny earring in one ear. He stood. Emma placed the skull on one of the desks and couldn't help but think how incongruous it looked in the sunny office.

"I'd like you to meet Waylon Randiger. He's my second in command here." Moore indicated the man in the short-sleeved shirt. Emma removed the socks and shook his hand.

"Is it real?" Randiger asked.

She shook her head. "No." She put the socks back on her hands and turned the skull over. There was a smoothed edge of the skull that bore the remnants of a manufacturer's stamp that someone had tried to file off. "It's fake. A good fake, but fake nonetheless."

"You took pains not to get your fingerprints on it," Randiger said, "but I'm sorry to say that we'll not be able to take an impression here. We don't have the tools."

"I think it's teenagers playing a prank," Moore said.

"The man in the garage was no teenager," Emma said.

Randiger looked at her in surprise. "What man?"

Moore gave Randiger a sidelong glance. "Ms. Caldridge was attacked by a man when she interrupted him in the process of destroying some of her things in the garage."

"And a woman who claimed to be a voodoo priestess."

"Voodoo? Was there an offering?" Randiger said.

Emma nodded. "A dead rooster and now this,"

Randiger frowned. "Whoever is doing this has to be stopped."

Moore waved her into a chair next to his desk. "Can you give me a detailed description? I'll enter it into our database."

Emma glanced over and saw that the office had a Springfed watercooler in the corner. For a moment she toyed with the idea of telling Moore about the deliveryman's comment, but decided against it. What the man had said wasn't relevant to the investigation, and she decided to stick to the facts. She ran down the intruder's basics, including the keening noise he made while chasing her. She described his strange, twitching face and upturned eyes.

"Was he staring up at the sky?" Randiger asked.

Emma nodded. "All the while he was swinging at me. It was creepy."

"It sounds as though he was mentally unbalanced," Randiger said.

"He had dreadlocks." Moore said this as if it was significant.

"So not an islander," Randiger said.

"Why not? Do none have dreads?" Emma asked.

Randiger shook his head. "None. And we don't have anyone claiming to be a voodoo priestess living here. They must have come from off island."

Moore frowned at the skull. "We're just past peak season, which ended on January sixth. Most of the owners have left already. Gone back to their main houses. While we register everyone arriving by plane, it is possible some could dock at night and sneak in that way. *Doubtful*," Moore emphasized the word, "but definitely possible."

"And the staff?" Ellen asked. "How do they arrive?"

"By boat if they come from a nearby island, or plane if not. It's not likely that they would bring troublemakers, though, because jobs here are coveted. Every staff member is given a thorough background check by us before they are allowed to accept a position." Moore shook his head. "I'm still inclined to think the skull is the work of a teenager. Maybe one that is still home from school and wants to create some excitement while here."

"If he's not an islander and not staff, how else could he have gotten here? Boat?"

"Maybe from the mangrove side, where no one could see them land a boat," Moore said.

Randiger pursed his lips while he thought. "Only way to access the mangrove by boat is to pass over the blue holes first. No one I know would willingly take that route."

"Why not?" Emma said.

Randiger looked surprised. "I presume you've heard the stories."

"That they're loaded with phosphorescent minerals that glow blue?"

"That they're guarded by a giant sea monster that will suck you down into the depths, never to be seen again."

Emma wasn't sure if Randiger was kidding. "Sea monster? Are you serious? First I'm attacked by a voodoo priestess and next you tell me there are monsters in the water? Just what is going on here?"

"Hey, you're on an ancient island that was uninhabited for most of its existence. Stories are to be expected."

"She's going to dive them," Moore said. Emma paused. She hadn't yet told anyone on the island of her plans to dive the holes. She wondered where Moore had gotten that information.

Randiger looked alarmed. "I don't advise that. Why do you need to go there?"

"I'm collecting plants indigenous to the island. My lab, Pure Chemistry, is always searching for new plants that we can utilize in high-end cosmetic products. The mangrove has unique forms of algae and seaweed that contain ten times the normal levels of vitamins A and D as well as some indigenous mud composed of minerals in an unusual concentration. We're assuming the minerals wash in from the blue holes. I'm not too concerned about monsters."

"It's folklore, granted," Randiger said, "but I can't help but think it derived from an actual event and the story just got more fantastical over the years. We did have a boat go missing a year ago."

"But that could be completely unrelated."

"Maybe. But others have spoken about a creature that lives in the holes. It's been described as similar to a kraken from old sailor lore."

"Something that pulls boats into the deep, never to be seen again?" Emma said.

Randiger nodded. "I know. Crazy, right? But those stories have been handed down for years through our ancestors. I know these people. Salt of the earth fisherman not given to hallucinations. If they tell the story, there must be some truth there. At the very least I suggest that you not go alone, and I can guarantee that you will have a difficult time getting anyone from the island to accompany you."

"Please don't worry, I'm not so foolish as to dive alone. As for company, what about Mr. Marwell?" Elliott Marwell was the head of Seahook Tours, a fishing company that specialized in deep-sea fishing.

Randiger looked skeptical. "Doubtful. He's never agreed before when other tourists have asked him."

"He's never agreed before because he's one of the tale-tellers," Moore said. Randiger looked surprised.

"Elliott? Really?" Randiger said.

Moore nodded. "He went out one day and got too close. Swears that his boat almost got taken in. He never went near that area again."

"That's what I need," Emma said. "Someone who's been there."

Moore shook his head. "Won't be Elliott."

"Still, I'll ask."

Moore shrugged. "Can't hurt." He indicated the skull. "We'll look into this as best we can." That's it? Emma thought. She probed a bit deeper.

"Will you inform the police in the neighboring islands about the two of them?" Randiger glanced at Moore out of the corner of his eye. Moore frowned.

"I'd hate to wind everyone up. I thought I'd interview the staff of the various houses first. See if anyone knows or has seen them. The one with the dreadlocks in particular, since he should be easy to spot."

"How many houses are on the island?"

"One hundred, not including the hotel and various boats that dock. Since we're past peak season now the population is shrinking daily as visitors fly home."

"News travels fast," Randiger added, "so don't be surprised if most have already heard it."

"I'm actually more concerned that the neighboring island police forces get a report so that they can keep an eye out for these two," Emma said. Once again she noticed Moore's discomfort at the idea. "I'm not looking to kill tourism, but if you're correct and they came from a nearby location, that seems to be an obvious choice."

"I'll be sure to let them know if it becomes appropriate." Moore's face held a stubborn look, and Randiger gave Emma an apologetic glance. It was clear that notifying the authorities would be last on Moore's list. Emma decided to let them start with the locals and work their way around.

"I guess that will have to do for now," she said.

Randiger walked her to the door. "In the meantime, it sounds as though you'd better lock your doors *and* windows at night," he said.

8

Kemmer stood in the dark in front of his partially gutted beach house and watched the solitary beam of light on the water draw closer. The fire department had gone and the girls were asleep in the big house. He was alone. His Akita hound sat at his side. Kemmer liked the dog, but unless it could suddenly learn to do a trick that would generate mounds of cash it was going to have to find somewhere else to live. His sister was enamored of all of his dogs and owned an estate five miles away. He would send them to her. The light pulled closer and he could make out the shape of a boat drawing near. When it reached the dock the driver cut the engine and brought it alongside. Another crew member jumped lightly onto the pier and secured the boat. He nodded at Kemmer, stepped aside to allow a tall, thin man to step past him onto the boards, then retreated into the cabin, leaving Kemmer and the thin man alone on the pier. Kemmer strolled up and thrust out a hand.

"Welcome to St. Martin," he said.

The man's narrow face, long nose, and hard eyes matched his nickname: the Vulture. He'd been given the name by some of his corporate victims; companies whose balance sheets had turned bright red when their profits dried up in the latest downturn. The Vulture dangled the carrot of investment capital at outrageous interest rates in front of the CEOs of the struggling companies, swooped in when a company failed to make a payment, and then picked clean the assets, leaving the employees, creditors, and shareholders in the dust. Kemmer had met him several times before but always made it a point to keep his distance. Of course, that was when he'd been flush with cash and had no need of the Vulture's bailout funds. Now, he wasn't so lucky. Without an immediate capital infusion, the entire network of shell companies that he used to hide the fact that he was broke would come crashing down. As so famously spoken by financier Warren Buffett, when the tide goes out, one sees who is swimming naked. Kemmer was naked and shivering. The Vulture was his last hope.

"What happened to the beach house?" the thin man asked.

"A bomb."

"Was Mr. Sumner in it when it exploded?" Kemmer had no idea who Mr. Sumner was, but he wasn't going let this man know that.

"No one was in the house."

"A pity," the man said.

"Come to the top of the hill. I have some fine brandy up there. We can sit and talk."

The man shook his head. "No. I have only a few minutes here. I'm headed further south to the Windward Islands. How much money do you require?" Kemmer did his best to hide his surprise at the blunt question.

"Ten million." The man showed no emotion at the figure.

"And the collateral?"

"The proceeds from my salvage company."

"What company is that?"

"It's called Deep Sea Treasure Hunters. We search for buried treasure from sunken Spanish galleons throughout the world." The man raised an eyebrow.

"And are you successful?"

Kemmer puffed up a bit. Treasure hunting was his passion. "Very. We just discovered coins from a shipwrecked Spanish galleon that will be worth millions at auction."

"How much are you allowed to keep?"

"Fifty percent of the proceeds."

"Why do you need my money, then?"

"It will take close to three years to catalog, verify, and auction the coins. I need the money by next week."

"I know of your tax trouble. This money will be confiscated, I'm sure. I want you to hand deliver the majority of the company's shares to me and then begin an expedition to the blue holes."

Kemmer was astonished. He'd thought he would be the one directing this meeting, but it was clear that this man had his own plans hatched. Still, he felt compelled to tell him that the blue holes were an unlikely spot for a shipwreck. The odds of finding treasure there were slim.

"There's nothing in the blue holes except mineral deposits." The man gave him a considering look.

"I understand that many believe them to be guarded by a sea monster. Are you afraid?"

Kemmer snorted. "Of monsters? No." He stared at the man a moment. The request was extraordinary. And easy to fulfill, given enough time. "How soon do you require this expedition?"

"In three days."

"What? Impossible. It's high season, my boats are booked for the next three weeks."

The man shrugged. "Then we have no deal." He turned to go. Kemmer grabbed his arm.

"Wait. If I arrange this expedition, you'll lend the money?"

"The expedition *and* the shares."

"As collateral only. They remain mine unless I default," Kemmer said.

The man nodded. "That is acceptable."

Kemmer felt something akin to elation at the idea that his immediate money troubles might be over. "You're on." The thin man turned back to his boat. "But tell me," Kemmer said, "what's in the blue holes that you want so much?" The man shot him a look from the corner of his eyes.

"Not what, who. Just prepare the expedition. I'll arrange the rest."

Kemmer watched him step back onto the boat.

The crew untied it and turned it back out to sea. Walking past his burned beach house toward the estate above, Kemmer couldn't shake the feeling that he'd agreed to something much more deadly than a simple expedition.

9

Terra Cay's harbor was unlike those of any Emma had seen in the islands. Pristine and well regulated, it only accommodated a few ships, a design created deliberately to control the number of boat owners requesting to dock. If you didn't have enough money to buy or rent a villa, the island didn't want your company.

Seahook Tours operated out of a blue painted shed at the dock's far end. She parked and started over to it, strolling in the sunlight. From twenty feet away she spotted Elliott Marwell on the deck of a beautiful white yacht. As she drew near, Emma saw the boat's name: *Siren's Song.* Marwell's dark skin gleamed under a white baseball cap. He wore a navy tee shirt, black cargo shorts, and a small silver hoop earring in his left ear. He glanced up and straightened to watch her approach. When she got closer he began to smile.

"Something tells me you're Emma Caldridge," he said.

Emma smiled back. "I finally made it here."

"Come aboard. It's nice to meet you in person." He came to the boat's edge and helped her onto the deck. His hand was warm and rough-skinned. She'd been in conversation with Marwell both on the phone and by e-mail for over three months in preparation for her trip and had arranged an expedition around the island's perimeter. She would use the time to scout good locations for her search.

The deck sported built-in cushions and tables in a configuration for casual dining, as well as side benches covered with outdoor fabric. Emma peeked into the main salon. Gleaming wood with shiny black, glossy painted trim lined the walls. A flat screen television complete with a built-in sound system ran along one side, and next to that, a granite-covered wet bar with a stocked liquor cabinet behind it. On the opposite side there was a modern couch, chairs, cocktail table, and credenza, and to the rear, a dining table with six chairs.

"This is stunning," she said. "It looks like some sort of penthouse in New York City. Not like a boat at all."

Marwell nodded. "It's an eighty foot Hatteras. It has two staterooms and two heads, along with a hot tub up top. It's a nice size. Of course, not as big as some of the others." He jutted his chin at two much larger yachts docked farther down. "But in some ways I like it better. When you're out on her you still feel as though you're boating. Those others feel like a floating hotel." She saw that he'd been pouring ice into a cooler. Next to it sat several six packs of beer and cans of soda. "Care for a drink? Take your pick." Emma shook her head.

"Little too early for beer."

He chuckled. "For the group that I'm taking it's never too early."

"And that would be?"

"Richard Carrow and his guests. Up on the West Hill."

"I've met him."

Marwell settled onto a bench seat along the boat's side.

"He's friendly. Been an owner here for four years, so I know him well. Some of the others in his crowd . . ." Marwell rocked his hand back and forth. Emma settled onto the bench next to him.

"Is this your boat?"

"No. This is Carrow's. The *Seahook* is over there." He waved at a much smaller boat a few slips down. It had two fishing rods locked into holders at the aft.

"Ahh. That one looks fast."

Marwell beamed. "She is. I like these big cruisers for comfort, but there's something about a fast boat that gets me smiling. We'll use the *Seahook* for your expedition." His comment gave her the opening she needed.

"My research into the island leads me to believe that the reason the seaweed here is so unique is due to the proximity of the blue holes. I think the same minerals that give them that blue glow are feeding the seaweed. Rather than do the perimeter tour, I'd like to head out there to dive them."

Marwell's face closed. "I can't take you there. The blue holes aren't safe."

Emma nodded. "I've heard the stories. Can you fill me in? Everyone seems to know the fables in general, but no one has the specifics. I'm told you might."

He sighed. "I used to get quite close to them. Not enough so that anyone could dive them, but close enough to get a glimpse. They're famous among the diving set and a lot of people wanted to explore them. The only thing that has stopped them is the fact that they would have to dock here to do it, and this island is too expensive for most." Marwell seemed reluctant to speak further. Emma decided to prod him.

"What's so dangerous about them?"

"Well, they've never been mapped, for one thing. Some say they extend all the way to the Bahamas, where there is a second set. Like an underground network of caves. Once inside, they stretch downward. It takes a better than average diver to attempt them. And the rumors of a sea creature have kept most of the locals in the area away."

"Do you believe the rumors?" she asked. Marwell rose, began to pull bottles from the six packs and shove them into the cooler.

"One time I got closer than usual. Was a sunny day, just like this one," he waved a bottle in the air, "and I didn't have a booking. I decided to head that way, and when I got near I thought, oh what the hell, I'll just go take a look." He shook his head. "It takes at least three hours to reach them, and when I did, the sky was still bright blue, the waves slow and easy, a perfect day for boating." He paused. "I was directly over them. They were beautiful. The sea takes on a deeper, richer hue where they are and seems to sparkle ten times more than usual. I wasn't there more than five minutes when I felt the boat give a lurch. It was as if something had grabbed onto the hull and yanked." Emma was surprised to see Marwell shudder.

"I threw it into gear, but the boat didn't move. Something was holding it in place. I opened the throttle all the way." He pointed to the *Seahook*. "You've got to understand that I have two powerful engines on that boat. I have to if I'm going to deep-sea fish. But the engines were whining and the boat didn't budge. Whatever had it in its grasp gave another yank and the aft section started to sink in the water, which should give you an indication of the incredible power of the thing." He put the bottle in his hand into the cooler.

"By this time I was in an outright panic. I leaned over the side to see what was there. The water near the stern was churning and foaming and there was a large black mass below. I ran back to the bridge and turned the steering wheel. The boat swung to the side and broke free. The twisting motion must have forced whatever it was to release its hold. I took off out of there as fast as I could go." Marwell wiped an arm across his face where he'd begun to sweat. He looked at Emma. "I hope you don't think I'm a coward, but I've never gone back there, and I never will."

Emma didn't know what to say. She didn't think Marwell was the type to lie, but she didn't know what to make of the story.

"Could it have been a sea creature?" She put up a hand. "*Not* a monster, you understand, but an actual creature?"

Marwell came back to sit next to her on the bench.

"I've thought long and hard since then, as you can imagine. I've actually spent quite a bit of time researching it, just trying to figure out what the heck it was . . . Did you read the recent story about a boat in an open ocean race in the vicinity of the holes?"

"The one that claimed a giant squid had attached a tentacle to the hull and they dragged it for miles before it let go?"

Marwell nodded. "That's the one. They actually saw tentacles and suction cups the size of dinner plates, because they had sleeping quarters and a cabin window below. I never saw anything like that, but it's the only possible explanation that I can come up with."

"Some Japanese fisherman photographed a giant squid just recently. It was over forty feet long."

"I've read about that as well. Forty feet is amazing. Just one tentacle of that size would wrap around my boat completely." Marwell shook his head. "The ocean is something mysterious, isn't it? It's why I love it." He frowned at Emma. "But whatever it was, I don't need to meet up with it again. It's too dangerous. That thing latched on within five minutes of me being there. It's waiting and watching."

Emma wasn't sure how to respond to Marwell's story. He struck Emma as a practical, rational sort of person not prone to flights of fancy, yet she wondered if the years of folklore about the blue holes had left him assuming he'd meet a creature there. Still, that explanation didn't entirely sit well with her either. She thought there was likely something in the holes. Nonetheless, she intended to dive them.

"I understand your concern," she said. "Is there anyone else that you think would be willing to take me there? I'm not so foolish as to dive alone, but everyone seems to be leery of the area."

Marwell shook his head. "No one I know will do it. I'm sorry." The sound of several engines reverberated through the air, and moments later four Jeeps screeched into parking spots near the *Siren's Song*. Emma watched Carrow, Warner, and several others pile out, all with tote bags. They headed toward the boat. When Carrow saw her, he broke into a smile and waved. As he approached he greeted Marwell.

"She ready to go?"

Marwell nodded. "Ready when you are."

Carrow turned to Emma. "Care to join us?"

She shook her head. "Wish I could, but I've got more collecting to do."

"Where?"

"She's thinking of diving the blue holes," Marwell said. "I'm working on talking her out of it."

Emma patted Marwell on the shoulder. "Thanks for the concern, but I've got to do this."

"Not alone you won't. Promise me," Marwell said.

Carrow tilted his head to one side. "No one will go with you?"

Emma shook her head. "No one."

"And you have to do it?"

She nodded. "It's my job. I'm certified. But of course I won't go alone."

Carrow smiled. "I'll go with you."

Marwell frowned. "Mr. Richard—"

"You will?" Emma was thrilled. "Are you certified?"

"I am," he said. Emma glanced at Marwell, who nodded.

"He's actually quite an experienced and careful diver, but that doesn't mean I think you two should do this."

"Do what?" Warner and a man Emma hadn't met were on deck now, standing next to Carrow.

"Dive the blue holes," Carrow said. The man cocked his head to the side.

"Cave diving? Isn't that a type of extreme sport?" he said. "I saw a television show about a cave that has over forty dead divers in it."

"That one is in Egypt," Carrow said. "It's legendary due to its danger. But the blue holes here don't have that reputation."

Warner grimaced. "Forty dead people? That's disgusting. Why do they do it?"

"It's a form of extreme diving," Emma said, nodding at the man who'd mentioned extreme sports. "The Egyptian caves represent a challenge that a lot of divers can't resist. Like the challenge that Mount Everest represents for mountain climbers."

"Lots of dead people left there too," the man said.

"I don't understand that obsession either," Warner noted.

"I can't go today." Carrow indicated the crowd that was forming on the cruiser's deck, "but I can anytime this week. You just let me know when." Marwell got an agitated look on his face.

"Both of you stop. This is dangerous. There's something out there. I've seen it. The risk is not worth it. Especially not for a job. Let the boss take his own risks."

"I can't," Emma said.

"Why not?" Marwell put his hands on his hips.

"Because I am the boss."

10

An hour later Emma drove up to the mangrove's edge. The day's heat was rising and the sun beat down on the car. Crawling through a mangrove was one of her least favorite things to do. The footing beneath could be treacherous, and in places one could sink deep into the brackish water. The twisted mangrove roots extended for several acres, their arching formation emerging from the water in a tangle of wood.

She hauled on her knee-high Wellington rubber boots, shoved a hat with an attached mosquito net onto her head, and pulled the strap of a messenger bag around her neck, settling it across her body. The area where she'd found a rich source of algae was located within the heart of the mangrove. The first time, it took her almost three hours to locate it, partly due to the difficulty in climbing through the swamp, but also because she'd been canvassing the entire grove to find it. Now that she knew the coordinates where it could be found, she hoped to cut the time in half. After opening her compass she started into the swamp.

It was slow going. She grabbed the branches above to assist her in clambering over the tangled wood below. The extensive root growth that was a godsend for the ecosystem because it saved the island from erosion was a hassle for Emma. Despite the obstacles, she moved ahead in a steady rhythm.

Two hours later she made it to the clearing. The mangrove trees there formed a circle, with an open area in the middle where the sun beat down. The water, formerly a brown, brackish color, took on a green hue with a slight turquoise phosphorescence that she suspected came from the blue holes miles away. Here, the sun beat on the water, heating it and causing the algae to thrive. She pulled some gloves and plastic pouches out of the messenger bag and began scooping up the slick tendrils that floated in the water by the water's edge. She listened to the buzzing of a bee somewhere to the right and saw a dragonfly zipping around ten feet ahead. The sun-heated air felt warm and moist, and the water made a splashing noise as she plunged her hand into it. She felt a peace settle over her as she collected the samples.

She looked up in time to see the man raise the machete.

The blade whipped down and she rolled right, crawling up onto her hands and knees and catapulting herself over a long mangrove root that twisted out of the swamp. The man's Rasta braids swayed with the exertion of his swing, and she heard the metal thump into a root. She only looked at him for an instant, but it was enough to see that his face was still twisted.

She leaped over another branch and landed with both feet in the muck, sinking lower as her weight pushed her into the ooze. She pulled her foot up and out with a sucking sound and grabbed at the branches over her head, using them to swing her way to the next opening. Behind her, she heard him splash into the water. Drops of the resulting spray hit her back.

The swamp consisted of ninety acres of wetlands, and she had spent nearly two hours hiking in. She was returning three times faster, but knew she still wouldn't reach the edge and civilization for at least another thirty minutes.

And he kept pursuing her. Emma heard his heavy breathing and splashes as he clambered behind. Every so often he vocalized a whistling wail and chills ran through her at the animalistic sound. She swallowed and kept going, refusing to waste the time it would take to turn around and look. Often they had to crawl through the swamp to move ahead. Emma took advantage of every small opening, hoping the forest of mangrove roots and limbs that grew in long lines next to each other would impede his massive shoulders and large body. She also heard him hacking at the smaller branches with his machete. The cracking noises of splitting wood only served to make her fear ratchet higher.

As an ultra marathon runner, Emma prided herself on the mental endurance she'd cultivated as part of her training. Ultra runs could be as long as one hundred miles and last over twenty-four hours. Often the mind gave out before the legs did. Self-doubt had no place in an endurance run. She knew this basic fact of endurance sports and had spent many hours teaching herself to think only those thoughts that would further her forward progress. If the idea to stop entered her consciousness, she would ruthlessly shove it back into the recesses of her brain before it could take hold.

Now, when the fear reached her throat and her eyes began to sting with tears, she did the same thing she did on mile eighty of a hundred mile run—she told herself that she would prevail because to stop meant failure. In this case, she knew that to stop would kill her.

Mud and stinking water covered her clothes. Her sodden shoes felt like heavy weights attached to her ankles. Her palms were slick with sweat and striped with green ooze that wrapped around some of the lower, underwater branches. She splashed down into the rank liquid and back up onto the twisted roots in what seemed an endless vista of misshapen branches.

Finally, she took the time to glance behind her to gauge his progress. All she saw were mangrove trunks in a wild, squiggly line pattern. He wasn't behind her. She slowed, trying to control the loud rasping of her own breathing in order to hear. There was nothing. Not the sound of splashing water, winded breathing, or cracking wood.

Once again he was gone as quick as he had appeared.

Emma slowed her pace and not long afterward emerged from the grove. She'd left her Jeep at the mangrove's edge but didn't see it in any direction and knew she was in the wrong place. After a moment she found her bearings and headed west, keeping out in the open and well away from the brush. She wasn't about to give the man benefit of cover. If he was going to attack again, he'd have to cross thirty feet of open field.

A butterfly landed on a nearby weed, its wings spread to the sun, and birds chirped all around. Her heart still thumped at an alarming rate despite the beauty and peacefulness around her. Deceptive peacefulness, she thought. This island was harboring more dark secrets than anyone suspected.

The midday sun beat down, creating shimmering heat waves on the pavement when she found the Jeep. The leather seats were hot to the touch as she gingerly lowered herself into the driver's side, then threw the car into gear and headed back toward her villa. Her clothes stank and her heart still raced. She mentally crossed off the rest of her required errands. She'd come to Terra Cay in the hopes that after collecting her specimens she could spend the rest of the holiday relaxing, but now all she wanted was to get back to her house in Miami Beach. She shoved the hands-free headset for her phone into her ear and called Moore.

"I found him," she said. "He's in the mangrove." She briefly described the attack and the location where she last saw the dreadlocked man. "I'm getting out of this area," she concluded. "I don't want to be alone if he returns."

"I understand. Randiger and I will take it from here. Go home and lock your doors."

Emma shifted the car into second gear as the Jeep started the climb to the top of the hill. She swung through the entrance guarded by two pillars and slowed when she saw a blue Aston Martin parked in her spot. Carrow leaned against the door, speaking on a cell phone. He hung up when he saw her. His expression was grim, his mouth set. His eyes were bloodshot and all of the exuberance she'd seen in him earlier was gone. She parked halfway on the grass next to his car, killed the engine and looked at her watch.

"Isn't it a bit early for you to be back?" she said. Carrow gave her a somber look, and seemed not to notice her disheveled state.

"We airlifted Martin out about two hours ago. He never woke up, and I decided not to risk waiting."

"I'm sorry to hear that," Emma said.

"And now Layton's asleep."

11

Layton Nalen was the band's bass player.

"Does he do drugs as well?"

Carrow nodded. "I checked for mandrake powder. Nothing."

"Oxy?"

Carrow sighed. "Yes. Cocaine when he can get it and some new prescription drug marketed to shift workers that are employed at all hours. It's designed to keep them awake. Of course then comes the alcohol to take the edge off and sleeping pills to bring it full circle."

Emma wasn't surprised at this last bit of information. What went up had to go down, and most addicts swallowed tranquilizers to get to sleep. She suspected that he had found the mandrake and dumped it into his alcohol as well.

"It doesn't sound as if you'll be recording."

Carrow shook his head. "We're under contract to produce another record, and soon. We're behind as it is. I called the studio on the mainland and we've arranged for a second crew to come here. Engineers, equipment, and two new musicians. They're on their way. We'll set up at the villa. And Layton will be airlifted out this afternoon. There's a tropical storm brewing. It's some miles away but could impact on our ability to get him out if we wait any longer."

"I'm sorry," she said. She sighed and reached into the back of the Jeep to get her messenger bag with the specimens. Suddenly she felt unbearably tired. Before she could lift the strap to her shoulder, Carrow reached out and picked it up for her.

"You look exhausted." He eyed her clothes. "Were you crawling through the mangrove?"

Emma shook her head. "More like running for my life. The man was there."

Carrow's eyebrows flew up. "Did you tell Duncan?"

Emma nodded. "I called him from the Jeep once I got back to it. He and Randiger were headed there to look for him. I decided to come here. I need a shower and some time to think. There's something strange about the entire thing."

"Were his eyes crazy again?" Carrow grimaced. "That sounded like the weirdest thing about him when you described him to me last night."

"They were. But I'm not sure what it is he's after. I just don't believe that it's me, because I've done nothing to merit the attacks."

"Maybe he wants you to stop collecting."

Emma nodded. "That's the only possible explanation. But what he wants is irrational. If I don't collect the plants, someone else will. They can't stop progress forever." Emma started walking toward the villa, and Carrow walked in step with her.

"Doesn't sound like rationality is something this guy's got in abundance, if you know what I mean."

Carrow's comment depressed Emma further. Her tropical island vacation was fast turning into a demented circus, and she was beginning to seriously consider abandoning the entire project. She would have, except the cosmetic company had paid her extremely well to embark on this mission. Collecting the plants was only phase one of the job. After that her lab was to formulate test batches of creams for the second phase. The final phase was to conduct clinical trials on the creams' antiaging effectiveness. Between all three phases her company stood to make millions, and keep her and her employees busy for the next four years. She hated to walk away from such an interesting and lucrative project because of a madman.

"I need a shower," she said. Carrow ran a hand through his hair.

"Can you help me search for the mandrake?" he asked. "I asked the landscaping crew, but while they don't know what it looks like, they insist that they do know every plant around my villa and it's not there. That doesn't mean it's not somewhere else on the island, though."

Emma paused. With everything going wrong, the last thing she needed was another plant to acquire. She was behind schedule before the midnight visitors, but now she would have to harvest ten more plants. It had taken her three days to locate the first batch, but she hoped to cut that time in half. Still, she needed to use every waking moment to complete what she was sent to Terra Cay to do. But something in Carrow's eyes made her reconsider. Behind his smiles and flirting with Johnson last night, there seemed to reside a fear. As if something was happening that he hadn't yet revealed. He caught her hesitation and put his hands up, palms out.

"No drugs or selling our souls to the devil, I promise."

Emma smiled. "You misunderstand. I'm only hesitating because last night's destruction and to-day's interruption has put me behind schedule. I'll have to head back to the mangrove and collect again no matter what the crazy man wants from me. Then I need to dive into the blue holes and scrape the walls for minerals."

"I promised to go with you, and I will, but I really would like you to look at Layton and find the mandrake garden first."

"So you don't believe the stories about the blue holes?"

He shook his head. "Not at all. But something strange is happening on this island. I don't like it."

"When does Layton get airlifted out?"

"Three hours."

"Then let's go now. Give me a chance to shower. Would you like some coffee while you wait?" Emma noticed that Carrow looked relieved.

"Love some."

They headed into the villa, passing through the kitchen. Johnson was there, cutting up a large fish. She smiled at Carrow.

"Why Mr. Richard, how nice to see you," she said.

"I'm here to drink some of your heavenly coffee." Carrow's smile and flirtatious manner was back. No one would believe that a few minutes ago he'd looked so grim.

"Right away."

Emma guided him out to a gazebo at the edge of the infinity pool. He settled onto a small love seat. A scorpion made its way from under the nearby cocktail table, scurrying through the grass and disappearing in the flower garden.

Johnson brought a wooden tray that held a coffee press and two cups. Carrow added cream to his, along with two heaping teaspoons of sugar, and took a sip. "Ms. Johnson, you've outdone yourself this time," he said. She smiled and walked away.

"I'll be right back," Emma said.

Twenty minutes later she was showered, dressed, and though her hair was still wet, the rest of her was at least presentable. She lowered herself into Carrow's Aston Martin and strapped on the seat belt. Once again he whizzed around Deadman's Curve back to his house. The sports car, though, took the bend in stride, hugging the road and cornering without slipping out from behind, as the Jeep had. The engine roared as he accelerated, and Emma felt every bump in the road from the combination of the tight suspension and the performance wheels.

A short time later he pulled into the driveway on West Hill that led to his house and parked the car in an area beneath an overhang. He turned off the engine and Emma soaked in the silence. He was looking at her, but it was clear that his mind was miles away.

"Great car," she said finally. His eyes focused and he smiled.

"Wonderful car. Growing up I dreamed of owning one." He shrugged. "It was so far beyond my imagination that I would try to stop myself from even thinking about it. But the vision kept coming back, over and over. And now," his smile broadened, "here it is."

He swung the door open and Emma joined him, the two of them walking to the house. The only sounds were the chattering of birds, the wind blowing through the leaves, and her shoes crunching on the gravel drive.

Carrow opened the carved door. The inside of the house was in chaos. Wailing came from a room in the back, and Warner, fully dressed in jeans and a nautical striped tee shirt, her feet bare, came running down the hall and straight into Carrow's arms.

"He's going to die!" she sobbed. He put one arm around her and gave Emma a shocked look.

"Who?" he said.

"Layton!" Warner's body shook with fear. Her panic seemed to fill the space, and Emma felt her own skin crawl, both at the image of the shaking Warner and the unearthly wailing in the house.

"Where's his room?" she asked.

"Down the hall, opposite Martin's." Carrow moved Warner to the side. She clung to him and he kept his arm around her neck as he started toward the open door and where the wailing seemed to be emanating. Emma stepped in behind them and saw a man, fully clothed, on all fours on the bed. His muscles jerked and he catapulted up three feet before landing again. His face held a terrified expression, his mouth was open, and he wailed in a long, wavering, panicked warble. His body jerked again and up he went into the air, landing on the bed.

Rory, the medium, stood on one side of the mattress, swaying and intoning a singsong chant. She wore a tee shirt and jeans and her feet were bare. Around her neck was a large wooden crucifix on a leather string. The song was a mixture of strange words sung in a minor key, almost like a Gregorian chant. Layton kept jumping, not noticing them though they walked into the room and stood at the foot of the bed.

"What the hell is going on here?" Carrow said. His voice was harsh. Rory stopped singing. Layton gave another piercing wail and his limbs jerked.

"He's possessed by evil spirits," Rory said. "Can't you see? I'm chanting to make them leave his body and return to the depths, where they belong."

"Did you call the doctor?" Carrow asked.

"Why would I? No doctor can help him," Rory replied.

"I did," Warner said. "Ten minutes ago."

The scene would have been unbelievable to Emma if it wasn't for the obvious terror on Layton Nalen's face. His muscles jerked again, as if he had no control over his limbs, the bedsprings creaking when he landed. His breath came in gasps and sweat glowed on his face. Emma took a step forward.

"Don't get near him!" Rory said. "Can't you see that he is inhabited by something evil? You both should put on a cross, immediately! You are vulnerable to demonic possession if you don't."

Emma couldn't help it; she snorted, both in anger and disbelief. Anger that Rory would simply stand and sing while Nalen fought his spasming body, and disbelief that she hadn't called an ambulance. Rory's face flushed red.

"This is nothing to laugh at. Can't you see he's fighting the demon inside?"

Nalen made a terrified, groaning sound as he jerked and jumped into the air, rising and falling on all fours again.

"I can see he's in distress," Emma said, "but I don't see a demon and I don't think you can assume anything. You should have called the doctor."

"You're wrong, he *is* possessed," Rory said. "Layton was in here calling out evil." She waved a hand in the direction of the bathroom. For the first time, Emma looked in that direction. Through the door she saw a red pentagram painted on the bathroom's white tile floor. It appeared to have been drawn in a streaky, red substance that, if it wasn't blood, certainly looked like it. At each point on the pentacle there was a black, votive candle. The flames glowed.

"He and the rest of the band play at devil worship," Rory said. She leaned in closer to Emma. "But evil is nothing to play with. He got what he conjured. Now we have to get it out of him somehow."

Emma didn't respond. She agreed that evil wasn't anything to play with, but whatever was in Nalen, she doubted it was a demon. She suspected he was experiencing a side effect from the cocktail of the many drugs Carrow had said the man took on a regular basis. She moved closer to the bed.

"Mr. Nalen, can you hear me?" she said. Nalen neither looked her way nor responded to her question. He just crouched on the mattress and panted, as if waiting for the next spasm. Sweat beads covered his forehead. Emma reached out to touch his arm.

"Don't touch him! The demon will transfer to you!" Rory said. Warner groaned again and Carrow stepped closer, dragging Warner, who still clung to him.

"I don't think that's going to happen," Emma snapped. Rory took a step toward her, and for a moment Emma thought the woman would hit her. Instead she slapped her hands together.

"I wash my hands of it. You deserve what you get. Don't come to me when you no longer can control the demon inside."

"I'll take my chances," Emma replied. Carrow firmly placed the clinging Warner off to the side and stepped closer to Layton.

"Not you, too," Rory said. "Don't put yourself at risk."

Carrow ignored her. "Layton, you hear me? Can you tell me what's going on?"

Nalen's body leapt again. He let out a high-pitched wail that ended on a whistle. It was clear to Emma that he was exhausted and in pain. He wouldn't be able to sustain the jerking action of his muscles much longer. The phone rang and she started in surprise. Carrow went to the bedside table, answered it, and after a brief conversation slammed it back down.

"That was the doctor. He says that he's on another matter that's serious and can't get here. He'll call in a prescription for a tranquilizer to the Acute Care Center. He said we need to sedate him, to get Layton's muscles to stop jerking."

"How far is the Acute Care Center?" Emma asked. "I'll go pick up the pills."

"Twenty minutes."

Forty minutes round-trip. Too long, she thought, but wondered if Nalen's heart would hold out. He was pale, shaking and sweating. He howled again and his panting increased.

"Anyone have tranquilizers?" Carrow asked. He looked at Warner. "Do you know where Layton kept his stash?"

Warner shook her head. "He told me last night that he was out." Nalen howled again.

"What about the mandrake?" Carrow said to Emma. "You mentioned last night that it was a narcotic. Will that work?"

She nodded. "It will, but it's risky. I have no idea how to administer it."

"I'll administer it," Carrow said. "We don't have the time to go to the clinic and back." He spun around and grabbed Warner's hand, pulling her with him toward the door.

It wasn't long before he returned with the mandrake powder in a small bowl. He held it in one hand, a glass of water in the other. Warner, who followed him into the room, held a set of measuring spoons.

"How much?" Carrow asked Emma. Layton wailed again, this time with an earsplitting shriek.

"Hurry!" Warner said. "He's getting worse."

"One tablespoon in the glass." Emma was guessing. Mandrake was so rare and so rarely used that the amounts needed to induce somnolence would be outside the normal dosing information available to her. She doubted even a Google search would produce any credible dosing instructions.

Carrow held the bowl out to Warner, who measured the amount and dumped it into the water. He swirled the liquid to mix it, handed Warner the bowl, and approached the jerking man on the bed. He waited until Nalen was once again between seizures and then put the glass to his lips.

"Drink," he said. Nalen's eyes didn't move but he must have understood because he drank.

Carrow held the glass and tipped it slowly, making sure that Nalen had time to swallow it all. Nalen jumped again, but this time the wailing didn't come.

Emma watched him and kept note of the time. After three minutes he stopped jumping. In five his muscles' violent twitching seemed to ease. After ten minutes his eyes began to droop and his arms collapsed. Carrow helped move him into a resting position on the bed. Five minutes later Nalen fell asleep.

The room was quiet. Warner quietly cried and Rory frowned. Carrow moved over to the bathroom and gazed at the pentagram, then returned to stand at the side of the bed.

"What fools we are," he said.

12

Carol Stromeyer piloted the boat across the water toward the small island of Anguilla. A slice of moon threw a glow onto the waves, and the air was warm as it blew across the skin on her arms. She still wore the balaclava over her face, even though Sumner had correctly guessed her identity earlier. She kept her focus on the GPS display for the boat and did her best not to dwell on the man she had just killed. Stromeyer was former military and had killed before, but that was a while ago and in battle. This was the first time since then, and she was doing her best to remind herself that he would have surely killed Sumner had she not shot first. She turned her mind to the problem of who had paid the two men to attack Sumner. Between the bombing and the shooting, it appeared that he was a target. She glanced his way. He wasn't looking at her, and she took advantage of that fact to take his measure.

Stromeyer had spoken to Sumner many times on the telephone, but had never met him in person. The first thing that struck her about him was his height. He stood over six feet two inches and had a straight but relaxed posture. She knew that he was a reticent man, and he lived up to that reputation now. He sat on a bench against the port side and remained quiet while staring out at the ocean. In fact he hadn't said much since the revelation at the dock, and she left him alone with his thoughts.

Stromeyer had been handling a volatile assignment in St. Martin for several months now, and felt no closer to her goal. The lack of progress had been frustrating until tonight. When she'd heard the man claim that he was paid to take out Sumner and Caldridge, a big piece of the puzzle fell into place. There had been rumors for over a year that large shipments of both guns and a new, highly dangerous weapon was soon to pass from South America through the Caribbean and on to the U.S. mainland. If someone wanted both Caldridge and Sumner dead, it was likely that the players in the sale would be from some past event where both were involved. Sumner had met Caldridge in the jungles of Colombia when an organization was arranging an arms trade, and again in Somalia when another group tried to steal a pharmaceutical drug that could be used as a weapon. Stromeyer would review both events again in search of a link between those scenarios and the present shipment.

Darkview had been hired by the Department of Defense to discover whether the rumors were true, and to stop the transfer. Edward Banner, her business partner and the president of Darkview, had accepted a contract with the understanding that the DOD wanted not only to halt the flow of weapons, but to obtain solid evidence of the money laundering and offshore transactions funding the sales. As a private company, Darkview was not subject to the same restrictions as the U.S. military operating in a foreign arena. Where a military action would be seen as a breach of international law, even an act of war against the island nations, a private company could act in any way it saw fit. But cracking the local banks and their money gathering operations was a lot tougher than it appeared. Several of the small nations in which the weapons were to pass refused to provide any assistance to Darkview's investigation.

"I thought we were going to St. Barths, but it's there," Sumner pointed to starboard, "and we're headed straight. What's your actual destination?"

"Anguilla," Stromeyer said. "British West Indies. It's less populated than St. Barths, and someone you know is there."

"Who?" Sumner asked.

"Edward Banner." Stromeyer saw the flash of Sumner's white teeth as he smiled.

"Your business partner."

"I don't know what you mean," Stromeyer said. She heard Sumner snort.

"Okay," he said.

Stromeyer navigated the boat past the tip of the island, where the island's only yacht club sat. In all the days that she'd been on assignment in the Caribbean, she'd never seen an actual yacht docked at the club. For that reason, it was the perfect place to both dock the boat and be left alone. Darkview had paid well to ensure that any employees would turn a blind eye to their comings and goings. At night it was deserted.

"Help me moor it?" she said.

Sumner got up and tossed the bumpers over the boat's wall. He gripped a rope that had been coiled on deck and when they were close enough leapt lightly onto the dock. Stromeyer reversed and drove forward in small movements until the boat was properly positioned. Sumner tied it down, wrapping the rope around the metal cleat on the dock, then did the same with a second rope at the stern.

"You've done that before," Stromeyer said after he was finished.

Sumner nodded. "I grew up in Minnesota and my family had a cottage on one of the lakes where I would go fishing and hunting."

"Were they hunters, too?" she asked. Sumner was a skilled sharpshooter. His talent seemed both natural and born of years of familiarity with guns. He smiled and nodded.

"Hunters, too." Stromeyer waved him to a motorcycle parked in the parking lot. It was a serviceable Suzuki, big enough to carry two and powerful enough to outrun a fast car if necessary.

"Get on. I'll take you to Banner."

A rooster crowed somewhere in the distance, but otherwise the world was quiet. The night sky was beginning to lighten and Stromeyer didn't need to check her watch to know that soon it would be dawn. She'd been working nights for over six months and was used to the strange hours, but knew she would need to sleep soon.

She swung a leg over the motorcycle and Sumner joined her on the back. She started the engine and winced at the grating roar the cycle gave before putting it into gear and heading out onto the frontage road next to the parking lot, driving on the left, as was the custom in Anguilla. She turned right, swinging wide before going straight. The road ended on a street that circled the entire thirty-five-square-mile island. After a short while she turned onto a gravel road. Palm trees and ferns surrounded them, and the scent of night-blooming jasmine wafted over her.

At the end of the road sat a house made of white stone cut into graceful arches at the entry that curved over the dark wood front door. Bougainvillea curled over the railing of the wide front portico. She pulled up to the front stairs and stopped.

The door opened and Banner stepped onto the porch. He held a cup of coffee in one hand and wore navy sweatpants and a gray cotton polo shirt. Like everyone else on the island, he was barefoot. In his mid-forties, Banner was six-foot-two and had salt-and-pepper hair trimmed close to his head. His blue eyes rarely missed any detail, and his expressive face revealed a sharp mind. His straight posture indicated his former military background, but his exceptional good looks sometimes confused those who met him into thinking he was less than the fighter that he was. Banner liked it that way. He'd once told Stromeyer that the tendency of some to dismiss him was a mistake he could exploit to his own advantage. Many an enemy had come to regret underestimating him. Banner's expression lightened when he spotted Sumner. He flicked a glance at Stromeyer and smiled.

"Nice mask. Is it Halloween and I missed it?" he said. Stromeyer turned off the cycle and punched down the kickstand.

"I thought it was safer to keep Sumner here out of the loop, concerning who he's keeping company with." Sumner strolled up the steps and put a hand out to shake.

"I told Ms. Stromeyer that I'm aware of who she is. The voice is distinctive, and I've spoken to her on the phone enough times to recognize it."

Banner's smile broadened. "And still she covers her face. Suspicious one, isn't she?" Sumner nodded. Stromeyer dashed up the steps and waved a hand at them both.

"This suspicious woman is going to sleep. Enjoy your breakfast." She slipped past Banner and headed to the back of the house and her bedroom.

Banner had rented the three bedroom villa in part because of its secluded location and its comfort. He used one room, Stromeyer the other, when she was not in St. Martin, and the third was converted into a home office where they kept their base of operations while in the Caribbean.

Stromeyer entered her room for the first time in a week. She removed the mask and sighed when the cool air hit her face. She was five-foot-seven and had light brown hair, streaked with blonde, that hit her shoulders. Though a bit younger than Banner, she had also spent time in the military. She knew how to shoot a gun, fight, and fly both airplanes and helicopters. The bulk of her military service, though, was spent at a desk in the appropriations department learning how to requisition, transport, shift, or decommission just about anything in the military system. It was her knowledge of the protocols and paperwork needed for a military contract that prompted Banner to offer her a job. His promise of the occasional field operation in addition was the reason she accepted.

Stromeyer walked to her closet and opened the panels, putting away her shoes, stripping off the dark clothes and dumping them into a hamper. She twisted her hair into a knot as she walked to the adjoining bathroom. After securing it with elastic, she washed her face, brushed her teeth, and threw on a nightgown that hung from a hook on the back of the door.

She shut all the wooden blinds and slipped between the cotton sheets with a sigh. The last image in her mind before she drifted off was of the woman's body hanging from the tree. She made a silent vow to find her killer.

13

Banner looked up from the table when Stromeyer walked into the kitchen. It was late afternoon and he estimated that she'd slept almost nine hours.

"Hungry?" he said. She nodded.

"Starving. Where's Sumner?"

"He took the motorcycle and headed to a hotel. Said he was exhausted from the night. He'll come back in the evening for dinner." Banner stood and pulled out a chair at the table for her. "Sit down. I was just going to make a late lunch. You want some?"

She sat and nodded. Banner thought she appeared pensive. He'd always admired Stromeyer's ability to work through a problem to its conclusion, even if that meant hours behind a desk coordinating paperwork and reading regulations. He preferred action. He headed to the refrigerator and started removing what he needed.

"Sumner told me about the threat made against him and Caldridge. That it was made against them both narrows the field of possibilities, doesn't it?" he said.

"Absolutely, but I don't think it's related to the cartel from last year," Stromeyer said.

"I agree. Since the leader's death, his foot soldiers have disappeared." He reached for a loaf of bread and removed two small plates from the cabinet. "No, it has to be either from the incident in Somalia or Colombia. Sumner and Caldridge were together during those two missions. It probably emanates from one or the other."

Stromeyer grimaced.

"I don't even want to think about Somalia. What a stressful time. Which reminds me to ask: how are we doing? New contracts flowing in? I've been out of the loop down here and it makes me nervous not to know."

In the past two years they'd been recovering from a devastating public relations disaster—an unknown force that seemed bent on portraying Darkview as a dirty player in the world arena. Congressional subpoenas demanding information about their DOD contracts were issued weekly and the IRS had weighed in, auditing their records. Luckily, Stromeyer's paperwork was impeccable and nothing had come of the probe, but the feeling remained that there was a person or corporation with an interest in destroying Darkview by manipulating matters behind the scenes. Neither Banner nor Stromeyer had ever taken the time to hunt down the perpetrator, instead pouring their efforts into obtaining new contracts and business to keep the doors open and the lights on.

They'd survived, and obtained not only this mission but two others, yet Banner remained on the alert. If someone chose to mess with his company again, he would not rest until he'd found out who it was.

"So far so good, but I don't have to tell you that we need to wrap this one up with an arrest. The Department of Homeland Security has tried and failed, and the CIA has been unable to trace the money. If we crack it, we'll be heroes. Mayonnaise?" He held up the jar.

She nodded. "Do we know where Caldridge is? She's never where you'd expect her to be."

"Sumner said she's in the Caribbean. Terra Cay. She's on the search for a miracle seaweed that when put into a jar will make every sign of old age disappear like that." Banner snapped his fingers and was pleased to hear Stromeyer laugh.

"And make her company millions, no doubt."

He smiled. "No doubt. I'd like to think she's safe for the moment, but I asked Sumner to call her and check." He placed the sandwich in front of Stromeyer.

"Are they still dancing around the personal issue?" she asked.

Like we are? Banner was too savvy to say it out loud. Stromeyer had no idea that his admiration for her ran deeper than on a business level, and he was determined to keep it that way. He'd never thought it was a wise idea to date one's colleague. Still, he was always happy when she appeared and sometimes couldn't help but tip his hand.

"They both seem set on building their careers

right now. You know how that goal can overwhelm all others."

Stromeyer threw him a glance. "Know? I've been living it since the investigation. Funny how financial troubles have a way of focusing one's attention."

"I can only hope that her company is making it, though. She employs almost one hundred people. She stumbles, and they all do." Banner joined her at the table and they ate in silence for a while. When they were finished he leaned back and looked at her. Circles around her eyes were evidence of the long nights she was keeping, and he was certain she'd lost some weight. "Tell me about the woman. Do you think it was Kemmer's work?"

Stromeyer sighed. "No. She's not one of his girls, and it occurred at the same time that the beach house blew up. At first I thought the events were related to Kemmer, but now I think that they both are pointing to Sumner. He's angered someone quite dangerous."

Banner got up and cleared the plates, placing them in the dishwasher. He grabbed the pot of coffee from the maker as well as two mugs by their handles. He put the cups in front of Stromeyer and poured. The black liquid was almost viscous. Stromeyer raised an eyebrow.

"What in the world did you do to make the coffee that thick?"

"Put new grounds over old. What, you don't like it?"

"Uh, well I don't know. Let's see." She went to the refrigerator and retrieved some cream, poured it in the coffee, turning it from black to espresso brown. She added quite a bit more. The coffee remained dark, but the liquid was hitting the rim so she dumped some into the sink, added more cream and took a hesitant sip. Her eyes lit up. "Wow. That's really good." She gave him an astonished look. "I had no idea that you made such amazing coffee."

He smiled at her. "Did you think I was just good for knocking heads together?"

"And hammering people into the ground and chasing them down and shooting them and—"

He put up a hand. "Okay, I get it." She smiled back, but then grew serious.

"Something tells me that we're both going to be tested, and soon. Between the bomb at Kemmer's house and the dead woman, it feels as though things are accelerating."

"And we're no closer to finding the guns, gunpowder, or the money train."

She shook her head. "Not yet, no." Banner leaned against the kitchen counter and crossed one leg over the other. He took a sip of coffee.

"I say let's take the fight to them."

"Okay. How?"

"We talk to Kemmer. It was his beach house they bombed. Let's find out why. If he's clean and it's Sumner they're after, then we'll deal with that next."

"And Caldridge?"

"Let's warn her. In the past few years she's become quite good at protecting herself." Stromeyer took another sip of the coffee.

"And if it appears necessary, I think we suggest to Sumner that he go to Terra Cay. The two of them together make a formidable force."

Banner nodded. "Like us," he said.

Stromeyer held up her coffee cup in a toast. "Like us."

14

Emma returned home in another car from Carrow's villa. It seemed that his cars were making a circuit between her villa and his. He'd send another driver to pick this one up later. The phone rang the moment she stepped into the foyer. She reached for the credenza and picked up the handset.

"I hope you're enjoying the lifestyle of the rich and famous," Sumner said.

Emma smiled at the sound of his voice. An image of him came to mind: about thirty, six-foot-three, with brown hair, rugged face, and a slender physique, he rarely smiled. When Emma had first met him he also had rarely spoken. He'd opened up more with her over the years but was still quite taciturn.

"I'm learning that the rich and famous are a lot more messed up than we actually know."

"Now there's a surprise."

"Yes, shocking, isn't it? What's up? I'm surprised that you're calling me. I thought you were working undercover and incommunicado."

"I was, but something's happened that I think you should know."

He gave her the story. Emma tossed her keys onto the credenza and headed to the kitchen while she listened. He finished by saying, "Keep your wits about you."

"Not a problem." She told him about the events of the last eighteen hours, focusing on the crazy man and the priestess.

"They sound like a couple of amateurs."

Emma felt a rush of gratitude. That Sumner wasn't buying the zombie and demon stories made her feel like a weight was lifted off her shoulders. She hadn't realized how tense she was until just that moment.

"They *are* amateurs, at least the voodoo priestess is. But I'm really concerned about the crazy man and the illness that seems to be making its way through Carrow's villa. I've never seen a man have a seizure as strange as Nalen had."

"Do you want me to fly down?"

Emma paused. She knew that as a member of the Air Tunnel Denial program Sumner was routinely sent on missions the world over to stop drug trafficking, and she felt bad asking him to put such a lofty goal aside to help her with a couple of crazies and an overindulged rock group.

"Aren't you working on something in the Netherlands Antilles?"

"I am, but that was before I learned that we have a mutual enemy. My cover is blown, anyhow. I would be happy to put the surveillance aside to watch your back if you need it."

"I think I'll be okay for the moment. My immediate mission is to find and collect some minerals from the blue holes."

"All right. You need me, you just call. It's a short flight from here to there, and I've never had the pleasure of partying on Terra Cay."

"I'll let you know."

Sumner hung up and Emma settled into a kitchen chair with a cup of coffee. She stared out the window at the lush foliage around her and tried to decide which was more dangerous: the strange malady at Carrow's villa or the strange man who was chasing her. In the end she decided that the man was the most pressing problem. One swipe of his machete and she would be dead. A disease could be addressed in a hospital. She sipped her coffee. After a few minutes she decided to take a run. It was the best way to keep an eye out for the mandrake, and she needed the exercise. She put on her running shoes and headed out.

The late afternoon was cooling just a bit. It remained light through eight in the evening, which gave her plenty of time to scout for the mandrake. She began to run, keeping her pace slow while winding her way down the mountain. The trail cut a more direct path to the hill's base then the road did, and she leaned back as she ran downward.

The trail flattened at the base and she stretched out, keeping her strides long and picking up the pace a bit. She eyed the plants on either side of the path but saw nothing out of the ordinary. As she ran she felt her muscles warm and her breath settle. The beginning of a run always felt a little strenuous as her body adjusted to the speed and exertion, but after ten minutes she could usually count on her system to settle into a groove. As an ultra runner, for Emma the groove could last at least three to four hours. After that her heart rate would climb, indicating that the exertion was taxing her reserves. While ultra runs could last twenty-four hours, today she only planned on one and a half, at best. She would run up toward the West Hill, back down, and up again to her villa. The uphill portions would provide the workout she required.

She hit the beach twenty minutes into the run. The ocean glistened at her left, and three gazebos, each with their own picnic tables and grills, were on her right. Several people hovered near the far one, cooking food and gathered around the table. As she neared she saw Rory and two others. Rory fixed her with an angry stare. The two others, whom she didn't know, turned to watch her run by. One of them smiled and nodded a greeting that she returned. To the left of the gazebo there was a stand of manchineel trees, each marked with a red-painted band around its trunk to indicate acid sap. The tree's white sap was so caustic that drops on one's skin could cause burns and even blindness. Columbus nicknamed the green apple fruit that the tree bore "death apples," a name that Emma thought was perfect in its explanation. Warning signs in several languages cautioned sunbathers not to rest under them. About twenty were planted in the sand and continued along the hill. For her, they were the only thing that marred the beautiful beach.

Running, she reached the next trail, which ran uphill from the sand. The going got steep and she felt a burn starting in her thighs as she pushed herself. Most of the plant life here was unremarkable and indigenous to the island. She hadn't yet seen anything even remotely resembling mandrake. Turning a corner, she stumbled to a stop.

She was staring at a small clearing filled with marijuana plants, planted in a circle twelve feet in diameter. The plants sparkled full and green and lush. This was a field lovingly tended. She began a circuit around it, looking for mandrake or any additional plants that matched it, and found them in a second, more secluded area.

This clearing was six feet by four feet and hemmed in by a hedge of oleander bushes in full bloom that formed a beautiful and deadly natural fence on two sides. This garden, too, was lovingly tended, with straight rows and plants arranged by category in each. The difference in this field was that every one of the plants was poisonous. Whoever planted the garden knew about nature, plants, and poison. Emma heard a noise and turned to see the woman who claimed to be the voodoo priestess standing at the edge of the garden. Her head was wrapped in a red bandanna but the rest of her outfit consisted of a simple white tee shirt tucked into a long skirt.

Once again she felt the rancid evil that flowed from the woman. Emma shot a quick glance around, searching for the man, but the woman was alone. Emma remained silent, waiting for the woman to speak first.

"You like my garden?" she said.

"Not particularly," Emma replied.

"I use the plants for medicinal purposes. The people come to me because modern medicine doesn't work."

"Nothing medicinal about them."

The woman snorted. "As if you would know."

"What makes you think I don't?" Emma asked.

"You're not a healer or a witch doctor. You told me that you don't believe in the spirit world." The woman took a step closer. "But I do. I know that the earth contains many things. Some that can heal, some that can kill. I don't need a laboratory and test tubes to create a drug, but you don't know how to do it any other way." Emma decided to let the woman in on her mistake. She pointed at the nearest plant.

"Foxglove. Also called 'witches glove.' We chemists know that it contains cardiac glycosides. Most people would recognize the name 'digitalis.' It causes dizziness, vomiting, delirium, and hallucinations. While it's used for cardiac conditions, a medicinal dose is so close to a lethal dose that it's tough to administer without killing the patient." She walked to the second row. "Jimson weed. This one saved my life once. My favorite story about it is the one where the Jamestown colonists used it on British soldiers. It causes hallucinations, delirium, insanity, coma, and death. The British survived, but just barely." She pointed to the next row. "Rhubarb. The roots make for a great pie but the leaves will kill you. And I'm not surprised to find this last one in your little garden." She pointed to the final row of plants. "Belladonna. If ingested, the result will be loss of balance, staggering, hallucinations, convulsions, and eventually death. Ten to twenty of the berries will kill an adult. Used by voodoo practitioners to create their so-called 'zombies.' How much did you give the man?"

The priestess raised an eyebrow. Emma waited. In her experience, when one was silent others would fill the void with talk. And she wanted this woman to talk. The woman shrugged.

"So you know plants. That won't save you. You're marked for death and it *will* come."

The outright threat shocked Emma more than anything the woman had said so far. While she saw the woman as the amateur that Sumner had called her, she wasn't about to let herself be brazenly threatened. Emma walked toward her and noticed the small skull voodoo charm dangling from a necklace around the woman's neck. The woman stood on the opposite side of a low lying oleander bush, and Emma stopped before her legs touched it.

"Death comes for us all one day, but I don't intend to let you or anyone else choose when. If I were you I'd watch what I say."

The woman smirked. "Are you threatening me?"

Emma shook her head. "Not at all. But words have consequences. All you're drawing to yourself is trouble. Take your fear tactics elsewhere. They won't work with me. And tell whoever is paying you to harass me that it won't slow the research into the blue holes. If it's not me doing the research, then someone else will."

"I've seen brave men shake and cry in front of a voodoo bokor. You will, too, when your time comes."

Emma wished she'd had her phone with her so she could have called Moore, but perhaps it was irrelevant. Even if she could have notified him, he would have been forced to traverse over a mile of the trail on foot. The woman would be long gone by the time he reached the garden. She decided to quit the conversation and turned to go back to the path. From the corner of her eye she saw the woman lean forward.

"The ritual is done, the curse is upon you, and the demons that I called forth to do my bidding are coming for you. When they do, you'll be scared. You'll see hell." Emma looked back. The black soulless eyes held triumph in them. Emma raised an eyebrow.

"I've already seen hell. I didn't like it, but I survived. And I hope that you chose your demons wisely, because I'm not going down without a fight."

She stepped out of the small area then, back into the marijuana field, and reentered the trail. She thought she heard the sound of an evil laugh echo behind her.

15

Emma ran the entire looping trail and saw nothing that resembled mandrake. After her discovery of the priestess's garden she assumed there must be another that contained the anesthetic plant. She made it back to her villa without incident, stripped off her running clothes, and took a long hot shower. The steaming water seemed to wash not only the sweat from her body but also the evil feeling the contact with the priestess had given her.

After her shower, Emma decided to drive by Island Security to see what was being done about the woman's male companion. As she pulled up to the building, she heard a plane in the distance and gazed into the sky, shielding her eyes from the sun. It was a private jet, one of the many that landed on Terra Cay daily, on approach.

Emma jogged up the steps and into the office. Randiger sat at his desk against the far wall and its bank of windows. He was looking out, watching the airplane approach. He glanced over and smiled when he saw her.

"Watching the planes land?" she said. "I'll bet that never gets old."

He smiled. "It doesn't. They taxi to this end and you can watch them step out. I once saw the Queen of England walk down the steps to a waiting car."

"What? You didn't make her check in through immigration?" A small covered but open air area served as the island's immigration point; one islander sat at a window checking in passengers. The entire process took three minutes and was completed with a smile. Terra Cay seemed far removed from the crime and stress of daily life. Emma wondered if it was her presence that was disrupting the idyllic existence.

"I didn't need to see her passport to know it was her," Randiger said. "A face known the world over."

"I wonder what that's like. Never having your privacy. Everyone you meet knowing who you are."

"I imagine Carrow knows a bit about that." Randiger grimaced. "Though I don't think I would like that particular brand of celebrity. The whole crew seems trapped in their skin."

It was an interesting observation. The more Emma talked to Randiger, the more she liked him. There was something solid and dependable about him. He stood up.

"What brings you here?"

"Just wondering if you caught the man who chased me."

Randiger grew serious. "No. But we did find evidence that he'd been living at the far end of the mangrove. There was a makeshift tent and some cooking pots along with a banked fire. The fire was our biggest concern. Something like that gets out of control, this entire island could go up in flames. The acres around it consist of mainly scrub, and our fire department is volunteer and small." Emma told him about her encounter with the woman.

"A poisonous garden?" Randiger rubbed his face and sighed. "I'll get one of the gardeners up there to rip it out. Along with the marijuana. We know it's being cultivated in small plots and we've been diligent about destroying it whenever we find it. It's not that we're so against the individual grower, but drugs inevitably bring dealers and violence. It won't do to let it get out of hand." Behind him, Emma saw the jet taxi to the end of the runway, coming to a stop just a few feet from the looming mountain.

"They almost fly right into the mountain, don't they?" she said.

Randiger nodded. "I'm sorry to say that a few actually have. But the majority of pilots who fly the route have been here before and know what to expect."

The plane began a slow turn and headed off to the side nearest the immigration area. As it did, Emma saw the navy crest with the word *Rex* in stylized calligraphy embedded in an elaborate logo.

"That's Carrow's personal plane, isn't it? His bass player was having a seizure earlier. Do you know if they airlifted him out?"

Randiger nodded. "Just a little while ago. Carrow

sent him on that jet. It's on the return. I've been told it should be holding the new crew that will be setting up the villa to act as a recording studio. Along with a new bass player and drummer."

"Was he conscious? Nalen, I mean."

"Oh yes. Awake and talking. Said the seizure was only a vague memory. He recalled Carrow speaking to him and being unable to respond or to control his muscles."

"Odd." She watched the ground crew work around the airplane. One man chocked the wheels while another rolled a set of stairs to the door. The setting sun threw a streak of red and gold across the plane's white shell. Heat waves shimmered off it.

"The general consensus seems to be that the cocktail of drugs he took didn't mix," Randiger said. He came to stand next to her and watched the ground crew work.

"Is their drug use an issue for the island? I haven't seen it full-blown, but I've heard that it can reach epic proportions."

Randiger threw her a glance. "It would be if it wasn't for Carrow's wealth and the fact that he is, overall, an asset to Terra Cay. He's given hundreds of thousands of dollars to the local library and instituted a music program at the elementary school set up for some of the weekly staff that bring their children with them." Randiger shrugged. "Frankly, he's done a lot more than some of the other owners, even those with ten times the amount of money that he has."

"Ten times? Is that possible? Carrow's loaded."

Randiger nodded. "We have a few billionaire owners. Carrow's three hundred million doesn't come close."

"What does a billionaire do with all that money if not donate it to good causes?"

Randiger shrugged. "Who knows? One has a yacht complete with a submarine and helicopter. Half the time he doesn't use it, though. He flies in."

"Are they nice? Friendly?"

Randiger rocked his hand back and forth. "Some, sure, but it depends. Many get here and then sit in their pool house taking work calls while their guests party. Guys with everything that money can buy, and instead of kicking back and enjoying it for a couple of weeks they spend their time here working. It can be sobering to watch."

The door to the jet opened from the inside and Emma watched as a steward swung it wide. She waved at the ground crew before disappearing back inside. The first man out of the plane stood for a moment on the stair, blinking in the setting sun. Emma gasped.

"What is it?" Randiger said.

Emma stepped closer to the window to peer at the man. After a moment she smiled. It was all she could do not to bolt from the office and head his way. She hadn't seen him in a while.

"I know that man." She pointed at the passenger as he headed down the stairs.

"What's his name?" Randiger asked.

"Oswald Kroger, but his friends call him Oz."

16

Emma stepped onto the porch and watched as Oz strolled down the stairs and toward immigration. He hadn't spotted her and she took advantage of his lack of awareness to take stock.

She'd met Oz the year before, when he was down and out, looking to run a shipment of marijuana from Mexico to the States. Both he and she had gotten caught up in a nightmarish journey with both the shipment and the cartel that controlled it. Oz had nearly lost his life. Now, though, he looked healthy, but still too skinny, she noticed. He had long brown hair to his shoulders and the face of an ascetic; angular, pale, and classic. She knew that he had the mind of a genius, but Oz's intellect was both his savior and his curse. He often struggled to fit in, and though in his late twenties, he was still at times awkward in a large group. His real talent was anything electronic; computers, circuitry, and sound systems. He'd always taken freelance work as an audio engineer, and she supposed that's what he was doing in Terra Cay.

He disappeared into the immigration area, reappearing five minutes later carrying a black duffel bag. Emma made her way across to the parking lot. Oz was looking around, taking in his surroundings. They were fifty yards apart when he spotted her. His face lit up and he dropped the duffel onto the ground. He jogged toward her with his arms out on either side and Emma heard him laugh. When he reached her, he grabbed her around the waist and lifted her off the ground, holding her tight against him.

"What the hell are you doing here?" he said into her hair. Emma squeezed him back. He lowered her to the ground but kept his arms around her waist.

"Working. You?"

"Working. I'm going to set up a studio for the band Rex Rain. They're here on the island."

"I know. I've met Richard Carrow. Didn't you run sound for him in the past?"

Oz nodded. "Once at a stop on his tour. Carrow's great. When he called and asked if I'd come, I jumped at the chance. The timing's perfect and I can always use some extra cash. Can you walk with me a minute?"

"I can do better than that, I can drive you where you want to go. Where are you being put up?"

"At Carrow's villa. They say he has some outbuildings and a guest house."

"I have a car over there." She pointed to her Jeep. "I'll take you."

"Great. Just let me tell the driver that I've got a ride."

He returned to snatch the duffel off the ground and held a brief conversation with a man in khaki pants and a white shirt with the sleeves rolled up, who stood near a black Range Rover. When he was finished he headed her way, tossing the duffel into the Jeep's backseat. Oz settled into the passenger side.

"You look good," Emma said when they were on their way.

"Thanks, I feel good. I'm back at MIT and just finished my core classes. Two more years and I'll finally get my bachelor's degree."

"Yes!" Emma put up her hand and Oz slapped it in a high five.

"Great, isn't it? Money's tight, as usual, but I'm getting a bit of a reputation as a sound engineer and jobs like this are starting to come my way. This one is ideal. I get paid to work on a beautiful tropical island and I'm on break, so it won't interfere with my classes." Emma shifted into third and continued along the airport road. "The only reason I got the job, though, is because the original plan for recording fell through. What's this I hear about two members of the band getting deathly ill? Do you know anything about that?"

"It's odd. Don't quote me, but they both seemed drug-related." Oz didn't seem surprised at that bit of information.

"Yeah, well that pretty much comes with the territory. Rex Rain isn't the worst, but they're among the top users, I'd say. Channel Surfeit is the worst. Their lead singer just tanked and they dumped him in rehab and cancelled the rest of the tour."

"There's something else going on," Emma said. Oz gave her a sidelong look.

"Mm. When you say that I get nervous. You still taking small projects for Banner?"

"On and off. When he has a job that I can fit into my schedule."

"Is your business here for Banner? Because if it is you can drive me right back to the airport. I don't need to be around anything that Banner is handling. He only gets hired when the situation is dire. Dire situations scare me."

Emma smiled. "Guess you're right about that. But don't worry, what I'm doing here is for the lab. It's a lucrative contract, and I don't need to tell you that it's important, given the flat economy."

"Business tough?"

Emma nodded. "Lots of cosmetic companies are dialing back on research and development, preferring to market their tried-and-true products. It's a prudent strategy for a tight economy, but it means that Pure Chemistry has fewer projects pending. I don't want to have to lay anyone off, so I've been belt tightening everywhere else. This contract came through at just the right moment."

"So what's going on?"

Emma told him about the bizarre man and voodoo priestess as well as Sumner's call.

"You were with me during my last adventure. Think it could be related?"

Oz seemed to ponder her question a moment, and she remained quiet to let him think. She had shifted into fourth on the main road but was beginning to climb the mountain. Deadman's

Curve was ahead, and she prepared to downshift. She flipped on the headlights, because the sun was almost gone and shadows were everywhere.

"I don't think so, but I've followed news of the cartel since then and by all accounts it's disappeared. This sounds like a couple of locals who don't want you muscling in on their action."

"That's just it, there is no action. No one currently mines the blue holes and the locals won't go near them out of superstitious fear."

"I'm talking about the mandrake. Maybe they think you'll start selling it directly to the members of Rex Rain and cut them out."

Oz's suggestion was a revelation to Emma. She hadn't even considered that the voodoo priestess was a drug dealer, but it made perfect sense.

"That is such a smart insight on so many levels that I'm embarrassed I didn't think of it before. She must be dabbling in drugs, because the zombies of voodoo lore are a result of local priestesses who administer scopolamine to their victims. I'll bet the man was under the influence. Oz you're a genius."

He smiled. "Nope. I've just been around rock and roll bands a lot longer than you have. They have drug dealers lined up in every town on the tour and they contribute mightily to the local economy while they're there. Miss Priestess is probably just trying to scare off the competition." Emma shifted into second and slowed for the curve. It was full dark and a bug hit the windshield. The night air was still warm but had cooled to a tolerable level.

They heard the pulsing music about a quarter mile from the villa. The heavy bass and rapid guitar wailing floated on the night air. The song was "Requiem for the Dead," one of Rex Rain's biggest hits and the title of their Grammy winning album. The pounding of the drums grew louder and then softer as Emma drove upward around the curves.

"They're jamming. Isn't it great?" Oz said. "But the volumes are all off."

"I like the guitar player. Who did they bring in?"

"Ian Porter. He's primarily a studio musician; one of the best in the business. He's a cult figure to guitar players the world over, and half the rock bands have tried to woo him to join them. He's always refused. Says he loves music but not the circus that is stardom. Carrow must be paying him well to fill in like this. Especially when he knows that Porter won't tour."

"Well, Martin might be recovered by the time the tour begins."

They reached the stone pillars situated at the beginning of Carrow's driveway and Emma slowly finished the final climb to the front door. She pulled the Jeep next to Carrow's Aston Martin and killed the engine just as the song ended. The sudden silence was startling. They walked along the path on the side of the house, headed to the pool area.

Over thirty people sat on reclining chairs, floated on inflated pool loungers, or milled around the area. The band was set up on a small stage, only one foot off the ground, on the lawn to the right. A second, low platform stabilized the additional equipment. Carrow stood front and center, wearing faded jeans and a black tee shirt emblazoned with the flag of England. His feet were bare and his skin glistened with sweat. His curls were spectacular, wild in the humid air, with ringlets hanging down to his shoulders. He looked a little bit like an untamed Medusa. He reached out to a high stool where a bottle of whiskey sat. He grabbed it and downed a mouthful, holding it out to the bass player, who took a swallow and then passed it back. Carrow offered it to the guitar player, presumably Porter, who shook his head.

Porter's hair was as dark as Carrow's was fair. It curled around his ears but was no longer than that, and he had a soul patch beard on his chin. A diamond stud earring was in his left ear and a small silver peace sign hung from a braided black leather cord around his neck. He wore dark jeans and a white tee shirt that looked like it came from a three-pack in the underwear department. He was taller than Carrow but almost as thin. Emma wondered if all rock stars were genetically programmed to be thin or if their lifestyle didn't leave a lot of room for adequate nutrition. Where Carrow's personality shone from the stage and one could see his lighter side, Porter seemed to be much more serious and introspective.

Two three-foot-high square speakers on a pallet with wheels sat on either side of the stage, and three small, low rise monitors lined the front.

Cables ran almost twelve feet from the speakers to a sound station set up on a folding card table.

Oz put down his duffel and walked to the audio equipment. He took in the flat sound board lined with black dials that looked like a series of eraser tips in perfect rows. He started adjusting several, keeping his head down, his concentration focused. His hair hung in front of his face, blotting out his profile. Carrow spotted Emma and smiled. He leaned into the microphone.

"I see that my favorite chemist is here. Or should I say my favorite *legitimate* chemist." A few people in the audience twittered in laughter. "Let's sing a song about chemicals, shall we?"

Carrow said something to Porter, and a pleased look came over the guitarist's face. He started into the introduction of the next song. It took Emma only a few seconds to recognize the song. It was "Siren," a song about a woman who pulls a man into her orbit and offers him drugs.

Oz glanced up from the sound board long enough to throw her an amused look. Emma lowered herself into a nearby chaise, knocked her shoes off, pulled her feet up and leaned back. The stars glittered in the sky, and the bluesy, bass song echoed in the night. The warm evening breeze blew across her bare arms. The bold scent of night-blooming jasmine perfumed the air.

After a moment a man Emma didn't know walked over and handed her a small glass. He held up a bottle of red wine as if to ask her if she wanted some and she nodded. He filled it, smiled, and strolled away without having said a word. Moments later the woman in the chair next to her passed her a joint. Emma passed it on without taking a hit. As a chemist, she had access to every type of drug imaginable and at phar-maceutical-grade quality. She knew the physical mechanisms in the body that the different drugs affected. She was well aware that the world's scientists had created wildly effective chemicals that played havoc with the human system. The easy access made her afraid that once she started, she'd spiral down a drain and wouldn't be able to stop. She didn't use any.

Carrow's voice was full and emphatic and he sang with a slight rasp that might have come from a combination of whiskey, cigarettes, and days on the road. As he sang, Emma felt herself being drawn in. She was mesmerized by his face. He was an attractive man, not handsome in a conventional way but when he sang it was as if conventionally attractive men paled in compari-son. It was as if he was the only man alive and worth listening to.

He kept his lips close to the microphone and his eyes half closed. His body swayed slightly from side to side and he had a hand on the mi-crophone even though it was on a stand. Emma felt a peace flowing through her that she rarely seemed to have these days. Between the pressure of her ongoing business, the dangerous situa-tions that were often the outcome of working for Banner, and the recent string of events, she'd had precious little time to just relax and be. She felt safe, both because Oz was there, and she knew he would help her if she asked, and because Sumner had called and offered his assistance. It allowed her to lower her guard and enjoy the music as the island's tropical temperatures and ocean breezes served to calm her. She placed the glass on a nearby end table and settled deeper into the chaise. Her lids lowered and she drifted off while Carrow started another quiet ballad.

She woke with a start. The moon was straight overhead, as was a man. He hovered over her with his hands on either arm of the chaise. His face was so close to hers that it took a moment to adjust her vision to identify him. It was Carrow.

"It's late. You fell asleep." He spoke low and soft, as if to avoid startling her. "I was just considering picking you up and carrying you to bed." His mouth cricked a bit at the edge as he waited to see her reaction. Emma raised an eyebrow.

"How kind of you to be concerned that I get enough rest," she said in equally soft and low tones. She smiled into his eyes and his own smile grew wider.

"Would you like me to sweep you off your feet?" he said. She held his gaze.

"That sounds *very* nice. But I should warn you, I rarely get swept away."

"That's a shame, because it's a lovely feeling."

"So I've been told," Emma said.

"By your girlfriends?"

"By the men whose feet *I* have swept off the ground." Carrow raised his eyebrows and then laughed in a low, whiskey-laden tone.

"I do like your style, Ms. Caldridge."

"And I do love your singing, Mr. Carrow."

Carrow moved his head closer to hers and Emma remained still, waiting.

"Are we headed to the beach?" Warner's voice came from somewhere behind Carrow. He stayed where he was, moving no closer.

"We're all going swimming. Care to join?" he said after a moment.

"I should go home," Emma said. "I have to work tomorrow."

Carrow nodded. He straightened and held a hand out to Emma. She reached out and a beach towel fell off her shoulders. She looked down at it in surprise.

"Oz covered you while you slept," Carrow said. She moved the towel to the side and clasped his hand. He pulled her to a standing position. Warner was nearby, patiently waiting for Carrow, and Emma felt a pang of remorse, though for what, she wasn't sure.

"Thanks for the concert," Emma said.

"You're welcome. Oz told me that you two know each other well. Please feel free to join us at the studio. But first, we'll head to the blue holes."

"What time?" Emma asked.

"Ten. That's practically dawn by my standards. I've already had Marwell outfit the boat with everything we need. Meet me at the dock?"

"I'll be there," Emma said.

17

Stromeyer huddled in the corner of the alley watching the casino's back door. Dumpsters lined the wall and the occasional rat ran back and forth along the edge. The smell of rotting garbage wafted to her every few minutes, carried on the night air, but she thought it was surprisingly contained considering the amount of waste the casino produced.

She'd driven the boat back to St. Martin the day after she'd spoken to Banner. Now she was dressed in her usual dark clothes and covered her hair with a hood from a zip up sweatshirt. She had her thin ski mask in her pocket, which she would put on in an instant if she needed to apprehend anyone.

Kemmer was in the casino playing craps. His driver and car idled at the alley's entrance waiting for him to reappear. Weeks of surveillance had revealed that he generally held a monthly meeting behind the casino. Most of the local authorities believed Kemmer to be a low level, fairly benign criminal. Though wanted in the Netherlands for tax evasion, his usual activities involved a modest gun-running operation and an equally modest escort service. The escort service was an offshoot of his legal prostitution business in Amsterdam, and was well run and unremarkable. He took credit cards for payment, and the Antilles pocketed a portion of the sales in tax. Though the local island tax officials suspected that he didn't pay all the tax he should have, what he did pay was substantial enough to mollify them. Paying companies on small islands usually were given some deference, because they had many options to choose from in the Caribbean and no island wanted to lose a business to their neighbor.

The door swung open and Kemmer stepped out. Stromeyer sat up straighter and pressed her back against the wall. She was hidden in a small space between two Dumpsters. She could see Kemmer from her position and was hidden from anyone who entered the alley.

A man walked past the Dumpster, heading toward Kemmer. He held a dark green duffel in his left hand and kept his right in his pocket, an ominous sign. Stromeyer took out her own gun. Kemmer and the man met in the middle of the alley.

"Did you bring a sample?" Kemmer asked.

The man nodded and held up the bag. He had his back to Stromeyer, which was a shame because she would have liked to see his face. The man put the duffel on the ground and crouched next to it as he unzipped it. He removed an Uzi submachine gun and held it out to Kemmer.

"No, no, I want to see the bullets. Can you show them to me?"

"Yes." The man reached into the duffel and removed a small bag that resembled a case for a laptop computer. "Here they are." He held something out in his palm. Stromeyer leaned forward as well but couldn't see what the man was holding. She felt excitement bubbling up in her. She'd observed several of Kemmer's weapon purchases in this alley and all were unremarkable. The usual crate of assault weapons and rocket propelled grenades changed hands with a wad of cash. She would pass on the information to the interested local authorities and they would move in, or not, as the case might be. This transaction, though, looked as though it would be different. Kemmer leaned forward to see whatever was in the man's palm.

"Do they fit into any gun?" he asked. The man nodded.

"Any gun that can fire their size, yes."

"What's the misfire rate? I've heard it's significant."

The man shrugged. "About thirty percent."

Kemmer's mouth fell open. Stromeyer could relate, because her own mouth was open. A thirty percent misfire rate was totally unacceptable. She certainly hoped Kemmer wasn't fool enough to buy a bullet that failed as often as that.

"That's outrageous. Awful, actually," Kemmer said. "I don't think any of my clients would accept such a huge failure rate."

The man shrugged. "They have to understand that they're buying an entirely new, cutting-edge product. Some kinks are to be expected. It's like buying the first model year of a new car."

Stromeyer's bent left knee felt tight, but she ignored it. The man's statement was exactly what she wanted to hear. The months of careful surveillance were finally yielding a meeting that might be what she'd been hoping for. She watched Kemmer frown at the man's analogy.

"Kinks, yes. Massive misfire, no. My clients need their weapons to work in all sorts of situations. They're often under fire themselves. That their gun won't work thirty times out of every hundred trigger pulls is like playing Russian roulette with their lives. You need to give me a discount."

The man shook his head. "Not a chance. These are extremely expensive to make. They're designed for unique situations where complete anonymity is required. I have several customers lined up to buy them, and if you don't want to pay full freight there are others who will. It makes no difference to me." He bent down and replaced what Stromeyer presumed was ammunition back in the duffel, zipped it, and picked it up off the ground. "Maybe next time, when I have something a bit more average, I'll call you." The man turned and started walking away. Stromeyer saw his profile only. A strong, hooked nose and pointed chin.

"Wait," Kemmer said. The man paused and looked back.

"Maybe you let me buy a few samples that I can take to my clients. Let them work with them. See if they like them. If they do, then perhaps we can arrange to buy some more." Stromeyer thought Kemmer's suggestion sounded reasonable, given the product's defect rate. She was surprised to see the man once again shake his head.

"No. These are a limited edition. The materials to make them aren't readily available and are very expensive to obtain. That's another reason they're so costly. I can only sell them in specially prepared batches. This is only one batch. There are others at a different location. Once this batch is gone it will take almost three years to manufacture another."

Kemmer seemed frustrated at the man's intransigence.

"Then give me twenty-four hours. Just long enough to get in touch with my clients and see what they're willing to pay given everything you've told me."

"No. You buy them now. Immediate and verifiable wire transfer, or I go elsewhere." Kemmer sighed.

"Then I'm sorry to say that we have no deal." Kemmer looked dejected. Something about his reaction made her think that the objections he'd raised to the buy were only based in part on the defect rate. She wondered if he had the funds to complete an immediate wire transfer.

The man nodded once and continued walking away. Kemmer spun in the other direction, opened the door to his waiting car and climbed into the rear seat. The car made a three-point turn and drove away.

Stromeyer rose, straightening her stiff left knee, and worked her way down the alley as quietly as she could. At the end, she peered around the corner in time to see the arms dealer closing the trunk of a new, dark-colored sedan. He entered the driver's side and put the car in motion, turning right onto the main road that ringed St. Martin.

Stromeyer's own motorcycle was parked in the same lot but farther from the overhead light. She jogged to it, put on her helmet with the full face mask, and kicked the cycle into life. A minute after the man's car had disappeared into the darkness she was on the road and speeding along.

She caught up with him at the second light. She didn't bother to memorize the plate, because the car appeared to be a standard, midsize rental. She doubted that the man had either paid for it or registered it in his real name. He took off again and she followed. It seemed he was headed to the area with both a dock and the airport, where she had been with Sumner just the night before.

Indeed, the car turned into the airport parking lot. She hung back as he maneuvered into a premium spot close to the main entrance. Then he got out, retrieved the laptop bag and slammed the trunk closed, leaving the duffel. Cycling into the lot, Stromeyer stopped at the front row of cars, to the far left of the parked vehicle. She watched the man stroll to the airport entrance and wasn't surprised to see him hand off the car keys in a brush-by technique to another man heading toward him. She locked the cycle and walked rapidly toward the entrance, keeping her face turned slightly away as the accomplice with the car keys opened the sedan's door and got in.

The Princess Juliana Airport in St. Martin had two levels of security. The first required visitors to show a passport and boarding pass to a customs agent before heading to the main security line. Stromeyer strained to see the man among the crowd.

Three minutes later she was in the terminal watching the arms dealer walk through the security line. He placed the laptop bag on the conveyor belt and it sailed through the metal detecting machine. The man sailed through as well. Five minutes after putting his shoes back on he was strolling toward the gates with the bag in his hand.

Stromeyer jogged back out of the terminal and ran to the motorcycle. She kicked it into gear and headed along the frontage road to a place on a slight rise where she could see the runways. She pulled out her binoculars and waited, sitting on the cycle, scanning the runway.

Forty-five minutes later her patience was rewarded when she saw the man with the laptop strolling toward a small plane. She noted the number and called Banner.

"Does Sumner have access to an ATD plane? Fast?"

"I think so, why?"

"I need him to intercept a flight." She rattled off the plane's identifiers.

"He's in St. Barths. I'll call him now. Any idea which way the plane is headed?"

"No, but I'm right here. I can head back and talk to the airport authorities."

"Don't bother. The ATD guys probably have access to all of that information online. Let me call Sumner. Hold tight."

Stromeyer waited. She kept her binoculars on the small plane and the phone to her ear. The plane's props started. It spun in a slow circle and headed toward a runway. Banner's voice came back as it lifted off.

"It's headed to Terra Cay," he said.

18

Emma got home and went in search of a snack. While Carrow's staff had served small appetizers, she hadn't eaten a meal. She headed to the kitchen to check the warming drawer. She often worked late and Johnson would leave a meal for her. There was a chicken pot pie and a kiwi cheesecake. When she finished eating she made the rounds, checking the doors and windows. She found the door that connected a small mudroom to the laundry room unlocked and secured it before heading to the master bedroom to sleep.

She rose from a deep sleep to a lighter, dream state to the sweet smell of decay. She opened her eyes and saw a creature that was preparing to attack her. The dark shadow hung above her, enveloping her in icy cold. The floating figure reached for her throat with long fingers—each one dripping with seaweed. She had a vague image of a head, of long, muscled arms and claw-like feet. Its breath held the scent of decay she'd smelled. The carbon monoxide detector started to wail and the beast opened its mouth and displayed a jagged row of teeth as it howled along with the alarm.

The slowly turning bamboo ceiling fan above the bed allowed Emma to breathe despite the gas-filled room. The rotating fan sent enough air her way to keep her alive. The alarm shrieked at an ear-piercing pitch, and she tried to force her muscles to function. Her head swam and her breath came in labored gasps. She jerked to the side as the beast lowered its jaws toward her face and she kept rolling to the edge of the mattress. The draped mosquito netting covering her, she fell straight down to the jute rug below, still wrapped in the mesh. The room careened around her, whipping in a blur as vertigo took over. The dizziness was so extreme that she felt her stomach clench in preparation for the dry heaves. She turned her head and gasped.

There was another creature under the bed. It stared back at her through malevolent red eyes.

She forced herself to crawl away, fighting her way out of the gauze, dragging herself across the rug, and when that ended, across the wooden floor. The beast's howls rose when it became tangled in the netting, and she heard a ripping sound as it clawed its way out. The room spun and her right calf twisted into a tight cramp. She groaned from the pain and pitched sideways, but her own voice sounded muffled.

She'd thrown the windows open earlier, to allow air to circulate while she slept, and now half rose and stumbled to them, plucking at the slatted wooden blinds, trying to unlock them and swing them wide to get to the outside and fresh air. She pulled the stops on the screen and shoved it open from the bottom. She smelled the decaying thing behind her, and its frigid aura hit her back as she crawled through the opening, snagging the edge of her cotton night shirt on the wooden sill and turning her body to clamber out. Dropping onto the ground, swaying and still disoriented, she crumpled to the grass and closed her eyes. While her brain told her to move, her body wanted to sleep.

Don't sleep, don't sleep, she told herself. The beast would be upon her. Her body, though, wouldn't respond. It was as if she'd been drugged. She kept her eyes on the window, watching. After a few moments, when the beast didn't appear, she felt her lids begin to lower. *I'll just rest for a moment,* she thought.

Her calf muscle twisted in a sudden charlie horse that made her sit straight up and brought tears to her eyes. She punched at it in a desperate attempt to get it to ease up as her foot curled. She hammered at it again, and when it subsided, fell backward and lay there, panting.

Did carbon monoxide poisoning cause seizures? She shook her head and tried to focus as her lids lowered again.

Emma woke to the sound of a mosquito buzzing in her ear. She opened her eyes to see the insect hovering next to her right temple. It was just a shadow in the wan light of the moon, flitting in and out of her peripheral vision. She glanced at the sky but saw only inky black dotted with stars, which meant that she hadn't been unconscious for long. The carbon monoxide detector's piercing shriek was gone but her head still pounded, possibly from the monoxide gas. Her vision was clear, though her dizziness remained. She rose.

The back lawn was quiet. Stars twinkled overhead. Emma leaned into the window and peered at her bed. The mosquito netting was bunched on the left side. She assumed that she'd pulled it in that direction when she rolled away from the beast. The room was quiet. Peaceful.

The doors were locked, so the only way back into the villa was to crawl through the window. Emma hauled herself over the sill but left the screen ajar and the shutters open, in case she needed to make another hasty exit. She moved toward the lamp on the nightstand, keeping her back against the wall and her eyes on the bed. She staggered with both exhaustion and vertigo. The shadows dissipated when she flicked on the light.

She reached for the netting and spread it wide. It was intact. No holes where the beast had ripped through it. She took a deep breath and lowered herself to the floor. The back of her neck tingled in fear, but she ignored it and peered under the frame. Nothing hid there.

She looked up at the ceiling and scanned the corners. The room had no carbon monoxide detector. And now she remembered that the villa had no furnace. There was no need for one. Terra

Cay villas needed air-conditioning, not heating. The ringing she'd heard must have been in her own ears. The beast in her mind. Her stomach twisted into a vicious knot, bending her forward with the pain.

Not carbon monoxide. Poison.

She got up and swayed to the bedroom door, heading to the kitchen, breathing in irregular gasps as she made her way down the hall. She kept her shoulder against the wall, using it as a support to stay upright. Another cramp hit her stomach and she bent forward. She felt her body heat climbing with fever. *Keep moving*, she told herself.

Emma stepped into the kitchen, the tile floor a shock of cold on the soles of her feet. She made it to the pantry, opened the door, and reached to the top shelf to grab a white plastic bin with a red first aid symbol on it. When she had it, she staggered backward and fell against the sink. She flipped the bin open and saw the dark brown bottle of Ipecac syrup.

Thank God, she thought, twisted off the top and swallowed a mouthful.

The heaving started within seconds. She vomited over and over into the sink, her diaphragm hammering into her spine with each convulsion. She'd never realized just how powerful her stomach muscles were until that moment.

When it was over she lowered herself to the floor and sat with her back against the cabinets. The dizziness was gone, the muscle seizures as well. She reached over her head to the edge of the sink and pulled herself upright, then managed to remove a large glass mug out of the cabinet next to the sink and fill it with water. She drank the entire glass, filled it again, and drank again.

Having thrown the remnants of the chicken pie and cheesecake into the garbage, she now pulled them back out and placed them into two plastic sandwich bags. While it was possible that the food at Carrow's villa had been tampered with, she doubted that was the case. The more likely scenario was that her late night snack was tainted.

Done securing the samples, Emma filled a pitcher with yet more water and refilled the glass. While she was drinking she heard the woman's low laugh. She glanced through the kitchen's sliding glass door that led to the backyard and spotted the woman silhouetted against one of the trunks at the corner of the lawn where the tree line began. The woman's figure began to undulate and then disappeared. Another hallucination, Emma thought. Her hands were clammy and her heart still raced with adrenaline.

She called Island Security and Randiger answered.

"I'm sorry to call so late, but I think someone broke into the villa again," she said. She recounted the hallucination and the possibility of tainted food, and told him that she'd found the laundry room door unlocked. She heard him give a heavy sigh.

"Do you think you can make it to tomorrow?

I've got three people who have fallen asleep and I'm dealing with their hysterical relatives."

"Carrow's villa again?"

"No. Three members of the staff of another villa. I've called the National Health Service in Nassau, Bahamas, in the hopes that they'll send a doctor. Honestly, this keeps up and we're going to have to issue a travel warning. I don't have to tell you how much trouble that would be for us."

"I'm headed out to the blue holes tomorrow," she said. "I'll bring the samples to you before I leave. Perhaps you'll have the doctor take them to a lab?"

"Will do." He rang off.

Emma checked the doors and windows once again, went into her room, locked the wooden shutters and grabbed her pistol out of the armoire. She rearranged the mosquito netting and shoved the gun under the pillow. While the dizziness had disappeared completely, her lethargy remained. She fell asleep within minutes.

19

Stromeyer sat in front of a computer screen and scrolled through picture after picture of known female operatives of the major intelligence agencies of three nations. The dead woman who had hung from the tree didn't match any portfolios from America, England, or Israel. She ran another search, this time looking for known international criminals. Once again she came up empty. She rephrased the search, looking for known terrorists. Nothing.

She sat back and stared out at the evening through the screen door that divided the living area from the terrace of her rental apartment in St. Martin. It was the top unit of a three-flat located halfway up the small mountain overlooking the harbor. Boats bobbed in the water below, illuminated only by lights set on pole supports every few feet along the dock. The balmy night was quiet and lovely, but a breeze blew through the screen, and Stromeyer was content to remain inside while she worked on the case. She wore her usual jeans and a white tee shirt, her hair in a loose bun and her feet bare. She paused when she heard a knock on her door.

She rose slowly, taking care not to move the chair's roller feet across the floor, and went to a messenger bag propped against a wall. It was teal blue on the outside, with a lime green interior, and nestled inside it was her gun. She removed it, checked the clip, took off the safety, and positioned herself next to the front door.

"Who is it?" she called.

"It's Sumner."

Stromeyer paused, thinking about how to proceed. While she hadn't wanted him to know who she was at the scene of the dock shooting, it would serve no purpose to cover her face now. He still couldn't testify that the masked woman at the dock was the same woman named Stromeyer who lived on the third floor of a walk-up overlooking the bay in St. Martin. She opened the door.

Sumner was framed in the entrance, dressed in a pair of dark jeans, a gray tee shirt, and a casual navy blazer. He wore black suede dress shoes with a square toe and his habitual serious expression. There was nothing frivolous about this man, Stromeyer knew, but she was unprepared for the full force of his intensity. It radiated off him and seemed to fill the space between them. She'd noticed his contained manner at Kemmer's compound and the dock, but the confines of the small apartment intensified that impression. He stuck out his hand.

"It's a pleasure to meet you . . . in person," he said.

She shook his hand. "Likewise. How did you find me?"

"After I tracked and intercepted a suspicious flight for Banner, he asked me to report to you first."

"Do you think anyone saw you return to the island? Whoever set that bomb for you could be back."

"I came in from the French side and in a rented boat. From there I went straight to the police department to check on the arms seller. I rode in the back of a paddy wagon here. I don't think anyone followed us."

She stepped aside and waved her hand. "Come in. Let's sit on the terrace. Can I get you a drink?" Sumner walked in and scanned the apartment while Stromeyer closed the door. The rental was small, with dark hardwood floors, a slowly turning ceiling fan, and wooden slatted blinds on the windows. Stromeyer went without air-conditioning as often as the ocean breezes would allow. Her private residence was in Washington, D.C., and she found St. Martin's balmy, tropical air a refreshing relief from the capital's oppressive humidity. "Are the authorities detaining the dealer?" she asked.

He nodded. "He's in custody here on the island. They confiscated his bag, but I managed to convince them to allow me to take one of the bullets he was trying to sell. I'm going to send it to the Southern Hemisphere defense guys. Let them analyze the material."

"Who is he?"

"He said his name was Martin Saint."

Stromeyer rolled her eyes. "Saint Martin backward? How original of him. Did he have identification that matched?"

"Excellent identification. He carried a Bulgarian passport that looked authentic. Has to be a false one, though."

"What would you like to drink?"

"I'd love a whiskey if you have it." She walked toward the narrow wet bar set into the corner of a wall on the opposite side of the living room. The screen on the laptop she passed still showed a woman in an obvious mug shot. Sumner walked over to look at it and gave Stromeyer a quick glance.

"I'm trying to identify the woman from the casino," she said by way of explanation. "The St. Martin authorities haven't been able to find any information about her. Are there any details that you can recall that might help?" She poured him a shot of Maker's Mark and herself a cognac and carried both to the terrace. Sumner joined her there and sat on a wicker couch that faced the view, while she sat in a matching armchair opposite him. He accepted his drink, took a sip and settled back.

"She was well spoken. At first I thought she was a high-end call girl working the casino crowd." He sighed. "But it soon became clear that she was far too intelligent for that. Perhaps an agent working for a foreign agency?"

"I checked. Nothing."

"And not one of Kemmer's girls. Though I ac-

cused him of it, I didn't really think so. Yet . . ."
His voice trailed off.

"Yet?"

"I still think she was someone's girl. Okay,
maybe not a call girl, but something higher class
along those lines."

"Mistress?"

He thought for a second and nodded. "Exactly.
Yes. Mistress. Not a wife."

"Why not a wife?" Stromeyer was intrigued.
She wanted to know Sumner's view of mistresses
versus wives.

"A wife wouldn't have been in a casino alone.
She would have had her husband with her. But
a mistress *would* be there alone. Perhaps waiting
for the man to get free and join her. A mistress
would keep herself busy gambling until he appeared."

"If you're right and she's a mistress, would that
be Kemmer?"

Sumner shook his head. "Kemmer doesn't have
one. He generally picks from among his girls.
Easier for him. He doesn't have to put himself out
for anyone, and the girl uses him and his money
until he grows bored and picks the next one."

"How depressing," Stromeyer said. Sumner
looked at her over the rim of his glass and his
eyes held a glint of humor.

"I don't know, maybe he has the right idea.
Choose from available options."

"Whoever said that had no romance in his soul.
I hope you're not in agreement."

"Well, since I'm chasing an option that may or

may not be available, I think we can safely say that I lean toward the less practical." Stromeyer assumed that he was talking about Emma Caldridge. She smiled but refrained from commenting.

"So what about Mr. Saint? Can the authorities hold him? Are they interrogating him?"

"They're in the process, but he's not talking. A lawyer has already weighed in and is screaming bloody murder."

"The guy's an arms dealer caught in the act of transporting illegal weapons. What can the lawyer possibly be complaining about?"

"Jurisdiction. He says I had no authority to intercept."

"Is that true?" Stromeyer asked. Sumner sipped again and nodded.

"It is. While we've been working in conjunction with St. Martin, we generally are supposed to only intercept suspicious aircraft flying in under radar. This flight didn't match the intercept criteria and his lawyer is crying foul."

"So he'll be released?"

"I assume so."

Stromeyer felt the soft air flow around her and the cognac warm her. Despite the calming effect of both, she felt a twinge of dread. The idea that the seller would walk free to attempt another sale of his deadly product was depressing.

"Ever feel that what we're doing is spitting in the wind? That it's never going to make a difference?"

Sumner inhaled slowly and exhaled just as slowly. "All the time." He finished his drink and rose. "I'd better get moving. As soon as I get any information on the bullet, I'll let Banner know."

"Watch your back."

"I'll do my best. You, too." He stood just as another knock came at the front door.

"I seem to be popular today," Stromeyer said. She checked her watch. "But midnight is a bit late. Cover the left side, could you?" She put her drink down and returned to the living room, once again grabbing the gun, which rested on the nearby credenza. Sumner pulled out his own weapon and positioned himself against the wall to the left.

"Who is it?" Stromeyer called through the door.

"Police. We'd like to speak to you." It was a male voice, inflected with an accent that Stromeyer couldn't place. She moved carefully to the door, looked through the peephole and saw nothing. The man had placed his hand over the viewer.

"I'll need you to place your credentials where I can see them," she said. "That means you'd better remove your hand from the lens."

After a moment of silence the door shivered as the man on the other side delivered a tremendous kick. The panel cracked and the dead-bolt lock ripped from its seat in the frame. Stromeyer dove to the left, where a hallway led to the bedroom.

Two masked men burst through the door. Both wore black, with bulky shirts covering what might have been Kevlar vests. In their gloved hands were guns. Stromeyer caught a glimpse of a silencer. Professional killers, she thought. Sumner crouched low and shot up at the first intruder, hitting him in the chest. The gun's noise cracked through the small apartment. The man took the hit and staggered, but raised his own gun, confirming Stromeyer's suspicion that they were wearing bulletproof vests. Sumner scrambled to his feet to run but his options were few in the enclosed space.

"Sumner, stay down," she said. He dropped to the floor and the second man's shot missed him. Stromeyer aimed at the first man's neck and fired, glad that Sumner was low and out of the line of trajectory. She heard the man grunt, but it was clear that while she had hit him, it wasn't a kill shot. From somewhere in the hall she heard the voices of her neighbors, an aging couple that had retired from New York City to the quiet of St. Martin. The husband said, "Call the police," and she hoped that he would stay well away from the apartment.

While Stromeyer was focused on the first man, Sumner had aimed at the second. This one was smarter than his buddy. He'd realized that the lack of places to hide in the small area worked both ways, and with two against two, his options to hide were few. He had been second in the door behind his friend, then angled around him and kept moving. He didn't wait to be shot but instead sprinted through the room and dove into the kitchen.

Stromeyer ignored the second man while she focused on the first. Sumner had managed to get behind the sofa. This put the first masked man between Sumner on his left and Stromeyer on his right. The man backed away, keeping his gun up and sweeping it back and forth to encompass both of them. He hit the door and disappeared. Stromeyer heard his feet thundering down the stairs.

"Loser in the kitchen." Stromeyer projected her voice in the direction of the man in that room. "There's nowhere to go and we've got the door covered." There was no sound. "Slide your gun across the floor and come out slowly, hands in the air." She heard what she thought was a knife being pulled from the block. A second later the gun skittered across the wood floor. Sumner was up and moving quietly to lean against the wall at the kitchen entrance, and Stromeyer took up position opposite him. She could hear police sirens in the distance. Her neighbor had called for help.

"Come out," Stromeyer said.

The man appeared at the doorway with one hand in the air and the other, the one nearest Stromeyer, held low near his thigh. Sumner put the muzzle of his gun at the man's ear, and Stromeyer let him take one extra step to clear the entrance. She reached down, grabbed the man's wrist, wrapped an ankle around his and yanked his foot out from under him. He staggered, and as he did, she pulled the butcher knife out of his hand. She used her other forearm to push against his back, which sent him crashing face-first to the floor. Sumner crouched next to him and pulled the mask up and over his head. He grabbed the man's hair and pulled it to the side so Stromeyer could get a look at his profile.

"Who sent you?" Stromeyer asked.

"Money guy," the man said.

"What's his name?"

"I don't know. He never said. I got the job through an ex-con just out of prison. He was hired but couldn't finish."

"Where is he?"

"Dead. He's the guy they found floating. Two days ago. You hear about that?"

"I shot him," Stromeyer said. The man groaned, and she leaned closer to him. He watched her with the eye that wasn't plastered to the wooden floor. "Just like I'll shoot you if you don't cooperate." She knew that the dead man had been a dealer fairly high up in the chain of command of a local gang, but she didn't recognize the one on the floor. "Who gave you this address?"

"The guy gave it to me. Called it in just an hour ago. "

"Where'd he get it?"

"I don't know." Stromeyer put the tip of the knife on the man's cheek and pressed. A tiny bubble of blood began to form. A look of panic grew in the man's eyes.

"He has a contact at the department. He said they gave it to him." Stromeyer watched as sweat rolled down the man's neck into his collar. She had no doubt that the combination of stress, heavy Kevlar vest, and the knife at his cheek was making him overheat.

"I have some handcuffs," she said to Sumner.

"What you gonna do to me?" The man sounded

panicked. Stromeyer felt little sympathy. Just two minutes earlier he'd been ready to kill her.

"Shut up," she said. The man clamped his lips together. She went into the messenger bag and removed the cuffs. She tossed them to Sumner to use while she jogged up the stairs to retrieve several bandannas. She gave one to Sumner. "Blindfold." She used another to stuff his mouth and a third to tie around his head. When he was trussed, gagged, and blindfolded, they moved him into a bedroom closet. Stromeyer kept a minimum of clothes in the rental. She tossed what she had into her roller bag and within ten minutes was ready to leave.

"Off the island?" Sumner said.

"For good, I'm afraid. If this guy is right, then someone in the police department is dirty." The sirens she'd heard before were louder now. "Let's get out of here before the next round of police comes. I don't want to have to decide which cop is clean and which is dirty."

Sumner nodded. Stromeyer thought about who might have known her location while in St. Martin. "It makes sense that the address leaked from the department. Darkview is working in conjunction with the locals, but I thought the mission was kept secret."

"Hard to keep a secret on an island," Sumner said. Stromeyer had to agree, but the fact annoyed her.

"They manage to keep the offshore accounts secret."

"That's because the holder of the accounts will

blow the bankers' brains out if they talk. Darkview doesn't operate that way. Well, I presume
the shooting at the dock was an unusual circum-
stance."

"Darkview doesn't hesitate when one of their
operatives is at risk."

"A fact for which I am extremely grateful,"
Sumner said. Stromeyer sighed.

"I'll need to set up shop elsewhere. Did you let
anyone besides Banner and the detective know
that you were coming here?"

Sumner shook his head. "No one."

"Let's turn this on, then." She reached behind a
small electronic tower set on a table near the front
door. "It's a dummy system. It's a stereo tower
that has a small camera built in." She showed
him a tiny LED display that lit when she pressed
a switch in the back of the machine. "We'll see
who comes through the door to check on our
hostage. Maybe we can flush the leak out that
way." She put the gun in her roller bag. "Shall we
go?" Sumner returned his gun to a holster at the
small of his back and nodded.

"Thanks for the backup. That's the second time
you saved my life this week."

Stromeyer smiled. "I'm on a roll." He pushed
aside the shattered door and stepped out of the
way to allow her to leave first.

"I don't mean to appear ungrateful, but here's
hoping that peace prevails and your roll comes to
an end."

20

Banner woke when he heard the door open and close in a quiet motion. He reached under the pillow opposite him, pulled out a gun and sat up. Wearing long black pajama bottoms and a loose gray cotton tee shirt, he kicked free of the sheets and stood. He moved along the wall and settled in next to the door frame just as the door swung open.

"Don't shoot me." He heard Stromeyer's voice. He rose and stepped out where he could see her.

"Thanks for the heads-up," he said. "I'd have been upset if I'd killed you."

"No sorrier than I would have been," Stromeyer said. Banner looked at his watch.

"It's three o'clock in the morning. To what do I owe the honor of your visit?"

"The crew after Sumner made an unannounced visit to my apartment while Sumner was there." She told him of the attack. "I think it's safe to say that the apartment is compromised, and perhaps my cover. We'll have to let the Department of Defense know that there's a mole in the police department."

Banner nodded. "If you're right and a source in the department revealed your address, then this location isn't safe either. Time to move elsewhere. Where's Sumner?"

"He went to meet with the Southern Hemisphere Defense group to analyze the bullet. He asked that you stay put long enough for him to get the results to you."

"How much time do you think we have before they come across the water here?"

She shrugged. "It's not as risky for us as it is for Sumner. They seem to be tracking him, not me. I've just been in the wrong place at the right time. My feeling is they'll focus on following him first and us second, if at all. Still, you should be ready to leave right after he delivers his report." She looked around the room. "I forget. Do you have an alarm system here?"

He nodded. "I do. Let me turn it on." She stretched, and Banner noticed that she looked tired. "Need some sleep?"

"Desperately," Stromeyer said. "I never realized until this mission how crucial sleep can be. Seems as though I've been up most nights. Arms dealers need to learn how to conduct their transactions in the daylight hours."

Banner smiled and walked to the alarm keypad located on the master bedroom wall. He activated it to trigger should anyone tamper with the perimeter. "There's a reason that sleep deprivation is a tried and true form of torture and mind control. Without sleep, people very quickly begin to hallucinate and then die."

"Now I believe it," Stromeyer said as she walked out of the room.

Banner headed down the hall toward the kitchen. He doubted that he'd be able to wind down very quickly. His body was still alert from the way he was roused, and he thought perhaps a glass of water would help. He didn't bother to turn on the light as he made his way through the house. The phone rang and the noise startled him. That can't be good news, he thought.

He picked up the receiver and heard the voice of Susan Plower, the Secretary of State. She'd risen through the ranks by virtue of a brilliant mind and unshakable loyalty to the former Secretary, Carl Margate. When Margate retired, he'd pushed for Plower to succeed him. While her mind was brilliant, her organizational skills were lacking. Things were better now that she had an entire staff to keep her on task, though, and Banner liked that she could see through the obvious in an instant and mine the deeper implications of an event. Hearing her pulled up a mental picture of Plower in his mind: a mousy woman with ill-fitting clothes and a thoughtful manner. She was surprisingly effective as Secretary, mostly because her quiet approach appeared to foreign dictators as the opposite of the brash American that they expected. She got her point across with a quiet insistence that leaders knew would be backed by the force of the United States military complex. Banner liked her.

"I know the hour is late and I'm sorry to wake you," Plower said. Banner held the phone between his shoulder and jaw as he reached into the kitchen cabinet for a glass.

"Not at all. What can I do for you?"

"Do you never sleep?"

"Only when off duty." He heard her soft laugh.

"I'm afraid I'm going to give you less time to sleep. There's been an incident in Saudi Arabia." Banner poured some filtered water into the glass and took a sip.

"Terrorist? I hadn't heard anything."

"That's because it's not the usual bombing or threat. The prince was walking from a restaurant to his car, and a robber tried to shoot him. The gun misfired and the man took off. They were unable to catch him, but they did find an unusual bullet."

"From a new material?"

"Yes, how did you know?" He told her about the strange arms seller that Stromeyer had stumbled upon.

"The Southern Hemisphere Drug Defense crew is on it," he said.

"The king is upset and there are rumors that the U.S. has had a hand in developing the bullet, which, by the way, can sail through standard metal detectors."

"Please tell me that the U.S. hasn't developed it. We're barely staying ahead of the criminals with standard bullets designed in the last millennium. The last thing I need is a better bullet."

"We're not involved, but we're as concerned as

the Saudis. The Secret Service is asking that we begin an immediate investigation. The President is preparing to travel to the G-8 conference, and they're concerned that their security measures will be inadequate."

"Stromeyer has set up a meeting with another buyer. Rumor is that there is a cutting-edge weapon available. We'll keep you posted if it proves to be the unusual bullet."

"Thanks, and please tell her hello for me. And to stay safe, both of you."

"You, too. I understand that one of the African leaders has a massive crush on you. Be careful that he doesn't have you kidnapped for his harem." Banner smiled at the sound of her groan over the line.

"State dinners with his country are excruciating. He sits too close, doesn't want to discuss politics, and keeps complimenting me on my clothes. Complimenting *my* clothes, can you imagine?"

Banner couldn't, but was surprised that she seemed to know that her clothes were shapeless. For the first time, it occurred to him that perhaps her lack of fashion was deliberate.

"A crush could come in handy, though. Maybe he will help with intelligence on the new weapon?"

"Unfortunately he's not that far gone, though I haven't put his affections to the test and have no intention of doing so. I'll rely on you and Stromeyer, if you don't mind."

"Thanks for the vote of confidence."

"Not at all. In the meantime, we'll try to keep the President within safe boundaries. Good luck."

She rang off, and Banner finished his water. He stared out the window and started cataloging in his mind the known countries and terrorists that would have both the financial wherewithal to fund research for a cutting-edge weapon and the knowledge base to fashion one. His list was short, but lethal.

21

The next morning Emma pulled into Island Security carrying the food samples. She opened the door and stepped into chaos. All the phones rang at the same moment and two women stationed at separate desks were picking them up, saying "Can you hold?" switching lines and saying "Can you hold?" over and over again. Randiger stood at his desk against the wall looking out onto the airfield while he held what appeared to be an intense conversation. He looked up, saw Emma, and waved her to him. He hung up as she reached the desk.

"You look good," he said. "Glad to see that the poison didn't get to you. Did you bring the tainted food?"

She held up the plastic bags. "I could analyze it myself, but I want it to be used as evidence, and I imagine it would be a conflict of interest if I did the testing." Randiger's phone rang again and he ignored it.

"What's going on? Seems frantic around here," Emma said.

"Two more houses have staff that fell asleep and can't be woken. The news has spread and the owners that remained after the holiday are leaving." He jutted his chin in the direction of the airfield, where one private jet after another was lined up for takeoff.

"What about the staff?"

"They're leaving as well, but the charter boats have a set schedule so they'll be here awhile longer."

"Any idea what's causing it?"

Randiger nodded. "I just got off the phone with a health service official in the Bahamas. He asked if the staff members do drugs. Of course, the families of the patients deny that they do." Randiger's voice held a sour note.

"And you don't believe them?"

"No. I know the guys involved and they all indulge. Nothing terrible, but a smoke here and there from some homegrown, if you catch my drift."

"So the official thinks it may be from the drugs?"

"They do." Randiger raised a coffee mug to his lips, looked into it, grimaced and put it back down. As he did, Emma saw that it was half filled with a layer of congealed cream on the surface.

"Do *you* think it's from drugs?"

Randiger rubbed his face. "I have no idea, but whatever it is, it seems to be spreading. Everyone's getting agitated. The islanders are going to local doctors for natural treatments."

"Is that code for the voodoo woman?"

Randiger nodded. "I think it is. I've been asking around for her, and no one claims to know who she is or where she's staying on the island, but frankly, I don't believe it. I think they're protecting her because they believe her potions can help them."

"Do they? Any success?"

He shrugged. "If there are, no one's talking." His phone rang again and again he ignored it. "Listen, I'm headed to interview a family of one of the patients. They say they found some sort of powder residue in his bedroom. Can you come take a look at it?"

Emma checked her watch. It was eight o'clock in the morning and she didn't expect to leave for the blue holes until at least ten.

"Sure. I'd be glad to help."

"Then let's go."

Randiger drove a short way before turning into a dirt access road hemmed in on both sides by trees. Every so often Emma would catch a glimpse of a sprawling compound and the back of a large mansion flanked by smaller houses.

"That house is massive," she said. "Is it the largest one on the island?"

"No. It's the second largest. The largest is owned by a newspaper and magazine mogul from the UK who also just recently purchased a large pharmaceutical company." Randiger mentioned the name.

"That's one of the biggest in the world. He owns it?"

"Yep. He provides the Acute Care Center with

most of its pharmaceutical supplies. Just about every home on the island has a medicine chest filled with his pills. He's in a bit of insider trading trouble right now and is spending a lot of time here."

"No extradition treaty on Terra Cay?"

Randiger chuckled. "Ahhh, yes. Hypothetically speaking, if a conviction comes down while he's on the island, it would take quite a long time and lots of paperwork to get Terra Cay to turn him over. Would buy him time to wait for the outcome of any appeals."

"Nice guy. And this villa over there is smaller than his?"

"By a fraction only. This one is owned by a financier and businessman from Russia. He's a recluse and rarely spotted off the grounds. He's a bit obsessive about security. Lots of closed circuit cameras and a couple of guard dogs. Because his house is beach level, he has his own private dock."

"Russian recluse financier? Interesting," Emma said. "What's his business?"

Randiger shrugged. "Lots of different things. Oil and gas, some gold speculation and several service companies. He owns a pool chemical corporation and supplies most of the houses here with their pool chemicals, and he also owns the Springfed water company and supplies the dispensers that you see everywhere. In addition, I'm told that he provides joint venture capital to companies around the world."

"Hmm," Emma said. Randiger threw her a look.

"I know what you're thinking," he said. "Russian mafia money."

"Well, yes as a matter of fact. You've got one guy from the UK hiding from an insider trading scandal and another from a troubled nation that's hiding from . . . who knows what. What's this one's name?"

"Ivan Shanaropov."

"Any of his staff affected?"

Randiger shook his head. "No one's contacted us as yet."

"Lucky him," she said. "So we're not going to his villa?"

"Right. We're headed to the villa owned by the English royal family. One of their gardeners is affected."

"Are they in residence?"

"Luckily, no. I wouldn't want Terra Cay to be the island responsible for harming a royal. That would be my worst nightmare."

"If it's a disease, then it's not as if you could have stopped it."

Randiger pulled into a circular drive lined with several neat, small town houses. He killed the engine and cast a glance in her direction.

"Try telling that to their subjects. These are the staff houses."

Emma followed him to the front door of the third house in the row. An aging woman, her white hair pulled back into a bun and with dark, unlined skin opened the door. She wore a flowered housedress over a voluminous body.

Her face held a concerned expression. Randiger smiled at her.

"Hi, Lorraine. I'd like you to meet Ms. Emma Caldridge. She's a chemist and I asked her to come with me. I'm here to check on Henry. He still sleeping?"

"He is. Nice to meet you, Ms. Caldridge. You're a chemist? I hope you can tell me what the powder is in my son's room." She waved them into the house. It was a shotgun design with living room, dining room, and kitchen in a row, and a staircase to the right that led up to a second level. She moved up the stairs slowly. At the top she entered the first door to her left. Emma stepped in after her, and Randiger followed.

A young man, no more than twenty-four years old, lay on the bed, sleeping. A sheet covered him to the waist and he wore a worn, white undershirt. Sun shone into the room from a window set in a far wall and a clock sat on a nightstand. Next to the clock was a saucer containing two small piles of powder and an ashtray that held an empty roach clip. A framed poster of Bob Marley hung on the wall above the headboard.

"That looks vintage," Emma said.

Lorraine nodded. "It's from one of his uncles. Henry loves Marley's music."

"This the powder?" Randiger pointed to the saucer.

Lorraine nodded. "There was some on the floor, too. At first I thought it was dust. And you know I don't allow no dust in my house."

Randiger nodded. "Yes, ma'am, I know." A flash of humor lit her eyes at Randiger's deferential answer, but it was gone in an instant and her serious expression returned. Emma leaned closer to the saucer. One pile was easily identifiable.

"That's mandrake," she said. She pointed to the dirty-colored pile that contained larger, coarser pieces mixed with the sandlike grind. "But that," she pointed to the second pile, "isn't." The second pile was a finely milled white powder.

"Any idea what that one is?" Randiger asked.

"It could be anything." She looked closer. "Well, not cocaine. Doesn't look like it."

"What would a voodoo doctor use?"

"Henry don't have any truck with voodoo." Lorraine sounded adamant.

"Now, Lorraine," Randiger said, "I know that, but maybe he got the powder from a friend. Could have been slipped to him." He sounded conciliatory. "Well?" he asked Emma.

"Possibly scopolamine."

"What's that for?" Emma hesitated. She didn't want to mention drug abuse or voodoo again in Lorraine's presence, but if the substance was scope, then there was a good chance that Henry was involved in some sort of drug trafficking or voodoo. She decided to have that conversation with Randiger when they were alone. For the moment she focused on the beneficial aspects of the drug.

"Divers use it. It stops nausea."

"Ah, sure. It comes in patches, doesn't it?"

Emma nodded. "Transdermal patches, yes. They work well."

"Could it be the reason that Henry's sleeping?" Lorraine asked.

Before Emma could respond, she saw Henry twitch. It was almost as if he'd heard his name. Emma kept her attention on him while she answered Lorraine.

"Possibly. Scopolamine can be used as a knockout drug when mixed with alcohol. Like Rophenol, or roofies."

"Think he mixed his own?" Randiger asked. "With the mandrake?" Lorraine's sad expression changed to one of outrage, and Emma was quick to head off the explosion.

"Hard to say. Maybe he had no idea what it would do to him."

"Henry doesn't do drugs," Lorraine said in a forceful voice. Randiger gave her a glance and flicked another at Emma, who bit her tongue. She was certain that Randiger recognized the roach clip for what it was, but it was clear he wasn't going to point it out to Lorraine, and Emma decided to keep silent about it as well. If Lorraine chose to remain deliberately blind to Henry's paraphernalia, who was she to enlighten her? Besides, Emma didn't think her son's current condition had much to do with marijuana. The scope and mandrake were the most likely culprits.

"Can you give me a Baggie with that powder?" Randiger asked. "Maybe we keep it separate, just like it is on the tray." Lorraine nodded.

"Let me get it for you." She left the room.

"So our Henry not only smokes pot, but he uses

scope and mandrake too," Randiger said when Lorraine was gone.

Emma watched, and Henry's face twitched at the sound of his name.

Randiger continued, unaware of Henry's reaction. "I don't know about the mandrake, but I don't like the scope. Henry doesn't dive much that I know about. Why would he need it?"

"It does give one a happy, intense high," Emma explained. "Like ecstasy. Like really bad ecstasy, though, because in the end it creates some wicked hallucinations."

Randiger took out his phone and snapped a picture of the powder. Emma leaned closer to Henry.

"Henry, if you can hear me, move your right hand."

Randiger gave her a surprised look but said nothing. He watched Henry's hand.

After a long pause, Henry's hand slid across the sheet a fraction to the left, then back. The movement was so small that Emma wasn't sure it was intentional.

"Again, please. I wasn't sure if you meant that," Emma said.

Henry stayed still.

"Henry, move your hand again, please," Emma said.

Henry's hand twitched once and stopped.

"Oh God, he's awake but paralyzed," Randiger said.

"He's definitely having trouble responding," Emma said. She heard steps from the hall as Lorraine returned.

"I'm going to have him transported to a hospital," Randiger said.

Lorraine carried a couple of plastic bags and a spoon. She carefully filled the bags and handed them to Randiger.

"You find out what this is and get my Henry to wake up."

"Has the doctor been here?"

She shook her head. "Not yet. He said he has three others to see first. Said to keep checking on him until he can get here."

"I think you should arrange to transport him to a hospital as soon as possible. Off island," Randiger said.

She nodded.

Emma followed Randiger to the car. When they were inside he turned to her.

"Is scopolamine also known as a zombie drug?"

Emma nodded. "I didn't want to say anything in front of Lorraine, but yes, it is. Mostly because it induces amnesia after the hallucinations are finished. When the victim comes to, they can't remember a thing."

Randiger put the car in gear and started the drive back to his office. Emma gazed out the window, watching the mansion flash in bits and pieces through the trees.

"Would the scope paralyze him like that?" Randiger asked.

Emma shook her head. "I don't think so."

"What made you think to ask him to move?"

"It was something that the voodoo priestess said when I confronted her. She said that the man with her responded only to her suggestion. It occurred to me that the priestess was being literal. That he could only move when ordered. Perhaps she'd given him a drug. How many people on the island do them?"

Randiger shrugged. "A few. The younger ones, mostly. Not much to do on a small island. They fish, boat, drink, listen to music, and flirt with the girls. It's a quiet life. Not too interesting for a young person."

"So it would be easy for someone to introduce a new, cheap high and have it make its way quickly through the population."

"Yes. Anything that is a novelty would be a welcome change for some of them. I'm going to really start pressing for information on that voodoo woman. Her magic is sickening people, not helping them."

"Maybe it's her drugs that's creating the sleep."

"If it's not, then I'm really worried."

"Why is that?" Emma said.

"Because the official said that his other theory would be a virus. And if that's it, then we would already be into pandemic-level numbers."

"What virus causes one to sleep?"

"I asked him that question as well. He didn't have an answer. And that worried me more than anything else."

Despite Randiger's ominous news, Emma drove down the hill with a feeling of lightness. She was eager to get off the island, even if only for a day and a night. She needed a break from the strangeness.

The day was perfect for a sail: shining sun, soft breeze, and a smooth, blue ocean. She grabbed her messenger bag from the front seat and headed to the *Siren's Song*. When she got there, she saw Carrow on deck along with Oz. Marwell was there as well, checking the pressures on a row of scuba tanks. He looked grim. Oz waved to her.

"Mind if I come along?" he asked. "Richard says he'll be diving with you and someone needs to stay topside. And I have this." He held up a metal device.

"That looks like—"

"A sextant," Oz said.

"Actually, I was going to say a protractor," she said.

He pointed it at her. "Well, you're not far off. Both are used for calculating angles, but this one will calculate the angle of the sun from the horizon."

Emma squinted at him. "And we need that why?"

"To do some celestial navigation. I'm going to plot a course to the blue holes using only the sun and stars for guidance."

Carrow walked up and gave Oz an amused look. "The boat has a GPS system and radar, mate. I don't think we'll need the sextant."

Marwell looked up from the tanks. "Never know when you'll need to navigate by the stars. Most long-distance yachtsmen can do it."

"Can you?" Carrow asked.

Marwell nodded. "I worked for the British Merchant Navy before coming to Terra Cay. It's still a required course."

Oz looked impressed. "I'm an avid astronomer. Didn't I tell you that?" he said to Carrow, who took a swallow of his energy drink.

"No, but let me just state for the record that I'm not surprised." He raised an eyebrow at Emma.

"All I knew is that you're great at computers," she said to Oz.

"Computers or just about anything electronic, sure, but I love astronomy second. I've always loved it, even as a kid. I spent hours poring over reproductions of old charts that the ancient mariners used. When we studied Christopher Columbus in eighth grade I prepared a paper explaining how he navigated to the new world."

"I spent eighth grade getting high," Carrow said.

Emma snorted. "Eighth grade? Isn't that a bit young?"

Carrow shook his head. "As I recall, it was just the perfect age."

Emma waved him off and focused on Oz, who never failed to surprise her. He had a genius IQ and brain power to spare, yet remained an easygoing, friendly man with a quick smile and sweet manner. He told her that as a young man his genius was a curse, because it intimidated most kids his age and as a result he had few friends.

"Didn't Columbus land somewhere around here?" Emma said.

Oz nodded. "Yep. Should be fun to see how

close I get with my calculations versus the computer."

Carrow got a dubious look on his face and then shrugged. "Whatever makes you happy. Ready?" He headed back to the fishing boat and Emma followed.

Marwell stopped fiddling with the scuba tanks long enough to help her on board.

"Thanks for setting us up," Emma said. He frowned.

"I still don't think any of you should be going out there—the place is dangerous—but if you do go, I want you to have functioning equipment. Is there anything I can say to talk you out of it?"

Emma laid a hand on his arm. "I appreciate your help and your concern."

He inhaled and then shook his head. "All right. Look here. This is your wet suit, belt, and tanks, and everything else that I thought you might need. I assume you don't intend to go deep?"

"No. My understanding is that the opening of the first cave is forty meters deep and lined with the mineral that I need. I'm just going to scrape it, collect it, and go."

"Agreed. You have four regular tanks, but these"—he pointed to a second row of tanks— "have mixed gases. The other one is for Carrow and the third for Oz, though he says he won't be diving. Here's your ascent line"—Marwell showed her a bright yellow rope—"to keep you on track with the boat. I've added some food and drinks in that cooler." He pointed to a large cooler strapped to one side of the boat. "There's more below. This boat is always well stocked. The radio works well and there's a GPS tracker and satellite phone. I'll be only a call away. Anything happens, you contact me."

"Aye aye, sir," she said. As she had hoped, his face softened a bit. Not quite a smile, but almost.

"And there's one more thing. Over here." Marwell stepped to a long, low, dark plastic toolbox. He unhooked the clasps and opened it. A rifle with a telescopic site rested in the case. She looked at him with raised eyebrows.

"What's that for?"

His expression turned grim again. "To shoot whatever grabs the boat and hangs on."

Emma didn't know what to say, but his words sent doubt through her. That Marwell was so certain they'd meet up with some creature that he'd arranged for a weapon made the danger all that more real. She shook off the feeling. She had one hundred people depending on her back at the lab to collect the mineral, and she didn't believe for a moment that a sea monster lived in the blue holes. Whatever was there was physical and quantifiable and she expected it to be explained by science. Nonetheless, she wouldn't scoff at Marwell. The world was filled with wonder, and even the things that science explained often awed her.

"Do you know how to shoot a rifle?" he asked.

"I do," she said. He gave her a considering look and then nodded with approval.

"Somehow I suspected as much. Mr. Richard," Marwell called to Carrow, "I'm off." Carrow stepped over and shook Marwell's hand. Emma noticed that Carrow had slight bags under his eyes, but nothing extreme. He seemed to have energy in abundance.

"Thanks for setting us up," he said.

"Keep your wits about you. All of you," Marwell said.

"Will do."

Marwell untied the ropes from the dock threw them to Oz, who caught them. Carrow started the engines and the boat moved off. He drove slowly until free of the harbor and then accelerated. Emma opened the cooler, pulled out an iced tea in a glass bottle. She uncapped it and went over to offer it to Oz, who sat in the companion chair. He flashed her a smile. Carrow already had an energy drink in his cup holder. He wore aviator sunglasses and kept his attention on the sea in front of them.

Emma grabbed her own drink and watched the island behind them grow smaller as they cruised away.

Over three hours later both the color and luminosity of the sea began to change. Emma worked her way up to Carrow at the helm.

"We're getting close, aren't we?" she said.

"Yep. Can you see the difference in the color?"

"It's beautiful."

"See any monsters?" Oz spoke in a mild voice, but Emma thought he seemed a bit nervous. Carrow grinned.

"Relax. We're not close enough yet." He checked a gauge on the dash. "About thirty more minutes, give or take, and we'll be right over them. You should know that the opening is dead center of the questionable area. Should anything occur, we'll need at least twenty minutes to get to the edge and away."

"You sound like you're leaving the option open for something to happen," Oz said. Carrow took a sip of his energy drink.

"I don't believe in sea monsters, if that's what you're asking. Do you?"

Oz was quiet a moment. Carrow gave him a glance and then shot a questioning look at Emma. She shrugged and waited. She'd learned that Oz usually thought before he spoke.

"It could be a large sea creature. That, I could believe, or some sort of phenomenon. The ocean is just so vast that I don't think we've learned everything there is to know."

Carrow seemed to consider Oz's answer. "But attacking a boat and pulling it down? I mean, how much strength does it take to yank a several ton cruiser underwater?"

"A lot," Oz said.

"I just can't imagine it happening. However, if it does . . ." Carrow pointed to the gun case. "Shoot the bastard."

"That's Emma's job," Oz said.

"Have no fear," Emma said. "A large tentacle curls out of the ocean at me and I'll empty an entire clip into it if I have to." Carrow laughed.

"Deal." He held up his energy drink can and Oz tapped it with the neck of his bottle.

The ocean became bluer and more illuminated

with every passing moment. Emma watched the churning wake and calculated the amount of product she'd need for her tests. She figured if she could get enough to fill ten gallon-sized hefty bags she could use one to run some initial tests at Terra Cay and send the rest to Miami. They traveled a bit more, and then Carrow cut the engines. The ensuing silence was welcome. The boat bobbed on the waves. Emma leaned over the side and scanned the water directly below them.

"Searching for a monster?" Carrow said with a smile.

"Actually, a shark," she replied.

Carrow groaned. "Thanks for that lovely thought."

"Statistically the shark is not very likely," Oz said. "You're thirty times more likely to get hit by lightning."

Carrow downed the rest of his drink and tossed the can into a garbage bag.

"That's what I like to hear," he said. "Death by shark versus death by lightning." He gazed around all sides of the boat. "Marwell was right, it's beautiful here. Can you see any of the caves?"

"No. Blue as it is, it's still too dark down there. Let's suit up?"

Twenty minutes later Emma and Carrow were ready. They'd lowered the anchor, attached a weight to the yellow ascent line and dropped it into the water. Her equipment was excellent, Marwell had given them the best, and she had a small yellow tank as a spare, an octopus regulator should something go wrong, and they had to share a tank and a safety sausage in case they drifted and Oz needed to see them at a distance. Carrow finished preparing and came over to assist her.

"We've got to do this in forty minutes and then ascend. We'll do a safety stop at about fifteen feet, okay?" he said.

"Sounds good." Emma checked her collection supplies and strapped on a wrist compass. She checked Carrow's wrists. "No compass?"

He reached down to a belt and showed her a compass attached to a lanyard on his dive belt. "I prefer this one." He looked at Oz. "We have safety sausages and I have this whistle as well." Carrow showed Oz a plastic whistle that also attached to him by a lanyard. "I don't expect us to drift too far out, but one never knows. I'll blow this first and only activate the sausage as a secondary measure."

"You'll yank on the rope when you're there?" Oz said to Emma.

"I will."

"Ready?" Carrow said.

Emma nodded. "Let's do this."

22

Kemmer steered the boat toward the blue holes. It had taken him two eighteen-hour days to get the boat outfitted and provisioned for the trip from St. Martin. An hour before he was to launch a man stepped onto the deck. About forty, with a wicked slash on his jawline, a head with hair trimmed in a close buzz and a rolling bag behind him, the man identified himself as "Joseph."

"I'm sent by your new partner," he'd said. "Do you have the guns on board?"

Kemmer had shown him the stash of high-powered sniper rifles, one with a bayonet attached, in a bag. "Good." That was the last thing Joseph had said since the beginning of the trip.

Kemmer distrusted everything about the man. His instincts flared whenever Joseph's beady dark eyes fell on him. Kemmer piloted the boat and did his best to stay quiet. The Vulture had made it quite clear that he expected only Kemmer and this man on the trip to the blue holes. Kemmer wondered what Joseph intended to do once they got there. If he was a diver he'd be disappointed. Kemmer hadn't brought any dive equipment on board, and it was clear that the roller bag was far too small to contain any. Finally, as they neared the site, Kemmer's anxiety got the better of him. He needed to know what Joseph intended to do.

"Are you planning on taking water samples at the site? Photos?" Kemmer said. A camera and a collection test tube were the only two things he thought would fit in the bag. Joseph turned his head and looked at Kemmer.

"No," he said.

"The locals think a sea monster lives there. Do you hope to catch a video or photo of it?"

Joseph gave Kemmer a look filled with derision. "Do I look like an ignorant local?"

"Not at all." Kemmer wanted to kick himself for even starting the conversation. Conversing with this man was a mistake. Still, he couldn't help himself.

"What's in the bag, then?"

"A gun," Joseph said.

"More? I didn't bring enough?"

"You didn't bring mine. I only fire that one."

"And the others? The ones that I was ordered to bring? What are they for?"

"For the others."

"What others?"

"The ones waiting at Terra Cay. That's where we're going after this."

That was news to Kemmer. He shoved aside his irritation at the fact that he hadn't been told about any others or that they were going to use his guns.

"Terra Cay won't allow us to use their dock with guns on board," he said.

"We're not going to use their dock. We're going to approach from the mangrove side." Joseph kept his eyes on the ocean ahead of them.

Kemmer did his best to keep his temper in check. Landing at Terra Cay from the mangrove side was dangerous. The water became shallow, and sharp coral outcroppings made for a difficult approach.

"That's a tough approach. Lots of rocks just below the water's surface."

Joseph shrugged. "I'll take my chances," he said.

Kemmer couldn't help but notice that Joseph seemed to think that he was the only one taking a chance on mooring at Terra Cay. Clearly the man thought he would do exactly as he was told; a fact that was true but still irked Kemmer. He returned his attention to piloting the boat, watching the gauges and keeping an eye on the compass. He'd be happy when the trip was completed.

"Are we in the Bermuda Triangle?" Joseph asked.

Kemmer nodded. "We are. The blue holes are located there."

"You been in the Triangle before?"

"Many times. Never a problem. The disappearances were pilot error, nothing more."

Joseph nodded, appearing content with the answer.

Kemmer didn't comment on the disappearances due to crime. He just hoped he wouldn't become one.

23

Emma jumped into the ocean after Carrow, who had already submerged. The clear, sparkling water was effervescent below the surface for several feet as she swam after Carrow slowly, taking care to descend in a leisurely fashion. A school of small neon-colored fish swam to and fro in front of her, moving in unison with rapid precision. A large slow-moving fish passed to her left. Its round eye seemed to look at her, then away.

She kept her breathing regular and calm. The biggest issue for her underwater was always the tendency to panic as she passed the fifteen meter mark. Her instructor had suggested that it might be nitrogen narcosis, a common condition that usually manifested at lower depths but could occur at any time. Every diver experienced it to some extent at depths below thirty meters, but the level and intensity changed for each person and each dive, and there was no way to train one's body to avoid it. The inevitability and unpredictability of nitrogen narcosis was what made it so dangerous.

The general symptoms for a diver were feelings of happiness or dread, decreased judgment, panic, the inability to remember the steps required to dive, and eventual unconsciousness and death. Divers had been known to think they could breathe underwater and take the regulators out of their mouths. In previous episodes, Emma's mild panic at depth had led to rapid breathing that depleted her tank quicker than it should have, but over the last three years she'd learned to expect the panic and force herself to continue to breathe slowly until it passed.

The sea darkened as they descended, and then the top of an arch came into view. Emma's depth perception was off, because the arch opening at first seemed as wide as ten feet but then appeared to narrow to three feet. She blinked, trying to discern if it was the angle of approach that made the arch move or if she was actually suffering from narcosis and experiencing the tunnel vision that was another marker of the condition. She focused on keeping her breathing even and slow, and her fins moving in a rhythmic, relaxing progression. After a few more feet of descent she saw the darker, round opening of the first blue hole. It lay directly at the base of the arch, about twenty feet farther below.

A shape attached to the left outer portion of the arch came into view. It was part of a boat's windshield hanging from the side of the arch. It seemed the windshield had snagged on a spiky section. Several small, bullet-sized holes pocked the glass, and the rest had shattered in a crazy pattern. Carrow reached the arch first and she saw him peer at the windshield. He ran his hand along the top of the arch before he continued down, toward the blue hole.

Emma approached the arch and also ran her hand along it. It was at least ten feet wide, and she realized that her perception of motion had come from the combination of the current that ran through it and the fact that a portion was broken off. It appeared to have been hacked at with an ax. She saw from the closest section that the sparkling blue mineral compound was only present in the first quarter inch of the arch. The rest appeared to be nothing more than a shell-like substance. From what she could see, there were only a few bits of the unique mineral left, and certainly not enough to supply an ingredient for a major cosmetic company's product.

She grabbed her tools and began scraping across the top, collecting pieces for later analysis. Perhaps the compound could be re-created in the lab in larger quantities. After filling a quart-sized bag she returned the tools to her belt.

She'd kept an eye on both her watch and her compass while diving, and now descended to the blue hole's entrance. Carrow was already there, staring to his right. Emma looked that way and her heart clutched. Slumped next to the opening was the body of a diver. It wore a black wet suit that ended at its ankles. The feet had been gnawed away, probably by fish, and the mask swayed in the water's current because no face anchored it. It, too, had been eaten. Emma couldn't see any evidence of the diver's oxygen tanks, but the remains of a regulator were clutched in the diver's right hand. Most of the flesh was gone but enough remained to see that the diver had been male.

Emma swallowed. She wondered if the shattered windshield and the dead diver were related. Perhaps an explosion caused the windshield to shatter and rip off from the boat? If so, she wondered what type of explosion. She glanced around, looking for any indication that the rest of the boat had followed the windshield down, but the area was clear. She knew they were actually on a promontory under the water. Maps of the area indicated that it extended over five hundred yards in all directions and then sloped downward, presumably all the way to the sea bottom. Too low for anyone to dive and low enough to swallow up the hull and remaining pieces of the shattered boat, if there were any.

She moved away from the body and back to the blue hole's entrance, put her hands on the edge and peered in. Carrow joined her. He stayed crouched at her right side as she collected more of the mineral. After six minutes on her watch, he floated up a bit, hovering over her head and looking around. He swam in a small circle above her. She thought he was marking time until she could complete the collection. Seven minutes later she was done. She put her tools away, attached the collection bag to her, and looked around for Carrow.

He was gone.

She experienced a moment of sheer panic. That he'd been floating above her one minute and gone the next sent her anxiety flying. She moved upward, forcing herself to swim in the same leisurely pace she'd used on descent. As she passed the midpoint of the arch's opening she spotted Carrow fifteen feet to her right, swimming away from her.

She checked her watch. They had five minutes left to explore and then would have to begin their ascent. She followed him through arch, but kicking fast, trying to catch up and warn him about the time. It wasn't until she was through the opening that she realized it was actually a tunnel, leading downward. Carrow was descending into it.

She caught up with him and lightly touched his leg. He stopped descending and she made the signal to ascend. He nodded but turned back into the tunnel. She touched him again, shook her head no and pointed back, out of the tunnel. He pointed downward. Again she signaled no. He made the sign for ascent and pointed downward.

Emma realized that he'd gotten disoriented. He believed that descending into the tunnel was ascending. She shook her head more vigorously, pointing upward. Carrow reached to his compass and held it in front of her, showing her its face.

The compass reading confirmed that they were to head farther into the tunnel if they were to ascend. Emma's entire being rebelled at the idea that the direction he pointed was correct, yet the compass verified what Carrow thought. She checked her own compass, but it appeared to be broken. She shook it, hoping to get it to function again, but it remained dark.

He watched her through his mask with a patient look on his face. Emma remembered Marwell's comment that Carrow was an experienced diver, and his calm in the face of her misunderstanding confirmed this fact, but she still believed that to continue to descend through the arch tunnel meant that they'd eventually use up all their air. Once they realized their mistake, they wouldn't have enough to complete an ascent. They'd die.

Emma's life had once been irrevocably altered by the lack of a compass. She'd been downed in a jungle and lost hers in the ensuing plane crash. Since that day she never traveled without one, and her belief in them as a lifesaving tool was unshakable. Yet now she struggled with the idea that Carrow's compass was wrong.

She grabbed him by the arm and shook her head no. Carrow's eyes first registered surprise, then concern. She saw him grapple with how to convince her that the direction she thought was the correct one was wrong. He shook his head very slowly, showed her the compass, pointed down the tunnel and began to swim in that direction.

Emma felt the low level panic she'd been working to control surge to the forefront. She swallowed in fear. If she followed, she would have to commit to the direction for as long as it took. She decided that her confusion must stem from nitrogen narcosis and so forced herself to go after him. She couldn't shake her belief that the compass was wrong, but the idea that a compass was broken in a way that showed the wrong direction entirely didn't seem likely. Either Carrow's compass was correct or there had to be another explanation. She followed with a feeling of overwhelming dread that they were going in the exact wrong direction.

Meanwhile, everything she knew about compasses ran through her mind. That they pointed magnetic north, for instance, not true north. Depending on where one was on the Earth, true north could be as much as twenty degrees east or west. While the deviation was small, over time and distance it could result in navigational mistakes of several thousand feet.

They were technically within the area that would include a tip of the Bermuda Triangle, and some claimed that a narrow band of the Triangle was one of the two places on earth where true north and magnetic north aligned, the other being the North Pole. In that case, there would be no deviation between the two readings. None of these facts, though, explained why the compass appeared to be sending them off course.

Emma glanced at her watch. In ten seconds they would have been swimming for five minutes. She had to make a decision to either try to convince Carrow one more time that the compass was wrong or follow him into what every instinct told her was the deep. She swam even with his shoulder and moved slightly ahead.

The tunnel opened into a large, cavelike area.

Stalactites and stalagmites pointed above and below them. The walls were jagged with dents and divots, and large pieces of the stalactites that broke off had fallen to the base of the cave. She saw three more bodies, their corpses in various stages of decomposition. All looked to be male. One had a collection bag gripped in his hand, and an ax lay next to the other. The cave provided proof that they had gone in the wrong direction, because they hadn't passed through it on descent.

Carrow turned to look at her and she saw the horror in his eyes. He grabbed at his compass and Emma reached for hers. The reading had reverted and now it confirmed that they had gone the wrong way. Carrow swung his hand up to show her the compass face. As he did, black liquid erupted from an opening at the far wall of the cave. It billowed outward, like the ink shot from an octopus. The current shifted, and Emma felt a riptide punch her in the chest and drag her back toward the tunnel's opening. She reached for Carrow's arm and held on tight as the vacuum pulled them upward, back the way they had come, but three times as fast as they'd descended. She tumbled in the water, hitting the tunnel's sides. Carrow slammed into her and then bounced back against the tunnel's wall and his arm yanked from her grip. His spare oxygen tank dislodged and hit her in the face before spinning away.

Emma tried to slow her ascent by grabbing at the smooth walls around her. She embedded her nails in it and felt the tips break one by one. Pain shot through her fingers and she felt a nail rip deeply into the cuticle.

The black ink compressed into the tunnel and filled the area behind them. It kept coming on, and she hoped it wasn't poisonous or acidic. She bit down on the regulator so tightly that her jaws ached. Reaching the end of the tunnel, she shot out into the open, getting a quick glimpse of the arch as the current continued to carry her up. Carrow followed, his arms wheeling as he tried to fight the surge. The ink spread, turning the water a dirty gray.

Emma turned her head to the side and kicked as hard as she could at a right angle to the riptide. Managing to break free, she swam away while doing her best to stay at the same depth. She saw Carrow using his arms in a motion opposite to the current in an attempt to slow his ascent. He curled his body into a ball and then kicked outward, managed to free himself from the concentrated stream and float sideways. But he was at least fifteen feet above her when she saw his body go limp. Unconscious, he began to float higher.

Emma swam up to Carrow and wrapped her fingers around his belt. She pulled him closer and checked his pulse and his tank. He was breathing but was dangerously low on air. Their rapid ascent made the lack of air the lesser of their worries, though, because now they faced decompression issues unless they could stay at this level for at least two minutes. The black ink was pooling below her and she didn't want to remain in the water when it reached their altitude. She held

Carrow in place next to her and checked her depth gauge. They were at eighteen feet, ideal for a safety stop. She hovered in the water, holding his belt, and did her best to slow her own breathing. A ringing in her ears indicated that she also was feeling the effects of their rapid ascent.

She watched the black ink work its way upward. A pool of fish skittered away, curving to avoid it. Emma swam up three more feet before checking her compass. She tried to settle her mind, focus on the steps she needed to take to compensate for the nitrogen narcosis that she presumed made her misread the device earlier, but she couldn't seem to think straight. She decided to watch her depth gauge instead, figuring there was time enough to locate the boat once they had safely surfaced.

A flash of yellow caught her eye. She swam that way and it became less fuzzy and more outlined. She felt tears prick behind her eyes when she realized that she was looking at the yellow ascent line attached to the boat. Wrapping an arm around Carrow's chest, she dragged him with her toward the line. When she reached it, she yanked on it, paused and consulted her watch. She'd risk it and wait two minutes, not three. The ink was approaching fast.

When it seemed enough time had passed to safely ascend again, she swam upward, bringing Carrow with her. The sun sparkled above her head and the boat's hull bobbed in the water. She reached the surface and removed her regulator and mask as Oz leaned over the side, his expression grim.

"I'm okay," Emma said, "but Carrow isn't. Can you help me get him on the boat?" She pulled his mask off and held him so his face was to the sun.

"Let me throw you a line," Oz said. "Wrap it around him and I'll try to pull him up." He threw a rope into the water and Emma curled it around Carrow and knotted it. Then Oz pulled him through the water to the boat's edge. With Emma's help, Oz was able to haul Carrow over the side. She scrambled up the ladder and immediately began retracting the line.

"We've got to get out of here, fast," she said.

"What happened down there? I felt turbulence, almost like an eruption, and the boat began to heave in the water."

"I can't describe it. I got hit with nitrogen narcosis and I think Carrow did too because we both misread our compasses and the next thing I knew we got caught up in a riptide."

Oz was bending over Carrow. He unzipped the wet suit, and Carrow took a deep, shuddering breath and opened his eyes.

"Oh thank God," Emma said. "You have to breathe some oxygen."

Carrow nodded and took the mask that Oz handed him.

"Oz, can you drive the boat?" Emma said.

Before Oz could answer, a gunshot cracked through the air.

24

The bullet slammed into the cooler holding the food and ricocheted into the air. Emma hit the deck, pulling Carrow's head lower as well.

"Stay down," she said to him. "Some nut on another boat is shooting at us." She did her best to remain calm, but her heart was thudding and her ears still rang from the rapid ascent. Carrow nodded and lay flat, never removing the mask from his nose.

"What the hell was that?" Oz said.

"Gunshot," Emma said.

"Are you joking?" Oz's voice was incredulous.

She scrambled to the helm, pressed the button to raise the anchor and flipped the engines on, keeping them in neutral while the anchor retracted. The other boat was far to their starboard side but coming on fast.

"Grab the wheel, I'm getting the gun."

Oz crouched low as he sidled over and took her place. "Pirates?" he asked. He kept his eye on the winding anchor as he spoke to her.

"Possible, but not likely. They're in the Caribbean, but not active over the blue holes. They're as afraid of them as Marwell is."

"Then why shoot at us?"

"I have no idea." She went to the gun box and removed the rifle, loaded it and headed to the starboard side, crouching behind the gunwale. She raised her head to look out and saw the boat speeding toward them. The engines on the cruiser turned over and Oz put the throttle down while steering them away from the other vessel. He remained low, driving the boat from his position next to the chair.

Emma took aim at the driver through the telescopic lens. She was an adequate shot under the ideal circumstances of a shooting range, but these circumstances were hardly that. The boat bounced up and down as it plowed through the water and bits of sea spray cascaded over her and the gun. The distance between the two vessels increased and Emma lowered the weapon. She hated to waste a bullet on an improbable shot. She made her way to the helm and grabbed the satellite phone. It was unable to make a connection. She slammed the receiver into its cradle.

"Satellite phone is down." She reached for the radio. "I'll send a mayday." She flipped on the radio but all she heard was static. She continued with a mayday, giving the coordinates for the blue holes. They were whizzing away, but any overhead craft might be able to fly in a concentric circle and find them. "Are we heading back to Terra Cay? I don't want these guys to herd us further out to sea." She glanced at the GPS tracker, but it was dark. "Damn, the GPS is out."

"What's wrong with the compass?" Oz said.

The compass on the dash was spinning erratically, twitching one way and then the other. Emma checked the compass on her watch and it, too, was alternating from point to point.

"I have no idea, but we've got to figure out which way is back."

Oz kept the throttle down. They'd pulled away from the other boat, but any slight advantage they might have had initially was fading as it gave chase. Emma watched it buck up and down as it hammered directly into the oncoming waves.

"We're in the Bermuda Triangle, right?" Oz said. "Did we cross the agonic line? Could the compasses be readjusting to the electromagnetic change?" He was remarkably calm as he asked the question. Emma wasn't surprised that he knew about agonic lines. As a student at MIT and an amateur astronomer, he must have discussed the phenomenon. The agonic line was an imaginary line where true north and magnetic north aligned.

"I checked into that before I came to Terra Cay. The agonic line has been moving for years. It's currently over the Gulf of Mexico. I doubt it could be affecting the magnetic compasses and it would have no effect on the gyrocompass. Something is, though."

"Check Carrow's. Maybe one is still functioning. I wasn't able to finish my calculations with the sextant. I just need a general idea of direction. We can fine-tune it once the instruments come back on line."

Emma crawled to the aft and grabbed Carrow's belt, which was lying near the back of the cruiser where they'd dropped it after hauling him on board. His compass was behaving in the exact same manner.

"No change. It's messed up," she called to Oz.

"They're gaining," Oz said. He'd risen to sit in the captain's seat. Emma went back to stand next to him. They *were* gaining. She estimated that they would soon be within range. She went to the back of the boat, grabbing a towel that was next to the cooler. Lowering herself down against the gunwale, she put the towel on top and rested the gun's muzzle on it. The towel's cushioning helped keep the muzzle on line, but the shot was still going to be challenging. Carrow had risen to a sitting position and removed the oxygen mask. He watched her. She targeted the other vessel's driver, took a deep breath, and held it in preparation to squeeze the trigger.

The engines seized and the cruiser gave a violent lurch. Emma flew sideways and hit the opposite side with her back. Carrow slid across the deck and slammed into the cooler. The engines whined and their gears clanged.

"Sounds like a rod is stuck in them," Carrow said. Emma, on her knees now, scrambled back to the aft section. Carrow joined her to peer over the transom at the engines.

The water behind the boat was black and churning, but the cruiser didn't move. It was as if something was holding them in place, trying to pull them underwater. Emma tried to see what was obstructing the engines, but the oily, dark water reduced the visibility. The boat gave another violent lurch, the stern shuddered, and the rear of the boat started to lower into the whirlpool that was forming.

"We're sinking," Carrow said.

25

Kemmer watched as Joseph lowered the rifle.

"I missed. The waves are throwing off my aim. Get the boat closer and I'll try again."

He spun the wheel and turned the boat toward the white cabin cruiser floating in the water almost a quarter mile away. Kemmer wasn't sure the weapon Joseph was wielding could accurately hit a target at that distance, but his immediate concern was doing what Joseph wanted. He cursed inwardly at his folly. The Vulture had taken advantage of his need for cash and gotten him caught up in attempted murder. Kemmer didn't know who owned the white cabin cruiser or why the Vulture had gone to such great lengths to intercept it on the ocean, and he didn't particularly care. His concern was that Joseph would kill him after he completed the assassination. The man didn't seem the type to let witnesses live.

Though he hadn't loaded dive equipment onto the boat, Kemmer did have a handgun in a compartment near the steering wheel, in addition to the bag of weapons he'd shown Joseph earlier. As he drove he plotted how he would retrieve the gun and shoot Joseph before Joseph would begin his cleanup. He had never killed anyone, but that didn't mean he wouldn't hesitate to dispatch Joseph if it meant saving his own life.

The water remained smooth and sparkling as Kemmer opened the throttle and began gaining on the cruiser. He watched the boat turn its nose away and start moving. He heard the distant roar of the engines. The cabin cruiser clearly had power, but it also had added weight in contrast to the smaller vessel that Kemmer drove. That weight would affect the larger boat's speed, and eventually he would gain on it. He urged some more speed out of his boat, and the engine's whine grew higher pitched as the machinery pulsed.

Joseph sat on a back bench seat with a sniper rifle in his hands and concentrated on the vessel ahead. Kemmer's speed made their boat slam into the waves and buck upward, sending both of them bouncing in the air. Joseph shot Kemmer an annoyed glance.

"Can't this thing stabilize? I can't be thrown around when I aim. I'll miss again."

"Why didn't you wait until we were closer? Now they're running."

"I don't need to get in a firefight. The more I can drop at a distance, the safer I am."

"You think they have guns on board, too?"

"I doubt it, but I've learned never to assume anything."

Kemmer wasn't pleased at that latest piece of information, but it made sense. If the boat ahead of him were cartel flunkies on a drug run, they'd have every type of weapon imaginable on board as well as the will to use them.

"Why are you after them? Who are they?" Kemmer said.

Joseph ignored both questions and remained silent.

"Did you hear me?" Kemmer said.

"It's none of your business. Just get this boat to stop bucking."

"Only thing I can do to settle the boat is ease off the throttle. We won't go as fast, so it will take us longer to pull even."

"No, keep it open all the way. I'll give you a signal when we get into a position that will give me a free shot. When I do, kill the engine."

"Okay. Figure at least twenty minutes. That cruiser's a lot heavier, but it also has a couple of powerful engines on the back. We'll gain on them, but slowly."

Joseph shrugged. "I don't care as long as we get there."

"Looks like there are a couple of people on board. Who are you trying to kill?"

"All of them," Joseph said.

26

Emma aimed into the churning black water.

"Watch out," she said to Carrow. Once he stepped aside, she fired. The water kept swirling and the boat sank a bit more. The waves started splashing over the transom's edge.

"Oz, jerk it to the right. Marwell said he dislodged his boat that way," Emma said. Oz spun the wheel and the boat turned sideways in a sluggish move. The rear still remained in place.

"Try the other way," Carrow said. Oz spun the wheel back and the boat began an equally sluggish correction, but whatever held it in place didn't release it. Emma glanced at the oncoming vessel.

"Get down." She lowered herself back against the gunwale and replaced the towel. The water was dangerously close to not only rushing over the side but engulfing her weapon as it surged upward. She aimed and fired.

The other boat veered to the left. She peered through the scope and saw that she'd shot through the windshield but missed the driver. The sound of a gunshot signaled return fire, and a bullet embedded in the boat's side. The driver wasn't shooting; another person held the gun. Emma could just make out the shape of his head by the vessel's edge.

Their boat kept sinking lower and more water splashed over the side. Emma ignored the deluge and kept her gun up, tracking the attackers as they drove in a large circle. Carrow went to stand next to Oz at the helm. Oz spun the steering wheel from side to side as they attempted to dislodge the boat. The engines whined and Emma smelled a combination of burning gasoline and oil coming from them, but the boat stayed in place and the black whirlpool by the stern seemed to whip around faster.

A third shot sailed over them. Seawater splashed into Emma's face and she wiped her eyes before firing back. The shooter remained out of sight and she doubted that she'd hit him. She was breathing fast and inadvertently swallowed some of the ocean spray. It burned the inside of her throat and she coughed. She didn't want to spare a glance at whatever was hauling them downward, but the thought that they were going to die by either gunshot or drowning passed through her mind.

The other vessel continued to track around them in a circle, driving straight into the oncoming waves. Its engines roared and then cut out as the boat bounced high. While Emma had a slight advantage—the immovability of the *Siren* meant that her shots had a halfway decent chance of landing near their target unlike the other shooter, who had to contend with the bucking motion of his boat—but she knew that her advantage would disappear when the shooter came close enough to pick them off. The attack boat straightened and came toward them head on. Emma squeezed off two more shots in an attempt to stop them. She shattered the windshield and hit the bow.

Water was all around her. She had the vague impression that Carrow was bailing it out but didn't want to remove her eyes from their attackers long enough to confirm it. Oz kept the vessel moving from side to side, but without the benefit of engine push the *Siren* still didn't move much in either direction. Carrow came to kneel at her side.

"What the hell do they want?" he said.

"To kill us. Why, I don't know."

She saw a flash of light as the sun reflected off the other man's weapon, and she targeted the location and fired. The other boat careened away once again, driving in a circle, but an ever tightening one. Soon they would be upon them and she would be embroiled in a firefight. She checked the clip.

"You might want to get below. They're almost on us, and up here you're an easy target," Emma said.

"Oz has an idea that he wants to try. He's going to straighten us out and lower the throttle all the way. We may burn up the engines faster, but they're close to overheating now and it's worth a shot."

Emma nodded without taking her eyes off the circling attack boat.

"What about the radio and GPS?"

"Still out. I've sent two more maydays." Carrow watched the other boat circle. "Those aren't pirates," he said in a flat voice. Emma glanced at him out of the corner of her eye.

"You sound positive. Why?"

"I just know. Intuition. They're after us in a very personal fashion. It's my boat. Perhaps me." He looked at her. "You have any enemies?"

Emma nodded. "A few."

He gave her an assessing look before glancing at the water in the stern.

"Can you see if it's an animal holding us?"

Emma shook her head. "It's too dark. But whatever it is, it's winning. We're going lower every three minutes or so. In ten this whole section will be under. From there the rest will just drop like a stone."

"So either be picked off by the shooter or go below and drown," Carrow said. It was as if he had read her thoughts. But she didn't want to agree, at least not openly.

"Or we try Oz's idea and hope for the best."

"I'll tell Oz to get on it."

"And then maybe get below."

Carrow shook his head. "I'll stay up here with you both. I'm not dying alone."

Oz looked over from the helm.

"I'm going to straighten her out and give it one more shot," he said.

Carrow left her side and returned to bailing.

The engines continued clanking and whining. Emma watched the other vessel approach and did her best to settle her mind and focus only on the boat. She ignored the rising water and tried to ignore the fact that something strange had grabbed hold of them and was dragging them into the deep.

She heard the other boat's engine seize. It, too, came to a dead stop. The man with the gun flew toward the front of the vessel and Emma heard him yell. The black churning wake formed around the back of the other boat and the aft section began lowering into the turbulence. Emma wanted to shout in exultation as she saw it shift violently. Its nose pointed upward and the stern down. Considerably lighter than the *Siren*, it was sinking faster. She heard the yell of the driver and for the first time the shooter stood up, seemingly heedless of the open target he'd become. He stalked to the rear of the boat, aimed his weapon and shot four times in rapid succession into the water. Emma could have told him not to waste his bullets. The boat continued to sink.

She felt a lurch, and the *Siren*'s aft section rose higher in the water. The engines gave a roar and the wake behind the boat grew even more turbulent.

"Come on, you son of a bitch, let go!" Carrow yelled. The *Siren* surged forward. It was as if whatever was holding them had heard Carrow and obeyed. Oz whooped and Carrow laughed out loud.

"Go, go, go!" he yelled. Oz kept the throttle down and the boat surged through the waves.

Emma kept her eye on the other boat, but the driver had joined the shooter at the back. He held a gun with a bayonet on the end and was repeatedly stabbing it into the churning water. The boat, though, didn't move. Even as they pulled away Emma could hear the misfiring of the other vessel's engines. She glanced at her watch. It had taken them twenty minutes to get whatever was holding their boat down to release them. They were some of the longest twenty minutes of her life so far. She could only hope it would take the other boat equally as long.

As they sped away. Emma watched the boat grow smaller in the distance. When they were out of range she emptied the gun and moved up next to Oz. She placed it on an undercounter shelf.

"Are the compasses still going haywire?" she asked. Oz nodded. He was pale, but his face had a determined look.

"I'm just going to try to get as far away from that boat as I can."

"I'm going to help Carrow get the pumps working," she told him. "How much fuel do we have?"

"Half a tank and two extra cans in the hold. That's thanks to Marwell. He overprovisioned us."

"Thank God for the gun," Emma said.

"And here we thought we'd be shooting monsters with it, not humans."

27

Emma joined Carrow to bail the deck, a task made much easier because they were once again floating on the water rather than being dragged down. The boat was no longer listing and they'd been able to start the bilge pump. They worked in silence and Emma kept an eye on the horizon behind them. If their pursuers were able to free their boat quickly, they could be tracking them.

"Is the radar working?" she asked Oz.

"No, and the GPS and compass are still down. You think they're following us?"

"I wish I knew. The radar would tell us. I can only hope that their equipment is acting as strangely as ours."

Carrow paused a moment and pulled a bottle of whiskey from the cooler, uncapped it and poured it into a small plastic glass. He handed the glass to Oz and began to pour another, which he gave to Emma. He poured the third and held it up for a toast.

"To life," he said. Emma and Oz repeated the toast and they all swallowed the shot.

"Think we'll outpace the shooter?" Oz said to Carrow.

"If they remain stuck. That boat was faster. If it wasn't for that lucky break it would have overtaken us. Do we have any idea where we are?"

Oz shook his head. "Not really. We haven't gone that far from the holes, but I can't tell you in which direction until the compass situation straightens out. What I will say is that we'd better get the hell out of this area before another incident causes the boat to stop." He looked at Emma and Carrow. "Any ideas about what it was that held us in place? Did either of you see a creature under water?" Emma slid into the companion seat at the helm next to Oz. Carrow took another swallow of his drink.

"I couldn't see a thing," he said. "The water was black and so disrupted that there could have been an entire herd of them and I wouldn't have spotted them."

"We're in the Bermuda Triangle," Emma said. "Before I came here I did quite a bit of research on the area. Lots of disappearances here and lots of theories as to why. Up until now I was on the side of the human error theory. Many planes and boats traverse this route and human error is bound to occur. Nothing supernatural."

"And now you've changed your mind?" Oz said.

"Absolutely. That was no ordinary event."

"Sea monster?"

"Hmmm, probably not, though I agree that visibility underwater was so poor, I can't rule it out definitively. But I have another idea. I think it was a methane eruption."

Carrow perched against the nearby counter.

"Is that an actual eruption or a Bermuda Triangle theory?"

"Well, both, actually. Methane eruptions are real, but there hasn't been one detected in the Triangle. Methane bubbles that naturally form at the sea's bottom float upward in massive quantities and eventually erupt. Methane gas eruptions cause the water around the explosion to grow much less dense, resulting in a sudden loss of buoyancy, and anything above it will sink. Oil rigs have been the primary victims of methane gas eruptions."

"They've sunk?" Carrow sounded surprised.

Emma nodded. "They have. No injuries. The sinking process was slow and the rigs were able to radio for evacuation, but it does occur. However, it's extremely rare and I wasn't willing to give the theory credence until now. Now I think that the eruption we experienced in the holes and the turbulence that Oz said he felt on the surface was a methane gas eruption. It's the only explanation that comes close, I think."

"So no sea monster?"

"Well, I *did* shoot, just in case."

Carrow held up his glass. "Amen to that."

Oz checked the compass. "The gyroscope is spinning less and less. Whatever is disrupting it is settling down. Maybe we're getting out of the zone. Which leaves me wondering why that other boat was shooting at us." He gave Emma a pointed look. She sighed.

"I think they were after me, though how they knew that I'd be diving the holes today is a question that I can't answer." Carrow refilled his whiskey glass as well as Oz's. He offered it to Emma, but she waved it away. If the attackers returned, she needed to keep her wits about her.

"All right, fire away," Carrow said. "Tell me why two murderous individuals want to kill a nice chemist like you."

Oz nodded. "I want to hear this as well. You assured me that you weren't working on a project for Banner."

Emma held up a hand. "And I'm not." She looked at Carrow. "In case you're wondering, Edward Banner is the head of a contract security firm that takes on difficult projects worldwide. I sometimes assist."

Carrow nodded. "I've spoken to Banner once, though I've not met him. He was looking for information on Oz."

"Banner's great, but I'm really working at Terra Cay on private business. Unfortunately, I've recently learned that someone is gunning for both me and another freelancer who works for Banner. We don't know who or why. I was told to watch my back."

"Old grudge?" Carrow asked.

"Very likely."

Carrow took another gulp and gave her a considering look. "You are just chock-full of surprises," he said.

"And not all of them nice ones, I'm afraid. I'm sorry to subject you both to this."

"You've saved my life in the past," Oz said. "If I can help you, then that's the least I can do." He gave her a reassuring smile. How lucky I am to have such friends, Emma thought. Oz returned his attention to steering the boat. Carrow took another sip of the whiskey and kept his gaze on her.

"What did you do that may have made these two gun for you?" he asked. Emma took a deep breath and stared out to sea. Though she was thinking about Carrow's question, she was also scanning the horizon. How quickly she fell back into old survival habits, she thought.

"I've done only two missions for Banner. Both of them ultimately saved lives. I'm proud to work at something that makes a difference. I only wish that innocent people like you and Oz wouldn't get caught up in it." She went to take a sip of her drink and was surprised to see that the glass was empty. She looked up and Carrow was standing over her, a serious look on his face and the whiskey bottle in his hand. He poured some into her glass.

"I've never done anything that I thought made a real difference," he said. "You're right to be proud." His voice was low and meant for her ears only.

"I don't believe that," she said. "Randiger told me that you've instituted music education in the school at Terra Cay. That makes a difference to a lot of children."

"Don't let that news get out. Will absolutely ruin my reputation among the rock 'n' roll set." He moved to sit on the open seat next to her.

"The radar's up," Oz said. Emma and Carrow both got up to stand at Oz's side.

"What a beautiful sight. Where are we?" Carrow moved closer and watched the radar for a moment.

"Ahhh, not good news, I'm afraid. We've gone the wrong way. In fact, the exact opposite way from Terra Cay."

"That's not as bad as it could be," Emma said. "We have extra fuel and lots of food. Even if it takes a while longer than we projected, we should be able to get home, right?"

"We have enough fuel, yes, but only enough if we cross back through the zone. I don't know about you guys, but I don't need to go through another methane eruption or whatever it was. And I definitely don't need to meet up with those two losers again," Oz said.

"Are they around? Is the radar picking them up?"

"No boats."

"Well at least that's something," Emma said.

"Do we risk the Triangle again? What's your vote?" Oz looked at Emma. She was up and pacing while she thought of all the possible angles.

"My biggest concern is that the radar and compasses will go down again once we reenter. Can we signal for help? Maybe we can get an escort to help us return?"

"The radio, compass, and satellite phone are all

down," Oz said. "I can't be sure that any message will make it to anyone."

"And there's something else," Carrow said.

"Out with it," Emma said. "We've been attacked by a monster and shot at by killers. It can't be much worse than that, can it?" She was having a difficult time thinking of anything worse.

Carrow sighed. "Maybe not, but that," he pointed to a mass entering the right of the radar screen, "is very bad news."

"Is that what I think it is?" Emma said.

"A tropical storm is coming our way."

28

Banner stood with Sumner in the kitchen of his rented house while Sumner laid a bullet on the table. It sparkled blue in the sunlight that shone through the window.

"This is what we confiscated from the airplane that Stromeyer asked us to intercept," he said.

"That looks like a glitter crayon," Banner said.

"You know how ammunition manufacturers have been trying to create a caseless bullet that can withstand heat and eject with accuracy?"

Banner nodded. "The Heckler & Koch, G–11 prototype came close."

"But it was expensive and never went into full production. As far as we can tell, this bullet is made from a unique mineral. It contains the usual propellant inside, but the casing is not metal. This material seems the answer to the prayers of terrorists the world over."

"Why?"

"It can withstand the heat generated in the chamber of a fired gun, but it's not metal." Banner picked up the bullet. It was sleek and felt cool to the touch but had a denser feel, almost like glass.

"Ceramic?" Banner asked.

"Not really, but close."

"How does it avoid the heat issue?"

"Far as we can tell, it has unique properties that allow it to disperse heat evenly and it doesn't retain as much as regular metal."

"Okay," Banner said. "So a better bullet. I don't want to sound jaded, but the bullets we already have create damage enough to keep me in business. Stromeyer said that it has a substantial defect rate, yet the arms dealer wanted top dollar for it, which is odd, because no one needs their weapon misfiring in the heat of battle. Seems to me this is just another prototype that may never become worth the cost."

"The bullet might not be worth the cost, but something else may really be happening here. I discussed this with the Southern Hemisphere Drug Defense guys and we came up with a theory. We think this bullet is only a small part of a larger problem. We think it fits into a gun manufactured from the same material."

Banner made the connection immediately, as well as the grave danger posed by the material if Sumner was correct.

"A completely nonmetal gun. Able to be smuggled through any metal detector the world over," he said. Sumner nodded.

"Even the ammunition won't be detected. It's like the legendary glass gun that the CIA claims doesn't exist."

"Reminds me of that movie," Banner said.

"*In the Line of Fire*," Sumner said. "The villain makes a plastic gun that he smuggles through security. But even in that movie he had to hide the ammunition because it would set off the detector."

"Still, to create a gun that unique has to cost millions. Is there a government behind the manufacture?" Banner asked. Sumner sat down in a chair.

"We're not sure."

"Because such a weapon—not to mention the ammunition—violates the Geneva Accords. They require a full metal jacket. Seems as though the major governments should band together to shut this particular technological development down. And who has the knowledge to both find the mineral and create the weapon?"

"We do know that it probably required a team of chemists to fashion the bullet alone."

Banner looked at Sumner, who was watching his expression closely.

"Chemists," Banner said. "And the arms dealer was headed to Terra Cay, where Caldridge is currently working."

Sumner nodded. "She just received a contract to find an unusual mineral located in the blue holes off Terra Cay. She was excited about the project, but dealing with some crazy stunts that I now think were designed to scare her off. Make her leave before she could go out and mine the holes."

Banner refilled his coffee cup and offered the

pot to Sumner, who nodded. Banner took a cup
from the cabinet and poured one.

"So they keep the mineral for themselves,"
Sumner said.

"Let's get her on the phone," Banner said.

Sumner pulled out his cell, accessed the con-
tacts list, and hit a number. He put it on speaker
and placed it on the table. After a few rings the
phone cycled into voice mail.

"I'll text her," Sumner said. "What do you want
me to say?"

"'Can the ATD program spare you for a couple
of days?'"

Sumner nodded. "I think my cover's been
blown."

"Then maybe you tell her that you're flying
over to Terra Cay. Something strange is going on
there, and I think it's time to dig a little deeper."

29

Emma sat on the back bench holding the rifle while Carrow drove the boat. They'd decided to risk crossing the blue holes again. The radar was back up, but the phones and radio remained broken. Night had fallen. Emma kept the gun at her side even though they hadn't seen the shooter's boat again. Carrow plotted a course a mile from the scene as a precaution and it seemed to be working. There was nothing that she could see or hear on the ocean.

Oz sat on a bar stool at the counter under the helm's canopy, making notes and glancing occasionally at the radar. The moon rose above them, full and bright. Emma shivered in the cool air and watched the whitish glow as it hit the waves. She couldn't hear much over the noise of their engines, but she still endeavored to listen for other sounds that weren't synonymous with nature. While she might not see the boat if it was far enough away, she knew that sound would carry and she might pick up the noise of an engine or the clank of machinery. She shivered again and rose to get a sweatshirt from her bag. She placed the gun in its case, closed it, and headed down to the cabin.

The spacious cabin had a galley kitchen on one side and a table and benches on the other. Emma put the heavy, fleece-lined sweatshirt over her head and sighed at the warmth. Since the dive, she'd felt the cold in her bones. Oz came down the stairs, lowering his head to avoid hitting it on the stairwell's low ceiling.

"You okay? You've been really quiet," he said. His hair gleamed in the lamplight and his angular, classical face contained shadings and shadows.

"I've been thinking about the shooter. Wondering what it all means. You've been quiet, too. What are you writing?"

Oz sighed and reached into a small refrigerator. He removed an energy drink and slid onto the bench to sit at the table.

"I've been figuring out the return trip by celestial navigation. Just in case the radar gives out again."

"Is it hard to do?"

"Not really. But there are twenty-two different calculations, so it's time consuming."

"Guys, come look at this," Carrow called from above. His voice held a strained tone. Emma headed up the stairs and joined Carrow at the helm. He pointed to port.

"Over there. I saw something floating in the water." He put the boat in neutral.

Oz and Emma leaned over the side. Bits of de-

tritus rode the waves, most of which was uniden-
tifiable, except for a small bench cushion from a
boat.

"You see that?" Carrow said.

"Is it from the shooter's boat?" Oz asked.

Emma strained to see the colors on the cushion
as it bobbed in the water, but the combination of
the movement and darkness made it hard to dis-
tinguish features. Oz grabbed a fishing net on a
six-foot pole and used it to snag what looked like
a piece of white tubing. He pulled the net toward
him, working hand over hand to bring the item
closer to the side. Carrow joined him and stood
next to Emma.

A man's arm lay entangled in the netting, and
the rest of his body dragged behind.

"Shit!" Oz yelled. Carrow leaned over the side
and looked at the man floating in the water.

Emma leaned over as well. "His arm looks like
a bit has been taken out of it."

"Shark, you think?" Carrow asked.

"Probably. I have an idea where he came from,"
Emma said.

"The shooter or his driver, I'll wager," Carrow
said.

"I agree. Has to be, don't you think?" Oz said.
Emma thought so as well.

"I can't tell if he's breathing. Let's haul him on
board."

30

Sumner lined up the small plane for approach at the Terra Cay runway. He knew the tight landing configuration and hammered the brakes down as he increased some drag. The plane rolled to a near stop several feet before the mountainous wall, and he turned it to taxi toward the small terminal. A signal man waved him into a parking spot, then he cut the engines and unlocked the main cabin door. He swung it open, lowered the stairs, grabbed his duffel and stepped down. A dark-skinned man in a police uniform stood about twenty feet to the side of the airplane. Sumner headed that way while the signal man started chocking the plane's wheels.

"I'm Waylon Randiger, Island Security. You must be Cameron Sumner from the Southern Hemisphere Drug Defense Agency." Randiger stuck out his hand. Sumner noticed that the man's demeanor was serious and his eyes were bloodshot. He looked tired and worried. Sumner looked back and saw a continuous line of private jets, all idling while they waited their turn to take off.

"It's a pleasure." Sumner looked around. "Lots of planes leaving."

Randiger's face became set. "We issued a travel warning early this morning."

Sumner raised an eyebrow. "Weather?"

"No. A health warning. We have a strange sickness sweeping through the Island. Lucky for us a big chunk of the residents had already departed after the New Year celebrations, but the ones who remained are leaving now. You sure you don't want to turn around and fly back out? I wouldn't blame you if you did." Sumner shook his head.

"I'll stay. Do I need to go through customs?"

Randiger nodded. "They know you're coming so it will be quick. Come with me and I'll take you through. After that I'd like to show you something. We can talk in the car."

Sumner worked his way through customs and headed to the small SUV that blinked its lights after Randiger pressed a button on his key fob. He tossed his duffel in the back and crawled into the passenger seat.

"I understand that you're a friend of Emma Caldridge's?" Randiger said.

"I am. I've been trying to reach her, but there's been no answer on her cell and the housekeeper at her villa said she's out on a diving expedition."

Randiger nodded. "She went out with Richard Carrow and another man this morning. There's a satellite phone on the boat, but they're not answering that either. Perhaps they're out of range."

Sumner glanced at Randiger. "Odd for a satellite phone. And do you mean she's with Richard Carrow the lead singer of Rex Rain?"

Randiger kept his eyes on the twisting road, but Sumner could sense his anxiety.

"I do. He's an experienced diver and he offered to take her to the blue holes when no one else would."

"What's everyone else afraid of?"

"A combination of the blue holes and the Bermuda Triangle area where they exist. Lots of superstitious folks in the islands." He parked the car next to a trail that led into a wooded area. "I'm going to show you something that will give you an idea of the problem."

"What is it?"

"Something that isn't pleasant." Randiger glanced at Sumner's shoes. "You don't mind getting those a little dirty? We're headed up that trail about five hundred yards." Sumner's black Superga gym shoes had seen more wear than just the trail.

"Don't worry. They wash up just fine."

"Then let's go."

Sumner followed Randiger into the woods, gaining almost immediate relief from the sun's heat. The smell of grass, wet loam, and the feel of moist air was a welcome change from the arid atmosphere inside the airplane. They reached a clearing and Randiger skirted the edges, doing his best to avoid stepping on the elaborate display in the center.

A series of stones placed in a circle about ten

feet in diameter filled the open area. Inside the circle were the remnants of a fire. Blackened and burnt wood lay in ashes in the center, and before it were the remains and entrails of a small animal. A viscous mass below the entrails contained a couple of feathers stuck into the mess, and Sumner assumed it was a bird that had been eaten. The entire display reeked of old smoke and new blood with a hint of the sweet smell of decay.

In front of the carcass lay a small, crudely woven doll, about a foot long and made from burlap. It had brown yarn for hair and had the letters EC drawn on the chest in black marker. Its neck was slit and the cut area colored with red marker to approximate blood. A kitchen knife protruded from its chest.

"It's voodoo," Randiger said. "The island's always had its practitioners, but they've stayed in the shadows and no one really discusses it. This, though, is the most recent event, and I think that doll is supposed to represent Ms. Caldridge."

Sumner walked around the display, checking it out from all angles. While he could see the threat implied in the defaced doll, he also felt as though the act was designed to vent rage at a distance. Sumner had been beside Caldridge when she'd had another's rage directed toward her in close confines. This indirect attack, despite its obvious menace, seemed diluted in comparison.

While he knew better then to ignore the threat, he also felt it was a childish act.

"Any idea who is doing this and why?" he asked.

"Ms. Caldridge interrupted a woman calling herself a hougan priestess and a so-called zombie destroying her lab."

"She told me about that. Seems as though they could have harmed her then, but didn't. Something tells me they want to scare her off, but not necessarily go any deeper into trouble to do it."

Randiger pursed his lips. Sumner could tell that he didn't agree but seemed hesitant to speak further.

"You look like you have something on your mind," Sumner said.

"There's another problem." Somehow Sumner wasn't surprised by this bit of information.

"Okay," he said.

"I'm the deputy sheriff on the island. Duncan Moore is the sheriff. He would normally have been the one to greet you at the airport, but he's sick. Really sick."

"What does he have?"

"He fell asleep last night and didn't wake up. He has yet to wake up."

"Coma?" Sumner said.

"Perhaps a type of one, but it seems as though he's just . . . asleep. His wife called me to say that she tried to wake him up and couldn't. This was at six o'clock last evening, and I suggested that she call the doctor. She did, but he's in St. Vincent and not able to get here until tomorrow afternoon. In the meantime, Duncan started to have seizures. His wife called the doctor back and he suggested a tranquilizer. His wife gave him one and it didn't work. Now she's asked that I contact Ms. Caldridge, because word is she had a good result with Nalen, the bass player for Rex Rain who had the same symptoms."

"What did Caldridge give him?"

"Mandrake powder. Problem is, we can't find any, nor can the gardeners at the various villas. Either they don't recognize it or it's not growing anywhere on the island. I have pictures off the Internet, but it looks just like any other weed to me. I don't suppose she mentioned it to you? Perhaps where she found it?"

"She didn't. I'm sorry. But she should return soon, shouldn't she?"

Randiger looked at his watch. "It's nearly six o'clock. They left early morning and told Marwell, our dockmaster, that they'd be back tomorrow morning at the latest. As I mentioned, I've been trying to call them on the phone and he's been trying to raise them on the radio, but they're not answering."

Sumner didn't like the sound of that at all. Caldridge was an extreme runner, but a novice diver. While he hoped all went smoothly, he knew diving could be a very dangerous activity.

"How experienced a diver is Carrow?" he asked.

"Very. He's maintained a home here for four years and dives quite a bit."

"What's his judgment like? His reputation in the tabloids is that he's wild as hell."

Randiger nodded. "Oh yeah, he's all that. But I don't think he'd horse around on a dive. We can ask Marwell what he thinks. He's been on several dives with him."

"Let's go."

Sumner followed Randiger down the path back to the SUV. The sun was setting and throwing shadows all around. He felt the loam under his feet and slapped at a few mosquitoes that tried to feast on his arms.

By the time they reached the dock the sun was a half penny lowering into the water line in the distance. They found Marwell in the dock office gazing at a radar screen set between a computer monitor on one side and a radio on the other. Randiger introduced Sumner and mentioned that he was a friend of Caldridge's.

"He's asking about Carrow," Randiger said.

Marwell gave Sumner a frank look of assessment, and Sumner remained quiet while he did. The older man seemed to be a no-nonsense type of person, which was the kind Sumner liked the best.

"What do you want to know?" Marwell asked.

"I understand he's a good diver, but his reputation in the media is that of a wild man. I was asking about his judgment."

"As a diver?"

Sumner shrugged. "In general."

"He can be crazy as hell and spoiled by the celebrity lifestyle, but I've never seen him make a bad decision on a dive, if that's what you're asking me. Besides, Ms. Emma seems capable of handling herself and him, if it came to that."

Well that was certainly true, Sumner thought.

"Even the most capable among us can find ourselves facing something formidable, though," Sumner said. Marwell nodded.

"You're exactly right. I'm worried about them. I warned her not to go to the blue holes."

"Because of the legend?"

Marwell seemed to bristle at the question. "Because of the uncertainty. You might think I'm nuts, but I've had my boat attacked there and I know it's no legend. It was formidable indeed."

Sumner was surprised at this piece of information. Marwell seemed the last person to believe in monsters, and Sumner felt a chill work its way through him. He mentally shook it off and directed his attention to the radar.

"Any sign of them?"

Marwell sighed. "No. And I still can't raise them on either the telephone or radio." Sumner looked out the window. Night had fallen.

"I'm a pilot. If they don't return here by dawn, I'll head out on a search."

Marwell got a dubious look on his face. "You may not be able to by then. There's a storm heading our way. It's slow moving, but gathering force as it does."

"Looks like I'll have to make that call in the morning," Sumner said. He turned to Randiger. "In the meantime can you take me to the hotel?" Before Randiger could answer, the door to the office burst open. A tall, thin woman with a beautiful, fine-featured face, thick hair to her elbows, and a panicked look stepped in.

"Mr. Randiger, please come to the West Hill. They've all fallen asleep."

31

Sumner followed Randiger and the woman—
he'd learned that her name was Warner—out to
the Island Security SUV. Warner rode with them
while she filled Randiger in on the problem at
the villa.

"The housekeeper, cook, and maid didn't show
up this morning. We got news that they all were
sick. I was heading to their quarters and found
a gardener asleep in the grass behind the pool
cabana. At first I thought he had passed out, but
when I tried to wake him he didn't respond, and
then he started to have the same seizures that
Layton had. I came right here."

Sumner listened to Warner while he ran a few
calculations in his head. The addition of four more
sick people meant that the total was approaching
eight with the same sickness. On a small island
with only two thousand occupants, that was a
significant number. Warner finished her explanation and turned to look at Sumner. After hearing her name he'd figured out why she seemed

familiar to him. She'd posed for the recent cover of *Sports Illustrated*, and he thought she was even lovelier in person than airbrushed, despite the deep circles below her eyes.

"I'm Cameron Sumner. A friend of Emma Caldridge." He shook Warner's hand and noticed that it was as slender as the rest of her. He knew that models remained thin in order to offset the illusion of weight put on by the camera, but he didn't realize just how unusual it looked in real life. While her face was beautiful, the combination of height and thinness made her body appear to be full of angles as opposed to curves. He estimated that she was only four inches shorter than his six-foot-three.

They reached the villa at the top of the mountain and Warner headed along a path that led to the pool area. She skirted the lounge chairs and jogged to the pool cabana.

Three people stood in a circle around a man who lay on the grass. His body twitched and jerked in a seizure. Another man in a green utility shirt and pants sat on the ground and cradled the sick man's head, and a woman knelt next to him. Sumner recognized the woman as Rory, the television medium. One of the standing men had a small soul patch beard and dark hair. Randiger introduced him as Ian Porter, and Porter gave Sumner a solemn nod.

"Did you call the doctor?" Randiger said to Rory.

"Yes, whatever good that did. He says he isn't here and can't get here until tomorrow. There's a nurse at the Acute Care Center and she's on her way with some tranquilizers. I doubt that they'll help. We heard from Duncan Moore's wife that they did nothing for him." Rory turned her dark eyes on Sumner, and he had a visceral reaction to the blankness that he saw in their depth. Every instinct told him there was something off about Rory. He cataloged the thought in the back of his mind and refocused on the man in front of him.

"We need to figure out what type of illness is making its way through this island," Randiger said.

Rory pointed at the man. "That's not an illness, it's possession. The voodoo practitioners and their black arts are permeating the very air that we breathe." Warner sucked in a breath, and the gardener sitting on the ground looked scared. Randiger pursed his lips.

Sumner could barely suppress a snort. The only thing that possessed this man was either a drug gone bad or a virus or bacteria. Rory must have caught his disbelief, because she directed her attention to him.

"You're a friend of the scientist, aren't you?"

Sumner nodded. He wanted to ask how she knew about his friendship with Caldridge, but he decided to remain quiet.

"You can ask me how I know about the connection between the two of you. I know because I'm a medium."

She gave Sumner a self-satisfied look. Indeed, he was impressed that she'd nailed his thoughts so accurately, but not for the reasons that she assumed. He knew he was a difficult man to read and kept his expression neutral out of habit. That she'd been able to discern his thoughts made him realize that she was very good at reading body language and expression cues.

"I know who you are, Ms. Rory," he said. "But I don't think this man is possessed."

"Of course you don't," she said. Her voice held barely contained contempt. Sumner felt a bit of anger begin to creep through him, but he suppressed it. What she thought of him was unimportant. He turned to Randiger.

"Could he be a voodoo practitioner? Perhaps he took a drug?"

Randiger looked at the gardener cradling the fallen man's head. "What do you think Leroy? You know him the best."

Leroy shook his head. "No way. Johnny here is god-fearing." The glance he threw Sumner was tinged with anger. "He don't mess around with voodoo."

"Yes he does," Porter said.

Sumner was interested to see the entire group's reaction to Porter's statement. Rory looked triumphant, Warner frightened, Randiger resigned, and Leroy outraged. Randiger coughed.

"Could you explain that, Mr. Porter? I understand that you just arrived on the island last night."

"We went down to the beach to swim late last night. I needed to . . ." he glanced at Rory and Warner. "I needed to relieve myself. I headed into the trees and I saw this man, a woman, and another man all kneeling around a campfire. They were chanting, and he cut the head off a rooster. I got the hell out of there."

"Did you tell anyone what you saw?"

"I mentioned it on the side to Carrow and he seemed unconcerned. Said that the locals had been practicing Santeria for years. He said it involves animal sacrifice but is different from voodoo."

"Is that true?" Warner asked Randiger, who nodded.

"To the untrained eye," he glanced at Rory, "it looks like voodoo, but it's actually an offshoot of Roman Catholicism that originated in Cuba. They worship the saints."

"Like I told you, Johnny is god-fearing," Leroy said. He gave Sumner another look filled with challenge.

"But what they were doing wasn't Santeria," Porter said. Sumner focused on Porter. He seemed sure of himself.

"What makes you say that?" he asked.

"They also had a doll in their hands and the second man was busy twisting the head from its neck. I told Richard that it seemed off to me. He agreed, but said he didn't know enough about the two practices to be sure. He told me to stay the hell out of there and he wrapped up the swim and got everyone back up to the villa."

Johnny stopped jerking and lay still. His breathing settled down and he seemed to sleep.

"You should look into diseases that induce coma," Sumner said. "I'm no doctor, but this looks viral or bacterial, doesn't it?"

"I'll call the hospital where they took Martin," Randiger said. "Perhaps they have some insights."

"You're just wasting time," Rory said.

"Perhaps you have another idea, Ms. Rory? Because if you do, I'd like to hear it," Randiger's voice was filled with annoyance.

She put her hands on her hips. "As a matter of fact I do. I think we need to conduct a white séance. It's a ritual that will call on the forces of good to begin to do battle with those of evil. I'm sure you think that it would be a waste of time."

Randiger put his hands up. "Listen, you're free to do whatever you wish. I'm not going to stop you unless what you do violates the law or the rights of someone else."

"We need at least four people to manifest the forces. Will you join?" she said to Warner. Sumner thought that Warner seemed less than thrilled by the idea, but she nodded. "And you?" Rory pinned Porter with a glare. He shrugged.

"If Mr. Sumner will, then I will."

"I imagine Mr. Sumner won't be joining us. Am I correct?"

Sumner shook his head. "Not at all. In fact, I'd be quite interested to observe the ritual."

"Then please meet me at the villa at eleven forty-five." Rory stalked off toward the house.

"Leroy," Randiger said, "can you get Johnny to his room without my help? I'm going to head back to the office and make a few calls."

"Sure enough. His brother's on the way over. I'll wait here for him."

Randiger looked at Sumner. "I'll give you a ride to the hotel."

"I'll do that for you," Warner said. She gave Sumner a small smile. "If you don't mind?" Sumner couldn't imagine that any man would mind being around Warner. He nodded.

"Thank you."

They headed back the way they'd come. Warner and Randiger moved ahead, and Sumner walked alongside Porter.

"Are you with Rex Rain?" Sumner asked.

"No. Studio musician. I try to stay independent. Being in a rock band can twist your head up, that's for sure."

"Are they all crazy, then?" Sumner asked.

"Not all, no. Some are quite talented businessmen. These days you almost have to be to stay alive in the industry. But when they're crazy, they're really over the top."

"Like Rex Rain?"

"Like some members of Rex Rain, yeah."

"Tonight should be interesting."

Porter grimaced. "Musicians may be crazy, but no one in Rex Rain is as crazy as that medium."

32

Sumner, Porter, Warner, and Rory sat on chairs in a circle in the center of the living room of Carrow's villa. Rory had lit a candle and put it on a small end table placed in the center. The lights were low and all Sumner could hear was the sound of the waves pounding onto the shore far below. It was five minutes to midnight, and he would have much preferred sleeping, but he wanted to see just what role Rory might be playing in the illness sweeping the island. Sumner wasn't ruling out poison or deliberate sabotage. What he couldn't figure out was the motive.

Rory started rocking from side to side and making a humming sound. Warner sat to Sumner's right. She wore faded jeans and a tank top and frowned at the candle. Porter sat to Sumner's left and never took his eyes off Rory.

The French doors leading to the pool area were open, but the screens were closed to keep the bugs out. The candle threw the only light, and shadows flickered across the circle as the breeze blew.

The tree frogs sang their song. Sumner thought the island had a beautiful, ancient quality about it, and he could see why those who could afford it built homes there. Each villa sat on an acre of land, at least, and Carrow's on several more than that, leaving the occupants in the villa with a great deal of privacy. Privacy and isolation. The privacy Sumner liked; the isolation not so much. A stand of trees shielded the main house from the staff quarters.

Rory's humming became louder and more insistent. Her body began to sway in a languid circle. Warner seemed fascinated with the process. Porter kept his expression closed. Rory gave a loud shriek and Warner jumped in surprise. The medium slumped in the chair, as if asleep.

"Go away," Rory said in a low, guttural voice that was so unlike her own that even Sumner wondered how she managed to transform her tones. None of the rest of them replied. "I want the woman and you"—Rory snapped to a sitting position and pointed at Sumner—"to go." The medium's eyes were open, but even in the poor light Sumner could tell that the pupils were dilated. They hadn't been that way at the beginning. He wondered if she'd put dilating drops in her eyes before joining them. He held her gaze, saying nothing.

"Why don't you speak?" Rory said.

Sumner maintained his silence. He had agreed to attend as an observer only; he had no intention of engaging in the charade. If Rory thought to scare him off with a parlor trick, it was best she learn the error of her ways early. Sumner didn't worry about ghosts or goblins or zombies or anything else of a supernatural nature. What he worried about was blown covers, front doors wired to explode, and dead women hanging from trees. When compared to those events, he considered a ghost or two a completely benign problem; interesting to experience, but ultimately unable to affect much in the present day.

"You have twenty-four hours. After that all will begin."

"What will begin?" Warner said.

"The death," Rory replied.

"Whose death?" Warner asked.

"The petit-mort." Sumner jerked at the unfamiliar voice. Silhouetted in the screen was the figure of a woman. She wore a colorful dress and her head was wrapped in a scarf. Feather earrings hung from her ears. Warner sucked in her breath and Porter shot Sumner a worried glance and sat up straighter.

Ah, the hougan priestess, Sumner thought. Interesting that she appeared in the middle of the séance. He wondered if Rory told her to appear or if one of the servants tipped her off.

"What's 'the petit-mort'?" Warner said. While she looked pale, Sumner thought she seemed less terrified than he expected her to be. She must have been made of sterner stuff than her fragile frame and appearance indicated.

"It's French. It means 'the little death,'" the priestess said. She chuckled. "It's another term for sleeping. Because sleeping is like death, is it not?"

"Leave!" Rory bellowed the word at the priestess in her guttural voice, and this time Porter jumped in his chair.

"Not until the chemist does." The priestess looked at Sumner. "And her consort." While Sumner didn't mind being called a consort, he did mind that the priestess thought she could demand that anyone leave. He stood and started to stride across the living room.

"Leave her! She's evil. Do not go near," Rory said. Sumner ignored the medium while he kept his eyes fixed on the priestess. She watched him approach, her head still held high, but as he neared she got a wary look in her eyes. He kept moving, watching for the moment that the priestess would back away from him. When he was within arm's reach of the screen she took a step backward. Perfect, Sumner thought. Let her be wary.

"I don't like anyone to threaten Ms. Caldridge," he said.

The priestess shrugged. "So you think you'll protect her from me?"

Sumner shook his head. "No. She can take care of herself. I think I'll protect you from her."

The priestess's eyebrows flew up. "Arrogant man. I have the forces on my side. Not you."

"Your forces are evil," Rory said from behind Sumner. "Mine are good. Mine will prevail."

"She's a charlatan," the priestess said.

"So are you," Sumner replied. "Both of you need to quit playing your games. I'm not amused and neither is Ms. Caldridge. The authorities have been notified. I see you around here again and I'll be sure to have you arrested."

"And what about her?" The priestess pointed a finger at Rory.

"She's a guest of the owner and hasn't threatened anyone, trespassed, or vandalized another's property. You have. Don't do it again."

"Do you think I am afraid of you?" The woman raised her chin.

Sumner nodded. "Yes, I think you are. And that's wise, because neither Ms. Caldridge nor I scare easily."

"I can send you both to hell," the woman said, her voice filled with venom.

Sumner shrugged. "No, you can't. We've both been there already. The devil kicked us out."

Once again Oz used the net to pull the body toward them. Carrow grabbed a rope and started tying a loop.

"Get him close and I'll try to wrap this around him," he said.

Oz drew the body forward, carefully pulling hand over hand. The man was fully clothed and wearing a life jacket. He had a stout body and a gold chain around his neck. When he got close enough, Carrow leaned over and ran the loop over his legs, working it upward until it was around the man's stomach. He tightened it.

"On the count of three," Carrow said. Oz joined him to pull on the rope.

"I'll grab at the vest once you're able to get him out of the water," Emma said. Carrow counted and they hauled the body up and over the gunwale. A wash of water followed. They laid him on the deck. Emma noticed that one of the man's feet was bare while the other was encased in a beige deck shoe. He appeared to be pushing fifty years old, with a thick head of salt and pepper hair. His eyes were closed and his lips blue. Emma knelt next to him and put her fingers to his carotid artery. She felt a pulse.

"My God, he's alive," she said. "Let's get him downstairs and get these wet clothes off of him."

They hauled him below to the stateroom reserved for the crew. Oz arranged the bunk while Carrow and Emma stripped the sodden clothes off the man.

"What's this?" Carrow said. He pulled a gun out of the pocket of the pants and held it up for Emma and Oz to see. "Great, we're helping one of the guys that tried to kill us."

"How's that for a bit of irony?" Oz said.

"He must be the driver," Emma said. "The shooter was bald. The last thing I saw was this guy with a rifle with a bayonet on the end stabbing at the water behind their boat."

"Do we throw him back?" Carrow asked.

"No. I, for one, would like to question him. But we definitely keep our eyes on him."

"And the guns away from him," Oz said.

Once they laid him on the mattress they covered him with two heavy, military green wool blankets. Emma grabbed the first aid kit and returned to the man's left side. She removed the cloth and examined the wound on his arm. It looked like a bite. It had taken a bit of the meat from his bicep, but it didn't appear that any veins had been hit. The blood had congealed but it was clear the wound needed to be disinfected and stitched soon. She wiped the area with alcohol, careful to avoid dislodging the lump of congealed blood. She used a strip of gauze to wrap it tightly before stacking a couple of pillows next to him and placing his arm on them. Through it all the man remained unconscious. When she was done she straightened.

"Let's take all the knives with us. I don't want to leave anything even remotely resembling a weapon within reach." Carrow was out of the room first and grabbed a set of knives out of the kitchen drawer. Oz dimmed the lights. They convened at the helm.

"The sooner we reach Terra Cay the happier I'll be," Oz said. "Radar's down again." Emma joined him to peer at it.

"Can you guide us by celestial navigation?"

Oz gave her an excited look. "I can. But I should warn you, it can result in a five kilometer spread. I'm hoping my calculations get us closer, but three miles can mean a lot when you're out at sea."

"I'll take it. By then I hope the GPS and radar will be back on line."

"Can you take the wheel?" Oz said to Carrow. They switched places and Oz bent to his calculations. He grabbed his notes and stepped out from under the canopy to look at the sky.

"Pays to be smart like him, doesn't it?" Carrow said in a low voice.

"Not too many people are *that* smart. Oz is unique."

"Are you nervous about going back through the Triangle?"

Emma shook her head. "No. Whatever happens

we'll deal with it. I just can't imagine two methane eruptions hitting us."

"What about two sea monsters?" Carrow gave
her a sidelong look.

"Can't imagine that either," she said.

"Uh guys, can you put it in neutral and get out
here?" Oz said from the deck.

"Which way?" Carrow asked. Oz took the
wheel.

"I'll steer." He drove and watched the sky and
some of his calculations as he did. Carrow leaned
against the nearby counter.

"How long?"

"Two hours, tops," Oz said.

"That's not so bad," Emma noted. She grabbed
the rifle out of the holder and returned to her position at the gunwale. Carrow tinkered with the
satellite phone.

"Still down?" Emma asked. He nodded.

"Makes no sense to me. Even if we're talking about magnetic disturbances, they shouldn't
affect the satellite."

Emma agreed. The entire area seemed rife with
electromagnetic disturbances of some sort or another. She wanted nothing better then to be out
of the triangle and onto dry land.

"Radar's up," Oz said.

"Excellent!" Carrow went to stand next to Oz.

"See anything? Boats nearby?" Emma asked.

"Yep. Something's blipping a quarter mile
away," Carrow said.

"Boat?"

"Most likely."

"What about our direction? Are we good?"

"Right on," Oz said. Satisfaction filled his voice.

"Good job with the navigation," Carrow said. In the next instant they both groaned.

"Down again," Oz said.

"Oh well, at least we got some useful information out of it," Emma said. "I suggest we steer away a bit from the other vessel. Don't need to meet up with the bald-headed shooter right now." She heard a noise from below. "Sounds like our passenger is awake."

She headed to the cabin, this time keeping her rifle with her. When she reached the bottom of the stairs she saw that indeed their passenger was awake. He was looking around and attempting to sit up. He paused when he saw her.

"Water," he croaked.

Emma propped the rifle against a seat bench in the direct line of his vision. As she had hoped, he glanced at it and back at her. His eyes held a cautious look. She took down a glass and filled it halfway with water. She approached him on his right side.

"Stay down. I'll just lift your head a bit." She ran her arm under his neck and lifted him enough so he was able to drink. His lips were cracked and covered with white, dried salt. He drank the entire glass in one, long gulp. She lowered him back to the pillow and went to retrieve some more. She repeated the process, and when he was done drinking the second glass, he sighed. She put the glass on top of a narrow ledge running along the angled wall of the cabin and settled back on a bench. The man watched her.

"Your arm's injured. I have it propped up against the pillows, but I suggest you not move until we reach land and can get you to a doctor. The blood has coagulated at the tear, but it could reopen at any time."

The man nodded. Carrow stepped into the cabin and remained in the doorway, watching.

"What's your name?" she asked.

"Ardan Kemmer," he said.

"Why were you and that other man shooting at us?" Emma asked.

He closed his eyes. "I don't want to talk right now. I'm tired."

Emma was having none of it. "And I'm inclined to toss you back overboard. Either answer my questions or be prepared to get up close and personal with another shark."

Kemmer opened his eyes and gave her an angry look.

"Wasn't a shark. Was some sort of massive octopus. It had our boat in a grip and ripped at my arm with its teeth."

"Octopuses are invertebrates. They don't have teeth."

"Well this one had arms and teeth, I'm telling you. It wrapped itself around me and tore at me."

"So a Lusca," Carrow said. He stepped into the light.

"A Lusca?" Emma said.

"A large creature that is said to live in the blue

holes. It has an octopus's arms and a shark's head and teeth," Carrow said. "It's a mythical being. Not real."

Kemmer snorted. "Mythical my ass! It was real enough to rip a chunk out of my arm, wasn't it?"

"Are you sure it wasn't an average, everyday shark that bit you?" Carrow said.

Kemmer nodded. "I'm the head of a treasure hunting company. I'm comfortable on a boat and I'm familiar with the creatures around here. I know a shark when I see one, and I know an octopus when I see one. I'm not mixing the two up."

Emma shrugged. "Whatever you say, Mr. Kemmer, but that doesn't answer my question. Why were you and that other man shooting at us?"

Kemmer sighed. "I don't know."

Emma had expected a lot of answers, but that wasn't one of them.

"Why don't you know? Who was the shooter?"

"His name was Joseph. That's all he told me. I was hired by another man to run an expedition to the blue holes; he didn't tell me why. I just figured he wanted to see them for himself and he hired me because no other captains are willing to make the excursion. I didn't know that this Joseph had a gun until he pulled it out and started shooting at you."

"What's the name of the man who hired you?" Emma asked. Kemmer's lips compressed. He didn't answer. She stood. "Get up. You're leaving."

Carrow gave her a surprised look but remained silent.

"Wait!" Kemmer said. Emma put her hands on her hips and stared at him. "I can't tell you his name. I don't even know his real name. I know his nickname, though. Everyone who needs the occasional off-the-books loan knows about him. He's a corporate raider called the 'Vulture.' He waits until a company is floundering and then swoops in and delivers the death blow. My company needed fast cash and I called a few people I know to find him. He showed up on my dock, offered me a loan, and then demanded an expedition. This one."

"Was he on the boat?"

Kemmer shook his head. "No. Just me and Joseph." Kemmer looked at Emma. "That Joseph's an assassin, I can tell you that. I didn't like the guy from the moment that I saw him. I tried to stay out of it—his fight isn't mine and I've got nothing against you. I don't even know who you are. Once the squid or octopus or Lusca or whatever the hell that thing was grabbed our boat he turned on me. One minute I was fighting alongside him and the next I was in the water. I begged him for a life jacket and he just laughed. That asshole was going to let me drown."

"You were wearing one when we fished you out."

Kemmer nodded. "That's because the fish got the boat low enough that water ran onto the deck from the open transom and one of the jackets floated right off it."

"Did the boat sink?" Carrow asked.

Kemmer shook his head. "Guy kept firing and

firing at the water like a madman. He emptied his clip, loaded another and just kept at it. Finally it stopped sinking. By then I was trying to swim away, because I knew he'd turn that gun on me. Luckily he'd dumped all his ammunition into the beast. He must have really pissed it off because it grabbed me and started tearing at my arm. I blacked out."

"The radar spluttered back on," Carrow said to Emma. "He's somewhere to our port side and headed this way." Kemmer gasped and struggled to sit up.

"Lay down. You'll open the wound," Emma said. Kemmer gave her a wild-eyed look.

"I don't give a damn about the wound. That guy comes and we'll all die. He's a killer. Get this boat moving!"

Oz pointed to the radar. Emma watched the blinking light that indicated another vessel.

"How far?"

"Less than a mile."

"Can you change direction?"

Oz nodded. "I already did. We're not heading exactly toward Terra Cay's dock, though. We'll be landing at the mangrove side."

"We can skirt around once we're closer, right?" Emma said.

"Sure. Assuming the weather holds up. According to the radar, we should be able to outrun the storm and reach Terra Cay before it does, which is a good thing. We should be on the island before it reaches land."

"How bad is the storm?"

"I'm not good enough at reading the radar to be able to tell you, but it's not swirling like a hurricane would be. The winds around us have picked up, but nothing drastic."

Emma grabbed a towel and returned to her position at the port side. She replaced the rifle muzzle on the gunwale. She agreed with Oz that in the twenty minutes that she'd been below the wind had picked up and the air had the heavy feeling of an impending rainstorm. She wondered if the other ship's radar was running or if he, too, was having sporadic outages. Carrow came to crouch at her side.

"Kemmer settled down."

"Good," Emma said. "It will keep him out of our hair."

"Can you hear the other boat?"

Emma took a deep breath and closed her eyes, relying only on her sense of hearing to pick out any noise of a boat. The only sounds that greeted her were those of their engines, waves, and wind.

"No. Can you?"

Carrow shook his head. "I hate knowing it's out there, though. Wonder what the guy has against us."

"Or me," Emma said.

"Think Kemmer was lying when he claimed not to know?"

Emma thought a moment. "Actually, I don't. His story seemed plausible. He needed money and didn't spend too much time asking questions of his angel investor."

"More like devil investor." The boat picked up speed, and Carrow rose and walked to the helm. "Why the increase in speed?" he said to Oz.

"Other boat is gaining on one side and the tropical storm seems to be moving in faster on the other. We're going to get caught in a pincer if we don't. We need to get back. How much more do you think this boat has?"

Carrow leaned in to look at the gauges. "A lot. I say hammer it. We need to hustle."

Oz increased the speed. The spray intensified, and Emma soon abandoned the idea of keeping watch. The water would eventually soak the weapon, and she doubted that the other boat was faring any better in the dark. Plus, the shooter was alone. He could either drive the boat or shoot a rifle, but he couldn't do both. She would handle the problem when it appeared. She stashed the rifle and went back to the cabin to check on Kemmer.

He was awake and staring at the ceiling. The gauze she'd wrapped around his arm was soaked through with blood. Emma held onto a rail as the boat slammed into a wave. Kemmer turned his head to look at her.

"He out there?"

Emma nodded. "About a mile to port."

"He's a killer and he's coming after us all."

"Not you. Why should he kill you?"

"I'm a witness."

"What's your business? The one that was in financial trouble?"

"Prostitution and hash. In Amsterdam. Legal." He inhaled deeply. "I should have just paid the damn taxes and been done with it. I tried to get creative with my returns and they caught me. So I saved a few hundred thousand here and there. Wasn't worth this." He looked at his stump. "Is that guy with you Richard Carrow, the rock singer?"

Emma nodded.

Kemmer coughed. "Now there's the life. Party all night long. Must be great. Happy life."

Emma didn't respond. She didn't think Carrow's life was all that happy at the moment. She wondered how the rest of his band were faring and if anyone else had taken ill. Something about the events at the villa bothered her. She doubted they were solely drug induced, but she couldn't imagine what was causing them.

"Where was Joseph from, did he say?"

Kemmer shook his head. "Had a New York accent. Not an islander."

"Think he knows how to drive a boat? Use the radar?"

"Doubtful, but it's not all that tough to do. He struck me as a shrewd guy and a real survivor. He'll figure it out."

"Did you supply the gun he was using?" Kemmer turned his head to meet her gaze.

"You calling me an arms dealer?"

"Yes."

"What makes you think that?"

The boat lurched again and Emma danced sideways as she tried to regain her balance. She sat down on a high stool at the corner of the galley.

"Guns go along with drugs and prostitution. Even legal drugs and prostitution."

"Yeah, well you've got a point there, but no. He brought his own weapon."

"So a pro."

"Through and through. What's the money man got against you?"

Emma sighed. "You mean the corporate raider? I have no idea. But something tells me it's about the minerals I was mining in the blue holes. Someone doesn't want me to gain access to them."

"So stop mining them."

"I do that and my company will be in financial trouble."

"Is your life worth the money?"

"Of course not, but I doubt that Joseph will back off now."

Kemmer coughed. "You're right. He's being paid to bring us down. He won't go back until he has. Could be he'll be killed if he fails."

"A circle of death. The snake swallows its tail."

"You were holding your own with the rifle. Think you can bring him down?"

Emma heard Carrow calling to her from topside and she stood.

"If he forces my hand I'll have to."

35

Banner's phone rang in his ear, waking him from a fitful night of tossing and turning. He answered it when he saw that it was Susan Plower.

"I have good news, bad news, and really bad news," Plower said. Banner reached over to the bedside lamp and switched it on. He plumped the pillow he'd been sleeping on behind his back and grabbed the one next to him, exposing the nine-millimeter gun he kept underneath. He added the additional pillow and settled in to listen.

"Give me the good news."

He heard her sigh. "We've learned that the unusual weapon is a limited production. Apparently the material needed to make it is in short supply."

"Well that *is* good news," Banner said. The clock on the bed table registered eleven-thirty in the evening. Plower was working late for a government official. "And the bad news?"

"We've gotten word that a sale will go down sometime in the next twenty-four hours. Recent intelligence has pinpointed a small island called

Terra Cay as the possible site. We believe the bidders are there already."

Caldridge's blue minerals. Banner felt pleased that she'd led him to the right location for the sale, even if by accident.

"I've got both Emma Caldridge and Cameron Sumner, two of my best agents, down there already. Can you give me an idea where or who on Terra Cay is responsible?"

"No. At least not with any real accuracy. They're going to have to root around."

"That's manageable. So if that's the bad news, what's the really bad news?"

"The CDC has just informed me there is a disease spreading across the island. Apparently people are falling asleep and not waking up. The first cases were members of the band, Rex Rain."

"What kind of disease makes you sleep?"

"There are a few. An African sleeping sickness brought on by a tsetse fly is one." Banner knew of that one. He'd encountered it in Africa when he was stationed there. "But we don't think that's what's happening at Terra Cay, and Rex Rain hasn't toured in Africa for over two years. And even then they remained in Johannesburg, which doesn't have a reputation for the disease.

"The CDC is cataloging other symptoms as well. The afflicted are having hallucinations, seizures, and engage in psychotic behavior before they fall asleep. They do match a rare and deadly disease called Encephalitis Lethargica. It swept through Europe and America in the early 1900s. Five million people contracted the disease during the years before the Spanish flu of 1918 and of those nearly a million perished. Of those that survived, many stayed trapped in their bodies, frozen like statues and unable to move unless directed. They lived in nursing home facilities until they died."

"Lovely. Any treatments work so far?"

"None. It's incurable"

Banner sat up straighter. "What's the plan? Because Sumner just landed. I can recall him before he gets infected, but Caldridge has been there for days."

"The CDC has asked the appropriate authorities in the area to quarantine the island, and they've agreed and are preparing the order now. It will be exit screening initially. No flights allowed out and no boats or planes from Terra Cay allowed entry at neighboring locations. The island is fairly remote, so the hope is that we can contain this thing before it goes any further. There's a tropical storm on the way, which has been helpful, because travel to the island was already tapering in its path. We've asked the local sheriff to fly to the Bahamas, where he'll be kept in a cordon sanitaire and debriefed."

"And the remaining islanders?"

"I'm afraid they're stuck waiting it out. And that includes your agents."

"What are their odds of contracting this disease?"

"I wish I could tell you. The CDC scientists emphasized that they have no idea how it's contracted or spread."

"What about the sale? Do you think it will

proceed? Whoever is involved has to have heard about the illness."

"One thing that we've learned about pandemics is that people don't react the way you'd expect. Our source says that the seller appears to think an empty island is even better. Especially if the local law enforcement is gone."

"Not worried about contracting it themselves?"

"Who knows? Maybe they think they can take precautions and be spared. The CDC says there will always be people who go about their day, blithely believing that whatever illness is out there won't affect them no matter how many dire warnings the CDC issues. It's a source of frustration to them."

"If the CDC thinks that people ignoring their warnings is frustrating, they should work in contract security, where everyone you deal with seems bent on killing each other."

Plower sighed. "It does seem hopeless at times, doesn't it? But what do you think? Do you think they'd stay and go forward with the sale? Or move it to a new location?"

Banner considered the question. "They'll stay. These guys are massive risk takers. They're risking apprehension, jail time, or even death, and they risk it daily. And they're right, it's a fantastic opportunity to conduct a sale free of interruption by the authorities. They'll roll the dice. How will the quarantine be enforced?"

"Initially by grounding the local transportation and notifying the neighbors to screen and turn away incoming passengers. The impending tropical storm will keep most casual boaters away and they'll take advantage of that fact. After the storm has passed the WHO is going to send a mission to collect samples and determine the status."

Banner heard the door to the house open and quietly close. Stromeyer was back.

"I'll get Sumner on the search for the arms dealers. In the meantime, can you keep me informed as to the quarantine status?"

"Will do," Plower said. She rang off and Banner headed to the kitchen, where he heard Stromeyer rooting around and the sound of cabinet doors opening and closing. He found her there, with a pretzel stick in one hand and a jar of horseradish mustard in the other.

"Hungry?" he said. She put the pretzel stick in her mouth while she used a spoon to place a small amount of the mustard on a saucer. When she was done she removed the stick and dipped it.

"Starving. I've been moving between St. Barths, St. Kitts, and St. Martin in order to shake any possible tails before I came here. And I have news."

Banner slid into a kitchen chair to listen. She put the pretzel bag in the center of the table along with the mustard dip. He waved it off.

"The woman hanging from the tree has been identified as Irina Canenov. Mistress of Ivan Shanaropov, a Russian billionaire."

"Where have I heard that name?"

"He's a financier that seems to have an unstoppable stream of money that derives from shadowy sources. It's likely that you've read about him before."

"Does he live in St. Martin? Is that why she was there?"

Stromeyer shook her head. "He lives in Terra Cay, where he has a massive gated estate."

Banner reached over and took a pretzel stick. "Well that's interesting. Is he there now?"

Stromeyer nodded. "He is. And sources tell me that he filed a missing person report on his girlfriend."

"Covering his tail."

Stromeyer nodded. "I thought that as well. Seems that Ms. Canenov is the third woman he's dated who has disappeared from sight."

"Really? Is no one keeping tabs on this guy?"

Stromeyer shook her head. "He has alibis for all the times that they've gone missing. He claims the Russian government is abducting them and holding them, with the exception of Ms. Canenov of course, in an attempt to lure him back home, where they will imprison him for manipulating the oil and gas markets there."

Banner snapped his fingers. "That's what I've heard about him. He's a speculator. Well, not to worry, I think he's met his match."

Stromeyer raised an eyebrow. "Really? Who?"

"Not who, what. Seems as though a disease is sweeping through Terra Cay that's putting everyone to sleep. If he's there, he's at risk."

"What about Caldridge and Sumner?"

"Also at risk, I'm afraid."

Stromeyer frowned. "Anything we can do for them?"

Banner shook his head. "It's incurable. Best we can hope is that they manage to avoid it."

"So they're trapped on an island with a Russian killer and a deadly disease."

"I'm trying not to look at it that way."

Stromeyer gave him a surprised look. "What other way is there to look at it?"

"He's trapped on an island with one of the brightest chemists in the world who is not afraid to pick up a gun when she needs to, and her friend is one of the best shots in the western hemisphere. If I were Shanaropov, I'd be worried."

36

Emma found Carrow at the port side staring into the darkness.

"Listen," he said. Emma closed her eyes and focused on the sounds around her. Somewhere in the distance she heard clanging in a repetitive rhythm.

"Think it's the shooter's boat?" Carrow asked.

"We're one mile from Terra Cay," Oz said from the helm. Emma didn't think the sound was from a boat, because she didn't hear an engine. It sounded like something repeatedly hitting something else.

"Bell attached to a pole? Maybe a buoy? Are there any type of landings on the mangrove side?"

Carrow nodded. "There's a dilapidated dock and a shed. Well, at least there were before the last hurricane three years ago. Hard to say if they're still standing. I don't remember a bell."

"How long until land?" Emma said to Oz.

"Ten minutes," he said.

Emma retrieved the rifle.

"Oz, is the radar up? Can you see where the shooter is?"

"It's down again. I'm guiding us in from celestial navigation. I don't hear anything around us."

Oz kept the boat moving almost directly into the oncoming waves. It hammered through them at a steady pace. Emma was back against the gunwale with her towel and the rifle.

"Expecting trouble?" Carrow said.

"I'm not sure, but I don't want to take any chances."

"What did Kemmer say?"

"That the guy on the boat brought his own gun and wanted us all dead. He didn't know why, but he doesn't think he'll quit."

Carrow nodded. He'd put his hair into a ponytail and was wearing a navy nylon windbreaker with reflective tape in a line across the front and back. He looked serious, but not grim.

"When do you get scared?" she said. He gave her a surprised look.

"What do you mean? I'm plenty scared right now."

She shrugged. "You don't look it."

"I'm well into the scotch."

Emma wasn't buying it. The answer felt pat. "I'm serious. Most people would be half out of their mind with fear. You don't seem as frightened as I'd expect you to be."

The boat slammed into a wave and pitched both Emma and Carrow up a bit. When it settled down he lowered himself next to her on the bench.

"Frightening is getting up in front of thousands of people and singing. You ever wonder why so many rockers have drug and alcohol problems?"

"I've always assumed it's a combination of easy access and money coupled with a nocturnal life-style."

"That's part of it, sure, but another part is the need to kill stage fright. You're up there night after night and expected to deliver a good performance. You start out in a bar with six in the audience and a broken-down van and end up in large arenas with a massive tour staff and a brutal schedule. You begin to sleep poorly and eat poorly and party hearty. It also creates the need to keep the adrenaline flowing in order to ramp up for the performance. We all become excitement junkies to some extent."

"This situation has nothing to do with that, but you still seem calm."

"I've always considered myself to be on borrowed time."

"Live fast and die young?" she said.

He nodded. "Isn't that what you're doing working for this Banner? And isn't your ultra running a search for adrenaline?"

Emma returned her gaze to the blackness around them. Carrow's insight rattled her a bit. She'd always relied on science to explain everything in her world. The workings of chemicals in any application fascinated her, but she was also proud of her intellectual achievements. It seemed the opposite of intellectualism to crave excitement. Intellectuals craved knowledge. Yet, he was correct. She could no more stop running than he could stop performing. She'd come to rely on the adrenaline surge, and adding the occasional job for Banner fed that craving as well.

"Maybe," she admitted.

He smiled. "You act like it's a bad thing."

"It's a crude craving for excitement."

"At least it's a healthy way to get adrenaline. You can see what's happening to the band."

"And you? Where do you fall on the spectrum?" she asked. Carrow began to answer and stopped abruptly when a beacon of concentrated light hit the boat's bow. "Get down." Emma shifted to get her head below the gunwale. "Careful," she called to Oz.

"It's coming from land. I can see the outline of trees," Oz said. The light began to flash in sequence. Emma watched it but was unable to decode its meaning, if there was any. Carrow left her side and headed to the helm. She followed, bringing the gun with her. The flashes revealed that they were only a little ways from the island. Emma could see the trunks of the mangrove in the distance. The light itself seemed to be coming from between the trees.

"It's a signal," Oz said. "I have a bad feeling that it's not really meant for us." Emma watched the erratic flashes, trying to discern a pattern. It wasn't an SOS.

"Then for whom?"

"Shooter?" Carrow said.

"I have no idea," Oz said.

"There's one way to find out." Emma held the rifle out to Carrow. "You can shoot?"

He shook his head. "Not at all."

Emma simply nodded and brought the gun with her as she went below. She entered the stateroom and found Kemmer still flat on his back. He was pale and anxious and his eyes darted about.

"Is it Joseph?" he said.

"I'm not sure. We're at Terra Cay on the mangrove side. Did Joseph ever say that Terra Cay was his final destination?"

"No." Kemmer looked to the side. He's lying, Emma thought.

"You sure? Because someone is signaling us from land."

"Signaling? In what way?"

"Intermittent light flashes. If it's Morse code, I can't read it."

Kemmer sat up. "Get me up there."

"You shouldn't move." Kemmer swung his legs over the side of the bed. He waved her over and she helped him stand. When they were shoulder-to-shoulder he started forward. They made their way through the galley to the stairs and onto the deck. Carrow glanced back at them from the helm and hustled over to take Emma's place at Kemmer's side.

"What's going on?" Oz said.

"Show me the lights," Kemmer replied. Oz pointed ahead. As he did, the beacon flashed.

"Get me to that chair, can you?" Kemmer said. Carrow and Emma moved him to the companion chair. Kemmer sighed as he sat down. It was clear that the effort to come above had drained him. He peered at the light, squinting when the flashes illuminated the bridge. He watched as the lights ran through the pattern.

"They're signaling that you should come straight on. They also say that there's an underwater hazard to your port side."

"Question is, friend or foe?" Oz said.

"Foe," Emma said.

Kemmer looked at her. "Why do you say that?"

"We're on the mangrove side of Terra Cay. No reputable dockmaster would be here, because the actual dock is on the island's other end."

"Probably a smuggler's landing, then," Kemmer said.

"Terra Cay is getting more interesting by the moment." Carrow leaned against the side wall. Oz turned the boat to run parallel to the island.

"We're not landing here anyway," Oz said. "It's dangerous and I don't have the skill to maneuver through any underwater hazards."

"Want us to help you back below?" Emma said to Kemmer.

"Yes, I'm going to fall over."

"I'll do it," Carrow said. "I'd feel a lot better if you and your rifle stay up here," he told Emma. He assisted Kemmer to stand and she watched them move across the deck to the stairs. A second beacon showed across the water, but this one flashed in a steady progression.

"That's the official dock. We're almost there," Oz said. Emma slid into the companion chair while they made their approach. Oz gave her a quick smile and she smiled back.

"What a relief," she said. She heard the first raindrops hitting the windscreen and awning above them. "Just in time, too. Hear the rain?" The rain increased and the wind picked up as the dock loomed larger. Emma secured the rifle in its case and went belowdecks. She found Carrow in the galley taking a shot of whiskey.

"I needed a bracer. We almost there?"

"We are. Is there a rain slicker I can borrow? The rain is picking up."

"Check the lockers in the staff room. Marwell keeps four. Britanni has one in the master stateroom as well."

Emma stepped into the staff stateroom and glanced at Kemmer. His eyes were closed but the regular movement of his chest up and down told her that he was either sleeping or had passed out. Either way, he was alive, and she hoped to keep him that way until they could get him to a doctor. She opened the closet and found four yellow slickers of various sizes. She put on the smallest and was pleased to see that it was only a size bigger than she needed. She continued to the master stateroom and found a pair of rubber Wellington boots on Warner's side of the closet. Though they were also one size too large, Emma thought they fit well enough. She headed back upstairs.

The wind whipped and the rain pelted her when she stepped onto the deck. The storm had picked up in the few minutes she'd been below. Oz was holding the boat off the dock, using the engines to keep it in place as the wind and waves knocked them about. Carrow was at the stern now, holding a mooring rope. Emma ran to assist him.

"Where's Marwell?" she said to him. She had to yell to be heard over the wind.

"I have no idea. Can you help? Grab this line. I'm headed to the bow." He gave her the mooring line and started toward the front of the boat, waving at Oz to begin his approach.

Oz moved the yacht into place. The rocking became stronger but the boat handled the waves well and both Emma and Carrow leaped onto the dock pulling it the rest of the way and arranging the bumpers. Emma wrapped the rope around the cleats. The wind pushed at her and the rain soaked her face and hair, but the slicker managed to keep her body dry. She felt a line of cold water drip down her neck from inside the collar and strands of wet hair covered her eyes. She reached into her jeans and pulled out a tie, pulling the sopping mass into a ponytail and securing it.

Lights glowed from within the dockmaster's office, but Marwell still hadn't appeared. Carrow headed that way and Emma hurried to join him. They reached the door at the same time and Carrow opened it and waved her through. He stepped in behind her. The room smelled of burnt coffee and damp wool. The computer monitors on a desk pushed against the wall were dark. Marwell was facedown on the wooden floor next to his office chair. Carrow knelt next to him and rolled him over. Emma reached down and checked his wrist for a pulse. It was there, strong and steady, and his face appeared relaxed and calm.

"His pulse is fine," she said.

Carrow gave her a grim look. "He's asleep."

"I'll call Randiger," Carrow said. Emma moved Marwell into a more comfortable position on the floor and looked around for something to place under his head. In a locker against the wall she found a sweatshirt. She balled it up and used it as a pillow.

"No answer," Carrow said.

"No answer from whom?" Oz said as he stepped into the shed.

"Island Security. Marwell's asleep."

"Who can we call for him?" Emma asked. "Is he married? Does he have any relatives on the island?"

"I think he's divorced, but I can't even be sure of that," Carrow said.

Emma stood. "We need to get Kemmer to the Acute Care Center as soon as possible and let them know to come here for Marwell. Say we split up? You and Oz take Kemmer and I'll go to Island Security and see what's happening there."

"Let's go," Oz said. He turned the knob and

fought the wind to open the door. Rain whipped into the office, driven nearly sideways with the wind's velocity. Emma hunched down into her slicker as she ran back to the boat to retrieve her duffel and fought her way back to her Jeep. The canvas top whipped open at one end where she'd failed to snap it on. It made a pinging noise as it smacked against the aluminum car body. She secured it before crawling behind the wheel.

The wind and rain made it almost impossible to see more than a few feet in front of the vehicle, and she switched on both her high beams and fog lights. The windshield wipers whipped back and forth but did little to clear the deluge that hammered into the glass. Emma wound around the hill to the airfield and Island Security. She drove in from above the airfield and was surprised to see only two jets parked on the tarmac. One was Carrow's *Rex* and the other was a nondescript plane with double props.

Lights shone through the Island Security office window, which buoyed Emma. She wanted to ask Randiger about the toxic meal remnants in addition to informing him about Marwell. She parked the Jeep in a spot and battled the rain to the front door. She opened it to a gust of wind at her back and struggled to close it.

The office was empty. She removed her slicker, releasing a shower of droplets onto the wooden floor as she did, and hung it on a wooden coat rack near the door. She slipped off the equally wet boots before padding across the room in her socks. Both desks held telephones and coffee cups.

The secretary's cup was empty and clean. Randiger's was full, but the liquid had a congealed layer of cream at the top. Emma touched it. The mug was cool. His telephone's message light blinked and the display showed that forty messages were pending.

Something was wrong, Emma could feel it. The cold coffee indicated that Randiger had rushed out of the office, possibly in response to a call. She wondered where Moore was. Shouldn't one or the other be on call during a crisis?

She picked up the phone and dialed Johnson. The call rolled into voice mail. Emma hung up. She decided to head to the villa and speak to Johnson directly. She threw on the slicker and stepped out onto the porch. The wind's intensity had increased and lightning streaked across the sky, illuminating the area. As it did she saw the man with the dreadlocks standing motionless in the corner. His eyes were open and he stared at her. His ever present machete was in his right hand. He raised it and started toward her.

"Stop!" Emma yelled the word over the howling wind. The man stopped with his hand in midair. He stayed there, like a statue. Emma swallowed and began to walk backward slowly. The man's throat convulsed and his eyes rolled upward. He gave a moaning sound and his lips moved. Emma kept moving away, keeping him in sight. She slipped on the first step and stumbled. She grabbed the railing to stop herself from falling down the rest of the stairs.

The man's throat continued to convulse. A

trickle of water seemed to run down the side of his face. Emma assumed it was the rain, but he was under the porch roof and the wind was driving the rain away from him. A second drop of water slid down the man's cheek.

Emma realized that the man was crying. Another incomprehensible garble of sounds came from his lips. He swallowed and tried again.

"Help me," he said. Another tear rolled down his cheek and Emma gasped. She took a step forward, back onto the porch, but still maintained her distance.

"What's wrong with you?"

The man swallowed. "Sleeping sickness. I can't move unless said."

"Unless said? Do you mean you can't move unless instructed?"

"Yes," he said. At that moment Emma realized that his arm was frozen in the upright position. He still held the machete over his head.

"Lower your arm and drop the machete," she said. The man lowered his arm and his hand opened. The machete clattered to the wooden floor. He stayed where he was. Emma ran through her mind the drugs that could cause partial paralysis. Many could, but none would allow movement only on command. The only possibility was scopolamine. "Did the voodoo woman do this to you?"

"The sickness first. She gives me a powder, too."

"Do you have family on the island?"

"No," he said.

The wind whipped around her, blowing her ponytail into her face. Emma pushed it away while she thought of what to do about the man. He belonged in the Acute Care Center.

"Come with me to my car. I'm going to take you to the clinic," she said. She turned and was relieved to see the man follow her. She held the door and he got into the Jeep, his limbs moving in an awkward motion. He kept swallowing. When he settled into the seat his eyes moved upward. "Can you lower your eyes?" she asked.

"No," he said. "And when the drug wears off my back will curve."

"What drug?"

"The one she gives me. I don't know what it is. It wakes me up, but only for a while."

"Would you have killed me that night?" Emma said. He turned his shoulders to her but his eyes continued to stare up.

"I was chasing you to get away from her. To ask for help." He swallowed again and closed his eyes. The pain on his face made Emma's throat constrict.

"I'm sorry, I didn't know."

"I heard you have drugs that will stop this from happening to me."

The man formed each word in a slow, halting progression. Emma could see the enormous effort he was making just to stay awake. She got behind the wheel, put the key in the ignition and started the car. She threw it into first, flipped on the headlights and started the wipers. She pulled onto the frontage road. The wind rocked the car, and the rain poured in a constant deluge.

"I don't know what you heard, but the only drug I have is an anesthetic. It will make you sleep." His hands clenched and unclenched and he swallowed several times. Emma could see that he wanted to speak but was again experiencing difficulty. It was as if strong emotion blocked the flow of his words.

"No sleep. I can't," he said.

"Why? Why can't you sleep?"

"If I sleep I'll never wake up. I'll die." Emma heard the absolute conviction in the man's voice.

"Did she bring the sickness?" Emma said.

"Maybe," he said. "She and the big man work together."

"Who's the big man?"

"The one on the island."

To Emma it seemed as though he was speaking in riddles. She could see that he was having trouble maintaining consciousness by the way his lids fluttered and his eyes blinked, but she needed more information. He gave up trying to figure out who the big man was and focused once again on the woman.

"Where is she now?"

"Mangrove," he said. He started to lean forward. Emma saw that his back was curving. She'd seen the phenomenon before, but only in endurance races. After twenty-four hours in a race, many competitors' torsos lean to the side from a combination of exhaustion and muscle weakness. She assumed the man was experiencing both, but she didn't know why.

"Please hurry. Soon I'll sleep again. I'm afraid

of the sleep." Emma put the pedal down lower and the Jeep shot forward.

"I can't go much faster. The roads are too slick," she said. He didn't respond. She drove around the mountain, headed to the Acute Care Center. She turned right at an intersection and wound through the swaying trees. Leaves blew across the road and the occasional tree branch as well. She kept her eyes on the road but couldn't help notice that the man was bending forward even deeper at the waist. She fought down her concern and did her best to focus only on the road ahead of her.

She turned another corner and was relieved to see the center ahead. The lights were on but the adjacent parking lot was empty. A neon sign with a red first aid cross symbol glowed through the rain. She pulled into the spot closest to the door and killed the headlights. The man was drooping, his eyes at half-mast.

"We're here. Can you walk?" He didn't respond. Emma pushed open her door, squinting against the driving rain that hit her face and ran down her collar. She ran around to the passenger side and pulled the door open. The man fell sideways and she caught him. His eyes were almost closed. "You need to walk," she said. "I can't carry you."

He stepped onto the tarmac but his back was bowed. She held him around the shoulders and moved him to the clinic doors. She hauled the right glass panel open and helped him inside.

The interior smelled of lavender, which was as welcome as it was unexpected. A curved reception counter in white Formica was unattended, and Emma directed the man to a beige couch set against the wall. He sat down and immediately fell to his side. He lay there with his eyes closed. She went through a door to the left of the counter that led into a hallway with numbered treatment rooms. The quiet inside unnerved her. The only sounds were the hammering of the rain on the roof and the muted howling of the wind. She opened each door and found no one. No Carrow, Oz, or Kemmer.

"Is anyone here?" she called down the hall. There was no response. She returned to the reception area. The man was sleeping. There was a throw on the back of the sofa and she arranged it over him. She hated to leave him but she needed to find Carrow. Not that she had any way of contacting him, because due to the privacy concerns of many of the residents the island didn't maintain a telephone book. She'd have to drive to the West Hill. She picked up the phone and once again dialed Johnson. The phone rang several times before rolling into voice mail. She dimmed the lights in the reception area and headed into the pouring rain.

38

Emma fought the wind and rain to the Jeep. The canvas top was a poor defense against the deluge. Water dripped from the right upper corner of the windshield and splashed onto the dashboard. She decided to head first to her own villa to take stock. She didn't like that Johnson wasn't answering. The wipers whipped from side to side but made little progress in clearing the glass. She drove with great caution. The last thing she wanted was to slide off the curving road, but what the Jeep lacked in coverage it made up for in traction. Its wheels grabbed the road, and when she encountered some fallen branches it crawled over them with ease.

She turned into the Blue Heron's drive and was heartened to see that the lights were on. The villa's location at the top of the hill meant that the wind whipped around the vehicle with even greater force than it had at the base. She stopped short of the garage. Her table with the lab tests was inside, and she didn't want to open the door and allow the wind to whip through while she parked. She decided to keep the car outside.

She ran along the path to the house and entered through the same French door that the man had chased her to just a couple of days ago. Stepping into the kitchen, she saw Johnson on the floor on her back. The cook held a wooden spoon in one hand, and the remains of what looked like a half-prepared loaf of bread sat in a bowl on the table. Emma knelt down to take her pulse. She was alive.

"Latisha, can you hear me? It's me, Emma. Can you sit up?"

Johnson's chest expanded as she took a deep breath. Her waist stayed down and she arched her back and slowly rose to a sitting position. Her eyes remained closed. "You've caught the sleeping sickness. I'm going to walk you to the spare room. If you understand, move your right hand." Johnson's right hand moved. "Good. Stand up and walk with me."

Emma pulled Johnson's arm across her shoulder and rose with her until they were standing. She walked with her down the hall and into the spare room, throwing aside the covers and lowering her onto the mattress. Johnson kept her eyes closed through it all. When she was in bed and comfortable, Emma covered her with the duvet.

"I'm going to find the island doctor. See if he's here and can help. If you understand, please lift your right hand." Emma watched as Johnson's right hand made a slow rise off the mattress and stayed there. After a moment it became clear that

Johnson was unable to lower it. "Thank you. You can lower it to the bed again," Emma said. Johnson's hand lowered. Watching the previously competent Johnson lose control of her ability to move knocked the wind out of Emma. For the first time she realized that all the assumptions she'd had about the disease were wrong. She'd assumed it was confined to the prodigious drug use of Carrow's crowd, but Johnson was not part of that and now she was as incapacitated as the band members had been. Emma felt a mixture of sorrow and alarm constrict in her throat. She put a hand over Johnson's.

"I'm going to find out what is causing this. I'll be back to take care of you." She watched Johnson's face but there was no sign that the woman heard her. Emma rose and dimmed the light on the nightstand. She glanced over at Johnson one more time and saw a tear rolling down from her temple into her hair. Emma put her cheek against Johnson's and felt as though she wanted to cry along with the woman. "Oh Latisha, I'm coming back. Please hang in there."

Emma raced to the villa's home office, where a computer sat on a far desk. The storm was intensifying but she still had Internet access. She blew out a breath of relief and typed in a search for the terms "sleep" and "disease." The first sickness was a rare disease attacking young people that caused them to sleep twenty hours a day for two weeks or more at a time. Called Kleine-Levin syndrome, it appeared to resolve in older adults and bore no relation to the symptoms she was seeing. The second was a sleeping sickness caused by the bite of an infected tsetse fly and ran rampant in various African countries. While this disease could have been spread by a human carrier, Emma doubted that it accounted for the strange symptoms of those on Terra Cay. She kept scrolling, adding words to the search, and the results showed a travel warning issued by Terra Cay regarding a suspected outbreak of Encephalitis Lethargica.

The notice emphasized that there was no cure.

She sat and stared at the words next to the blinking cursor. *There is no cure.* She wanted to jump up, call an ambulance, get Johnson to the tarmac and fly her to a hospital. The idea that the vibrant, efficient woman who handled the caretaking duties of the villa with such efficiency and good cheer could end up frozen in a nursing home until she died was unbearable.

"It can't be this disease." Emma said the words out loud. The wind lashed at the windows and the rain poured down the panes. She jumped when the villa's doorbell rang. Leaving the Web page open, she headed to the front door and peered through the peephole.

Sumner stood on the stoop. She swung the door open and he hurried inside, bringing a shower of cold rain with him. He wore a dark black oiled trench coat that reached below his knees and his head was bare. He held a gun in one hand and gripped the neck of a bottle in the other. His soaking hair was plastered against his skull, dark circles rimmed his eyes, and his lips were chapped despite the island's humidity.

Emma thought he was one of the best sights she'd seen in ages. The relief she felt at his mere presence was so strong that she wondered how she'd managed to survive the stress of the last few days without him. He smiled at her, and even in the dim hallway light she could see how his eyes lit up as he did.

"I'm ridiculously happy to see you," she said. He leaned over, bending at the waist to stay far enough away to keep the coat from dripping on her, and gave her a kiss on the lips. She felt his rough skin and its warmth, and the storm and uncertainty faded from her consciousness as she kissed him back. For a moment the world receded, but just for a moment, because Sumner had only kissed her a few times before, when the universe had been preparing to explode around them. He moved back and held up the gun and the bottle.

"I bring you artillery, alcohol, and bad news. In that order."

So here comes the explosion, Emma thought. She noticed that the alcohol was the Laphroaig that Carrow had brought the first time she met him.

"That's Richard Carrow's. Is he with you?"

"No. I understood that he was accompanying you to the blue holes."

"He did, but the last time I saw him he and Oz were headed to the Acute Care Center."

"Oz? Oswald Kroger? He's here?" Sumner knew Oz from a run in with him during Oz's drifter era. The men had met briefly.

"He came to run some audio for Carrow. Is the scotch for you or me?"

"I only intended to bring the gun, but Carrow's girlfriend suggested that I bring the whiskey along in case Carrow was with you." He shrugged. "Seems as though Carrow isn't often seen without it."

"He's not. What's the bad news?"

"It's a long tale. Let me get out of this jacket." Sumner shrugged out of one sleeve and Emma helped him take the entire coat off. She placed it on a hanger in the nearby closet.

"Come into the living room. I'll pour the scotch."

He nodded. She noticed that all traces of humor had left his face. She led him to the living area. Sheets of water poured down the tall French doors that lined the wall facing the ocean. They rattled occasionally when gusts of wind buffeted them. Emma switched on two table lamps and sank into the long low couch. Sumner sat next to her and she settled in to face him. He took a sip of the drink and closed his eyes.

"That good?" she said.

"I needed a bracer. It's been a long twenty-four hours," he said. Emma frowned. Sumner's news must be more than just bad. She took a sip as well and welcomed the burn as it slid down her throat.

"The island's under quarantine," Sumner said.

Emma groaned. "Since when?"

"Since yesterday evening. The rumor that it was going to happen started earlier in the day, and the owners along with the locals rushed to leave. By the time the boom was lowered there were only one hundred people left on Terra Cay, and of those, sixty are asleep."

"Sixty-one," Emma said. "When I arrived here I found the cook on the kitchen floor."

"Sixty-one." He took another drink.

"What's the disease?"

Sumner shook his head. "The officials don't know. They're running tests on the first victims—the Rex Rain band members—but they've not been able to determine anything. Whatever it is, though, it's got the potential to be a pandemic. The authorities are alarmed by the rapid dissemination. They're trying to find the source."

"Where's Randiger? He's from Island Security. Have you met him?"

"He flew off the island to meet with government officials to discuss the outbreak. The quarantine was issued shortly after he left and he's not allowed back. They're holding him in a sterile location until they can determine if he brought it with him, and they're trying to contact everyone who visited the island over Christmas."

"And us?"

"We're going nowhere. Everyone else has to stay put as well. The airport and dock are closed."

"Who's asleep at Carrow's?"

"Everyone except Ian Porter and Britanni Warner. Belinda Rory is weaving in and out of consciousness. I expect her to be asleep next. All the staff is gone. They either fled before the quarantine or disappeared to their homes."

"Marwell is asleep. We found him when we docked." Emma gave Sumner a shortened version of the events on the ocean.

"An assassin?"

"Definitely. A pro, too. Kemmer said he brought his own weapon. Do you know Kemmer?"

"I do. He's a hash dealer, pimp, and arms merchant. The first two he does legally in Amsterdam, but the last one is definitely not."

"My biggest concern is that this guy was headed to Terra Cay after he successfully eliminated us. If he was able to wrench his boat out of whatever had a grip on it, then he likely came straight here. There's a rickety dock on the mangrove side that he may use."

Sumner picked up the gun that he'd laid on the cocktail table in front of the sofa.

"That is where this comes in handy."

The windows rattled as a strong burst of wind hit them. Emma could smell the wet loam and leaves that blew along with the breeze. The idea that Joseph was out there somewhere waiting to kill her was the final touch that made the moment seem surreal. She thought about the voodoo priestess.

"There was a woman claiming that she was a bokor priestess."

Sumner grimaced and slumped against the back of the couch with his legs spread. He held the glass on his stomach.

"Unfortunately that one is still awake. She's running around claiming that the sickness is a curse that some voodoo god has placed on the island. She is, of course, selling fake potions and amulets that she says will protect those who use them. She's a real prize."

Emma had to agree. "Has she threatened you yet?" He nodded.

"Twice. Once in the middle of a séance that Rory was conducting. I told her to take off and she got a bit angry. She kept trying to rattle me with her talk of the devil and curses." He gave Emma a wry look and took another sip.

Emma knew, better than anyone perhaps, that it took a lot to rattle Sumner. He faced challenges with a grim determination that would be appropriate in a seasoned soldier but were highly unusual in such a young man. She thought he could be described as an "old soul." He was not light-hearted by any means, but she welcomed his intensity. What Sumner lost in affability he gained in dependability. If he had your back, your odds of surviving went up exponentially. Emma had relied on that survival bump in the past, and something told her she'd be relying on it again.

"We need to find Oz and Carrow," she said. "They have Kemmer with them and he's in need of a doctor."

"The doctor's asleep," Sumner said.

"Not good," Emma said.

"Not good at all. Have you looked into this? Warner said that you administered some mandrake to Nalen and word is he not only stopped having seizures but also woke up a few days later."

"That was a bit of dumb luck, I'm afraid. The only disease I've found is incurable," Emma said.

She told him about the travel notice's mention of Encephalitis Lethargica.

Sumner frowned. "Incurable? I hate the sound of that."

"Then you'll hate the nicknames for the disease as well."

He took another sip of the whiskey, swallowed and said, "Hit me with 'em."

"There are two. The first is called the 'Aurora syndrome.' Aurora was Sleeping Beauty's name in the fairy tale. Some doctors think that the legend came from an actual case during the Middle Ages."

Sumner snorted. "Another scary as hell story that kids end up reading for pleasure. Like that song."

"Song?"

"Ring around the rosy. Don't some think it's a song about the Black Death? And there we all were, in the playground holding hands running in circles and singing it." He drank again. "You said there were two. What's the other one?"

"Sleeping Beauty Death," Emma said.

Stromeyer drove to the deserted dock in a black BMW M5 with a turbo 560 horsepower V8 engine, shaded windows, and a special glove box with a built-in pistol case. It wasn't armored by Stromeyer's specific request. Armoring slowed down the vehicle's response time, and she wanted speed rather than safety. She was back in St. Martin, taking a risk, she knew, but willing to do so to get some more information. Rain had just started to fall and the windshield wipers slid from side to side in a delayed pattern. The radio console glowed with the numbers of the marine station that she'd turned to in order to keep abreast of the oncoming tropical storm. The feeder bands were just beginning to lash at the island. She figured she had thirty minutes to complete her transaction before the storm began in earnest.

She pulled into the dock next to the long black limousine that idled at the farthest parking spot and flashed her brights once. The car flashed back. She heard the notification for an incoming text on her phone, and the words *Come inside the limo* appeared on her phone screen.

"Squeeze play," Stromeyer muttered. She'd expected as much, but to crawl inside another's car meant losing all control over both the situation and environment. The cramped interior would leave no room to maneuver should the seller wish to simply slide a knife in her ribs and take off.

She opened the glove box, removed the pistol along with a black balaclava to cover her face. Before she left the car she also grabbed a small leather rectangular clutch that contained over thirty thousand dollars, give or take, depending on the exchange rate, balanced equally between American currency and euros. The seller wanted to cover all financial possibilities and to bury his cash in various countries.

No. Meet me halfway, she texted back.

It's raining. More comfortable inside.

No, she texted. And waited. The limousine door swung open and she pulled on the handle and swung open the BMW's door as well. She stayed in the seat, however, watching to see if the seller was armed.

A man emerged wearing a long tan trench coat with a hooded sweatshirt underneath. The hood was pulled low over his face and he wore sunglasses despite the fact that it was night. He walked to the center point between the cars, the briefcase in his hand swinging back and forth as he walked. He stopped and waited.

Stromeyer put the gun in her shoulder holster

and covered it with her blazer. The air was warm despite the rain; she didn't bother with a coat, instead grabbing an umbrella. It was a small one designed to fit into a tote, and it popped open and was almost immediately blown inside out by the wind. She turned it to face the wind and did her best to hold it steady while she walked to hit her own spot on the pavement. When she was three feet from the man she stopped.

"Do you have the gun?" she said.

"I do, but not here."

Stromeyer felt her irritation rise. Her sources had pointed to this man as a direct contact to the seller of the iridescent blue bullet that Sumner had shown Banner. She was told that he claimed he could deliver the latest in weaponry: a gun that could pass through electronic sensors without eliciting a reaction. She'd let it be known that she would pay well for such a weapon. Now she thought that she'd been hoodwinked into bringing cash.

"Where is it?"

"It's in a safe place. There's going to be an auction. You want in?" The wind whipped up a bit stronger and Stromeyer had to clutch the umbrella handle tighter in order to keep it from bucking back and forth.

"I understood that we were going to close this deal here. Now."

He shook his head. "It's a very valuable weapon and the materials to make it are extremely rare and difficult to obtain. There's to be an auction. Several buyers have already flown to the auction site. If you would like, I can go there as well to represent your interests. To bid on the gun."

"I'll go. Tell me where."

"They won't let you in. Only trusted people are allowed to attend in person."

"So add me on the phone."

"I can't. Only live bidding. No phones, no Internet, no wire transfers. Nothing that can be traced."

"I can't just give you the cash and hope that you'll do your job. I'm not that stupid."

His lips, which were all that Stromeyer could see under the tip of the hood, stretched in a parody of a smile, but there was no warmth behind it. She wondered if the man ever truly smiled.

"A letter of credit held in a numbered bank account in the Cayman Islands will do. You can leave instructions that it may not be drawn down until delivery is completed."

Stromeyer rolled her eyes. Such an arrangement was common among legitimate corporations doing business, but she wouldn't depend on it for an illegal transaction. The seller could just as easily obtain the money by putting a gun to the head of the bank branch manager and force him to release the funds, or, more commonly, create a fraudulent release and dupe the manager into releasing the funds.

"Forget it. I'll deliver the cash when you hand me the weapon. It's that simple." Up until that point the seller had kept his head down, using the hood to shield both his face and his eyes. Now he raised his chin a bit, and Stromeyer caught a glance at his face. She had an impression of a scar on one cheek and a narrow nose.

"Then you tell me how much you are willing to pay. I will bid on your behalf, but be cautioned, should you win the bid, I, and the actual owner, will expect you to make good on your promise to pay."

"Of course. Where is the auction to be held? You forgot to mention it." His lips stretched again in the hideous imitation of a smile.

"I didn't forget. I didn't wish to say." He shrugged. "But I suppose now it is of no consequence, as no one can access the location in any event. The sale is to be held on an island called Terra Cay."

Stromeyer did her best to keep her expression impassive while her mind raced with this new information. It seemed that Susan Plower's intelligence source was on target, and it confirmed Banner's suspicion that the bullet must have been fashioned by the mineral found in the nearby blue holes. The seller's comment about lack of access, though, seemed the opposite of what he'd said initially.

"If I can't access Terra Cay then how am I going to bid? And why can't I access it?" Stromeyer waited to see if the dealer mentioned the quarantine.

"It's under quarantine due to a spreading illness. No immigration official in any country will clear an arriving visitor from Terra Cay, and no legitimate air or boat company will travel there either."

"So how do you intend to make it to the island in time for bidding if no one will take you there?"

"I said no *legitimate* company will take you there. I don't use normal channels."

The wind buffeted her small umbrella again and this time it swung in her hand. The breeze caught it and it spun around, shedding water droplets and allowing the rain to hit her face. She wrestled it back under control.

"And risk the disease?"

He shrugged. "In this line of business I take worse risks than that. As you can imagine, some buyers of arms believe they can simply threaten me or kill me to obtain my wares. Compared to death, disease is a lower concern. So, do I bid on your behalf?" he said.

Stromeyer nodded. "Yes. Up to five hundred thousand. Greater amounts need to be cleared by me first. Use the number I gave you for this meeting."

He nodded. "Don't cross me. You'll learn why I'm still upright while others that have tried are not."

"I have no intention of crossing you, simply because I need that weapon."

"We'll see if you're the highest bidder. Good evening." The man turned away and crawled into the limousine. Its lights flashed once and it drove away.

Stromeyer remained where she was until it disappeared from sight. When it was gone she returned to her own car and called Banner, who was waiting for a report of the meeting.

"Glad to hear you made it through," he said. "Did you get the weapon?"

"No. There's going to be a live auction. In person and by invitation only."

"Where?"

"Terra Cay."

"Well well. So Plower's source was right. Was he aware of the quarantine?"

"He was and, just as you thought, he was more than willing to take the risk."

"Sometimes these guys are absolutely depressing in their predictability. With any luck the buyers will all fall asleep and Sumner and Caldridge can just waltz in and arrest them all."

"Something tells me that at least a couple will escape the infection." Stromeyer turned on the car and switched on the wipers.

"Why do you think that?" Banner said.

"Because you know the saying, 'Only the good die young.'"

40

Joseph stood dripping water on the marble floor in the massive entrance foyer of one of the largest villas on Terra Cay. He had landed on the mangrove side twenty minutes ago and proceeded straight to the sprawling compound. He wanted to deliver the bad news of the woman's escape to his employer before anyone else tried to twist the information. He watched as a large, pale, and bald man shuffled toward him from the back of the house. The man wore green work pants, a gray shirt, and a blank expression on his face. Joseph recognized the expression for what it was: a complete lack of original thought or force of personality. He had dealt with such men before. They killed with impunity and a careless ease, primarily because they lacked the imagination to see their victims' despair. He killed with impunity, too, but he liked to believe that he put some creativity and panache into his work. The man lumbering toward him showed no sign that he had enough intelligence to do anything except take orders.

"Come with me," the man said. He turned and headed toward the second door on the left. Joseph followed, still dripping water, but not as much, and clutching his rifle. It was the only thing he'd been able to salvage from the boat. It was his prized gun. He would rather have gone down with the ship than leave it behind.

He followed the lumbering idiot to the door and walked through it into a large, imposing library. Books lined every wall from floor to ceiling. The remaining areas were paneled in a rich, dark wood. Long, elegant windows formed a bay area directly in front of Joseph, and a fire burned in a fireplace to his right despite the warmth. In front of the fireplace stood Joseph's employer. He only knew the man by reputation, that he was called the Vulture because he swooped in and picked the bones of struggling corporations dry. He waited until they had no more options to obtain funds, offered a loan at exorbitant rates, foreclosed when the companies could no longer pay, and then sold off the assets piece by piece. He wore a ten thousand dollar bespoke suit and his eyes were two hard marbles in a vicious, thin face. The man stared at him.

"Why are you here?" he asked. "I thought I made it clear that you were to complete your mission and then stay out of sight. Not show up here soaking my floors and stinking of seaweed."

"I wanted to deliver my report in person."

"So it's bad news that you bring me," he said. Joseph felt a flicker of fear. The man spoke in a mild tone, but the menace was unmistakable.

"You didn't tell me the boat would capsize."

The man raised an eyebrow and a smirk crossed his face. He'd known about the danger, Joseph thought, and he felt his own anger start. He'd been told that the stories of a monster in the area were merely sailors' tales, but now he realized they were true.

"I didn't know that it would. Did Kemmer use a faulty vessel? If he did then he deserved to die. I assume that you did kill him at least, did you not?"

Joseph nodded. "I threw him overboard. But the boat wasn't damaged. Something grabbed at it and started pulling it into the ocean. I had to empty my gun into it to make it release. When it finally did, the chemist was gone."

"Did she have time to mine the holes?"

He nodded. "She was finished." The thin man stalked to the windows and looked out. Joseph didn't like the silence and so he filled it. "I'll kill her here. I'm almost certain they came back to Terra Cay." Joseph watched with dismay as the man's eyebrows slanted downward in displeasure.

"I need to confiscate what she mined first. Get that from her before you kill her. And get it done soon. The buyers are here and the auction will begin. I intend to offer the remaining raw materials to the highest bidder as well. What she has may be the last." Joseph did his best to contain his relief. He would be spared. His mistake wouldn't cost him his life.

"Where's Kemmer's boat?" the thin man said.

Joseph hesitated and the man turned to look at him. "Where's the boat?" he said again.

"It sank when it hit a shoal near the mangrove. Without Kemmer, I didn't know how to navigate through the rocks. It was lucky that I made it at all."

"Lucky," the man said, his voice filled with sarcasm.

Joseph fingered his gun and did his best to contain his anger. He felt a vessel in his temple begin to throb with the exertion. His rage bubbled below the surface, as it always did. Self-control was something he had never owned in abundance. He'd learned it only after being locked in a prison in Brazil and it was clear that the other inmates were as vicious as he was, but with the added benefit of knowing the ropes. But he'd adapted, and before he escaped had killed four inmates and two guards. The guards were the two that weren't bribed. They didn't look away as the inmates disappeared into the tunnel they had been digging for over three long years.

"You need me. I've heard that she has backup. A man named Sumner. Rumor is that someone—I think you—paid two different men to try to take him out and both failed. You should have paid me."

The thin man snorted. "Pay you? I just did and you failed as well. You've got a lot of nerve." The windows shook in response to a hard clap of thunder, as if the storm was trying to punctuate the thin man's words. Joseph twitched with the effort of containing his anger.

"No one can shoot better than me. I am the best and you know it. *Everyone* knows it."

The man pointed a finger at him. "All I know is that she has managed to avoid getting killed on three separate occasions. Once against long odds. She's smart and she's wily. I want her dead, Sumner dead, and the minerals brought here. Do you understand?"

"I understand that you didn't give me fair warning about the risk at the blue holes. Perhaps you hoped that I'd kill her and then the creature in the holes would do the dirty work of eliminating me as well?" Joseph took a step toward the man. His anger boiled. If he didn't want the money so much he would have killed the man. But the amount offered far exceeded his usual fee and he wanted it. The skinny man sent him a look filled with derision.

"Quit talking nonsense. There is no creature in the blue holes. The area is subject to unusual natural phenomena. It doesn't happen every time someone passes over the area. There's no way for me to predict when it will occur. Besides, I wanted you to kill her, climb on board her boat, take the minerals and bring them to me. How would you have done that if you were dead?"

"Something grabbed onto the boat. It nearly pulled the entire thing underwater. If not a creature then what was it?"

The thin man shrugged. "I have no idea. But you knew the fables before you took the job, so don't act as though this is the first time you've heard of it and don't accuse me of duplicity."

"Why don't you just have your stupid giant kill her? If she's here, she sleeps less than a mile away."

Even as Joseph suggested the solution he knew why the Vulture hadn't simply killed her. Men like him wanted to pretend that they were as well educated as the others in the corporate world. He moved in the same circles and cultivated the image that he knew how to create the wealth and services that the others did, but in reality all he could do was earn money trading on the black market and troll for those businesses that were floundering. The Vulture sold the assets because he didn't have the true intelligence or skill to make a company thrive. And he knew it. And Joseph knew it too. Joseph knew that the man was another version of himself in a tailored suit, nothing more. The difference was that he didn't care if others branded him a killer. This man, though, wanted to appear an upstanding citizen of the world. He wanted to kill and remain anonymous while he did it. To obtain that result required hiring someone else with the ability to plan a killing with surgical skill and the willingness to wallow in the mud. Joseph knew he had both character attributes, and he didn't care how deep the muck got as long as he was compensated.

"I paid you well to do the job and leave no tracks back to me," the Vulture said. "That's what your reputation says that you do. I didn't expect you to not only fail, but to come here. What if someone had seen you?"

Joseph pointed at the window. "The storm covers all and the island is quarantined. No one will learn that you're the one who arranged their death."

"Get the minerals and kill Caldridge and Sumner."

"And the others on the island?"

The man shrugged. "I don't care if they all die. The plague will do a large part of it for me, but kill them all if you think it's necessary. Just make sure no suspicion flows my way."

"It doesn't work that way. The more you kill the more clues you leave."

The Vulture nodded. "Then you'd better choose your victims wisely, hadn't you?"

"You don't get it. I'll kill them all. I'm not the one who cares if they figure out that I did it. You are."

"Do what you must. The blame comes my way and you won't get paid. It's that simple. Now get out."

41

The villa's phone rang and Emma reached to the end table. She heard Stromeyer's voice.

"I have some bad news," she said. Emma sighed.

"You too? Sumner just told me about the quarantine."

"Not that. Different bad news. We have reason to believe that a major arms sale is going to proceed on Terra Cay within the next twenty-four hours. If we're correct, the weapon will be transferred there into the hands of someone very dangerous. Sumner knows the details of the weapon. We'd like you and Sumner to check it out."

"You think they're here despite the lockdown?"

"I do. And I've done some research on the various owners on the island. Most of the residents are well-known businessmen and celebrities. Lots of information on the Web about them all and nothing that would indicate someone as dirty as this sale implies. However, I did find three possibles among the land records. All three villas were purchased by nominees in various blind trusts."

She gave the locations of the three properties. The last was one that Emma recognized.

"You can scratch the West Hill property off the list," she said. "That one is owned by Richard Carrow, the singer."

"Ah, I see. I presume that he had the property purchased by a nominee to ensure privacy. Do you recognize the other two?"

"I know where they are. One is the largest villa on the island by far. It's owned by some Russian billionaire. Very reclusive guy who's obsessed with security."

"Ivan Shanaropov."

"Yep, that's him. You know of him?"

"He's our main person of interest right now. His mistress was found hanging from a tree in St. Martin."

"Found? By the police?"

"By Sumner. Let him tell you the story, but he should know that she's been identified. So maybe you look to the Shanaropov estate first. Carefully, of course. And we're paying standard Darkview rates."

Emma rang off and glanced at Sumner. His head had fallen back against the sofa and his eyes were closed.

"Sumner!" Emma cracked out the word and his head snapped up. Relief washed over her. "Sorry, I got worried. I thought you were asleep."

"Just resting." He took a sip from the glass.

"It was Stromeyer on the phone. She said there's a weapons sale that is going to occur on the island and she wants us to check out two villas."

He raised an eyebrow. "And if we find it?"

"Then we're supposed to stop it from going forward."

Emma felt a mixture of concern and exhilaration. The entire project on Terra Cay had seemed doomed from the start, but now she had a chance to salvage the week and put some money in the coffers. Darkview occasionally used her as a consultant, and paid her well. She was happy about the payday but concerned about the danger. "She said you knew about the weapon. Why don't you run it down for me?" She listened as Sumner told her about the bullet and its properties.

"The good news is that it's very valuable and so it's doubtful they'll use it to shoot at us. If they do, the other good news is that it has an extremely high failure rate, so our odds of getting hit are lower than with regular bullets."

"And the bad news?" she asked.

He inhaled. "Well, they *are* arms dealers."

"And will be well provisioned with conventional weapons that will work just fine."

"Exactly," he said.

"Stromeyer didn't know how many people we're dealing with, but my guess is that Joseph the Assassin is among them." Emma started pacing the length of the room. "I don't think you can just march up to the villa and take a look around. They'll pick us off as we do. And there's just two of us and God knows how many of them."

She paced back and forth, planning. The rain hammered into the windows and thunder cracked all around them. Sumner kept silent,

watching her as she paced. "We'll need to infil-
trate the villa. Maybe lure them outside. Distract
them. While they're running around, we slip
inside and take stock. We're in luck that most of
the island staff has left. Fewer people to see us."

"The rain's going to be troublesome."

Emma went to the kitchen and retrieved an
island map from a drawer. She brought it back
and spread it out on the cocktail table in front of
Sumner.

"Here are the two villas that she mentioned. The
first is at the base of the West Hill by the beach.
It's a huge estate and there's a path cut into the
mountain that goes right past it. I know because
I've run it. The second villa is here." She pointed
at the map. "As far from the first as you can imagine. The owner of the first has a reputation on the
island of being a recluse." She looked at Sumner.
"And it was his mistress that you found hanging
from the tree in St. Martin. I think that's where
we'll start," Emma said.

Sumner moved the map toward him and studied it.

"Explain the topography to me. You say there's
a beach, but is there anything else?"

"The first estate has its own private dock. It's
one of the few houses on the island that does, because most are built up the side of the mountain
in order to maximize the view of the ocean."

"Any hazards?"

"Plenty. The witch woman has a garden of
earthly poisons situated on the trail and halfway
up the mountain. That makes me think she must

live nearby. I wouldn't want to stumble upon her if I could help it. She's never threatened me with a gun, so I hope she won't be a factor here, but one can never tell. Other than that, the only other hazard I can think of is the beach itself. The path at the bottom runs along a large stand of manchineel trees that separates the beach from the property. They have acid sap that pours off of them in the rain. They form an effective natural barrier between the beach and the house itself."

"Acid sap," Sumner said. "Lovely. So avoid running under them."

"Exactly. The path is close, and if the rain continues to blow as hard as it is," Emma waved a hand at the windows, "it's not impossible that some will spray you. However, I think that this side of the house probably represents the best chance we have to approach, because it's likely that the owner is relying on the trees to fend off any trespassers. Warning signs mark the area and no one would pass under the trees if they could help it."

"Would the raincoats and hats be enough to protect us?"

Emma shrugged. "For the most part, but the blowing rain and wind would mean that we'd have to be completely covered. Even a small drop can raise a blister. Maybe we wrap scarves over our faces and use sunglasses to protect our eyes."

"What if a drop gets in our eyes?"

"That can cause blindness. Probably temporary, but in large amounts it could be permanent."

"Sounds too risky. What about the rest? Security system?"

"Closed circuit cameras and guard dogs. We can carry meat to hold off the dogs, but the cameras present a problem."

"You said Oz is here. Can he help with the cameras?"

"Perhaps. But if this storm continues, it may be our best ally. It's likely that if his guards perform patrols, they'd be suspended and the rain will cut down on the cameras' visibility. We couldn't ask for better cover. Of course if the electricity goes off, then we have an even easier time of it."

"He probably has a generator, though. Houses of that size usually do."

"Much easier to disable a generator. But whatever we do requires that we get onto the grounds."

"What about the dock?"

"I never saw it so I can't be of much help."

"How bad were the waves when you docked? Can they be navigated?"

"The storm was just starting out when we docked so it's hard to say, but I would guess that *Siren's Song* is capable of riding out the waves. However, I have no idea how deep the water is on approach. There's a chance of shoaling at several island locations, and the situation may be the same here." She thought for a moment and then shook her head. "On second thought, Marwell told me that Carrow's boat was actually one of the smallest on the island. It follows that a Russian billionaire likely has a large yacht. If he docks his own then it's probably safe to assume the area leading up to the dock is safe enough for a boat the size of the *Siren's Song*."

"But there's still the problem of the cameras."

"And the guard dogs."

"And the guards themselves."

"And the other arms dealer guests."

Sumner frowned. "This one requires a SEAL team, not two contract security personnel."

Emma took a sip of her drink. "No chance of that happening. It would take too long to assemble one and get it here. By the time they do, the sale will have been completed."

Sumner rubbed his face and stared at the map. "Can we do it?"

Emma looked at the map, too, and again ran all the obstacles through her mind.

"I think we can. Worse comes to worse we look in the windows, see if we're outnumbered, and hightail it out of there before they come for us. Make a calculated retreat."

He touched his glass to hers. "To thoughtful retreats. May they not be necessary."

"Amen," she said.

42

Kemmer stared out the Jeep's window and tried to focus. He felt light-headed and his arm was once again bleeding.

"I need a doctor," he said. "Why the hell aren't we going to the Acute Care Center?" Carrow pulled into the driveway of a two story villa, modest by Terra Cay standards, and killed the engine.

"He didn't answer the phone so I assume he wasn't there. This is his house. Let's go," Carrow said. Oz helped Kemmer out of the car and dragged him to the front door. The rain made Kemmer squint as it hit his face. He was thankful for the support of Carrow and Oz, as he wasn't sure he could walk on his own. They reached the door and pounded on it. No sound came from within. Carrow grasped the knob and turned. It swung open, revealing an empty hallway.

"Dr. Zander, you there?" Carrow called down the hall. No response. "There's a small office in the back of the house with supplies. He sometimes takes patients there, let's go." They helped drag Kemmer through the house to the back. Kemmer hated the silence and the emptiness.

"The guy isn't here," he said. They opened the office door and switched on the light. Kemmer blinked to adjust his vision, which was swerving in and out of focus. A man slept on an examination table, his white coat fallen open to reveal a polo shirt underneath and khaki pants.

"So much for the doctor," Carrow said.

"I need stitches. Bad," Kemmer said.

Carrow looked at Oz. "Can you do it?"

Oz shook his head. "I would rather not. You?"

Carrow sighed. "No, but it may be time to change the bandage. Let's move Zander into his own bed and shift Kemmer onto the table."

Twenty minutes later Kemmer watched with dread as Carrow began to unwind the field dressing that Emma had fashioned. The edges of the bandage stuck to the wound and Kemmer hissed in pain as Carrow pulled on it.

"Oz, can you find any scissors in the cabinets? I'll cut it off rather than pull it off," he said.

Oz started rooting through the cabinets and removed a pair of doctor's shears.

"Want me to sterilize them?" he asked.

"Good idea. Dump some alcohol on them," Carrow said. Oz took a bottle from a nearby counter and held the shears over a sink as he poured the alcohol. He handed them to Carrow, who clipped at the stuck portions of field dressing. "That's done. Get ready, because I'm going to pour alcohol on it and it's going to sting like a bitch." He handed Kemmer a bottle with an elaborate label.

Kemmer looked at it in disbelief. "Port? What kind of sissy drink is this? You're going to burn me up with alcohol and all you got to give me is port?" He shoved it back at Carrow. "Forget it. Get me some morphine."

"I doubt that the doctor keeps morphine in his home. It's a controlled substance, so likely under lock and key back at the Acute Care Center."

"Then take me the hell there." A crack of lightning lit the room.

"I don't have the combination for the safe."

"Then get me some from your villa. Everyone knows that rock stars have the best drugs."

Carrow snorted. "By now every line's been inhaled, I can assure you. Best I can offer is this port or a drive up the hill for some mandrake powder. Which is iffy, for a lot of reasons. It hurt my drummer, but helped my bass player. You're welcome to take a long, bumpy ride up to the West Hill to get it, but I can't guarantee that you'll survive the trip. You've lost a lot of blood."

Kemmer put a hand out. "Give it to me." Carrow handed over the bottle and Kemmer drank a deep sip. He lowered the bottle and started to cough. "Damn, that's nasty." He waved Carrow over. "Get it done."

Carrow nodded and bent to the task of pouring alcohol on the wound. Kemmer stayed sitting and averted his eyes. He groaned when Carrow started, but kept the port bottle at his lips and drank. When it was empty he tossed it into a nearby sink situated under a cabinet of supplies. It hit the ceramic with a loud clanging noise. He leaned back on his good arm while Carrow continued.

Carrow was applying a fresh piece of gauze when Kemmer's eyes went out of focus and he felt himself wobbling on the one arm that held him upright. He turned his head to look over Carrow's shoulder, out the opposite window. From the darkness he saw a face form in the window, and before he could scream Joseph used the handle of his gun to smash the glass.

Tiny glass shards flew in all directions. Carrow stumbled backward and Kemmer rolled off the examination table, dragging the replacement gauze roll with him. He dropped the three feet down to the floor. Staying low, he scrambled on all fours to the open door. Bigger pieces of glass rained down on him as Joseph kicked the rest of the window out of the frame.

Joseph fired a shot without aiming, mostly to prove a point to those inside. He wouldn't put it past Kemmer to have a weapon on him. Hauling himself through the opening, he led with the gun hand first. A young man with hair to his shoulders was slumped in the corner next to the door, unconscious. Kemmer had disappeared through the open door. Joseph was surprised that the man had survived, but for the moment he didn't care about him. All he wanted was his money, and that would require recovering the minerals and killing the chemist, in that order. He pointed the gun at Carrow.

"Give me the minerals from the blue holes and you'll live," he said.

"I don't have them, mate," Carrow replied.

"Where is she?" Carrow looked at the gun in Joseph's hand. Joseph watched him struggle to decide what to say and thought he needed an additional incentive. "Tell the truth or I'll blow you away."

"She's at Island Security."

Joseph paused. He recognized Carrow now, and for all his hubris back at the villa and his claims that he'd kill everyone in his path, he didn't think killing a well-known celebrity was a good idea. It would bring a shit storm of trouble his way. For sure he'd never get another job once his face was plastered on an Interpol most wanted list. The people who hired him expected discretion. "That your Jeep outside?"

"Yes."

"Then take me there." Joseph aimed at the man in the corner. "Who's the pretty boy?"

"That's my bass player," Carrow said. "Known the world over. You kill him and every police officer in the universe will be hunting you."

"Shut up. You think I care?" Joseph wanted to shoot the man just to prove to Carrow that he was capable of it. He gave the man in the corner another glance. He couldn't recall the faces of the other band members, but the man looked the part of a rock musician, with his long hair and pretty face. His unconscious state puzzled Joseph. He appeared to be out cold, and that seemed odd. His initial bullets hadn't hit him as far as he could tell. He gave a mental shrug. Another one he could deal with later. "Let's go."

He followed Carrow out of the house. Wind-driven rain bit at his face the moment he cleared the entranceway. Carrow's hair worked its way out of a ponytail and started whipping around his head. Joseph winced against the storm's on-slaught and kept his gun pointed at the singer's back. Carrow stepped farther out and stopped. There was no Jeep in the drive.

"It's gone," Carrow said. Kemmer, Joseph thought. He swore.

"Back in the house." Joseph herded Carrow back inside. A small table near the door held a charging station and three phones, along with a wallet and a set of keys. Joseph reached out and scooped up the keys. One of them carried a Ford logo. "To the garage."

The wind worked at them again as they struggled their way to the garage. Joseph hit a button on the keychain and the door slowly began to lift. Inside they found a small blue Ford Focus. Joseph held the keys out to Carrow. "You drive."

"To Island Security?"

Joseph shook his head. "No. To the villa called the Blue Heron."

43

The phone rang again and Emma hated to have to answer it. Her reluctance must have shown on her face, because Sumner said, "Want me to get it?" She picked it up.

"Joseph just broke into the doctor's house and kidnapped Carrow," Oz told her. "He wants the minerals and you. Carrow said you were at Island Security, but I just called and no one answered. I figured you were back at the villa. Get the hell out of there."

"Are you safe?" Emma asked.

"Yes. I played dead. And Kemmer took off. He's in bad shape, but Carrow switched up the bandage on his wound. I don't trust that guy. I think it's fifty-fifty that he throws in with Joseph and his crew."

"I agree, he's not to be trusted. Sumner's here with me and he has a gun. You stay safe." She slammed the phone down.

"The killer made it to the island," she told Sumner. "He's headed to Island Security, but when he discovers that I'm not there he'll come here. I have a gun in the bedroom." Emma hurried to her room and grabbed her weapon. Sumner was right behind her, holding his gun.

"We need to get out of here," he said. "There are too many windows and too many entrances. We can't cover them all."

"Okay, but where?"

"Where will he go if he can't find you here?"

Emma thought a moment. "To Carrow's. The West Hill. It's the logical next place because he knows that Carrow was with me on the boat."

"Then we'd better get there before he does. He'll take anyone left in the villa hostage and use them as bait to get you to do what he wants."

Emma was heading back to the front door as Sumner spoke.

"God forbid he does, because it will work. I won't let them die to save my own skin. He can have the minerals, for all I care."

"I doubt that's all he wants. I think he wants you and me dead. We need to warn the others and then get off this island," Sumner said. Emma threw on the rain slicker she'd taken from the boat and slipped back into the Wellington boots. She checked her gun's magazine.

"Do you have any more ammunition?" Sumner had his own coat back on.

"No. I've got seventeen rounds. You?"

"Thirteen. This isn't my weapon, it's the owner's, and I don't know where he keeps his extra ammunition."

Emma waved Sumner to the back of the house.

She was halfway through the villa when she heard the sound of an engine revving in the distance. It accelerated and stayed at that intensity before reducing.

"Sounds like they're stuck."

"With any luck, they are."

The noise of the struggling auto diminished as they reached the back of the villa. They ran past Johnson's closed door and Emma said a small prayer that the killer would leave her alone. They stepped into the kitchen.

The lights were off, but a crack of lightning illuminated the room. Emma gasped when she saw that the bokor priestess stood in the center of the kitchen with both palms out flat in front of her face. Emma felt rather than saw Sumner directly behind her.

"Duck," Emma said as the woman blew on her hands. A fine white powder flew outward and settled on Emma's face, while a portion of it hit Sumner. Too late, Emma thought. She heard Sumner cough. He stepped past Emma, grabbed the woman by one arm, spun her around, cranked her wrist into the middle of her back and pushed her forward. The priestess stumbled into the far wall next to the French doors. She cackled loudly. Her laugh sounded mad.

"Devil's Breath hit you. You be mine now," she said. She cackled again. Sumner pressed her face-first into the wall and looked back at Emma.

"What was it?" he asked.

"Probably scopolamine," she said.

"Burundanga," the woman said.

"Burundanga is the native name for it," Emma said.

"What does it do?"

Emma moved back in line with the hall that led from the kitchen to the front door and checked for intruders. The rest of the house stayed dark. In a few long strides she was once again at Sumner's side by the wall.

"It's an anticholinergic. Hallucinations and delirium along with amnesia afterward." She could smell the strong scent of the woman's patchouli oil perfume and hear her heavy, erratic breathing.

"She sounds like she's on some sort of drug herself." Emma leaned over to look out the glass panel and checked the backyard. She heard the sound of a car door slamming.

"They coming for you," the woman said. "Now they kill you."

Sumner let go of her arm and shoved her aside. Emma hauled open the French door and ran onto the terrace. It was three steps down to the lawn, which had turned into a sea of mud with two inches of water rushing past. She placed her gun in her coat pocket to keep it dry and splashed into the streaming flow while working her way to the garage. It was still closed and the Jeep still parked in front. Water formed deeper pools on either side of the asphalt drive, but the vehicle's high clearance kept the bulk of it dry. Sumner, who had followed her, crawled into the passenger side while she got behind the wheel.

Headlights from another vehicle illuminated

the edge of the property. Emma fired up the
engine and hit the gas, turning the Jeep in the
opposite direction from the house. She flipped
the transmission into four-wheel drive.

"I'm going to drive over the lawn and through
the trees to the access road. It's made of dirt, but
hopefully four-wheel drive will be enough to get
us out of here." Sumner leaned between the seats
while he watched out the back of the car.

"Go," he said.

Lightning cracked through the sky, illuminating the lawn to Emma's immediate left and the
pool farther left of that. She hit the gas again and
they moved out. The Jeep slowed as it transi-
tioned from the asphalt to the grass, but only for
a moment. It sank a bit lower in the water-sogged
lawn but to Emma's relief kept moving forward.
She drove past the pool and toward the trees in
the dark, using the wipers but keeping the lights
off. The car slipped sideways a couple of feet but
corrected when she eased off the gas.

"How long before the drug kicks in?" Sumner
asked. He kept his eyes on the area behind them.

"With any luck it won't. Scope inhaled in
powder form is a weak way to administer it."

"I got some in my mouth and swallowed it,"
Sumner said.

"Oral ingestion is a much more efficient form
of dosing."

"Well that's just great," he said. "And if it does
work?"

"You'll feel it in half an hour, maybe forty minutes." The rear tires slipped a little lower when they hit a depression in the lawn and the car shifted its weight to the back.

"You think she told the truth? About what it was?" Sumner asked.

"I hope so, because the alternatives are much, much worse."

"What else could it be?"

Emma didn't want to think about that, but she kept her eyes on the approaching tree line while she answered.

"You mean what poisons are available to her on a tropical island?"

"Yes."

Emma inhaled. "Any number of deadly plants and animals grow in a tropical environment. One of the worst would be a tetrodotoxin. It's the poison in a puffer fish." The car slid to the left when it hit another depression. Emma pressed on the gas and mud flew in all directions.

"Hallucinations?" Sumner asked.

"Not really. More like paralysis and deep coma. Depending on the amount, death."

"Well let's hope the amount was low."

"Let's hope she told the truth and it was Devil's Breath. That's bad enough."

She heard the first gunshot as she entered the tree line.

"They're here," Sumner said.

44

Once in the trees, the wind lessened but the darkness was worse, if that was possible. Emma turned on the lights and swerved to avoid a flailing tree branch that had cracked but not broken off. It swung back and forth in disjointed arcs. Some of the trees made creaking noises as the wind hit them. At one point the trunks were spaced so closely that the Jeep couldn't squeeze through.

"Tuck the sideview mirrors in," she said. Sumner, still facing toward the back of the car, turned and opened the window on the passenger side. He flipped the mirror in while Emma did the same with hers.

"Does that buy you enough space?" he asked.

"We'll see," she replied. She inched forward. The car fit but the trees moved and scraped along the driver's side. The wheels slipped and the car shifted, causing the back of the car to hit one of the trees. Emma grimaced at the scraping sound but kept the car moving. After a few seconds they were past the narrowest portion of the opening and she could breathe easier again.

"They're on to us," Sumner said. "I see head-lights coming our way. Bet that the voodoo woman told them our direction."

"I hate that woman," Emma said.

"She's got a screw loose, that's for sure."

Emma turned onto the dirt road and depressed the gas pedal. The car moved out, flinging dirt and mud in all directions. She flipped on the fog lights, deciding that visibility was no longer an issue. The woman, she thought, must have told Joseph their direction.

After a few minutes on the access road she reached the asphalt. She had an overwhelming urge to hammer the pedal down in order to make the best time possible but fought the impulse. Water rushed across the road, and the combination of the wet and grease would mean she'd be hydroplaning in an instant.

"You'd better turn around and buckle up," she said to Sumner. "We'll hit Deadman's Curve in a couple of minutes. I'm going to take it as fast as I can." Sumner reversed and sat down, snapping the belt into position.

"Wish we had a better car," he said.

"I know. This thing is top heavy. Carrow has an Aston Martin that turns on a dime. I would love to be driving that one right now." A branch cracked and fell onto the right side of the road and Emma swerved to avoid it.

"But the Aston wouldn't have the clearance you need to avoid the debris," Sumner said, "so that might not be the right one either." He lowered his window and rain sleeted into the car. "The rain is falling almost sideways." He returned the mirror to its normal position and closed the window. Emma did the same with hers and wiped her face once the window was shut.

"How good a shooter is this guy?" Sumner asked.

Emma slowed for another turn. "Kemmer seemed to think he was a pro. I can't tell. He fired and missed, but both boats were bucking up and down so much that it was nearly impossible to get a decent shot off."

Sumner had his phone in his hand, and the small screen lit up the car's interior.

"I'm calling Stromeyer," he said. "I hate to expose them to whatever virus is spreading on this island, but we need both her and Banner. They should be able to get clearance to land despite the quarantine."

"Isn't it dangerous for them to fly through the storm?" Emma downshifted into second on the curve.

"It's risky, but I think Banner can do it. He's a competent pilot. Of course, if the wind gets any worse then the only guys who will be flying are the hurricane hunters. Ah, no. I can't get a connection."

"You can use the one at Carrow's villa."

"If we get there," he said.

Emma turned onto a fairly long straightaway and shifted back up into third. She glanced into the rearview mirror. The road had curved once before straightening and she couldn't see more than fifty meters behind her. No car appeared, but she could make out a glow that lit the area.

"Think that's their headlights?" she said. Sumner checked the sideview mirror.

"I do. What car did Carrow drive?"

"His own Jeep. Just like this one."

"So we won't be outclassed by their vehicle."

Emma caught a glimpse of headlights as the car behind them appeared on the short stretch of road that was visible before it was once again blocked by the mountain. She returned her attention to driving, because they were hitting the first part of Deadman's Curve.

"The car that's behind us isn't a Jeep," Sumner said. "It looks like a standard four-door."

"Then it will take the turns better, especially in this wind. It'll be less top heavy," Emma said.

She eased off the gas and waited until the Jeep slowed to press lightly on the brake. To her great relief they stayed in contact with the road and the vehicle slowed in response. They weren't hydroplaning. Yet.

"Here we go," she said.

The road in front of her disappeared around a tight portion of the mountain, and she slowed into the turn. The car skid a bit but made it around without incident. At the second twist it slid out farther but she corrected and they made it around. "Last one," Emma said. Her hands were sweating on the wheel and her throat was dry. The interior of the car lit up, telling her that their pursuers were close, but she didn't take the time to check the rearview mirror to determine how close. She was nearly through the turn when a massive tree branch tumbled down from above. It landed in a flurry of leaves and bark and wood.

Emma hammered the brakes but it was too late. She felt the Jeep shudder in a shaking motion while it slid forward. They drove directly into the branch with a sickening, cracking sound. The Jeep spun 180 degrees and she saw the residual glow of their pursuer's headlights growing brighter. The Jeep shimmied sideways to the edge of the road. It teetered precariously for a moment, the body parallel to the mountain, before it started sliding down.

"Shift your weight to this side," Sumner said. He grabbed her right arm and pulled her toward him, but Emma was still strapped into the seat and had no time to unhook the belt. She felt the car tip, and then her window slammed into the ground and glass flew into her cheek. The air bags deployed with a booming sound and smoke billowed into the cabin. The Jeep, though, wasn't finished falling. It rolled again onto its hood, and she heard the sickening creaking of bending aluminum and steel. The canvas roof above her head ripped off, but the side supports held. The steering wheel air bag deflated and she caught a glimpse of Sumner. His face was hidden by his own air bag, but she could see his shoulder and a portion of his head. The car rolled onto the passenger side and he grunted at the impact. He's still alive, she thought.

The Jeep frame collapsed some more and bits

of leaves and mud oozed through the broken window. The windshield cracked and popped and a crazy kaleidoscope of fissures snaked across the glass. Emma's head slammed against a side support that had buckled inward. She felt warm blood run down across her temple.

Then the car picked up momentum, the creaking and straining noises of the frame louder as the body took the beating. The only sound that eclipsed it was the booming of thunder. Lightning flashed in a strobe light effect that lent a terrifying new level to the crash, because Emma could see the chaos all around her in short bursts. Mud was everywhere, and she felt it hitting her face and coating her clothes.

The Jeep slammed to a halt, but her body was still in motion and she felt the seat belt cut into her neck as she strained against it. She whipped sideways and then jerked violently back when her body met the immovable force of the belt. The driver's side was up and the passenger side pressed into the mountain against some sort of protuberance. She hung above Sumner, who was slumped against the ground and what was left of the passenger window. He didn't move.

Emma hung there catching her breath. Rain poured in through the missing window and ripped canvas cover. She grabbed at the frame above her shoulder to steady herself and reached down to try to unhook the seat belt, but it had contracted so tightly that she couldn't get enough play in it to unsnap it. She pulled on the frame with her left arm to lift some of her weight off the belt while pushing on the button. It unsnapped, releasing the right side of her body but staying wrapped around her left armpit. She fell against Sumner.

"Are you okay?" she asked. Sumner inhaled and she saw his eyes flutter open.

"I'm alive. I can't tell if anything's broken," he said. He sounded groggy.

Emma took stock. Her head injury felt raw but the blood had congealed a bit on her cheek. She moved her toes and fingers and twitched her arms and legs. It all felt intact. She knew that the muscle ache would begin once the shock wore off, but for now all she wanted to do was get out of the wreckage.

"I'm going to climb out, carefully. We're stopped, but nowhere near the bottom of the mountain, and I'm afraid to dislodge us and finish the ride." Something hit the side of the car. "What the hell was that?"

"Where's my gun?" Sumner said. Emma looked around but saw nothing that resembled the pistol.

"I don't know. I put mine in my pocket. With any luck it's still there." Something else hit the undercarriage of the car with a clanging noise.

"What is that sound?" Sumner said.

"Maybe rocks rolling downhill? Whatever it is, we need to get out of this car."

"Look up before you move. He could be watching from above."

Emma paused. Sumner was right. She had forgotten about Joseph. She moved higher, doing her best to keep from any violent movements, and peered into the darkness. The car shifted and sank lower into the muck. Rain hit her face and she kept wiping her eyes, waiting for the lightning to illuminate the area. Finally it came and she saw that they were fifty feet down the mountain. From her angle she could only see the edge of the road and the rest of the mountain as it continued upward. Two people stood in a pool of light thrown by the headlights of a parked car. One had a gun.

45

Emma lowered herself back down.

"Joseph is there with Carrow." She fished in her pocket for her gun and found it. Her hands were unsteady but she was able to release the safety. She rose again and peered out. The two men were gone, as was the car. "They left. I can't see anyone." She put the gun back in her pocket and her foot on the console between the seats that housed the gearshift. She hoisted herself up and out of the wreckage. It sagged and began to slip, and she grabbed at the remaining frame.

"Hold it. I'm getting out," Sumner said. She dug her heels into the mud and held on while Sumner unbelted and stood up. He hauled himself out of the window, swearing when the remaining shards of glass snagged at his wrist. He swung his right and then left leg out onto the dirt and stood a moment, swaying. He held onto the car's wheel.

"You look shaky," Emma said.

"I am." He glanced to his left, said, "Oh shit,"

let go of the wheel and staggered back. Emma felt her own nerves take a jump and she hauled her gun out of the coat pocket while looking up at the road above their heads.

"Is he there?" she said.

"Not the killer. The beast," Sumner replied.

Emma turned back. Sumner was staring at a spot farther down the mountain. Lightning skated across the sky.

"There's nothing."

"Where the hell is my gun?" Sumner said. "I do *not* want to face that thing without it."

"Sumner there's nothing there," Emma said. "But I'll help you find the gun because we're going to need it." She worked her way around the car, doing her best to keep her feet from slipping out from under her. The muscle ache began and she felt the injury to her head begin to throb. Cold drops of water ran down her neck and seeped under the coat collar and she shivered. She looked inside the vehicle for Sumner's gun. A flash of lightning lit up the interior and she saw it in the rear foot well. She reached through what used to be the roof of the car and snagged it by the trigger guard.

"You don't see that?" Sumner pointed to a spot farther down the mountain. Emma squinted in the pouring rain.

"All I see is a bunch of scrub and a few trees. What do you see?"

"A misshapen beast-type creature with long claws for fingers and huge, pointed teeth. It's coming this way."

"It's the scopolamine. You're having a hallucination." She handed him the gun.

"I want to shoot it," he said. Emma reached out and took the gun back.

"Absolutely not. Don't you dare waste a bullet on an imaginary creature."

"It looks so real, it's amazing." The car began a slow slide downward, stopping again after three more feet. He looked at it. "There's a thing with red eyes peering from inside the car."

"More hallucinations. Interesting, though, because what you're describing are exactly the two beasts that I saw when that witch poisoned my food."

"Can people have identical hallucinations?" he asked. Emma came around to him and wrapped his arm over her shoulder.

"I've never heard of it, but anything's possible. Come on, let's go back up to the road. But on the other side of that branch."

"Creepy." He leaned on her and they started upward. He looked back down the mountain. "Slouching toward Bethlehem."

"Are you quoting Yeats?"

"'The Second Coming,'" he said. He slipped and Emma kept him upright.

"In the poem it has a lion's body and a man's head," she said.

"It's meant to be the devil returning. That's what this beast looks like. A creature from hell." He twisted his head to look behind them. "It's starting to move. Coming toward us. It has long, thin, bent legs with claws for feet, but it stands fairly upright."

"There's nothing there, you've got to believe me. Think about Joseph. He's the one we need to worry about, not random beasts."

"With any luck Joseph thinks we're dead," he said. Emma kept dragging him up the slope. Her feet sank deep with each step and she pulled them out with a sucking sound. He turned his head again.

"The red-eyed one is crawling out of the car." Emma felt a chill run along her spine.

"You need to stop telling me about it. It's creeping me out. Focus on something else."

" 'And what rough beast, its hour come 'round at last, slouches towards Bethlehem to be born?' " he said. He slipped and dropped to his knees, taking Emma down to hers as well. She rose back up and they kept moving.

"Almost there." She felt him twist again to look back. He inhaled sharply.

"They're gaining on us. The red-eyed one has the same body, but it's crawling on all fours. Moving fast."

"Stop looking back," Emma said. Her thighs burned from dragging the heavy rubber boots out of the mud and walking up the steep incline.

"Give me the gun," he said.

"No. We need the bullets."

"They're only five feet away. I've got to shoot them."

Emma dragged him the final few feet onto the asphalt road. Only then did she look back. She saw something flit into the trees a few feet lower to her left.

"The big one is gone. The red-eyed one ran into the trees," Sumner said. He looked at her. "You saw the one go into the trees, didn't you?"

She didn't want to encourage him in his hallucinations, but she didn't want to lie to him either.

"I saw something but it could have been an animal. Besides, I got hit with the scope, too. It's likely I'm having hallucinations as well, but milder than yours."

He raised an eyebrow and put out his hand. "My gun."

"You promise not to shoot at beasts?"

"I promise nothing. But if I see a beast, I'll verify its existence with you first." Emma handed him his weapon. He checked it. "It looks like it's been dragged through the mud."

Emma nodded. "It probably was while the car was sliding on its side."

"I hope it fires. I don't have the time to clean it." He shoved it in his coat pocket, straightened and looked around. "Do you see all the bats?"

"No bats."

He rubbed at his face. "This isn't exactly a recreational drug, is it?"

"Not at all."

"Which way?"

Emma pointed down the road. "Further down four miles and then back up about five if we stay on the road. We can cut that in half by running down the road one more mile and then hiking straight up."

"Then let's go."

46

Joseph dragged Carrow back into the Blue Heron villa. He marched him into the kitchen, where the voodoo priestess was sitting at the table, humming and swaying over a plate of various objects.

"What the hell are you doing?" Joseph said.

She looked up at him. "Curse. He be mine, too." She pointed at Carrow, grabbed a handful of white powder, stood to face him and blew on her palms. Carrow coughed twice before sucking air in a deep gasp. The woman turned toward Joseph and he aimed his gun at her and pulled the trigger, hitting her dead center in the chest. She jerked backward, got a look of surprise on her face and slowly slumped to the ground.

He stalked to the watercooler in the corner, pulled off a cup from the holder and drank a full cup. He filled it again. When he was done he saw that Carrow was staring at the woman's body. His face was pale and stress lines bracketed his mouth.

"That's what will happen to you if you cross me. I don't care who you are, do you understand?"

Carrow looked at Joseph and nodded.

"This long way around, will it take us past the mangrove?"

Carrow nodded again.

Joseph smiled at him. "What, cat got the famous singer's tongue?" He looked around the kitchen. "Anybody else in this house I should know about? Where's the staff?"

"Gone," Carrow said.

"You sure? Maybe we check each room. I'm not leaving any witnesses."

"I'm sure," Carrow said. "I know everyone on this island."

Joseph shook his head. "No you don't. You don't know the one guy who's brought all this hellfire down on your heads. If you did you wouldn't have let him on this fancy island."

"Is he staff or owner?"

Joseph snorted. "Owner. He owns everything. Except me. He only rented me." He tossed the wax-covered cup into the sink. "Let's go. Bring it."

"It?" Carrow asked. Joseph waved the gun in the direction of the corpse.

"Put it in the trunk of the car."

Carrow walked to the corpse and put his arms under the body's armpits. He began to drag her across the floor, through the house, out the front and to the car. Joseph kept his gun aimed at him the whole time. Carrow arranged the body in the trunk and closed the lid.

"Now back."

"Into the house?"

"Yes. Time to clean." Joseph watched with satisfaction as Carrow cleaned the floor on his hands and knees, using paper towels and floor cleaner. Joseph sat in a chair and drank some more water. "I read once that you guys worshiped Satan. Word was that you embedded satanic ritual sayings in your albums. That if they're played backward the words 'God is dead' can be heard. That true?" Carrow got to his feet and tossed the used paper towels in the garbage. He walked to the sink and washed his hands.

"It's not. It was all we could do to arrange them when played correctly. We had no idea what the albums would sound like if they were played backward."

"But the Satan worship. That true?"

Carrow looked at the spot that he'd just cleaned and swallowed. "Martin did some."

Joseph stood up. "So you got what you asked for. You got me." Joseph was pleased to see a flash of despair cross Carrow's face. He needled him further. "I mean, you wanted what Satan does, right? He kills. Like me. You prayed for me and Satan answered." He put his arms out. "I'm the answer to your prayers." Joseph laughed. He loved his joke. After a moment he stopped. The skinny singer was looking at him as if he was strange. Evil. Joseph felt his mood swing to angry in a second. "You're not better than I am. Don't forget it." He waved at the hall. "Back to the car. You're going to drive."

They worked their way through the house and Joseph kept the gun on Carrow while he buckled up.

"Which way?"

"Just take this road back around. I'll tell you when to stop."

Carrow raised an eyebrow but said nothing. He drove with precision, dodging branches and twigs. The windshield wipers slapped against the glass and the wind howled around them, occasionally buffeting the car. When they were still some distance away, Joseph told him to stop.

"Get in the trunk."

Carrow gave him a look. "What? The trunk?"

Joseph nodded. "You heard me."

"There's no more room."

"Make room. Unless you want to see where we're headed? In that case, I'll have no choice but to kill you. No witnesses, remember? So you can either get in the trunk with your girlfriend or you can die." He put the gun up against Carrow's cheek. He waited for Carrow to flinch, but Carrow stared back at him with a solemn look that lacked fear. He has some guts, Joseph thought.

Carrow pressed the trunk release and opened the driver's door. Joseph angled out on his side and kept the gun on the singer while he pulled the lid open. He pushed the body farther into the trunk, arranging the woman's limbs. Then he folded himself into the trunk as well, keeping his back to the corpse. Joseph pointed his gun at the emergency trunk release inside the space. "Touch it and I kill you, understand?"

Carrow flicked a glance at the handle but said nothing.

Joseph slammed the trunk closed, got behind the wheel, and drove the rest of the way to the villa. He pulled into the front under the portico and got out to ring the bell. After a couple of minutes the door opened. The large idiot stood in the doorway and looked at him with his dead eyes.

"Tell him Caldridge and Sumner are dead. The minerals are back on the boat at the harbor. I want my money. I'm getting out of here."

"Tell him yourself," the large man said.

Joseph waved at the car. "I got a guy in the trunk that I have to watch. Unless you want to?"

The man turned and disappeared into the house. Joseph returned to the car and leaned against it. Leaves blew across the yard and the rain kept hammering down. He couldn't wait to leave the stinking island behind him. After ten minutes the front door opened and the large man emerged.

"He says you're wrong. They aren't dead."

Joseph pushed off the car. "You lie!" he said. The man smirked. Joseph pushed past him into the house.

"What about your package in the trunk?" the large man said.

"I don't care. Where am I going?"

The large man glanced at the car, shrugged and closed the door. "Follow me."

Joseph followed behind the man and did his best not to urge him to go faster. The man ambled in a loose-jointed slow manner. When he reached the back of the house he turned left and went back to the library door where Joseph had last seen the Vulture. He opened it and stepped inside.

The thin man sat behind a desk in the corner of the room tapping on the front of a paper-thin tablet computer. A green accountant's light lit the desk pad.

"Why are you lying to me?" the Vulture said, but he didn't look up from his computer screen.

"I'm not lying. I saw them go over the side of the mountain. The car rolled down at least fifty feet, maybe more. I watched it for a few minutes and no one moved. They're dead."

"My contact at the West Hill says they both just appeared there at the door."

Joseph gritted his teeth together to contain himself. If what the man said was true, then he looked like a liar. Worse, he looked like a traitor. He had no illusions about what this man would do to him if he thought for a second that he was being double-crossed. He felt the first inkling of fear run through him.

"Where's Aiesha?"

"The voodoo lady?" Joseph asked.

"Yes."

"Dead," Joseph said.

The man raised an eyebrow. "Really dead or presumed dead?"

"I shot her. She's dead. She's in the trunk of my car. Want to come see for yourself?"

The man got an annoyed look on his face. "I might still have had some use for her. You shouldn't have killed her without my permission."

"She used her powder on Carrow. I didn't want to be next."

"Her knowledge of plants might have yet come in handy. Especially if the chemist is still roaming around."

"She won't be. Not for long."

"One can only hope. Now get rid of the body. Throw it into the sea, and then go back and finish the job or I'll finish you. Take Carl with you."

"No, I work alone," Joseph said.

"Not anymore you don't," the thin man replied.

Joseph turned away and looked at the large idiot Carl, who seemed even less enthused about the idea than he was.

"I have to watch the cameras," Carl said. "The security team left in the evacuation."

"Don't bother. There's no one left on the island. Go with him and make sure the chemist is dead," the thin man said. Joseph strode past Carl into the hall and back down to the front door.

"You have a gun?" Joseph asked. Carl nodded.

"How could you have let her get away twice?" Carl sounded disgusted.

"No one told me that she could shoot. I was told that she was a scientist."

Joseph opened the door and bent his head while he fought the swirling wind back to the car. Carl followed. When they were both in the vehicle, Joseph started it, put it in gear and began to drive. After they'd traveled a couple of feet there was a pinging sound and the image of a car with its trunk lid open appeared in red on the dash. Joseph slammed the car into park. He got out and walked to the rear. The trunk lid hovered open an inch from the clasp. He swung it upward and started breathing faster. The trunk held only the corpse. Carrow was gone.

He was breathing in and out so fast that he started to feel light-headed. He wanted to slam the lid down and scream his frustration to the sky, but he didn't want the fool in the passenger seat to know that he'd lost control of the hostage. This job was becoming a series of disasters.

Joseph slammed into the car, threw it in gear and floored the gas pedal. The car wheels spun on the wet cobblestones before grabbing. He turned toward the ocean.

"I'm going to the dock. You can help me throw the piece of trash in the trunk into the sea," he said to Carl.

"Do it yourself," Carl said. "I didn't kill her."

Once at the dock, Joseph slammed out of the car and opened the trunk. He grabbed her arm and dragged the body forward. He picked it up, slung it over one shoulder, and walked to the beginning of the plank walkway.

Ten-foot-high waves crashed over the wooden structure. The skinny man's yacht was docked on one side, and it bobbed up and down in the turbulence. Joseph took two steps farther onto the pier before bending over and tossing the body. It hit the water with a smacking noise and a wave slammed it against the round wooden dock supports. Joseph didn't stay to watch. He returned to the car and was relieved to close the door on the driving rain and howling wind.

He drove down the long driveway to the main road and turned to continue around the mountain. Carl gazed out the passenger window and remained silent. The whole time that Joseph navigated the mountain turns he boiled with anger. He wanted to hit something until it died. Anything to release the well of rage inside him. He focused on the chemist. She was the key. Find her, retrieve the minerals, kill her and take off.

As he drove his anger abated and he started thinking a bit more rationally. He thought about how easily the Vulture took the news that the voodoo bokor was dead. How completely expendable she was to him. Was that how he viewed all those who worked for him? It occurred to Joseph for the first time that the thin man had no intention of paying him. He would collect the minerals and have him killed.

He wouldn't take that risk. He'd steal the minerals for himself, kill all the witnesses, and take off in a boat. Once away he'd arrange his own sale.

And keep all the profits. He smiled in the dark as he drove to the West Hill.

47

Emma watched Belinda Rory stagger around the living room of the West Hill villa. She was alternating between talking to herself and crying. Sumner stood next to Ian Porter at the wet bar and stared at the corner of the room with an astonished look on his face. Emma could only imagine that he was seeing more beasts. Porter shoved a rocks glass in Sumner's hand.

"Drink," he said. Sumner drank, all the while keeping his eyes glued to the corner. Porter poured another shot and walked over to Emma. "For you. Glad to see you're in one piece." Emma still wore her soaking, filthy coat and her hair was plastered against her face. Wet strands hung in front of her eyes. She sipped the drink, which was a smooth orange brandy, while she watched Rory. The woman had moved in front of a framed black-and-white photo of Carrow onstage that hung on the wall and was muttering to it.

"What's wrong with her?"

Porter sighed. "I haven't the slightest idea. She

keeps saying that the dead people are all around us and they want to make us join them. She's been talking this way for hours."

"Where's Warner?"

"Asleep."

"Oh no," Emma said.

"Sorry, I meant normal sleep."

Emma brightened. "So the disease hasn't hit her?"

"Not yet."

Rory let out a shriek and pointed to the corner. "Do you see the beast?"

Sumner nodded. "You bet I do."

Porter frowned. "He's got it, too?"

Emma shook her head. "The witch woman drugged him with scopolamine. He's having hallucinations."

"How long will that last?"

"I have no idea, but I hope not much longer, because we all have to leave the island and he's the only one who can fly the plane."

Emma felt an overwhelming exhaustion settle over her. She knew that every moment she stood there was a waste of precious time, but she needed to regroup and think. She hoped that Joseph thought they were dead and she could buy some time. She went over to Sumner.

"Do you think you can fly a plane in this condition?"

He tore his eyes from the corner and looked at her. "I can fly a plane in any condition." He spoke in a matter-of-fact manner. If it was anyone else but Sumner, she would have assumed that he was bragging, but she knew him to be an excellent pilot.

"We have to collect all the people who are still awake, load them on the plane and get the hell out of here," she said.

"My plane only holds six. We should take Carrow's jet."

"Can you fly in this storm?" Porter asked. Sumner looked out the row of French doors. The rain was still a deluge, and the lightning and thunder continued unabated.

"I think I can. It's going to be unpleasant, though." He returned his gaze to the corner. "Oh no, the beast is gone."

"Is that a problem?" Emma said.

"I like to keep it in my sights. I hate to have it roaming about the island." He gave her a wry look. Emma couldn't help it, she smiled, and his lips crooked in amusement as well. He followed it with his usual serious expression. "But we can't fly away just yet. If we do, then we won't get done what Stromeyer asked us to do."

"I've been thinking about that, but realistically, would the sale go forward under these conditions? With a quarantine in place and a tropical storm?"

"Those are ideal conditions. Especially if the buyers were already on the island before the quarantine was put in place." He shivered. "Before I decide anything, I'm going to shower. I'm freezing and my stomach is rebelling. Could either symptom be from the drug?"

"The nausea, for sure."

He put his drink down. "Then I'm going to see if I can settle it down." He asked Porter to show him to a spare room. Emma decided to follow his lead. She shrugged off the coat and continued to a different room to shower.

Thirty minutes later she was clean, dry, and wearing a robe while she waited for their laundered clothes to dry. She sat in a chair in the spare bedroom and stared out at the rain, brooding. She'd come to a decision. There was a soft knock on the door and Sumner entered. He was dressed and holding a pile of clothes.

"Yours," he said. She crossed the room to take them from him. They were still warm from the dryer.

"Hallucinations gone?"

He shook his head. "No. They keep popping up at odd times. I wonder how long a half-life this stuff has. Maybe it's like LSD and can keep affecting you months later."

"I think you should fly everyone out of here and let me check out the two villas that Stromeyer asked us to," Emma blurted out.

Sumner frowned. "No."

"Let me tell you why I think it's a good idea."

"Don't bother. It's a terrible idea. Joseph is still out there somewhere, not to mention a handful of arms dealers bent on buying a weapon that will allow them to pass undetected through metal screening. While I know you can shoot—due to my fine instruction, I might add—I doubt that you can shoot as well as this Joseph. I, however, can."

"There are too many people at risk and no one else can fly Carrow's jet."

"I'm not leaving you here alone to face them," Sumner said.

"I'm only going to do half of what we discussed. The reconnaissance. See which villa is hosting. We can call back to Stromeyer to arrange for her to take it from there. It's not ideal, because the buyers could disappear, but at least we'll know who the players are, and that might be enough information for Stromeyer to track them. I can handle this. You need to get these people out of here."

"I know you can handle it, but I'm still not leaving."

Emma blew out a frustrated breath and headed to the attached bathroom to dress. When she emerged, Sumner was gone.

She found him in the kitchen, standing at the sink and cleaning his gun. He nodded at her when she entered before returning to the task. Every few seconds he glanced at the corner of the kitchen with a grim expression on his face.

"Beasts?"

He nodded. "I don't suppose you see them."

"No."

He sighed. "It's all that I can do to stay calm."

Emma walked up behind him, put her arms around his waist and laid her cheek against his back. His body vibrated with tension. She held him and tried to give him the strength he needed to keep ignoring what his brain told him was true. He stilled. They stayed that way for a minute or more. He put down the gun, placed his hand over hers at his waist and wrapped his fingers around her palm. She listened to the pounding rain and the murmuring voices of the others in the villa and felt his regular breathing and warm body heat. Someone coughed, and Emma turned to see Porter standing in the doorway.

"Sorry to interrupt, but you wanted to know if anyone approached the villa," he said. She still had her left arm wrapped around Sumner's waist, and felt his stomach clench in alarm. She stepped away from him.

"Yes. Is there?"

"The entrance gate has a camera mount. Come take a look."

Porter hurried through the villa to the front hall, where a small screen was attached to the wall near the door. It showed a man making his way through the trees.

"Is that Joseph?" Sumner said to Emma.

"Who's Joseph?" Porter asked.

Emma watched the man working his way around the ten-foot-high brick boundary wall. The pouring rain and shadows from the trees made the image blur. She couldn't see the man's face clearly enough to be sure. After a moment the man disappeared from the screen. She shook her head.

"It's hard to tell, but he had the right body shape and height. My gun's in the bedroom. I'm going to get it."

"Who's Joseph?" Porter asked again. "And why do you need a gun?"

"We think he's a hired killer," Sumner said.

Emma glanced back and paused when she saw Porter's stunned expression.

"Please tell me this is all a bad dream," he said.

"Go get Warner and Rory," Sumner said. "I'm going to cover you while you run to the garage. Take the first car you can and drive away as quickly as possible." Porter started down the hall to where Emma was standing.

"Where are we going?" he asked her.

"To the airport. Get inside Carrow's jet and wait for us there."

"Are you coming with us?"

"Not right away. I have something to do first."

"*We* have to do something first," Sumner said. He gave Emma a pointed look. Since she couldn't exactly force him to go with the others, she just nodded her assent. There was no time to argue with him. She looked back at Porter.

"Give us an hour. If we don't arrive, leave the jet and get over to the *Siren's Song*. Take it out. You don't have to go to sea, but you should go far enough so that he can't find you easily. Oz is at Island Security right by the airport. Please don't leave without him."

"The sound man?"

"Yes."

"I can see someone lurking in the backyard," Sumner said. His voice was low.

"Porter, go!" Emma said. Porter ran down the hall.

"Meet me in the kitchen," Sumner said.

Emma sprinted to the bedroom and grabbed

her gun from the coat. She ran into the living room to check on Rory. It was empty. The bank of French doors lacked any curtains and so she shut off the lights in order to make it more difficult for someone outside to see in. She saw a man working his way through the trees at the lot line. He seemed taller and bulkier than the man she remembered as Joseph. The lawn was illuminated from a lightning burst as the man turned to look at the house. Emma gasped and ran back into the kitchen. She found Porter and a sleepy-looking Warner standing there.

"Where's Rory?" she asked.

"I don't know. I couldn't find her anywhere," Porter said.

Sumner was against the wall next to the bay window keeping an eye on the lawn. "I was just telling everyone to go out through the front. I'll keep him pinned down here."

"Forget it. I have some bad news. He's got an accomplice. I've seen this guy before. His name is Carl. He works for the water company." She waved a hand at the Springfed water dispenser in the kitchen corner. "We're going to have to stage a distraction."

Sumner nodded. "Makes sense. What do you have in mind?"

"You're the sharpshooter. I think you should stay focused on Joseph and I should draw the other one away. He's on the side with the pool gazebo, which is good, because it's far from the garage. What do you say that I draw him out and you cover the rest while they run to the garage."

"How do you intend to draw him out?" Sumner looked at her with suspicion.

"On foot. I'm going to run into the trees. There's a trail that leads from the villa down to the beach. I've run it before. It's the one we talked about, with the poison garden and the manchineel trees at the bottom. If the big one follows me, he can't keep up, and with the wind and the rain I doubt he'll be able to get a clean shot. I don't know anything about him, but he didn't seem the type to be superskilled."

Sumner nodded. "Okay." He looked at Porter. "Hit that garage, head to the airstrip, and don't look back." He looked at Emma. "Just concentrate on running as fast as you can."

Emma checked her own weapon. "I need a flashlight. I'll kill myself on that path otherwise."

Porter walked to a pantry and returned with a heavy Maglite flash.

"This one should work," he said. Emma put a hand on Sumner's arm.

"Give me a moment to get some glasses and cover up my face from the manchineel tree sap. Can you take the second car and go to the dock and get Marwell? Meet us all at the airstrip?"

Sumner nodded. "Let's do it."

48

Emma shrugged into her coat, pulled on the Wellington rubber boots, and picked up the flashlight.

"I need a scarf to cover my face and some sunglasses," she said.

"I'll get them," Warner said. Two short beeps rang in the house.

"What was that?" Sumner said.

Warner turned pale. "The alarm pad. It's on chime, which notifies you when someone's opened a door or window." She went to a keypad located on the wall next to the French doors. A series of words ran across the LED screen.

"What does it say? Where is he?" Sumner asked.

"The far west bedroom window."

"He's driving us toward the other guy," Sumner said.

"Forget the scarf and glasses, I'm gone," Emma said.

"Let's go. Now," Sumner said. Emma nodded

at him, pulled the doors open and ran into the backyard.

The storm's increased intensity took her by surprise. It was one thing to watch it through the windows while safely inside a house and quite another to experience it firsthand. She bent against the wind and had to turn her face from the driving rain. Visibility was so bad that she thought it unlikely that either she or Carl would get a shot off. The lawn flowed with water and she splashed through several deep pools that had formed in various places. She began to run, her feet slipping in the grass and the heavy boots slowing her down. Still, she was glad for the protection, however minimal, that they provided.

She headed toward the area where she thought the trail began. She was only able to see a few feet ahead of her and didn't want to turn on the flashlight to pinpoint her location until she was near the trees. The intermittent lightning helped. Each time it flashed she looked at the ground ahead of her and did her best to remember what she'd seen. When she got to the tree line she turned back toward the villa and switched on the flashlight. She played the beam of light around, making sure to point it in the direction she'd last seen Carl running.

The light hit him full in the face. He stood twenty feet away from her. His small eyes narrowed as he squinted in the glare of the beam, water streaming down his face. He moved his arm as if to raise the gun and Emma darted into the tree line. She ran, keeping the flashlight in her hand and pointed in front of her. She heard the crack of a gunshot, but nothing hit around her and she kept moving. The tree branches above her head bent downward with the storm's force but acted as effective windbreaks, making it easier to run. But her boots sank with each step and their cumbersome weight made her usual graceful stride awkward and lurching. She consoled herself with the thought that her pursuer was also stuck with the same conditions.

The trail continued downhill, and she leaned back to keep from falling face-first. The path curved right and then left before going lower in a steep angle. Her boots lost their grip and she started to fall. She caught herself with her free hand behind her, her fingers sinking into the ooze before she got back up.

It didn't work, she thought. He's not following.

A beam of light hit a tree trunk next to her head and she leaped forward. Another cracking noise pierced through the cacophony of howling wind, crashing lightning, and booming thunder. She kept running, keeping the flashlight on. The path became steeper and slicker. Water ran down her neck into her coat collar and down her back. Her hair was in a ponytail, but pieces had fallen out and the wet strands stuck to her face. The boots were covered in layers of mud. They were even heavier than before. Her thighs began a slow burn with the effort of pulling her feet up and out from the sucking mud over and over again. She wished she could discard them altogether, but the manchineel trees were ahead of her and she didn't want her feet covered in blisters. She'd be unable to move at all if that happened.

She reached the poison garden and stopped with a cry.

The voodoo priestess hung from a tree branch. Her face was black and her tongue protruded from her mouth. Emma opened hers to scream and the vision was gone.

Emma started to shake. She kept going, keeping her eyes on the trail and avoiding looking up into the trees. She'd always relied on science and rationality to get her through the challenges she had to face. Intellectually she knew that the hallucinations weren't real, but emotionally she reacted as though they were. The events felt like black magic. She could only imagine what Sumner was experiencing at the dosage level he'd ingested.

Emma came to the last portion of the trail before the beach. This section of the path wound through an open meadow, and once again the wind pummeled her. It yanked at her coat tails and drove water into her face. She turned off the flashlight, because the open field provided no cover whatsoever. She was counting on the poor visibility to keep her alive until she made it to the bottom.

The manchineel trees came into view on her right. She stopped, put the flashlight in the pocket that didn't contain her gun and ripped off her coat. She put it over her head and held it closed under her chin as she ran. Within a minute she was even with the first of the tree stands. The wind swirled around her. She felt rather than saw the milky white sap hit the side of her coat. It made a heavier, stickier sound than the pounding rain. After a moment the tip of her nose began to burn as the wind blew the acid sap her way. Her eyes were next. They felt as though needles were stabbing into them and they began to tear. She kept blinking, but that seemed only to coat her eyes with the acid.

She tripped over something on the path, stumbled and fell face-first, tumbling down onto the grass. Her forearms hit the ground and took the brunt of the fall. She rolled and sat up, then looked back to see what she had fallen over.

Belinda Rory laid on the path, her face and arms a mass of blisters, and her mouth moving but making no sound. Emma crawled the few feet to the woman and knelt next to her head, trying to shield Rory's face with her body.

"It's me, Emma Caldridge. You can't stay here. The rain is blowing the acid from the manchineel trees onto you," Emma said.

Rory's eyes were swollen so badly that they would soon be shut and she'd be effectively blind. She moved her lips again, and this time Emma could tell that she was forming words.

"You need to move," Emma said again. "Get up. You can't stay here. The acid is deadly."

"The dead," Rory said. Emma grabbed at her arm to encourage her to sit up.

"I said deadly, not dead," Emma told her. "The dead aren't here. Get up."

"They *are* here. They say I'm in hell. They're burning me."

Emma reversed around the woman to kneel at her head and did her best to push her shoulders. To her great relief Rory sat up.

"Good. Now stand up. We've got to go. There's a man after us that wants to kill us. You have to move. Now."

Rory nodded. "Yes, he comes because I called him. He's the messenger for the devil. They said that they would send him." Emma felt a coldness run through her at the woman's words.

"What do you mean, you called him?"

"I called and told him where you were. The evil man. Now he's coming to kill you *and* me. The dead are saying that I was wrong. That the burning is hell. I've been sent down."

Emma looked back up the path. She saw the flickering of Carl's flash at the top of the meadow. He was only 150 yards up the mountain.

"The burning is acid from the trees. Get up and run." Emma felt several drops hit her skin and she almost groaned out loud at the sudden pain from the acid.

The woman shook her head. "I borrowed money from the skinny one. A loan. But I couldn't pay and he told me that he would waive some interest due if I stayed and told him when you and Carrow were going out to the blue holes. I did. And now I called him. I shouldn't have, but he was going to tell everyone about me. That I don't see the dead. That it was a hoax. I didn't, that's true, but I do now. And I see Lucifer. The skinny one is Lucifer in human form."

"Get up," Emma said. She gave the woman a shove, and Rory staggered to her feet. Emma dragged her along down the path. Rory wore flip-flops that slipped with every step.

"You're wrong. The dead are here. There's a man at your shoulder. He looks frightened for you." Emma focused on the path and keeping both her and Rory on their feet. "He says you need to avoid the water."

A gust of wind from the direction of the man-chineel tree stand hit them and the part of Emma's exposed forearm wrapped around Rory's waist erupted in a scatter shot of burning pain. A portion of a nearby branch exploded and bits of bark showered them. Rory screamed as each piece landed on the skin of her face and neck. The burn in Emma's exposed arm increased.

"He's shooting at us," Emma said. "Keep moving. You'll be a tougher target."

"The dead man says not to use the water to make your green grass tea."

Emma's heart plunged and she gasped. Memories of Patrick, her deceased fiancé, flashed through her mind. How he'd bring her boxes of the special tea that she loved and complain that it tasted like grass. An image of his body twisted in a car crash when he was hit by a drunk driver followed, which she knew was her imagination. She'd never seen a picture of the wreckage. At the time, she was too crazed with grief to even attempt to look at it.

Now tears clogged her throat and she swallowed. She hadn't thought about Patrick for nearly six months, a record for her. With Rory's comment about green grass tea she'd felt herself slipping backward, returning to the dark place where she was when it all began. Before Patrick died she'd been a conservative, careful woman looking forward to a life of the lab work she loved and marriage to a wonderful man. After, she became the daredevil in search of excitement that she now was. She pushed her body to run ultramarathon distances and took projects from Darkview. She ran her own company and drove herself to exceed in every way, mindless of the toll it would take on her.

A second gunshot sound brought Emma back to the present.

"Keep moving or we're going to join the dead," she said.

Twenty feet from the beach she stopped.

The beach was gone. In its place was twenty feet of water slamming against the mountain.

"Watch out for the water," Rory said. A third gunshot rang out and Rory jerked. Her body sagged. She was dead.

49

Emma lowered Rory's body to the ground, the frothing ocean in front of her. To the left there was a vertical drop too steep to traverse. It would be a challenge on a dry sunny day, but impossible under the present conditions. To her right lay the manchineel tree stand, and beyond that the mansion. She only had two options: either reverse and go back up the trail and into the arms of the killer, or risk even more acid burns by running through the manchineel trees. One thing she was certain of, though: the man would encounter as much pain as she would if he decided to chase her through the trees. He wore no hat and his head, forehead, eyes, and face were exposed.

Emma could see the weak glow of the mansion's lights through the cascading rain and tree trunks and headed in that direction. She pulled the coat back over her face as she ran. The already present burns began to blister. Her eyes were her most precious asset, and she kept the coat's edge low, to her eyebrows. What she lost in peripheral vision she gained in safety. If the acid reached her eyes she would be blind for as long as it would take to heal. The coat over her head concentrated the sound of her breathing, and it echoed in her ears. She listened to the ragged breaths and kept her legs moving. The burn in her muscles remained, but she was used to the type of pain that came from a grueling run and ignored most of it. Plunging on, she kept her pace even and her face covered. After what seemed an eternity she reached the tree line on the mansion side. Still, she kept moving, running away from the trees and their spraying acid sap as fast as she could.

Emma came to a halt for a moment on a rise that faced the side of the mansion. It was shaped like a crescent that curved toward the ocean on each end. Behind it and closest to her was a pool and pool cabana. Beyond that were tennis courts, and beyond that another row of trees that hid the staff buildings from the main grounds. The mansion's outdoor lights were on, but the drenching rain dimmed their brilliance.

A second section of trees crowded around the side. Emma took a deep breath and ran toward them. The ground leveled out at the hill's base, where large sections of the lawn had disappeared under inches of rainfall. She hammered through several standing pools of water. When she was far enough from the manchineel trees she lowered her raincoat and glanced back.

No flashlight beam bisected the area behind her, and a flash of lightning revealed only dark tree trunks and flailing branches. She saw nothing that resembled the shape of a man or that could be described as man-made illumination. Emma felt a certain satisfaction at the idea that her guess had been correct; he hadn't wanted to risk passing through the acid trees. His only option was to take the path back up, which would at least buy her some time to get an idea of whether this mansion was the one hosting the auction.

She skirted around the side, keeping low and jogging through the water. Meanwhile, she listened for the howl of dogs, but doubted that the animals or their handlers would be patrolling the grounds. If they were, she was counting on the chaos of the storm to render the dogs' noses less useful and their hearing less acute.

She made her way to the side of the house, darting from tree to tree. A camera mounted at the corner of the mansion faced the back. As she had suspected, the owner was relying on the manchineel trees to protect the house's flank.

The final twenty feet to a side window was open. She made it there and peered inside at a bedroom with a king-sized bed and an armoire. Light from a nearby door flowed into the room. She could see a bit of marble through the opening. It was an attached bathroom, and every so often the light would alter, indicating that someone was there. Emma crouched back down and ran along the side to the next window. This one was a tall piece of glass. She pressed her face against the house's exterior and peeked inside.

She saw an ornate library. Floor-to-ceiling shelves held books, and a couch and nearby leather club chair were arranged in the center. On the far wall there was a desk next to a bay window that faced the back of the house. A slender, dark-haired middle-aged man with a narrow face sat at the desk frowning down at some pages. Sitting on the paper, she saw a pile of small, blue, bullet-shaped objects.

Gotcha, she thought. She backed away from the window and ran along the wall toward the water. She reached the corner and took in the view.

The front lawn sloped down onto a portion of what must have been the sliver of beach but was now just water pounding upward. To the far side of the house she saw a dock. A large yacht bobbed in the pounding waves and three more were anchored offshore. Presumably the others were owned by the buyers. If she could get to the dock unobserved she might have been able to get the names of the boats. She could then transmit that to Banner and Stromeyer for later follow-up. She counted windows, trying to determine whether an occupant in the library would be able to see the dock and determined that he probably would notice her pass by. The house design maximized the view, and probably every room on that side would look out over the water.

She watched the waves crash over the dock. Even if she could reach it undetected she wouldn't be able to run to the end to get closer to the offshore boats. In the driving rain it would be impossible to read the licenses from the shore. The potential gain wasn't worth the risk.

Emma backtracked to the first tree line and

began working her way around the lawn toward the staff quarters. She breathed a sigh of relief once she plunged into the darkness of cover and jogged past the various staff buildings until she reached a utility building at the back. Like a large barn, there were two ride-on lawn mowers parked outside in the rain, as if someone had forgotten to put them away. She checked for cameras, saw none, and ran to the door.

It was open, and a relief to get out of the rain, if even for a moment. She stood still in the dark room, pulled out her gun while letting the water flow off her coat, then flicked the flashlight.

The shed contained yard equipment in one corner, pool cleaning equipment in another, and a section that appeared to be spare nets and paraphernalia for tennis court maintenance. Piled alongside this was a wet/vac vacuum cleaner, and next to that an industrial fan shaped like a snail shell. She walked down the open aisle, scanning it with the flashlight. At the far end of the room she saw a stack of firewood wrapped in burlap carry bags and a double door shed with a cabinet inside. She opened the cabinet and found rows of bottles and mason jars. Several contained dried leaves and were marked with labels. She recognized most of the plants grown by the voodoo woman.

Emma closed the door and looked at the firewood. Next to it was a basket with a lone, half-rotted apple from a manchineel tree. She took a closer look at the firewood and spotted a leaf left on one of the sections. The wood was manchineel.

Emma took a step back, heard a noise and spun

around, gun raised and ready to shoot. The beam of her flashlight fell on Richard Carrow.

"Don't shoot," he said.

Emma swallowed. "What are you doing here?"

"Hiding. I managed to get away from Joseph. The owner here hired him to kill you and Sumner. I don't know why." Carrow told her about the voodoo priestess and overhearing Joseph's claims that she and Sumner were dead. "She hit me with her powder."

"Any hallucinations?"

Carrow nodded. "A few. But nothing as awful as reality. He made me ride in the trunk with her dead body."

Emma closed her eyes. She couldn't imagine a ride so horrific.

"I've been sitting in here trying to think of ways to kill him. And his boss. He's the owner of this villa. His name is Shanaropov. I've never met him and I doubt many on the island have. He's been a loner. Now we know why."

"He may be an arms dealer looking to sell a revolutionary new bullet that can pass undetected through metal screening devices. The auction is tonight. I've been asked by a contract security company to derail the sale."

"We won't get off this island alive if we don't do something drastic. Joseph is still out there and I watched him leave with a second man."

Emma nodded. "Carl. He's one of them." She looked at the stack of wood. "I've got an idea."

"Whatever it is, I'll help you."

"Let's start a fire, shall we?"

50

Kemmer headed back to the dock and the *Siren's Song*. He wanted off the cursed island and away from them all. While the storm was dangerous, he figured he could take the boat offshore far enough to be safe from Joseph but not so far as risk capsizing. He'd stay in the protected part of the harbor until the rain lessened and then strike out for St. Martin, leaving the nightmare behind.

He made it to the dock and onto the *Siren's* deck. The boat pitched and rolled and water washed over the sides, but it seemed seaworthy. He went below, closing the door against the wind and rain with a sigh. He froze when he saw Joseph standing in the living area holding a cushion from the nearby sofa. The cabinets in the wet bar were thrown open and bottles, napkins, and glass were strewn all over the floor. Joseph had unzipped the cushion's cover and seemed to be about to cut the pillow open with a knife. His rifle was propped against the sofa's arm.

"Where did she put the minerals?" Joseph asked.

Kemmer swallowed. His throat was suddenly dry. "In the cooler abovedecks." He was lying, trying to buy some time.

"I already looked there."

"Then she must have taken them with her."

Joseph dropped the pillow, picked up his gun.

"Don't!" Kemmer said.

He felt the bullet enter his chest in a flare of pain. A second shot rang out and he watched Joseph stagger and then fall. Kemmer looked behind him and saw his tenant from St. Martin holding a gun. In two strides he was at Kemmer's side and caught him as Kemmer began to slide to the floor. The man helped him into a comfortable position.

"Let me get something for the wound," he said. "Don't move and don't close your eyes." The man disappeared and seconds later returned with a dish towel that he wadded up and balled against the wound.

"What's your name?" Kemmer said. "I guess it's not the one on the lease." The man gave him a grim smile.

"Cameron Sumner," he said. "The wound looks bad, but I'm hoping he didn't nick an artery. I'm going to load you in the car and get you to the airstrip. We're flying out of here."

Kemmer nodded. "I always said you seemed like a useful guy to have around."

Then, despite the warning not to, he closed his eyes.

51

Ivan Shanaropov rose as his guests filed into the library. There were four, one African from Sierra Leone who dealt in blood diamonds, one Romanian who acted as the Eastern European business manager for a Somali warlord, the head of a vicious drug cartel from Mexico, and the lieutenant of an equally vicious rebel stronghold in Chechnya. Of them all, Shanaropov distrusted the Chechnyan the most, probably because he'd dealt with the breed many times over the years and they inevitably would attempt to double-cross him in one way or another. He continued to deal with them only because, as a Russian living close to their borders, they were impossible to avoid. All of the men took in the room, gazing at the bookshelves and expensive furnishings with approval and respect. The Mexican's gaze was locked on the sparkling blue bullets that Shanaropov had deliberately placed on the desk in full view. He nodded at each of them and reached for a cigar box.

"Gentlemen, please take a seat, and may I offer you a smoke?" He spoke in English. The Romanian, African, and Mexican all nodded and chose a cigar before moving to the library's sitting area. Only the Chechnyan refused. Getting ready to screw me and not willing to accept any gifts? Shanaropov thought. Or too ignorant to understand English? He kept his face neutral, however, closed the box and replaced it on the desk.

"They are Cuban. I hope you enjoy them," Shanaropov said. He bent his wrist to look at his watch. He wore a Patek Philippe Platinum World Time watch worth over two million dollars. Shanaropov had never agreed with the standard view that one was born with class, one didn't purchase it. He'd proven the adage wrong time and again. His homes were on the finest, most exclusive islands, his cars were exotic, and his watch was considered one of the most expensive in the world. Wealthy men came to him when their businesses floundered and were happy to accept his loans in order to avoid the disgrace of bankruptcy. These men would rather pay usurious rates of interest than let the world know they were failures. He routinely loaned the funds and then destroyed the businesses when the inevitable day came that the assets were forfeited to him. Many never knew that their businesses had foundered not because they were bad businessmen, but because he had paid well to disrupt their contracts and destroy their reputations and customer base.

Only two companies that he'd recently at-

tempted to undermine managed to continue as
going concerns. One was Pure Chemistry, a small
laboratory run by the Caldridge woman, who
had interfered with a past mission of his, and the
other was Darkview, a much larger company that
had thwarted many of his more shadowy operations worldwide. Neither business was aware of
his backdoor manipulations, of course, but Shanaropov had every intention of prevailing against
them. He'd sell the bullets and then devote his
entire attention to destroying the two. The Darkview company, in particular, would be a wonderful asset to acquire. Shanaropov knew that
Edward Banner employed some of the best and
most unique set of contract security personnel in
the world. Shutting down their operations would
leave him free to continue without anyone hin-
dering his progress.

"Are those the bullets?" The Mexican pointed
to the desk, and his comment snapped Shanaropov out of his reverie.

"They are," he said.

"I have heard that they have a tremendous
failure rate. Is this so?" the Romanian asked.
Shanaropov shrugged in his best imitation of
nonchalance.

"While they do misfire at times, this is to be
expected given their construction. I think we all
know how difficult it is to create a bullet without
the usual metal jacket. Some reduction in performance is to be expected." Shanaropov took out his
own cigar, cut the end, and lit it. He puffed for a
moment while he thought about what to say next.

In fact the bullets failed nearly ninety percent of the time. He'd told his salesmen to claim a much lower misfire rate in order to lure potential buyers. His own venture partner, a pockmarked Bulgarian who assisted him from time to time with arms sales, had told him to forget about selling them. The minerals to make them were rare, difficult to mine, and the resulting product so poor as to be nearly useless. Shanaropov, though, had decided to go forward with the sale. He would use the excuse that the bullets were so rare that he couldn't allow anyone to test them as a way to avoid revealing the true extent of their failure.

One of the long French windows rattled as the wind pummeled it. Rain sheeted down the glass.

"Filthy night," the Romanian said. "Will this storm turn into a hurricane?"

Shanaropov shook his head. "It's predicted to taper eventually."

"What about the quarantine?"

Shanaropov waved his cigar. "Not to worry. No one in this villa has contracted the disease, and the rest have left the island." The last was a lie. Ten of his staff slept and one had already died, but he saw no need to alarm his guests. "I can't imagine a quieter, or safer, place to host a transaction such as this, can you?"

The Romanian nodded. "You have tremendous luck. First to create the ideal bullet and then to have a deserted island to yourself to auction it."

The Chechnyan eyed the ammunition. "How much?" The blunt question was what Shanaropov expected of the uncouth rebel.

"The bidding starts at one million dollars each."

The Mexican snorted. "Are you crazy? For one bullet?"

"For one bullet. They cost at least half that to make, so consider it a deal." This wasn't true, but none of the men before him could possibly have determined what the bullets cost to fabricate.

"And the gun?" This was from the African, who hadn't blinked at the cost. Shanaropov had chosen that one wisely. Money flowed in Africa, just not to the average African.

"Ten million," he said.

"Ridiculous," the Chechnyan said.

Shanaropov focused on him. "Too much to pay for a gun that can sneak past the Russian prime minister's metal detectors and security systems? I think not." He looked at the Mexican. "Or for you to do the same with your country's president?"

The Mexican got a gleam in his eye as he stared at Shanaropov. He had boatloads of money, Shanaropov knew, and spent most of it on elaborate villas complete with zoos. Cost was not a significant factor for him.

It was, though, for Shanaropov. He'd made some improvident loans and the borrowers had defaulted, as predicted, but when they did it became clear that they'd claimed assets far in excess of reality. Shanaropov had been taken in, given the loan, and discovered the truth only after the defaults. On three different occasions the men's businesses were revealed to be nothing more than Ponzi schemes. Multibillion dollar

Ponzi schemes, yes, on a vast scale, certainly, but schemes nonetheless. He had been furious. When he'd found out about the deception he arranged for one to die during his morning swim and another shot after writing his own "suicide" note. Still, the money was gone. While Shanaropov was far from broke, he never missed an opportunity to make more money.

The windows rattled while the men sat and contemplated the deal. Shanaropov's phone rang and Carl's name scrolled across the screen. He moved away from the others and answered it.

"The Caldridge woman is headed your way. She should be through the manchineel trees by now and roaming somewhere on the grounds."

"Does she have a gun?" Shanaropov asked quietly while stepping away from the long window. No need to be shot through it.

"Hard to say. I chased her part of the way and she didn't fire, but that may not mean anything."

"Find Carrow's boat and get the minerals she collected. We need those," Shanaropov said.

"Fine, but the roads are bad. It'll be a while before I can get there and then return to the villa." Shanaropov turned back to the room and looked at the collection of killers in his library.

"I'll handle it," he said.

Shanaropov crossed to the desk, grabbed the bullets, poured them back into a wooden box and headed to the door.

"Wait here," he said to the buyers. He carried the bullets into a separate den, where a two-foot-by-two-foot safe, built into the wall, hung open. He placed the box inside, next to the small gun case that held the pistol fashioned from the minerals, and closed it. The electronic keypad lit, and after the door locked he walked to a far wall, where a glass case held a selection of rifles, ammunition, and several guns. He opened the door and selected three AK-47s, one nine-millimeter pistol, and one rocket-propelled grenade launcher.

When he returned to the other room, Shanaropov found the buyers in the same seats as before. Cigar smoke hung thick in the air. The African eyed the guns hanging off Shanaropov's shoulder and shot to his feet.

"What are you doing with those?" he asked. His hand went to his waistband in what Shanaropov supposed was a purely reflexive act, searching for a gun that wasn't there, because they'd been frisked and disarmed before docking at Terra Cay.

"We have company. Emma Caldridge. A sometime agent of the Darkview company. She's somewhere on the grounds, and it occurred to me that I have four men known for their efficient handling of obstacles. I brought the weapons to assist you in shooting her down."

"I hate Darkview," the Romanian said. "Edward Banner has deployed his mercenaries throughout the shipping industry, and my employer's pirates are being killed before they can get near a boat. Business is suffering."

Shanaropov nodded. "Then you understand why I want his agent dead. I've heard that there is another on the island as well. Named Cameron

Sumner. I have my own assassin working on killing him, but you should take precautions."

Shanaropov handed out the AKs to the Mexican, Romanian, and African. He gave the Chechnyan the nine-millimeter.

"I want the RPG," the Chechnyan said.

Shanaropov shook his head. He'd be damned if he was going to give the Chechnyan the biggest weapon he had. As it was, he took a massive risk, arming these killers. Any one of them could turn on him, shoot him, and spend the rest of the evening attempting to blast open the safe. But it couldn't be helped. Joseph had already failed to kill the chemist and Sumner was out there somewhere. "I'm going to use it."

The Chechnyan frowned. He analyzed the weapon in his hand. "I need another magazine."

Shanaropov handed him one.

"Where is she?" the Mexican said.

"I don't know. Somewhere out there," Shanaropov pointed to the windows that faced the yard. The wind still buffeted the glass and rain poured down.

The Romanian huffed. "Senseless to go out in that looking for her."

"Better to wait for her to come to us," Shanaropov said. "I have no doubt that she will."

"Why is that?" The African puffed on his cigar.

"Because she wants to stop the sale and take the bullets."

"So they're that valuable?" The Mexican had a gleam in his eye. Of the three, Shanaropov thought that the Mexican would be the highest bidder. His hatred for the Mexican president was legendary.

Shanaropov nodded. "They are. She'll come. You'll see."

The African ground out the cigar stub in the crystal ashtray on the desk.

"So where do you want us? We're not going to simply sit here until she decides to appear."

"In the adjoining rooms. To the left and right of the hall. I'll leave this light on. She'll follow it, like an insect to a bulb. When she shows, fire on her."

The men filed out of the library. Shanaropov waited until they were positioned in each room before he returned to the entrance and lowered himself to the floor. From that position he could see into the library, but at the first sign of trouble he would be able to withdraw into the hallway. He propped the RPG against the wall, removed a pistol from his pocket, and settled in to wait.

52

Emma rooted around in the shed, looking for work gloves. She found some in a basket near the garden supplies and handed a set to Carrow, keeping another pair for herself. On a far shelf she saw a row of cans and boxes containing herbicides, fertilizers, charcoal lighter fluid, and paint thinner. She grabbed the lighter fluid and doused the burlap-bag-covered bundles with it. Each bundle, secured with a rope, contained about four pieces of wood. When she was finished she looked for a wheelbarrow and found one in a corner.

"Should we load them up in that and haul them to the house?" she said. "That way we'll be able to make one trip rather than many and reduce the chances of someone spotting us."

Carrow shook his head. "The wheel will get bogged down in the mud. We should just carry as much as possible."

Emma saw his point. "Okay, but be very careful. One touch and you'll regret it." She was already regretting exposing her arms to the acid. Both of them burned from the elbow down. Every movement of her arms brought them in contact with the sleeves of the coat, which only increased the agony. "And here." She handed him a hatchet from the tools hanging on a pegboard. "Cut them into smaller sections. It will make them easier to carry."

Carrow took the hatchet and started hacking away at the first bundle, dodging bits of wood as he did. He sliced through the first section and sap started oozing from the cut.

"Don't touch that. It's pure acid," Emma said. She grabbed a bucket and dumped the cut pieces into it. "This way we can collect it in one place."

Carrow nodded and continued hacking. While he did, she peered out of the door at the villa.

The rain had reduced the lawn to large puddles of standing water, and lightning still cracked overhead. The palm trees bent with the force of the wind. From the right she saw the lumbering form of the deliveryman. Emma watched him slog through the muddy lawn and enter through a side door. Through it all the lights of the library glowed.

"We need to lure them outside. I don't want to confront them in the house," she said. Carrow stopped hacking at the wood.

"Perhaps it's just safer to notify the authorities off island."

Emma nodded. "I thought that's what I'd do, but I hate the idea of them getting away. His boat is right there. Once this storm lessens they'll all be long gone."

"I hate that idea, too. They should all have to ride in a trunk with a dead body, just like I did."

Emma glanced at Carrow. His mouth was set and he frowned at the bundle of wood that he'd been attacking with the ax. His face was grim. She couldn't help thinking that he'd be forever altered by the events of these past few days. The happy-go-lucky rock star was gone, replaced with a man bent on revenge, or perhaps justice, though the two seemed the same at the moment. She looked at the house and plotted.

"We need to smoke them out," she said.

Carrow stopped hacking at a bundle, looked up and smiled.

"Perfect."

"Molotov cocktails," Emma said. "Acid-drenched Molotov cocktails."

Carrow held up a small brick of wood. "Like this."

Emma nodded and returned her attention to the house.

"We'll run along the tree line to the center of the villa. There are at least ten windows. Two large bays on either end of the crescent, three French doors with sidelights on either end, and five windows interspersed between. I think the second window on the far side, just before the bay, is at the end of a hallway. We're going to head there, break down the glass, light the wood and throw it in. Then I'm going to keep a couple of bricks for the far bay."

Carrow was busy arranging the pieces of wood in stacks in order to make it easier to carry. He had laid a large plastic lawn and leaf garbage bag down first.

"What's in the far bay?" he asked.

"The library. He's in there." She watched Carrow wrap the garbage bag around the bricks. "That's a good idea."

She did the same with her bundle and put as many pieces into the bucket. When they were done she opened the side door, shoved her gun back in her pocket, and looked at Carrow. He'd taken another plastic bag, ripped a hole in the top, put the entire thing over him and was working on ripping two holes in front for his arms. She did the same, but didn't bother with armholes. Instead she simply shoved the plastic over her coat to the shoulders but no lower. She wanted room to maneuver her gun out of her pocket. While Carrow suited up she rooted around in a toolbox for a hammer. She found a ball-peen with a point at one end and slipped it in her free pocket.

"Remember, after we throw the wood, head to the manchineel stand. Run straight through it. There's a path on the other side that goes up the mountain to your villa. Ready?"

He nodded with a gleam of anticipation in his eyes. Emma marveled again at his apparent lack of fear.

"Don't get overconfident," she warned. "Carl is there and we'll need to cross the lawn quickly. If you see any movement just drop the sack and run. A retreat alive is better than an advance and dead."

She lifted the bucket with the bricks and slid

out the door. The storm still raged, but she felt it less. Or perhaps she was just so wound up that it only appeared that way. She broke out of the shed and began jogging toward the villa across the great expanse of lawn. Water poured down her face and lightning cracked overhead. A bolt snaked to the ground three hundred yards to her right, and she gasped when she felt the air hum with static, as if electrified. She sprinted, feeling the burn in her thighs as the ground sucked at her shoes and once again she struggled to pull each foot out of the muck. Carrow stayed behind her but she could hear him huffing and puffing with the effort of slogging through the mud.

She stepped within ten feet of the first window, breathing heavily. Her pulse raced with the exertion and adrenaline. Somewhere inside the house Carl and a group of arms dealers lurked, along with a cache of weapons.

She removed the hammer from her pocket, swung the ball-peen end and smashed the pane. An earsplitting alarm started and floodlights on high poles placed in various locations on the lawn sprang to life.

"Glass break sensors!" Emma had to yell to be heard over the noise of the storm. She worked at the window, opening a large hole. She threw wood through it, followed it with a second and stepped back. Carrow reached in and flicked on a lighter, touching it to the bricks. They ignited with a whooshing sound.

"Watch out for the smoke," Emma said to Carrow. She glanced up into the room and saw a large black man, ten feet away, holding an automatic weapon.

She didn't think, only reacted, grabbing at Carrow's tee shirt and hauling him to the side, out of the line of sight through the window. She heard the rattle of the weapon as it fired and saw quick flicks of movement as the bullets whizzed by. Pieces of the window frame exploded, with chips flying outward. When the firing stopped she heard spastic retching from the man inside. The smoke was doing its work.

She picked up the bucket of bricks and ran, Carrow next to her, to the next bay. This time she pressed herself against the wall, taking care not to frame herself in the window in case another attacker was lurking. She straightened her arm, swung the hammer, broke the glass, but instead of placing the brick first before lighting it, she held it out to Carrow. He lit it and the wood ignited with a satisfying whoosh. Emma could feel the heat of the fire penetrate her work glove as she tossed the brick through the broken window.

Noise was everywhere. The villa's alarm shrieked and the wail managed to eclipse even the cacophony from the storm. She heard a man, screaming in pain, though what he was saying was unintelligible. She took a deep breath and ran past the window. In her peripheral vision she had the impression of a man, bent and stumbling as he held his hands to his eyes, but she didn't stay to watch.

Reaching the final bay, she pressed herself against the wall before peering inside. The library was empty.

Not good. After encountering a man in each room so far, she was suspect of this empty space, where a deal was being negotiated just minutes before. She pulled out her weapon and turned to Carrow.

"Stay back," she said. "I'm going to switch it up this time. Fire into the room first. Then we'll light the brick and toss it." She swung the hammer in a wide arc. This window smashed and she reached out, aimed her gun inside, and squeezed the trigger. Smoke curled out of the glass and immediately her eyes started burning. "Light it!" Emma said. She heard the brick whoosh to life as Carrow followed her instructions. He stepped past her and lobbed it into the room. Emma stepped into the opening, looking for the bullets that she'd seen resting on the desk. Instead she saw the thin man, aiming a weapon at her. Smoke from an adjacent hallway poured into the room and the man's eyes were streaming with tears.

He began to cough, and the mere act of opening his mouth sent him into a fit as the smoke hit his mucous membranes. He bent forward, hacking and retching and stumbled backward.

Emma didn't stay to watch. She dodged right and began running to the manchineel trees, with Carrow next to her. They were halfway there when another man stumbled outside followed by the two that Emma had encountered. She could hear them moaning in pain from the smoke.

"I'm blind! I'm blind!" one man yelled. Emma didn't look back. From her right she saw Carl holding a gun in one hand and the leashes of two large German shepherds in the other. He raised his weapon and Emma raised hers. She fired and he spun around. He got off a shot that grazed Carrow in the fleshy part of his hand. He grunted but kept running. Emma fired again, and hit Carl in the upper chest. He dropped to his knees and let go of the leashes.

The dogs sprinted toward Emma and Carrow at an angle that would allow them to intersect them before they would be safely within the manchineel forest. Emma ran faster, and Carrow did as well. He raced along beside her, his arms flying. The rain hit Emma's face and she instinctively turned her head. When they were twenty feet from the tree line she saw Carrow pull the garbage bag poncho higher to cover his entire head. Emma did the same with her makeshift poncho, pulling it over her head to her eyebrows.

They were ten feet from the trees when the spray from the rain hit them full in the face. Emma felt the water sluicing down the plastic bag. The first dog's howls turned to shrieks of pain. The second dog dug in and refused to go any closer to the trees.

To Emma it seemed as though her entire world consisted of making it to the poisoned tree line. She plunged into it and kept going. Carrow remained close. She looked back after bursting into the manchineel stand and saw that Carrow was lagging. A bright flash illuminated the sky and she thought it was lightning but saw with horror that it wasn't.

The Russian was standing on the back lawn aiming a rocket-propelled grenade thrower at them. It was as Sumner had predicted. They'd come fully prepared with conventional weapons. The devil wasn't ready to give up his bullets, Emma thought.

53

The grenade whizzed into the manchineel trees, slicing off branches and sending sprays of bark everywhere before it exploded in the center. Despite being dampened from the rain, two of the trees began to smolder.

"Keep running," Emma said to Carrow. "That smoke hits us and we'll be blinded."

Carrow, though, was flagging. He moved but had slowed to a jog and seemed to be going slower every few steps. Emma ran back, wrapped her hand around his bicep and dragged him forward. The wind blew in crazy directions and the smoke wafted toward them. Emma's eyes began to burn and she felt the membranes of her throat begin to swell.

They hit the edge of the stand and she kept hauling him upward on the trail. They passed Rory's body on the side, but Emma barely noticed and thought that Carrow didn't see her at all. They'd reached the poison garden when she heard the second grenade explosion.

"What are they shooting at us?" Carrow asked.

"Rocket-propelled grenades. The basic weapon in every arms dealer's arsenal."

"Is it that thin bastard?"

"Yes. He's not giving up."

"How far can they fly?" Carrow was huffing and puffing and could barely get the words out.

"Over nine hundred feet in the hands of an expert. And we have to assume that we're dealing with experts," Emma said.

"I don't think I can run any faster," Carrow said.

The trail branched out to the right and Emma took it. It had the advantage of running along the side of the mountain instead of uphill. To her relief, Carrow picked up the pace again once he was no longer climbing. They burst out onto a road.

"Where are we?" Emma asked him. He put his hands on his thighs and bent over, breathing heavily. He pointed down the slope.

"That goes to the airport."

"Then let's go," she said.

The downhill run was easier. Emma's eyes continued to burn but her throat hadn't closed yet and she thought perhaps she'd caught a break. Carrow ripped off the poncho and Emma got a look at his face. There was no mistaking the determination there. Ten minutes later they were nearing the intersection and the Acute Care Center as a car pulled out in front of them. Emma's throat went dry with fear and she scrambled in her pocket for her gun.

The car window lowered and she saw that Oz was driving.

"Get in."

Carrow and Emma tumbled into the car, with her in front and him in back. Oz hit the gas.

"Thank you from the bottom of my heart," Carrow said. "I didn't know how I was going to run down that hill."

"Did Sumner leave?" Emma asked. Oz shook his head.

"We saw the fire and heard the shooting. It was all I could do to get Sumner to stay put in the airplane. I had driven up to the Blue Heron to look for you and all I found was Ms. Johnson, asleep. I put her in the car and drove her to the airport. Then I told him I would drive up this second road and look for you both while he warmed up the jet. It should be ready when we get there."

"The *Rex*?" Carrow said.

"Yes."

He turned a corner and the airport came into view. The *Rex*'s lights were on and Emma could see that the ladder was down.

"Head straight for it," she said. "There are several very pissed-off arms dealers gunning for us. We need to get out of here, fast."

Oz drove to the airport and directly onto the tarmac. When they got out, Emma ran with him and Carrow to the plane. She hurried up the stairs and Carrow showed them how to secure the door.

"All aboard?" Sumner yelled through the open cockpit door. Emma made her way up to him, holding onto seat backs and the wall because the plane was turning to get into position to take off.

"Get us the hell off this island," she said.

Sumner swung the plane around and started taxiing down the runway, gaining speed. Emma lowered herself into the copilot's seat and watched. From the right, halfway up the hill, she saw a car spin to a stop and the door open. The thin man stepped out. He reached into the passenger seat. The *Rex* moved past and Emma couldn't see anymore.

"Trouble to your right," she said. "The Russian just pulled up. He was reaching into the back and I'll bet he's getting an RPG."

"Ten seconds more and we're airborne," Sumner said. The rain pummeled the plane harder as they increased their speed and Emma snapped into a belt and clutched the armrests. They lifted off and she heard sporadic clapping from the cabin followed by an explosion. The jet shivered. A warning alarm went on and the dashboard lit up in red.

"We've been hit with something," Sumner said as he kept climbing.

"Can we fly?"

"Yes, but we're leaking fuel. Get Stromeyer on the phone. I'm going to have to land soon."

54

Banner and Stromeyer sat around a speaker-phone on a conference call with Susan Plower.

"We need to have them land somewhere," Stromeyer said.

"They're arriving from a quarantine zone. No one wants them, I'm afraid," Plower said. "Can they make it to Guantanamo?"

"Not enough fuel," Banner said.

"Listen, Encephalitis Lethargica is quite dangerous. It's a sleeping sickness that causes catatonia, mutism, psychotic events, sleep, and death. There's no cure and no way to tell who will survive and who will die. You can understand why I'm getting no takers for them."

"Yes, I do understand," Stromeyer said. "But we have to do something."

"You aren't exactly making this easy on me. How the hell am I going to sell that to anyone?"

"But the good news is that we don't know how it's spread. Perhaps it's not easily contracted from one human to the next."

"That's not what happened in 1915. The CDC is telling me that over five million died."

"But that strain hasn't been seen since. Or, at least only extremely rarely. It's entirely possible that this version isn't as deadly," Stromeyer said.

"Or maybe not. I've already called the British Virgin Islands and the Bahamas. No one wants to expose their populations to this scourge and I don't blame them. Can they attempt a water landing?"

"I don't think so," Banner said. "The seas are rough as a result of the tropical storm. It's likely they'll die if they do."

"What about returning to Terra Cay?"

"There's an entire team of angry arms dealers just waiting to kill them. That's likely suicide."

"I'll work on it. How long do they have before they run out of fuel?"

"Half an hour," Banner said.

"Why didn't Carrow fill the damn thing up?"

"They did, it was hit by a grenade and it's leaking."

"I'm on it. Let me make some calls." Plower hung up.

Carrow sat behind Emma and Sumner in a jump seat in the cockpit.

"What's the plan?" he said.

"We need to land," Sumner replied. "The nearest airports are denying us access."

"Can't we just land anyway? What are they going to do if we ignore them?"

"Blow us out of the sky before we do," Sumner said.

"I'm an English citizen. Half these islands are territories of the British Crown. Hell, the Queen is a neighbor on the island. They'd better not blow me out of the sky." Carrow sounded outraged.

"They can and they will," Sumner said. "We need an airstrip that can handle a jet and a friendly nation."

"Does the phone work?"

Emma nodded. "It does."

"Then let me call my friend."

"Who?" Emma asked. Carrow named an actor known the world over.

"He owns an island and he's got a landing strip."

"He owns the entire island?" Sumner said.

"Yes. He owns the entire island."

Emma handed him the phone. "Get the coordinates."

Carrow dialed the phone and after a terse conversation said, "hold on," and quoted the coordinates. "He says he doesn't know how long the airstrip is, but he can land his jet. It's a bit smaller than this one, but it may work."

"Is anyone on the island? If so, tell them to stay far away from us and the plane," Emma said.

"He's at his LA house with his family. There's only a skeleton staff there at the moment and they live off island, so he thinks we're alone. I told him about the quarantine and he's asking that we stay with the jet after we land."

"Ask him if he thinks the runway lights are on," Sumner said.

The plane gave a lurch as a gust of wind hit it. Emma's stomach lurched as well. Carrow braced himself against the back of Sumner's seat as he carried on his telephone conversation. He leaned toward Sumner.

"There should be directional lights on at the runway, but he's been having a bit of trouble with the utilities and he said there's no guarantee they're working in the midst of the storm. Will we make it there and can you land it?"

"We'll make it and I can land anything," Sumner said. "But first get the creature off the controls."

"No creature," Emma said.

Sumner glanced at her. "Right."

"What the hell are you talking about?" Carrow asked.

"He was drugged with Scopolamine. He's having hallucinations."

"Please tell me you can see the controls." Carrow's voice was strained.

"I can," Sumner said. He kept his eyes on the instrument panel and Emma watched as the plane began to descend. In the distance she saw a row of flickering lights. Sumner adjusted the jet and pointed straight at them.

"Everyone strap in. We'll land in three minutes," Sumner said. The warning alarm on the panel switched to a louder, more strident pitch. The noise set Emma on edge.

"Is that a new problem?" she asked.

"No, it's the same problem. The fuel is just about finished."

Emma watched the runway lights grow clearer. The wind still lashed at them and the plane bumped with the gusts, but Sumner kept it on the line of trajectory and the ground grew closer. Emma held her breath as they prepared to touch down. They lowered onto the runway with only a small bump and the plane slid along the tarmac and ground to a halt at the end. It was a near perfect landing. Glare from a nearby spotlight bounced off the windshield. Sumner killed the engines and the annoying alarm fell quiet.

No one spoke. Rain poured off the windshield, sheeting downward. Emma slumped in her seat with a sigh of relief.

"You are one hell of a pilot," Carrow said. "And I need a drink."

Emma sat in the sunny kitchen in a small house located on the island. It remained devoid of people with the exception of Sumner, Stromeyer, and Banner. The last two had arrived after a decent interval, when it became apparent that none of the remaining group on the airplane had contracted the disease. After much negotiation on the part of Susan Plower, Marwell, Johnson, and Kemmer had been collected and transported days earlier to the Bahamas, where they were kept in the same cordon sanitaire with Randiger. Out of the forty cases on the island, twenty-five people died, including Martin from Rex Rain.

"How's Latisha doing?" Emma asked.

"Well. The doctor says he expects to discharge her shortly," Stromeyer said.

"And the arms dealers?"

"Two contracted the disease and died. Shanaropov and a Mexican survived. The Russian took off on his yacht and is at large. Plower has put resources behind a manhunt. We'll see what comes of it. She's also arranged for the Mexican to be transferred to Guantanamo."

"Bad for the Mexican," Emma said.

"But nothing more than he deserves," Banner said. "We recovered the bullets and the gun. None of it worked very well, but even if one had been smuggled through a metal detector and used to hit a target it could have been a disaster."

"What about the encephalitis? Is the island still quarantined?"

Stromeyer shook her head. "It will be lifted shortly, since no new cases have appeared. It has disappeared once again, as quickly as it did before."

"Still no cure?" Banner said.

"Still no cure and no answers, I'm afraid," Stromeyer replied.

"So science can't explain everything yet. The world retains its mystery," Emma said.

She sipped her coffee and eyed Sumner. He was his usual taciturn self, but she thought that his hallucinations had tapered off. He caught her staring at him, held her gaze and smiled.